daughter of the ninth line

The Complete Novel

Lines of Ebrus
Book One

grace mcginty

also by grace mcginty

Stand Alone Novels and Novellas:

Bright Lights From A Hurricane / The Last Note / Inside The Maelstrom / Pay-Per-Heart / 8 Seconds to Fly / Make My Heart Race / The Daymakers / Hunting Isla

Hell's Redemption Series:

The Redeemable / The Unrepentant / The Fallen

Damnation MC Duet:

Serendipity / Providence

The Azar Nazemi Trilogy :

Smoke and Smolder / Burn and Blaze / Rage and Ruin

Dark River Days Series:

Newly Undead In Dark River / Happily Undead In Dark River / Pleasantly Undead in Dark River

Eden Academy Series:

The Lost and the Hunted (Prequel) / Heart of the Hounded (Prequel) / Rebels and Runaways (Book 1) / Sweethearts and Savages (Book 2)

Shadow Bred Series:

Manix / Frenzy / Feral / Crave

Penalty Box Players:

Sticks and Stone / Break My Bones

Omega Lottery:

Tryst In The Dark

Hanging By A Thread Duet:

Tangled Threads Of Fate/A Single Thread of Hope

Offbeat Omegas

Ruffled Feathers/Dodging Bullets

For the Patrons.

Thank you for trusting me with your hearts. I promise not to break them.

(…too badly)

Norths Edge
Ozryn
Herelean Cliffs
Alutian Sea
Pillago Pass
Rewill
Fortaare
Lake Vale
Bine
Cyne
Tenby
Hamor
Eaglehoth
Boemouthe
Eelrood
Ovl
Doend
Boellium
War College
ERRIS

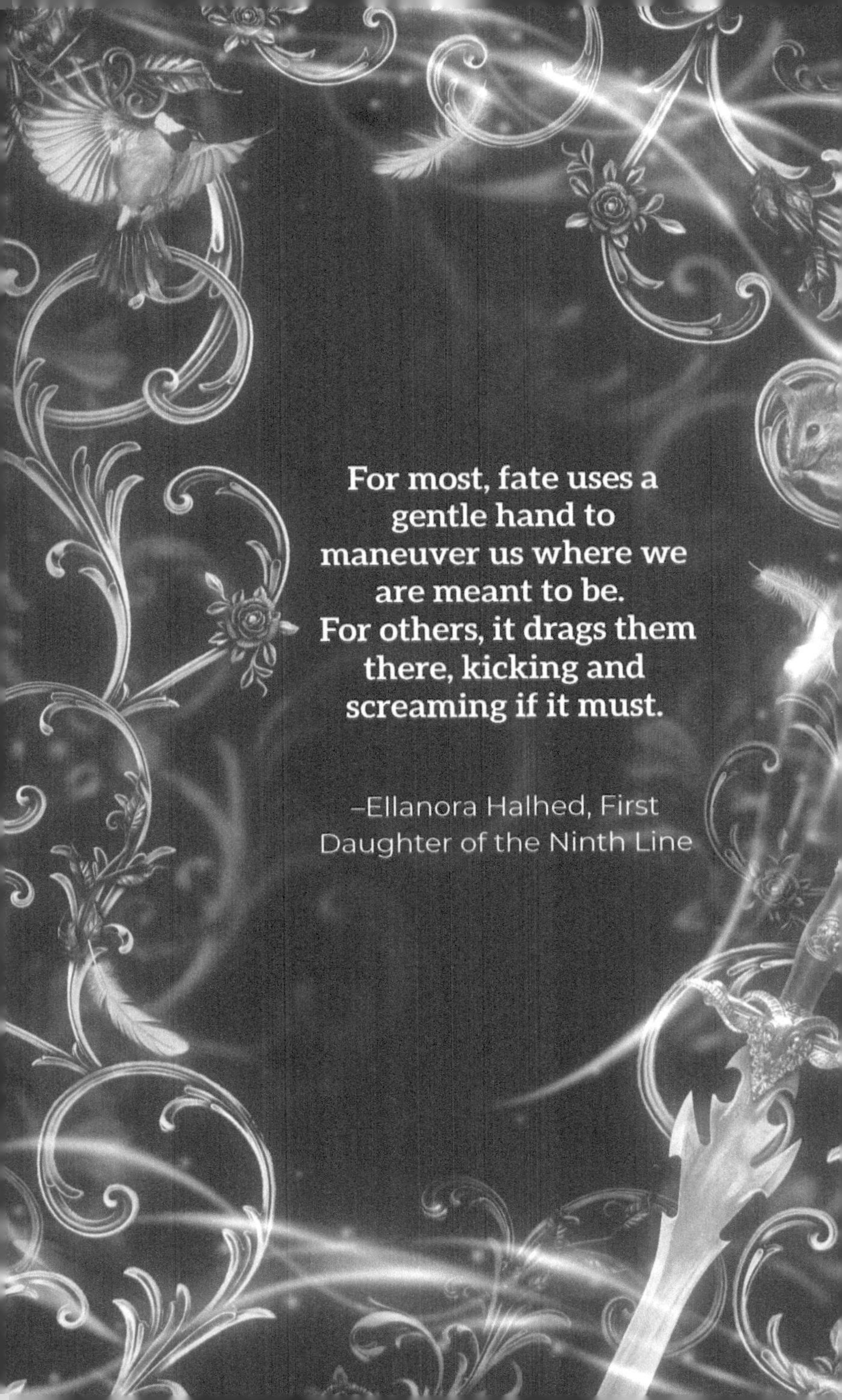
For most, fate uses a
gentle hand to
maneuver us where we
are meant to be.
For others, it drags them
there, kicking and
screaming if it must.

–Ellanora Halhed, First
Daughter of the Ninth Line

chapter one

Avalon

conscription day - the first day of spring

THERE WAS blood pooling on the cobblestone entrance of the Boellium War College. I shouldn't be surprised, given the baying of the crowd jammed into the front courtyard, and the man suspended in the air, bleeding steadily from his nose. The ruby liquid fell in huge drops, splashing on the ground beneath him with a gruesome dripping sound. Once the puddle of blood became too much, someone with water abilities seemed to wash it away.

That would definitely explain the pink stones.

The guy in the air, bound with invisible ropes, looked at me imploringly. "Help me," he gasped weakly.

I met his eyes, keeping my face shuttered and neutral, then timed my steps to walk under his blood droplets so they didn't splatter on me.

Someone huffed a laugh, and someone else muttered, "That's cold," but I ignored them all. I wasn't here to be someone's savior. I wasn't here to change the status quo.

I was here because I was *the useless daughter*.

Every one of the Twelve Lines had to enrol a child into the Boellium War College every year, and once a decade, it had to send a young person from the leading family of that Line. If I had to guess at their reasoning, I'd say it was so they didn't all send simple farmers' sons and create an army of uneducated cannon fodder.

Some Lines sent their most gifted children, either physically or mentally, in the hopes they could make advantageous connections or better still, marriages.

But that was for the Upper Six Lines. I was the youngest daughter of the current Baron of the Ninth Line. I was barely better than pond scum to these people. The only thing worse would be if I was from the Twelfth.

So I didn't care who was hanging up there, dripping blood for the cause; I couldn't help them. I didn't want to help them. I wanted to learn to fight, then go home to where there were fewer people and smaller egos.

I'd spent hours reading journal accounts of prestigious Ninth Line warriors, who talked about coming to Boellium War College like it was the best and worst time of their life, so I knew what to expect. I knew this was part of the hazing, helping to sift the weak of stomach and will from the strong contenders.

I knew that a little blood was going to become an

everyday occurrence for me. That was why I kept walking. It's why I avoided the eyes of the milling crowd, and closed my ears to their muttered commentary.

I wasn't cold. I was *realistic*. A tender heart in Boellium would soon bleed out, and then it would be their blood painting the courtyard's cobblestones red. That wouldn't be me.

I hefted my pack further onto my back and pushed through the heavy front doors. Again, I wasn't surprised that there was more carnage to walk through. There was a delicate balance in the power structure of this institution, and in the Lines themselves.

I didn't see him in the crowd in the courtyard, but the second son of the First Line would be out there, traumatizing the new recruits like it was his right, and I guess it was. The ruling family of the First Line, the Vylan family, ruled Ebrus with unwavering ruthlessness, maintaining their position of power through any means necessary, including their elemental abilities.

Means like suspending a man in the air and slowly allowing him to exsanguinate.

However, the second show of power would come from the next most politically powerful family. The Third Line. The Second Line had been assassinated by the First Line centuries ago, thus securing their power as the ruling body forever. None of us could stand against their rule, and really, none of us tried.

That made them sound like dictators, but they weren't so bad. They were ambivalent to the country outside of the Upper Six Lines, and their own lifestyles.

They left the rest of us alone, except for taxes and the conscription of one person per year per Line to Boellium.

A deep growl let me know that my mind had wandered, which was dangerous in this institution. In front of me were two large hounds, easily coming up to my shoulders. Their fangs were bared, their ears pinned back. My limbs locked, but my face didn't so much as flinch, a skill I'd been working on for as long as I could remember.

I didn't think the college administration would let them tear me apart, but how could I really know? Still, I stood my ground, staring down those hounds, until a whistle pierced the air and they turned, moving with purpose toward their master.

I'd passed whatever test that was; it equally could have been an assessment of my courage or a measurement of my bladder control.

The Taeme family of the Third Line were the Lords of the Beasts, and rumor had it, they were little more than animals themselves. If the Vylans were cold as an ice wind, then the Taemes were their polar opposite. Hot-blooded and uncontrollable.

I was going to stay out of the way of all the Upper Six Lines. I meant less than nothing to them, and I intended to do my two years here at the war college and return home, not even a blip on their radar.

Forgettable. That's what I was aiming for.

As I walked through the large atrium toward the administration offices, the hollering in the room echoed like a madhouse. Screams and cries, fighting animals and chilling sounds of pain. It grated along my already tightly strung muscles, but I kept my face impassive. This was nothing. The first few steps in going back to my life.

Show no weakness. I'd repeat it like a mantra until I believed it.

That was going great, until just outside the door I needed to pass through was a large war cat of some kind, cornering what looked like a stolt, a weird little hybrid between a tiny ferret and a rat, but a unique purple color.

They were elusive, and avoided people, so I knew someone must have brought it here purely to feed to the war cat, for whatever reason. The big cat had it cornered in front of the door, and the stolt looked terrified, standing up on its hind legs, slapping at the air like it was ferocious and not ten inches from nose to tail.

Something twisted in my gut, but again, I kept it from my face. I had to go through that door, the one blocked by the war cat. That was the only reason I stepped between the big cat and the stolt. The fact you didn't cower in front of a predator was the only reason I stared down the enraged feline, baring my own teeth. I was just being stoic when I didn't react to the tiny stolt running up the fabric of my long skirt, like it knew I was its one chance at survival. I put my hand on the door once it made it to my hip, and the soft scratch of its claws probably broke the skin.

Feeling eyes on me, I couldn't help looking over

my shoulder at the crowd. A set of forest-green orbs met mine across the room, and I knew enough about public affairs to know that it was Hayle Taeme, the third-born son of the current Baron of the Third Line. I held his gaze for long enough to convey that I wasn't scared of him, but not so long that it was a challenge. Turning away, I stepped through the door into a hallway.

The silence inside was almost as grating as the noise of the atrium. Only the clock ticking above the administration office door broke the sound vacuum. Checking there was no one around, I reached under my skirt and pulled out the stolt.

It scrambled against my hand, its whole body rigid with fear, and I looked at it dispassionately. I should just let it go here and be done with it. I'd given it a chance; the rest was up to nature. But for a reason I didn't really understand, I found myself opening one of the wide, deep pockets of my skirt and allowing it to scurry in, hiding deep in the fabric like a burrow.

I'd take it out to the woods later and release it.

Straightening my shoulders, I hefted my bag back onto my back and knocked on the office door. Someone barked to enter, and I did so with my chin raised high. Boellium wasn't a place to cower or show weakness. It gave you the respect you demanded. At least, that's what the journal of Hildor Halhed had said.

I stepped through the door and met the eyes of a woman with a shaved head and a wicked scar curling her lip, the effects of which made her look like she was scowling. She only had one arm and wore modified battle leathers.

"This frog shit never balances." Okay, maybe the expression on her face had less to do with her scar and more to do with the cursing she was throwing at the ledger in front of her. Slamming it shut, she looked at me and opened a different ledger on her desk with a heavy thump. "Name?" she snapped.

"Avalon Halhed, fifth child of the Baron of the Ninth Line."

Flicking through the book in front of her, she reached the desired page and wrote down my name. I leaned over a little and saw name after name of people from my Line. Some were my kin. Some were people who fell within our Line's Barony.

The administrator didn't look impressed by my pedigree, and I wasn't surprised. "Take this. It's your classes. If you're on time, you're late." She flicked her fingers at me, a clear dismissal. "Go down to the third subfloor. Surprisingly, you seem to be the only person from the Ninth Line in the college at the moment, so you might find it a little quiet." The *don't complain* was written so clearly on her face that she didn't even need to say it out loud.

I knew that last year's Ninth Line conscript had died in war games before he'd even graduated. It had upset the families in the Barony, which was why Father had promised to send his darling daughter this year as the conscript. *Yeah, right.* It had a double boon for Father; he appeased the barony and got rid of me in one move.

If I played this right, I wouldn't have to go back to the house I grew up in, the one that held nothing but bad memories. He'd promised that if I survived and wasn't called up to fight in some imaginary war, he'd give me land on the very outer edge of Ebrus, right where our barony turned into the wilds of the North. That's all I had to do. Survive two years here and go home. I just had to hope that nothing went wrong.

I shuddered at the echo of an old memory.

Lifting my chin in acknowledgement of the woman behind the desk, I turned and left the administration office. Looking left and right, I searched for the stairs that would lead down to the Lower Line dorms. I knew from the journals in Father's library that the Lines after the Sixth Line were housed in subterranean housing. The dorms went six floors below my feet, and the very idea made my skin itch. At least I wasn't of the Twelfth Line, stuck down in the pits of hell.

To the left, there was a large sweeping staircase that went up to what I would assumed were the other six dorms. To the right was an archway, with stairs down. That would be my path then. Straightening my shoulders, I walked toward the curling stairs, but not before catching a glimpse of what was going on in the atrium.

Some other poor soul—who'd probably been forced to join Boellium too—was being confronted by the hounds. Instead of holding eye contact and standing tall like I had, this fool turned and ran.

You don't run from a predator. That was the first thing they taught you where I came from. A predator will chase you down and tear you to pieces, just for the sport of it.

Which was exactly what those hounds did to the guy, dragging him to the ground before he'd even made it back to the door. Clearly, I was wrong—the college *would* allow them to tear apart new students.

Pushing down the kernel of pity that formed in my chest, I descended the stairs to my new home, and ignored the man's screams as he was eaten alive.

chapter two

Avalon

THE ADMINISTRATOR HADN'T BEEN wrong about my floor being empty. It was covered in dust and looked like someone had used it for storage for the last few months, with large boxes and stacks of chairs piled up in the communal area. Moving around the boxes and assorted crap, I picked out a bedroom. There were six on this floor, all shooting off the main communal room. They didn't separate us by gender, only by Line, so maybe on some of the more populous levels, it was just one big orgy all the time.

I wouldn't have that problem, thank the Goddess.

Deciding on a room that was the furthest from the staircase landing, I put my bag down on the bed and scooped the stolt out of my pocket, placing it on the rough-hewn desk that made up the only furniture in the room, besides a skinny wardrobe.

Theoretically, I could fill out every single other wardrobe on this level too. There wouldn't be anyone else until next year. The Ninth Line weren't as desperate to send their sons off to die as some of the other Lines. The area around our lands was tough and rugged—to eke out a living in the wilds took all the strong hands our barony could muster.

That was why I'd been sent, not one of my brothers. That, and Father hated me. Some part of me even understood it.

I'd murdered my mother, and it was hard to love even your own child after that.

The stolt sat cautiously on the desk, sniffing around, before leaping down and scurrying beneath the bed. Well, clearly I wasn't setting it free in the forest anymore. It would make its own way back to wherever it needed to be.

"How's that for gratitude..." I muttered to myself, walking into the kitchen portion of the communal room. There was a cafeteria here, but I'd start smuggling snacks down to my dorm as soon as possible, so I didn't have to spend too much time with the other conscripts. There were already a few cans of vegetables, some kind of dehydrated stew in a jar, and things that had gone moldy and I didn't want to think about too hard. I guess no one had time to just clean out some random kitchen.

On the wall to the left of the doorway, the names of past Ninth Line conscripts had been carved into the wood paneling. There were some family names I recognized. Lorson. Mertridge. My own cousin, Mattlock Halhed. He'd gone on to be a high-ranking member of the army—well, as high ranking as someone from the Ninth Line could get. I'd read his journal years ago.

Next to some of the names were X's. The conscripts who'd never made it out of Boellium War College. Walking to the kitchen, I grabbed a knife from the drawer and scratched an X beside the name Sly Lorson. He hadn't returned home from this hellhole and would serve as a warning to me. Keep my head in the game, or it would be my own name with an X beside it.

Getting to work, I carved my name at the bottom of the list. *Avalon Halhed*. Daughter of the Ninth Line.

That ritual completed, I changed out of my traveling skirt, which had blood soaking the hem already, and set it in a bucket to soak. Walking to my bags, I pulled out a pair of my pilfered pants. I wasn't going to die in this place just because I was hampered by the voluminous skirts favored by my Line. I'd stolen these from my brothers, and while they were a little long in the legs, they fit well enough. I folded up the hems and noted that I'd have to cut and re-hem them tonight, as well as the others I'd stolen.

Not that my brothers wouldn't have given them to me if I'd asked; they didn't hate me the way my father did. Whatever had happened to my mother, they'd mostly been too young to remember, except for Kian.

My older brother and the Heir to the Ninth Line had been ten when our mother had died. He remembered every moment, but had never blamed me. More than once, he'd hidden me from my father's enraged grief. He'd ensured I was cared for, fed, safe. I'd been barely more than a toddler, but I'd known that Kian meant safety, even at that young age.

No, I'd stolen my brothers' pants, not because they wouldn't have just given them to me, but because I knew my father had forbidden them from providing me with any aid. My preparation for war had begun as soon as I agreed to come to Boellium. I'd had my wits, what I could gather with my charisma or by theft, and a long walk down south.

Shoving the melancholy thoughts from my mind, I slipped the pants on and buttoned them up. They were snug across my hips, but they fit better than they had when I'd left. Starving on the road would do that to a girl.

I was hardly a girl anymore, and that's probably why my father had sent me here. I was twenty-three, and no one would marry me. I wasn't a son. I was useless for anything but conscription fodder to him.

Sighing heavily, I shook off the thoughts of my family and my obvious father issues, and climbed the stairs back up. I was old to be entering the Boellium War College, though not the oldest. You could offer anyone between the age of sixteen and twenty-eight. Some Lines sent their conscriptions young, before their best years were gone, before they had wives and children and emotional attachments to anything but the idea of being a badass warrior. Others waited for as long as they could—the more humane option, I believed, considering there was a chance we wouldn't return. You had a chance to live your life before it was stolen from you.

Reaching the main landing, I cursed the fact that no one had given me a map of this place. I looked at the crowd, the setting sun, and decided to just follow the majority of the other students in the direction they were going.

The food here was free, and if nothing else, the Lower Six Line conscripts wouldn't miss mealtime. Food wasn't plentiful in the outer lands of Ebrus. We struggled and toiled, and some years, we just plain starved. It was bad for us in the North, where the Ninth Line barony was, but I knew it was even worse for the other Lines lower than us, relegated to the most barren outer rims of our country.

We moved from the main building of Boellium to one of the large outbuildings. It was basically a stone barn, a thatched roof holding tight against the ocean breeze. Boellium War College was on an island, ostensibly to protect it from marauders in the early days, but I suspected it was to prevent us from escaping once conscripted.

Something about the sea breeze was reassuring, though, reminding me of home. Crashing waves against the cliff sides and the loud call of seabirds were the lullabies I'd fallen asleep to for most of my life.

As someone jostled into me from behind, I gritted my teeth. The ocean of people before me, however, was far too new. Until Ovl—the sea port governed by the Fourth Line, which supported the only ferry from the mainland to Boellium—I'd never seen more than a hundred people in a room together. The lands of the Ninth Line were vast, and our population was sparse. It was a rare occasion that would bring us altogether to the Keep.

But on that one dock in Ovl, there'd been more people than I'd seen in my whole life. Hundreds of people from different classes, Lines, and professions, all crammed together perilously on a dock that I was sure couldn't hold us all. It was by sheer will that I hadn't had a panic attack right then and there.

Too many people. Too much noise.

And it smelled like ass.

Ass and rotten fish.

The misery of the day had been exasperated by the fact that I wasn't a natural seafarer. I'd spent half of the six-hour ferry journey throwing up over the side and feeding the marine life in the Alutian Sea. All that meant I was starving now.

Walking into the food hall, I saw the room was segregated by Lines. I didn't need to ask which one was mine; it was the only one that was empty in a sea of people. Heading over to the trestle tables that ran along the sides of the room, I grabbed a tray and a traditional Falain dinner plate. They were segmented plates with high edges, so you could scoop many different types of food into the one dish without any of the items touching, unless you wished. They were popular mostly here at Boellium War College, and more particularly on Boemouthe Island, the home of the Tenth Line, who cared for the college and lived out here in social exclusion by themselves.

Despite their isolation, one look at the Tenth Line table showed they were happy enough with their lot in life. Twelve conscripts sat around their table, which was a lot, but I could understand it. Many would come to work here at the college, or join the armed ranks that protected it. To the Tenth Line, Boellium War College was their way of life.

The next most populated table had twice that many people. Maybe more.

"They're the Twelfth Line," the girl behind me in the food queue said. "They're in the middle of a famine after all their crops failed for the last three years running, so they've sent as many of their young people as they can to Boellium. Better to die at the end of a sword than from a hungry belly."

I lifted my head in agreement, but didn't turn to answer her. What a decision to make out there in the far Western plains of Ebrus. To send away all your young people, or hope the next year's crop took so they wouldn't die.

"I heard that Master Proxius is turning them away now," the next guy down the line added, and the girl behind me sighed heavily.

"Be real, Jacob. They're never going to turn away cannon fodder for war."

Normally, I'd agree. But that was the weird thing about our conscription laws; we weren't actively at war. Hell, we hadn't been to war in over five hundred years.

But we still maintained a highly skilled army, and if I was a betting woman, I didn't think it was for use against forces outside Ebrus's borders.

I finished piling food on my plate, then turned from the buffet tables without responding to the people behind me. Their words, however, played on my mind, and I couldn't help but look at the Twelfth Line table once more. The conscripts were stacked on top of each other, two to a small chair, with some even sitting on the table as they ate. I could see which ones were fresh recruits because they were so gaunt, their eyes sunken into their skulls and their hair stringy. They were falling on their food like savages.

In comparison, my table was empty. What felt like the collective gaze of the whole room on my back was a heavy weight as I placed my tray down and steadily began to eat. I didn't meet anyone's eyes, just held myself stiff and pretended they weren't there at all.

The food was surprisingly good, some kind of thick stew full of vegetables and chunks of meat. I ate it slowly, hungry after so many days on the road, but not wanting to embarrass myself like the Twelfth Line conscripts.

The eyes on my face began to burn, and I chanced a quick look and fell straight into blue eyes, cold and sharp. Hair so dark, it seemed to absorb the light around him, perfectly curling up from his forehead like a wave, as if a wind had tousled it, even though there were no elements inside the building.

I didn't need anyone to tell me that this was an Heir

of the First Line. He screamed privilege, from his ridiculously unblemished skin to the way his body had the musculature of someone who'd had bountiful food forever. His sapphire eyes met mine, holding me almost unwillingly in his gaze. I was like a deer, caught in the light beam of a hunter.

I was prey to this man, inside these walls. I knew it in my bones.

He didn't know me, though. I didn't care what Line he emerged from—I refused to be prey. I was going to keep my head down, but I wouldn't become a victim to do it. I kept my chin high as I dragged my gaze from his, hoping he didn't know how the very action made a shiver run down my spine, and went back to slowly demolishing my stew.

By the time I looked up again, the room was mostly empty, and the Prince of Ebrus was gone.

chapter three

Hayle

THE NINTH LINE conscript had stood out like fleas on my cousin, Lucio. I'd noticed her immediately, first when she walked through the atrium and stared down my hounds, followed by Lucio's war cat, then she'd been nearly impossible to miss as she stared down Vox Fucking Vylan.

Physically, she was unremarkable. The slightly too pale skin of the Ninth Line, with dark brown hair that was too unkempt to fall smoothly, but was thick and full. The fire in her eyes was something else, even if she was trying hard to stay under the radar like the rest of the Lower Lines.

Not that I blamed them. They could be the greatest warrior this school had ever seen, and the best rank they would ever achieve in our army was somewhere in the upper middle. Maybe Captain. They were here as troop fodder, not to jockey for influence like the rest of us. Because no matter how well you fought, when you were up against someone who had strong Line abilities —like Vox and his damn elemental strength—you may as well be one of the straw dummies we practiced against. I wasn't saying it was right. It was just how the world worked, so it was best if they didn't make waves and stayed in their own lane.

However, despite how hard she was trying to blend in, I knew this girl—this *nobody*—from the Ninth Line was going to stir up trouble, and I was here for it.

I sent my hounds to find her, and they happily went. They had good instincts, and they liked her scent, according to Braxus. They liked that she'd saved the stolt from Elaine, Lucio's war cat. There was no love lost between the hounds and the war cats. They would fight beside each other when it counted, but they bickered like a bunch of toddlers outside of their duties.

Alucius, Braxus's mate and my second hound, sent me a snapshot through our connection of the girl in the training arena with the new recruits. She was around my age, not one of the usual fresh faces that the various Lines sent.

I wanted to know her story, and there was one sure source of information. Slipping from my own training exercises, I called down my raven, Quarry. I was one of the strongest beastmasters of our line. The Third Line was known for its affinity with animals; our strong connection with some of the most powerful predators in Ebrus made us a formidable foe for our enemies, thus demanding respect from the other Lines.

However, a Line-wide secret was that the direct

members of the Taeme family could shift into animals themselves. Lucio was a wolf, but I was something even more fearsome. Something that hadn't been seen in so long, our historians had needed to delve into the history books to confirm what they suspected.

Quarry swooped down and landed on my outstretched arm as I walked back toward the main building of Boellium. "Is Svenna in her office?" I asked him, and he made an affirmative grunt. I nodded my thanks as he flew back to whatever tree he was sitting in today, keeping watch on what was happening on the college grounds and even the surrounding island. I stomped through the courtyard, which was much quieter in comparison to yesterday, though there was still blood in the crevices of the stone.

Alucius and Braxus had attacked a new recruit yesterday, permanently maiming him. I hadn't interfered. The hounds had better instincts than most people, and whatever threat they thought he posed to me or our Line was probably true.

He was still alive, but he wouldn't fuck with the Third Line again anytime soon.

Striding through the atrium, I entered the administration office, where Svenna was cursing at a ledger like it had personally insulted her grandmother. She'd once been one of the greatest warriors in the Dawn Army, and whatever punishment had led her to be stuck here in these four walls with only ledgers and students as foes was cruel. She was wildly unsuited to being a glorified secretary. It had nothing to do with the fact she only had one arm, and everything to do with the look she was giving me right now, like she wanted to set me on fire with her mind.

"What do you want, Taeme?"

I didn't know what Line she was originally from, but all the leaders of Boellium War College gave up their Line allegiance to become devoted only to the Dawn Army and the college itself. I couldn't imagine any role that would make me forsake my Line. They were my family. My life.

I gave her my most charming smile. "Maybe I just wanted to see you, Svenna?" I purred.

Svenna was scarred and had lost her arm in some battle or another, but beneath her constant scowl was what once would have been a fearsome beauty. Her blonde hair was cut shortish, but her blue eyes sparkled with intelligence and a ruthlessness that I found admirable.

"I was in the same class as your mother, and you piss me off more than a boil on my ass cheek. So spit it out, I'm busy."

I laughed, dropping the pretense. "I want to know about the new girl from the Ninth Line."

Svenna snorted. "Hardly a girl, Taeme. She's basically a spinster, by your standards."

I waved a hand. "You know what I mean. Who is she?"

Rolling her eyes in my direction, she slammed the ledger in front of her shut. "That's none of your fucking business, Hayle Taeme. You want to know more about the Ninth Line conscript? Go and ask her yourself."

Huffing, I sat in the chair in front of her desk. "People lie, Svenna. I want my information from a vetted source. I can make it worth your time."

She frowned, the ridged scar on her face pulling tightly at the skin of her cheek. "You have nothing I want."

That was untrue. Reaching into one of the many pockets of my pants, I pulled out a small jar. "The scar cream you wanted from the village, the one they said was no longer being made."

Svenna eyed the cream, and something flashed in her eyes. Desperation. "You're very annoying, you know that? Fuck the Third Line and their spying eyes. I'm using a more accessible tincture now, so you can take that cream and shove it up your own puckered assh—"

I held up a hand to stop her tirade. Normally, I'd have had the hounds take a chunk out of someone for disrespecting my Line with so little care, but this was Svenna. She hated *everyone*, and that kind of removed a little of the sting.

Pulling out a piece of paper, I slid it across the desk so it sat next to the jar of cream. "And the recipe to make it yourself." I was playing my hand a little early, but I was motivated. Besides, I liked Svenna. I didn't want to extort her any more than necessary.

She muttered something under her breath. "Fine,

but get your little furry minions to stop spying on me, or I'll start making winter coats out of them."

Yeah, my father wasn't going to go for that. Svenna was a key figure in Boellium, and he liked to have his finger on the pulse of every major institution in this country. "I can't do that. But I can give you a week?"

She made a rude gesture. "A year. The Third Line does know how invasive that shit is, right?"

I grinned. "We are all well aware, and don't worry, we aren't immune from it either. A dormouse told my brothers when I jerked off into a sock." I smirked at the memory of the shit I'd gotten for months after that. Even now, I checked for little spies before I jerked off. "I can give you a month, but that's it." Reaching toward the cream and the recipe like I was going to take them back, I wasn't surprised when she slapped her hand over them and dragged them back to her side of the desk.

"Fine. Dick." She stood and grabbed a different ledger. This one, I recognised as the admissions ledger. She pulled it from the shelf with her one remaining hand, and despite the fact it was huge and heavy, I didn't offer to help. I liked my balls where they were. She had incredible strength in her remaining hand and arm, and hardly struggled as she walked it back to the desk. "I'm going to leave this here, open to a certain page. Do not turn the page. In fact, don't even *touch* it. You get two minutes."

She swept out of the room, and I chuckled. *Surly.*

Walking around her desk, I looked at the page, open to the section for admissions for the Ninth Line.

Avalon Halhed. So nobility then, not that you'd know it from the way she dressed. You could definitely tell from the way she held herself, though. Youngest daughter of Baron Halhed, unmarried and twenty-three. A spinster. *Interesting.* Normally, daughters were married off in their teen years up there in the Northern perma-frost, to keep the Line varied and to share around the mouths to feed during the long, cold winters.

She had three older brothers, none of whom had ever come to Boellium War College, I noted, along with one elder sister, who'd been married off to some other lordling of their backwater barony. A description of her physicality—identifying features such as the birthmark at the base of her spine and the small scar she had on her chest—was listed on her page to help identify her body, should she be killed in training in a way that made her face unrecognizable.

A note was included under Psychological Fitness about the death of the Baroness Halhed. Just a brief line about Avalon being present at the death of her mother when she was a toddler. I guess growing up motherless could be a cause of some kind of psychological stress, but half of Boellium had lost a parent, either to infighting between the Lines, starvation, disease, or one of a multitude of other ways you could die in Ebrus. It was probably only listed because she was nobility. It was noted that she was the first female conscripted from her Line, however.

Other than that, her file was completely unremarkable, and I was a little pissed that I'd given up so much of my leverage for very little reward. It was the gamble you made sometimes in the information business.

Svenna stomped back into the room what felt like seconds later. "Time's up, Taeme. Get the fuck out of my office."

Giving her a cocky grin, I moved back around the desk toward the door. "A pleasure as always, Svenna."

She flipped me a rude gesture. "Shut the damn door on your way out."

Braxus was waiting for me outside the administration door when I stepped out. "Aren't you meant to be watching the girl?" I asked him, quirking a brow.

He yawned and sent me a mental picture of Alucius lying in the shade of a tree, watching the new conscripts fumble with their swords, including Avalon Halhed.

Huffing a laugh, I tilted my head. "Fair. I guess it doesn't take both of you to watch one girl." I paused at the stairs. One set went up to my floor, with another set going down into the bowels of Boellium. "Actually, I have another job for you, and I think you'll enjoy this one a little more. I know how much you love playing hide and seek."

Braxus gave me a toothy grin, his tongue lolling out as I described what I needed. Maybe I had a better source of information after all.

chapter four

Avalon

I'D NEVER HURT SO MUCH in my entire life. There were muscles in my body that I hadn't known even existed until they felt like they were on fire today.

"Lift your fucking sword higher, Ninth, before someone chops off your damn head!" the instructor—Kika, a hardass originally from the Sixth Line—shouted at me. I gritted my teeth and did what was asked, despite the fact that I burned. I wanted to vomit, and I wasn't the only one. Most of the class had already leaned over the rail of the training ring and lost their breakfast. I swallowed hard; I really didn't want that to be me.

My older brother, Kian, had taught me a little swordsmanship, enough that I could protect myself if we were invaded. Or if my father got into a drunken melancholy and came after me again. It had only happened once, back when I was eight, but if Kian hadn't stumbled upon us as my father pinned me to the hearth with the tip of his sword at my chest, I would've been dead.

Sure, Father had apologized—more to Kian than to me, but I'd taken it. That wasn't good enough for Kian, though. After that, I was never alone in a room with my father without one of my brothers there too. From that point on, Father had looked at me with guilt mixed in with his normal sadness and hatred.

All this was to say that I'd been overly confident coming to Boellium War College. I had held a sword before, and there were people from the Eleventh and Twelfth Lines who didn't even have that small experience.

But swinging a sword with my brothers once a week did not make me a warrior, and the defensive moves Kian had taught me were only half the skills I'd need. I screamed in my mind and lifted my sword, striking at the dummy in front of me.

Finally, the instructor gave a high-pitched whistle to signal the end of training, and my arm went limp. I couldn't drop my sword. My fingers were locked around the hilt, seized from the sheer will of holding my muscles taught.

The punishment for dropping your sword in practice was missing three meals at the food hall, and I had to admit, it was a ruthless but effective incentive for the starving Lower Six Lines. The Upper Six didn't seem to worry so much, laughing and joking with each other, their muscles strong and their faces full of good health. They joked and teased each other, and a couple even harassed the Lower Six recruits for their weakness, their ragged clothing, their inability to hold the bile from rising when exhaustion took over.

Fuckers. They didn't understand what it was like to put every ounce of your energy into just surviving another day.

I pushed the thought away and worked on releasing my sword. I did one finger, then another, and someone chuckled beside me.

"Do you need assistance?" The voice was smooth and cool, like a light snow flurry before a blizzard. Looking up, I met the eyes of the man from last night. The First Line Heir.

I shook my head. "I'm fine." Years of etiquette training had me choking out a strained, "Thank you."

He lifted a perfect dark eyebrow. Black hair. Blue eyes. Skin like a frozen lake. It was an intimidating, yet attractive package. "Do you know who I am, Ninth?" he asked haughtily, and I nodded, finally removing my fingers from my sword and letting it drop to the dirt of the training ring. "Then why do you meet my eyes so freely?" It was a pompous demand from a man who had lackeys instead of peers.

I tried to stop the intrusive thoughts, I really did. I wasn't here to make enemies, especially those of the First Line. Instead of deferentially lowering my face, I met his gaze once more as I said, "My apologies. I'll do my very best to avoid them in the future." Then I held his eyes a heartbeat longer, because fuck this guy.

The Heir—Vox Vylan—grunted in the back of his throat as he reached for me, a sneer already on his face. *Shit.* I'd fucked up already.

Suddenly, there was a giant hound between us, its body blocking the Heir from me. Vox scowled down at the large canine, somewhere between a wolf and something even more wild. And huge. "Stay out of this, Taeme," he said to the hound, and I looked at the dog between us, like it could actually be an Heir to the Third Line. "Or I'll turn your little pet into a throw rug."

The hound growled and bared its teeth, snapping its jaws, completely unfazed by the man in front of us.

Huffing, Vox rolled his eyes. "Learn your place, Ninth. I don't want you to end up like the last of your brethren."

Clenching my jaw, I turned my back on the Ebrus Prince and hurried away. We didn't really have princes, or royalty, but if we did, he'd be as close as we'd get. I didn't take a breath until I was around the corner and out from beneath the icy glare of Vox Vylan.

Looking down at the hound that was still at my heels, protecting my back, I narrowed my eyes at it. "While I appreciate your assistance, I don't need your help."

The hound's eyes glittered, and its tongue lolled out of the side of its mouth. If a dog could give you a skeptical look, this one was calling me out on my bullshit.

Huffing out an irritated breath, I grabbed a stick of the jerky I'd placed in my pocket earlier today. I'd known the training would be tough, and that I'd probably need to start stockpiling fuel to take down to my dorm. Oh well, I'd start hoarding food tomorrow instead. I held out the jerky to the hound, who took it gently between its teeth and laid down before me, chewing at the end.

"Now we're even. And tell your master that the Ninth Line can care for itself. I am in no way indebted to him for today's little stunt."

"I'm sure he'd never even suggest you were."

I stared down at the hound. Had it just talked?

The hound sighed audibly, and looked over its shoulder as if it worried about my ability to survive life. Hayle Taeme stepped around the corner, a cocky smirk on his face.

There was something incredibly wild about Hayle Taeme. His presence made the hair on the back of your neck rise, and raised goosebumps on your arms. That primordial awareness wasn't lessened in any way by the easygoing smile on his face.

I straightened my spine, meeting those arresting forest-green eyes. "Good. Then we're in agreement." I needed to get the fuck out of here before I ended up a snack for his hounds. For the second time in fifteen minutes, I held my breath as I hurried away from a predator, heading toward my dorm.

I was starving, because they'd made us train

through lunch, but worse than that was the gritty, abrasive feeling of dirt in the crevices of my body. I'd go and sit at the bottom of the shower stall until I felt moderately human again, then I'd climb the stairs to the food hall.

Striding through the atrium of the main building, I avoided the eyes of the other recruits. I'd had enough human interaction for one day. The trip down the stairs to my dorm level felt interminable, and halfway down, I wondered if I'd done this whole thing backward. How was I going to climb these stairs on rubber legs later? I needed to build my food stockpile fast, especially if more of today was to be expected.

I stumbled onto my floor and straight into the washroom. It was just one big open room with three shower heads jutting from the walls. Stripping off my clothes, I set the spray to skin-peeling pressure. I needed something to pummel my muscles back to life.

The water down here was icy cold, and I gritted my teeth as I stood under the spray. I could deal with cold showers; I might be a Baron's daughter, but we lived in the mountains. Ice baths were a way of life. Though that didn't mean I wouldn't give my left tit for a warm tub right now.

The cold water chilled my overheated skin, and I tried to push my interactions with the lordlings of Boellium from my mind. I was just a novelty, the lonely Ninth Line recruit, and they'd get over it, especially when they realized I didn't want to play any stupid political games with them. I didn't want to marry either of them, or join their courts, or do any of the other shit people jockeyed for here at Boellium. In fact, if I didn't talk to them for the next two years, I would consider my time in this hellhole a success.

When my skin began to prickle from the coolness of the water, and my fingertips were numb, I turned off the stream, wrapping myself in one of the drying rags that hung on the walls. I tried not to think about who'd used them last, and whether or not they were actually clean. I'd have to find the laundry here sooner rather than later, because if I kept sweating through my clothes at the current alarming rate, they would be stiff and putrid before the week was out.

Moving naked toward my room, I was kind of glad for my forced solitude. This was the most privacy I'd had in… well, ever. No maids, housekeepers, or brothers. Just me.

Opening the wardrobe, I sifted through my clothes. Pulling out another pair of men's pants, I screeched as something furry fell out of it. "Fuck!"

The purple stolt glared up at me, like I was the problem here.

"Are you fucking *kidding* me right now? Don't be mad at me just because *you* decided to sleep in my damn clothes, you tiny hairball. You could have been a war cat's dinner if it wasn't for me, so have some gratitude."

Despite my chastisement, I reached into the pocket of my dirty pants and split the remaining chunk of jerky between the two of us. It grabbed the little piece of dried meat in its jaws and disappeared beneath the bed. Guess I had a housemate after all.

I managed to pull on my underwear, but that was it. I laid down on the bed and tried to shuffle on my pants, but soon enough, I flopped back, exhausted. Maybe I'd rest for a little while, just to get my strength back.

chapter five

Avalon

WHEN I WOKE, my clock said it was almost midnight, and my stomach said it was about to crawl up my throat and find a better person to live inside. Also, there was a girl sitting on the side of my bed, staring down at me.

"What the fuck?!" I screeched.

She tilted her head. "Your boobs are out."

I recognized her from the Twelfth Line. I ground my teeth together, pulling a blanket across my body. "That's because I'm in my room, in my bed. Alone."

Shrugging, she stood. "We were worried about you when you didn't turn up for dinner. I volunteered to come and check you hadn't died after training."

That was oddly sweet. "Uh. Thank you?"

Grinning at me, the girl thrust out her hand, palm up. I stared at it stupidly, until I remembered that it was the traditional farewell of the Twelfth Line. Placing my palm to hers, I slid it along and then curled my fingertips against hers. It was a gesture that they did when they parted ways, one small clinging motion that said they longed to see you again, or something. See, etiquette lessons weren't a giant waste of time.

The girl turned and walked out of my bedroom, with no other explanation or even telling me her name. I slumped back against the pillow, weighing up whether I should go back to sleep, or find my way to the kitchen and hope I could sneak in and raid the shelves without alerting the staff.

My stomach gave another painful cramp. I was starving, and I needed food.

Decision made, I stood and pulled on a long-sleeved black shirt that hit my knees. Another one of Kian's shirts. He was going to have to go to the tailor sooner than he normally would once he realized I'd stolen a large portion of his wardrobe.

Slipping out of my room, and then the Ninth Line dorm, I began to climb the stairs. *Holy Mother of the Great North, my thighs...* I hadn't even been working my thighs in battle training, but they hurt with every single movement as I climbed the ancient stone steps.

By the Seventh Line dorm, I wanted to puke, but I kept pushing until I reached the atrium landing. My knees were shaking so badly, I almost collapsed on the slate flagstones. Dragging myself out the doors, I noted how quiet Boellium was at night. The solid stone building insulated any noise from permeating the quietness of the atrium. Or maybe it was magic.

Magic wasn't something the Lower Six Lines had

much experience in. The First Line had more magic in their little fingers than the rest of the rest of us combined. The unfairness of the whole thing burned at times. Magic could have changed the lives of all of us.

The Eleventh and Twelfth Lines wouldn't have to starve if they had the same elemental magic that several of the Upper Six Lines had. They could bring on the rains, or promote the growth of their crops. They wouldn't have had to watch their children wither and die from lack of food and fresh water.

The night animals made a quiet soundtrack to the witching hour as I crossed the cobblestone courtyard to the food hall. Not another soul stirred, which suited me just fine. While I might be slowly adjusting to the sheer amount of people housed in the college, I still found the quiet stillness of being by myself a physical balm to my soul.

Surprisingly, the food hall was unlocked, though the door creaked so loudly, fear ran up my spine. I stilled, waiting for the sound of footsteps, or for someone to magically appear and send me back to my room, or kick me out or something, but no one came.

I stepped into the hall and walked softly across the heavy floorboards. The scent of dinner still permeated the room, making my stomach growl nearly as loudly as the door. First, I went and looked at the section that held snacks, but it had been completely raided. There were two nut squares left, and I pocketed those, but my churning stomach told me that probably wouldn't be enough.

Slipping behind the large trestle tables that held the dishes at mealtimes, I walked down a short hall and a set of stairs to the kitchens. A large fire was burning, kept burning by magic and not by a hearth boy.

My Keep had one of those, a little orphan who tended the fire during the night. Cerri was small for his age due to malnutrition, and had been found wandering through the town when he was little more than five. The Keep had taken him in, and now he was a constant in the Keep's kitchens, being fed up by the cooks and doted on by the maids. He was a sweetheart, but everyone in the North had a job, no matter how young or old.

My job was to be a sacrificial tribute.

Pushing the negative thoughts away, I went to the cool locker, again spelled by magic. I pulled out a huge hock of smoked ham, and my mouth watered. Finding some slabs of bread, I was well on my way to making myself a sandwich that I'd have dreams about forever when a throat cleared behind me.

Dropping the knife with a clatter on the countertop, I spun toward the noise, my spine jamming ramrod straight when I came face to face with the Heir to the First Line for the second time that day.

Although he wouldn't become the ruler, every direct descendant of a Line Baron was called an Heir, and could be called up to lead if something happened. Technically, even I was an Heir, but my father would rather rule as a corpse than let me become Baron of the Ninth Line.

"Theft? Surprisingly cliché for a Lower Six conscript." The Heir's tone was filled with disdainful boredom, and it might have been because my blood was already pulsing with adrenaline, or maybe because he was so dismissive of the struggles of the people of Ebrus, but it made me irrational.

Sneering at him, I picked up the knife again and turned my back to the powerful Heir. "Willfully blind to the suffering of his people. Surprisingly cliché for an Upper Six Heir," I snarked back, rushing through finishing up my sandwich while keeping my actions even and slow. He'd never know that I was halving my toppings. Maybe I just liked ham and cheese.

He sniffed. "I could have you thrown from Boellium for insulting me."

I rolled my eyes, but thankfully, he couldn't see me. "That's your prerogative, *my liege*." I used the title with my own disdainfully bored tone. Fuck, I needed to reel back in my tongue before I ended up hanging by my feet from the rafters, bleeding out from my nose. "I'll inform the kitchen staff of obtaining my own food tomorrow morning. I was... otherwise engaged during the mealtime service." Let him think I was actually doing something important, and not passed out from exhaustion.

He raised an eyebrow. "With Taeme from the Third? Don't think you're special. He's had every female recruit on their back at one point or another. Some of the staff too," he informed me with an irritated sniff.

Don't say it. Don't say it.

"I'm sure he'd have you on your back too, if you asked nicely." My tongue was in control now, leaving my good sense behind in the dust. I was a fool. A dead and buried fool. "Now, if you'll excuse me, I have to get back to bed, if I'm to be a stellar student in this fine institution."

I went to move past him, but suddenly, it was like moving through quicksand. Bands of air tightened around my body, holding me still. *Oh fuck.* I'd lasted one whole day at Boellium before dying. It wasn't a record, I knew that, but even so, it was a record for our Line.

Vox leaned in, his lips so close to my face, he could probably bite off my nose. His eyes sparkled with anger. "If you think Hayle Taeme would be on top, you know very little about me, Low Class."

That's what his issue is?

He leaned forward and took a bite of my sandwich, still suspended in front of me. Then he plucked it from my fingers and threw it on the ground, striding with a confident swagger from the kitchen.

I struggled against the invisible bonds, but it was futile. I was here, at the mercy of anyone who walked in. Despite logically knowing it was useless, I pushed and strained until I was making a wounded animal noise, tears leaking from the corners of my eyes.

I was trapped as easily as a mouse by a barn cat.

A soft noise had me straining to look over my shoulder. I saw the hound first. The same one from today during training, I thought. It had a purple stolt in its mouth, and I recognized its tiny white socks as my stolt. Or the stolt that lived on my floor. Not mine. I wasn't attached to the rodent.

"Drop it," I hissed, and both the hound and the stolt cocked their heads at me.

But the hound indeed dropped the tiny creature. Unlike with the war cat, the stolt didn't run away. It sat on its haunches and indignantly smoothed all the canine slobber from its coat.

I glared at the stupid creature. "You must have been the dullest stolt in your whole litter."

On the stars, I swear the hound grinned back at me, like it thought my comments were hilarious. The hound —which was a she, I thought—shuffled closer to me and sniffed the magic surrounding me. One of her lips peeled back from her canines, and I knew I was about to die. It was the surprise of my life when she let out a giant sneeze, shaking her head in disgust at the scent of magic and covering me in hound snot.

"Agreed. It does stink." I stopped struggling and let my body slump against the bindings. If Vox wanted to waste his energy keeping me suspended all night, I could sleep like this. *Dick.*

Footsteps suddenly sounded outside the door, and I froze. I was fully aware of how very vulnerable I was right now. What if Vox had sent someone down to beat the shit out of me—or worse—while I was incapacitated? What if it was someone completely unrelated, and they took advantage anyway?

Sensing the spike in my anxiety, the hound wrapped

herself comfortingly around my legs, while the stolt stood by, cleaning its butthole.

I was almost relieved when Hayle Taeme appeared around the corner. He looked dishevelled, like he'd been asleep, or if Vox was to be believed, mid-fuck. The grin he gave me made me believe it was probably the latter. A man as handsome as Hayle wouldn't sleep alone.

"We have to stop meeting like this," he murmured, coming closer to poke at my invisible bindings. "You pissed off Vox, I see."

Straightening, he pulled out his necklace. There were two chains, one empty and one laden with talisman charms. There must have been twenty charms on the second necklace, each attached by a tiny silver clasp. Without looking down, he slipped the empty chain over his head, then moved his fingers along the chain remaining around his neck until he found the charm he wanted. With deft fingers, he unclasped it and hooked it onto the empty chain.

That many *tals* must have cost his family a small fortune, but I guess the Third Line had a lot of wealth, so why not deck out your favorite son with enough talismans to ward off the hand of death itself?

He reached toward me, and I flinched away. I didn't know if they were offensive or defensive talismans, and in the dim lighting, I couldn't make out the details on the swinging charm.

Noting my flinch, Hayle raised his hands. "It's an elemental *tal*. It nulls the effects of bindings that use one of mother nature's elements." Easing toward me, he slipped the necklace gently over my head. "Earth. Fire. Water." The talisman fell against my chest, and the binding broke immediately. I would have dropped to my knees if Hayle hadn't been there to catch me. "And air, of course." Steadying me back on my feet, he gave me a once-over. "What did you do to annoy everyone's least favorite Ice Prince?"

Well, I couldn't exactly tell Hayle that I'd insinuated that Vox wanted to fuck him, so instead, I flushed and went with the next closest truth. "I may not have shown the proper respect that an Heir to the First Line feels is due. I might've suggested he was willfully blind to the state of his people."

Hayle raised a brow, but didn't say anything else. "I would avoid pissing off Vox Vylan. You are playing outside your league, Avalon Halhed." He grinned at me. "But I find it kind of hot." He gave a soft whistle, and I realized the stolt and Hayle's hound companions —I hadn't even noticed the other one appear—were all eating my sandwich.

I glared at the stolt. "Seriously?" Sighing, I let them have it. I had my nut squares still in my pocket; that would have to tide me over tonight.

Hayle laughed, looking at the animals near our feet. "You have yourself a loyal companion. He came to find my hounds when he realized you were stuck. You should name him, though. It's a show of respect." With that, he let out another low whistle and turned. "I'll be seeing you, Avalon Halhed. Stay out of trouble and away from the bastard prince."

Then he was gone, yet again.

I looked down at the stolt curiously. Was it more sentient than I gave it credit for? "Should I name you, or are you returning to the wild now?" As if answering my question, it picked up a piece of ham and stuffed it in its mouth. It was a wonder any more food would even fit. "I'll take that as a sign you're staying. I guess Hayle is right. You need a name."

I started walking back toward the entrance of the food hall toward my dorm room. I guess I couldn't call him *It*. Or Stolt. Or like, Fuzzy, or anything that lame. He reminded me of the purple and white epsirialle flowers that grew in the cook's garden back home. Epsirialle might be a little girlish, though. Hayle had suggested it was a he, and as a Master of Beasts, he'd probably know.

"What about Epsy?" I suggested to the tiny creature.

He flicked an ear at me and ran up the side of my pants to perch on my shoulder. When had he gone from terrified of me to an unintentional fur scarf? "Epsy it is." Tentatively, I reached up and scratched his ear. "Thanks for the save. I appreciate it."

Epsy just curled his long, fluffy tail around my throat and dug his little claws into my shirt, still chewing on the food stuffed in his cheeks.

Apparently, I had already accrued one friend in this shithole. But that was my limit.

chapter six

Vox

THE GIRL from the Ninth Line was a distraction. I couldn't put my finger on what exactly it was about her that riled me so badly, but every time she was in my presence, my blood burned hot with irritation.

Like right now, in the weekly briefing from the headmaster of the college, Master Proxius, my skin itched as my eyes burned into the side of her face. She wasn't doing anything, per se. No, her disinterest in me bordered on disrespect.

My brothers would roll their eyes at the fact that I was riled by a person not showing me the due amount of respect and awe. It was vain and ridiculous to feel this way, especially as I'd spent the better part of my childhood trying to avoid the crowds of people who were desperate to make a connection with an Heir of the First Line.

I growled at myself and focused on Proxius's welcome speech. "This year, we've had one of the highest enrollment numbers ever in Boellium's esteemed history. Thirty-seven students from across all eleven eligible Lines have begun training to protect Ebrus far into the future..."

Blah blah, so on and so forth.

I'd once asked my parents why we had the conscription laws when we were never actually at war, and my father had merely given me that disappointed look he was so fond of when it came to me. It had been my mother who explained that the conscription rules made sure the people felt connected to the safety of Ebrus, and it also kept the other Lines from getting too unruly. Because mounting a coup was all fun and games until you were facing your nephew across the military fronts.

We also weren't stupid enough to think we were the only civilisation out there, with First Line astronomers creating countless books about planets and moons beyond stars. It was good to be always ready for an attack, because as soon as you let down your guard, that was when the enemy emerged. Or something like that.

Proxius continued. "And for the first time in quite a few decades, four out of the eleven eligible Lines sent us their best and brightest, with Heirs from the Lines themselves within our college walls. The First, Third, Sixth and Ninth Lines have all sent direct descendants, and we appreciate their Lines' sacrifice."

All eyes turned to me, and I transformed my face into what I considered my political mask: bored, superior, and more powerful than they could even comprehend. Not necessarily untrue on any front.

Besides, it was hardly a sacrifice. There was no way I'd ever see a battlefront. At the very worst, I'd be in the commander's tent, pretending to be helpful while they organized battle strategies.

I looked over at Hayle Taeme. I doubted he'd see much battle time either, but the Third Line weren't known for strategy—more for their ability to fight. Barely more than beasts, that was what my mother had always muttered whenever we were forced to receive them at the palace. My cool, aloof mother would think that; she held herself apart from everyone, even her children. The sheer level of physical affection the Third Line showed each other would be enough to turn her stomach in disgust.

Hayle Taeme was a cocky son of a bitch, but my opinion differed to that of my parents. They thought the Third Line were basically rabid, but I'd seen the scheming that Hayle Taeme had done here at Boellium, and he wasn't fluttering around blindly like a dog in heat. No, he had almost as many spies and informants as I did, and if rumor was to be believed, maybe untold more.

Those hounds of his were more self aware than any street dog I'd ever seen. They watched me with intelligent eyes, and I knew whatever connection they had with Taeme, they were an extension of the threat the Third Line Heir posed to me.

Edgar Marlee was the sixth son of the Baron of the

Sixth Line, who had weak mental abilities, but strong alliances with the First Line. Father called them our walking library, with their eidetic memories. However, politically, it made them a threat to the First Line, because while they had almost no physical abilities to rise up against us, they remembered everything and were not easily bamboozled.

It also made them fundamentally boring. They were very black and white; things were historically accurate or they were plain wrong. The Sixth Line played politics very poorly, which was a blessing for the rest of us.

And then there was the Ninth Line. My sources told me her name was Avalon Halhed, the youngest daughter of the Baron of the Ninth Line, who, until she came to Boellium, had never left her home in Rewill.

My sources also told me that there was some kind of animosity between the girl and her father, and despite appearances, there was no love lost. Given the way she had no respect for her betters, I was unsurprised that her father didn't have a lot of affection for his daughter.

The Ninth Line had very low-level psy-abilities, a touch of foresight, but usually only within a few minutes of the future, and only one possible outcome. Nothing that a bit of self-awareness and the ability to read a situation couldn't already divine.

But that was the way of it in Ebrus. The further you got from the First Line, the less powerful you were.

No, the Heir to the Ninth Line was little better than the Twelfth, who had no abilities to speak of at all. Not even luck. What they did do was procreate at an alarming, obviously unsustainable rate. Without the benefit of true magic, they had little to trade, and everything they had was achieved with backbreaking labor.

Avalon Halhed's words from last night were coming back to haunt me. Not the thing about Hayle Taeme; I was definitely the more dominant Heir both in and out of the bedroom, of that I had no doubt. No, it was what she'd said about me being willfully blind to the suffering of the people we ruled.

My father believed in a hands-off style of leadership. He let the Lines govern themselves, leaving their fates in their own hands, as long as they never attempted to rise against his ultimate rule and they paid their taxes promptly. But last night, while I couldn't sleep, I wondered if their fates really were in their own hands. The Line with the least amount of power had basically been banished to the farthest outreaches of Ebrus, to a climate with long, harsh summers, followed by dry, cold winters.

When my ancestors had been dishing out land to the other Lines, they'd done it strategically. Keep your friends close and your enemies closer. And of course, we'd given ourselves the prime real estate, because that was the boon of the victor. So those least able to withstand the harsh environment had been sent to the worst possible land, because they had no power to stand against us, and we'd stood idly by for decades as they starved under the guise of not interfering.

I looked at the Twelfth Line students now, and told myself that I would take more time to get to know the

Lower Lines. Not that I would ever rule Ebrus, but I would advise my brother; we could try and make life better for those weaker than us. Maybe set up a task-force of weather manipulators to go to Eelrood, the seat of power for the Twelfth Line, and aid in the growth of the crops. Any alternative was better than sending whole generations of children to Boellium just to prevent their starvation.

Avalon Halhed's spine was ramrod straight, like she could feel my eyes on her, and I sent down a tendril of air to wrap around her body, squeezing her tightly. The sound of her gasp echoed around the room, but she swallowed it down before anyone but those directly around her could pinpoint the exact location of the sound.

It was hard to keep the smirk from my face, but as she turned slowly to look at me over her shoulder, the fire in her eyes would have singed me if she'd had any form of elemental power.

I stared back, haughty and unaffected by her disdain. She needed to be reminded of who was the one in a position of power here, and of her place in the hierarchy of not just Boellium, but Ebrus as a whole. She was so far down the Lines of power that she wouldn't even be allowed to be my mistress, let alone be anyone in a position of authority.

Not that I'd want her as a mistress. She was far too plain. Like a length of coarsely woven cotton in a world filled with bedazzled silk.

The feeling of eyes on me prickled against my

awareness, and I acknowledged that I'd spent too long looking at Avalon. Turning toward the glare burning my skin, I was unsurprised to see the wild eyes of Hayle Taeme on me. If anyone could match me in power, it was Taeme, but even he fell below me. Maybe I should teach him a lesson too, show him that while he might be powerful, he fell short of my own strength.

His eyes held mine, a silent battle of wills with the droning voice of Master Proxius going through the upcoming events of the college. I didn't care. It would be the same as last year, and probably the year before that. No, this was far more important.

Neither of us would yield, but Taeme tilted his head down to the front of the auditorium. At the girl? Was he actually fucking her?

Whatever was between them, his meaning was clear. *Stay the fuck away from Avalon Halhed.* I felt the corner of my lip curl. His interest had just made her a thousand times more interesting.

Game on, fucker.

chapter seven

Avalon

DESPITE MY LOVE FOR READING, historical battle strategy had never been my topic of choice, which I was regretting now as Instructor Perot glared at me.

"I'm not sure, Instructor," I said for the eleventh time during this lesson. Why he kept calling on me when I was obviously inept at the subject seemed vindictive in a way I didn't understand.

"What were you learning up there in the home of the Ninth Line? How to knit?" His tone told me how useless he thought that skill was, but down here in the warmth of Boellium, he didn't know that being able to fashion warmth from the harsh wool of our mountain sheep was a life-saving skill. Perhaps even more so than being able to swing a sword, and definitely more than being able to recall thousand-year-old blood feuds from memory.

But I didn't say that. Instead, I apologized once more and wore his mockery like a coat of shame.

I wasn't sure what I'd done to piss him off, though. Maybe it was the mere existence of my Line. Maybe I should have paid more attention to the ancient blood feuds, because apparently, he was trying to start a new one.

The college wasn't huge, which meant that we didn't do separate classes. If it was time for Battle Strategy, the whole college was doing Battle Strategy. If it was combat training, the whole college was fighting.

Which meant I got no reprieve from the heavy presence of Hayle Taeme or the sharp looks from Vox Vylan. I wasn't sure where I'd gone wrong; instead of keeping my head down, I'd attracted the attention of the two most powerful conscripts here.

One of Hayle's hounds was lying under my chair, and the conscripts around me were either looking at me with curiosity or with concern, like I'd done something terribly wrong and was now under constant guard. It was never the same hound—they seemed to take it in turns—but no matter how many times I told them to leave, they'd sit doggedly at my heels with defiant expressions. Yep, the hounds had expressions. They were obviously not ordinary beasts of burden.

I'd had to come to terms with the fact that if I wasn't in my dorm, there was a hound beside me. Hayle hadn't said anything about it. In fact, I hadn't even spoken to him in a week. Boellium wasn't that big, so I had the suspicion he was purposefully avoiding me so I couldn't confront him about his furry shadows.

"Miss Halhed, who was the General for the Fifth Line during the Battle of Cregmire in the year 602?"

Who the heck would even know that? I sifted around in my brain for anything I knew about the Fifth Line, which was pitifully not much. The current family line was Ingmire, so I was just going to have to take a wild stab at it. "Ah, General Ingmire, sir?"

"Is that an answer or a question, Miss Halhed?"

I gritted my back teeth, wishing I had an elemental ability so I could set the churlish instructor's pants on fire. "An answer, sir."

"The wrong answer, yet again, Miss Halhed. I'll thank the Goddess every day that the Ninth Line only ever produces grunts and not ranking officers, because I am fairly sure your ilk would have us walking off the Herelean Cliffs."

My cheeks flushed red at his derisive words, and the hound at my feet let out a rumbling growl, so low that I felt it more than heard the sound. I buried my fingers in his fur, which was either going to soothe the beast or get my fingers bitten off. I figured if they were ordered to attack me, I would've been dog food by now.

The hound looked up at me, disgruntlement in his gaze, and I gave him a quick smile. "It's okay. His opinion of me doesn't matter." I said the words low, so no one could judge me for talking to an animal like I was from the Third Line instead of the Ninth. The hound huffed and put his big blocky head back on his paws.

I took notes and tried to comprehend as much as I could in the class, but Instructor Perot wasn't wrong— I'd been learning to knit and keep house instead of history and politics. I'd been learning to dodge flying fists instead of memorizing the different alliances and great battles. I *hated* feeling this inept.

So when the class ended, I waited until everyone left before I stood up and walked down to the instructor. "Sir, if I may have a quick word?"

Instructor Perot looked annoyed, but he cast a quick look at Braxus, the hound guarding me today. Everyone had known their names except for me; they were clearly something of a legend among the Upper Six Lines. Trained to work as a pair, Braxus and his mate Alucius were efficient machines of death. They could take down even the biggest prey, tear apart an enemy in seconds. People looked at them with equal parts awe and fear.

I understood the feeling, really. They were at least six feet long from nose to tail tip and five feet from paw to the fluff at the tips of their ears. Braxus might have been even taller. When we walked, his head was at my shoulder. They were terrifying, but something about them made me feel safe rather than scared.

My own stupidity, probably.

"Yes, Miss Halhed?" Instructor Perot's tone was clipped and icy.

Sucking in a deep breath, I swallowed down my pride. "You're correct in thinking that I am lacking in this facet of my training, and I was wondering if you had any reading materials that I could work through to catch up on what I assume is basic knowledge." It was bullshit. I'd seen the glazed looks on the faces of the rest of the new conscripts; this wasn't common knowledge, despite the derision of the instructor toward me. Still, I didn't want to spend two years being his chew toy for this class.

He eyed me, silent for a long moment. "Your mother was from my Line, did you know that?"

I pulled back in shock. I hadn't known that. I knew almost nothing about my mother; only the soft memories of Kian, and they were the memories of a boy who missed his mother. I remembered a soft scent, like lilacs, and sometimes I thought perhaps that was just my own delusions.

Sadness swamped me. Anger. Hurt. Regret. "I didn't, no. I'm sorry."

The apology was automatic; they were words that always followed mentions of my mother. *I'm sorry she's dead. I'm sorry I killed her. I'm sorry, I'm sorry, please, don't hurt me again.*

I shook the panic from my limbs, and Braxus huffed, stepping closer to me, his teeth baring at the instructor.

Instructor Perot wasn't perturbed by Braxus's rising aggression, or perhaps he couldn't feel the tension in the hound's body the way I could. "My cousin. She married your father and was never allowed to return home. She died within a decade of marrying him. He didn't even tell her parents she'd passed."

My mouth felt dry, and I licked my lips nervously. I didn't know what to say. Didn't know what to do. The instructor's obvious hatred of my family was palpable between us. So I just went with the truth.

"He wiped her from our lives. I don't remember her, or know anything about her, only her name and the stories my older brother could tell me. That she was kind and beautiful. That she grew flowers and loved the water. That my father was devoted to her, and he became a monster after she died. He doesn't ever talk about her, but he made sure we all felt the pain of her death." Mostly emotionally, but sometimes physically. "I don't even know what Line she came from, or you, for that matter."

Grief flashed briefly in Instructor Perot's eyes. "The Fifth Line. She was from Cyne, third cousin to the Ingmire line. She downgraded considerably, marrying Halhed, but she loved him, she said." The pain in his voice made my heart constrict in my chest. He'd obviously loved my mother, if the pain of her loss still put that look on his face after nearly two decades. Would he turn into my father if he knew that it was my fault she died? "You look like her."

Shock had me stepping back. No one had ever told me that before—not the staff who'd been in the manor when she died, not my brothers, and definitely not my father. I'd never seen a portrait. She had always been a ghost to me, or maybe a spectre that haunted me through no fault of her own. When I was younger, I'd hated her. She was the reason I was hurt, or hungry, or despised.

No one had ever said I looked like her.

"I... I didn't know."

Instructor Perot turned away, his shoulders stiff. He scribbled on a piece of paper, which he handed to me. "These are books available in the library to get you caught up on your severe lack of education." All vulnerability was gone from his face now, and he turned and walked out of the classroom. Away from me and the open wound he'd just inflicted on my soul.

Braxus whined, nudging me toward the door, and then I ran. I ran out the door, through the hallway. Past the other conscripts and instructors. Past the food hall and the open gate in the fortress wall. I ran through the village around the outer rims of the college and down the sand dunes until my feet were in the ocean. I didn't even care that my shoes were getting wet, or that soft, sucking waves were pulling me further and further out into the ocean.

Braxus was right there; he took my wrist gently in his mouth, the waves splashing up on his midnight fur, holding me so I didn't walk any further into the ocean. I collapsed down to my knees in the waves and allowed my salty tears to be dragged away by the sea. Braxus whined, but didn't release my hand. I realized I was sobbing, and he came around, putting his body between the ocean and me. Burying my face in his stiff fur, I cried even harder.

I don't know how long I cried. Minutes. Hours,

maybe. But suddenly, strong arms were picking me up out of the water and walking me back to the shore. I wasn't surprised to see Hayle, even though I hated that he would see me like this. I scrubbed my eyes and wriggled in his arms, but he just tightened them around my body.

"Be still," he ordered, and I didn't want to fight the command. When he sat on a rock, instead of putting me down beside him, he rearranged me in his lap. I turned my face into his chest, trying to wipe the tears from my face and hoping he'd just think they were ocean water. "What's wrong, Avalon? Why are you crying like your heart's breaking?" he asked softly into my hair, and any control I had over my tears disappeared.

"I'm cursed." My voice was shaky and weak, but I couldn't even find it in me to care. "I murdered my mother, and now I'm cursed."

chapter eight

Hayle

WHEN BRAXUS HAD SENT me images of Avalon trying to walk into the ocean, my heart had tried to explode out of my chest. I'd never run so fast, drawn on my power so deeply, as I had in that moment. I'd ordered Braxus to stop her, and he'd sent me the mental equivalent of snapping teeth. He liked the girl, that much was obvious; they both did.

Alucius had been mad that I was too slow—despite running faster than any other person in Boellium could ever contemplate, it still wasn't fast enough for my hound. She seemed aggravated that she had to watch my back instead of running ahead and helping Braxus with the girl. She kept circling back, nipping at my heels, urging me to go faster. I'd have been annoyed if I wasn't so panicked. That didn't make sense either.

Neither did the pain in my chest when I saw her from the top of the dunes, kneeling in the water, crying into Braxus's fur. I'd flown down the sand and had her up in my arms, safe against my chest, before I'd even consciously thought about it.

I'd carried her away from the unpredictable ocean, away from the temptation to walk into the waves and just keep going. I carried her to the long, flat rocks that the people on Boemouthe Island used as seats when they came down to this beach. The conscripts of the college had used this very bay as a place to party more than once.

There was room beside me, but I couldn't bring myself to put her down. Not yet. Her clothes were plastered to her body, her shoes a soggy mess around her feet. The cool sea breeze was whipping around us, and I worried that she would get sick if she didn't get back to her dorm room soon and change.

Even with all that, I couldn't let her go. I wasn't sure why, but I didn't fight the urge. Her pain was so thick in the air that I could almost taste it on my tongue.

"What's wrong, Avalon? Why are you crying like your heart's breaking?"

Her sobbing increased, and she murmured so quietly, I wondered if I misheard her. "I'm cursed. I murdered my mother, and now I'm cursed."

What the actual fuck? I thought about what I'd read in her enrollment ledger, about her witnessing her mother's death, but it had mentioned she was a toddler. I didn't know much about the powers of the Ninth Line, but I'd met my fair share of toddlers, and they couldn't shit by themselves, let alone murder their parents. "What do you mean?"

She just shook her head. "I don't remember it. But she fell off a cliff and into the ocean."

"That sounds like a terrible accident, Avalon, not murder," I said softly, and she shook her head, crying harder.

"They said I pushed her." Shock had me blinking in stunned silence, but I didn't release her. "Her maid said I lured her to the edge, then pushed her off."

What the hell did I even say to that? *I'm sure you didn't mean it? You were basically a baby.* Something about this whole thing seemed off. "I'm sure she was mistaken, Avalon. She was a grown woman, and you were a baby. I've never met any toddler who could push me over, let alone right off a cliff."

She was shaking her head again. "Doesn't matter whether it's true or not. It's what everyone believes, and it's followed me through my life, like a cloak of darkness I can never emerge from. I thought coming here would be different, but it's followed me here too."

I looked at Braxus, who was licking the salty water from the pads of his paws, and my companion sent me an image of Instructor Perot, followed by flashes of pictures that I deciphered to mean that Perot and Avalon's mother were related, and he held some resentment for her death.

I was going to kill him. I didn't care if he came around by the end of the conversation or not. He'd caused this turmoil in Avalon, and that was an offense I wasn't sure I was willing to let go. I couldn't explain this feeling in my chest, this urge to protect a girl I barely knew.

Alucius gave me an eye roll like I was still an errant pup and not her master. Well, kind of master. To the rest of the world, they followed my commands; in reality, our goals merely aligned and they did what I asked out of respect.

Alucius sent me an image of two wolves licking each other's muzzles and then her and Braxus fuc… "Alucius!" I snapped, and she gave me a toothy grin.

Avalon sat up, startled, and she looked over at my hound who looked completely innocent, lying on the sand like a stuffed toy and not a killing machine.

I got Alucius's point. She thought we were mates. Or at least that I was attracted enough to Avalon that I should fuck her. It would explain the ache in my chest at her pain, I guess. It was pretty inconvenient, though.

My parents would not be impressed if I brought home a mate from the Ninth Line. It would be like bringing home a sea cucumber and telling my parents we were soulmates. Still, we respected the Goddess and her plans more than any other Line, so they might dislike the idea, but they'd still accept her.

I gave into the compulsion to breathe in her scent. She smelled really nice when she wasn't covered in sweat and dirt from the arena.

I sat her up. "I haven't known you very long, Avalon Halhed, but I've been watching you enough to know a little. Someone who'd murder their mother would not save a stolt from being eaten. In fact, they'd probably stay to watch. A person who would purposefully harm another would not share their food with the conscripts from the Twelfth. Or with my hounds. You might pretend to be an ice queen, but you have a big heart that you're trying to hide." She snorted disbelievingly, and I wondered if she didn't actually see it. "Your family... They don't believe that you murdered your mother, right?" Anyone with two working brain cells would know it would've been an accident.

But the darkness in her eyes told me that they did. "My father—" She broke off, like she didn't know what to say, and honestly, if she told me that he believed a tiny toddler could push a fully grown adult anywhere, I would run all the way to Rewill and kick his ass myself.

"Your father?" I prompted.

She sucked the back of her teeth, looking back over the ocean. I held her tighter around the waist, the fear of seeing her neck-deep in the water earlier coming back full force.

"He believed the maid. He went crazy. He stopped everyone from taking care of me from the moment she died. My brothers told me he'd scream that I'd murdered my caregiver, and I'd never have another."

Shock made me stiff again. Well, shock and a rage so strong that I could feel it singe my veins. "He ordered everyone to neglect an infant?"

The idea was insane to me. In the Third Line, family was *everything*. Community was everything. Our bonds were our very lifeblood, and central to that was the idea that every child was a gift, to be loved and cared for by the whole Line. There was nowhere inside Hamor that a child could not go by itself and be one hundred percent cared for and protected. Anyone who committed violence against someone vulnerable would die a very painful, drawn-out death.

The idea of a father ordering their child to be neglected, despite the chance of death, was abhorrent to me.

She was nodding, no self-pity in her eyes. Like she believed she deserved it. "My eldest brother, Kian, defied him. He took care of me, with a little secret help from the staff, until I could care for myself. Kian stood up to my father, as his Heir, even though he was only ten."

I tried to imagine how much courage it would have taken a boy to stand up to his father. I wanted to visit her family, to shake her brother's hand and murder her father slowly. There would be no doubt who killed him.

"Your brother believed you didn't kill your mother?" I asked, and when she winced, I regretted my careless words.

She shrugged. "Maybe? He said that it was irrelevant whether I pushed her or she fell. What mattered was that she'd loved me with all her heart, and she'd want me to be cared for. So that's what he's done. He cared for and loved me, and made sure my siblings did too, despite our father's rage. We became closer for it; we had a bond born from death and violence."

I was silent, but I held her tightly, until her stomach

rumbled and the warm sun began to set behind the castle, making the chill of the wind even colder.

I forced myself to release her. "Come on. Let's go get you changed into something dry and feed you." I held out my hand, hoping she'd take it. But for the first time in my life, I wasn't sure the gesture of friendship, or something more, would be accepted.

Eyeing my hand like it was a rattlesnake ready to strike, she eventually placed her small palm in mine, and I tried very hard to hold back my smile.

In that moment, I made a silent vow to her. One that I would tell her out loud when the time was right. She would never be alone again—I would stand between her and her ghosts like a shield, until she was ready to fight them herself.

chapter nine

Avalon

HAYLE TAEME HAD FED me and put me to bed after my emotional breakdown. To thank him, I avoided him like he carried the pox over the next two weeks. Shame heated every inch of skin when I remembered him holding me like a child as I poured out my deepest, darkest secret. He now had something over me, not that it wasn't common knowledge back home. But Rewill was basically another country to the people down here; I doubted the hushed rumor had made it all the way to the walls of Boellium.

There was a stolt in my pocket and a hound on my heels, and I wondered if maybe I was an honorary member of the Third Line now, with the amount of animal companions I had. My body felt stronger after being here for a month. A month of regular meals, rigorous exercise, and sweet sleep. I was basically a new woman.

However, a month was how long my loner mystique

had kept away the other conscripts. As someone sat down opposite me at my table in the dinner hall, I kind of expected Hayle. Instead, it was the girl from the Twelfth who'd checked up on me. The one who had seen my boobs.

"Viana." She said the word like I was meant to know what it meant.

"What?" I asked around a mouthful of mashed potatoes.

Shaking her head like I was the ill-mannered one, she sighed heavily. "My name is Viana. You never asked. It's kind of rude, if you ask me, considering I went to check if you still lived."

"Avalon," I replied. "And thank you, I guess?"

Viana plucked a bread roll from my plate, but replaced it with a muffin. "You need the sugar for energy. Everyone knows who you are, Avalon. Even if you weren't the only Ninth Line conscript, you have one of Taeme's hounds following you around at all times. It's made you a bit of a topic of conversation.."

Great. So much for keeping a low profile and getting through this without making waves. "Not my choice." I looked down at a grumpy Braxus. "Not that I don't enjoy their company," I told the hound, and he gave me a toothy grin.

Viana looked between me and the hound like I was nuts. "That shit right there is why everyone knows who you are. Also, why everyone is too scared to approach you. But I've got nothing to lose, and you look like you need a friend."

I wanted to argue with her, but if I was honest, loneliness was hitting me harder than I'd thought it would. I'd always lived a solitary lifestyle, people avoiding me to stay out of the firing line of my father's wrath. But I'd still spoken to the cook and my brothers and the maids. The stablemaster. The shepherd. They weren't more than acquaintances—except my brothers, of course—but they'd helped stem the loneliness.

Purposefully isolating myself here had been different. I ate alone. Trained alone. Lived alone. And it was harder than I'd thought.

Shaking my head, I reminded myself of my goal. Get through this with no ties. I wanted to disappear after this. I didn't want to emotionally connect myself to someone I'd lose all too soon.

"Thank you, but I'm fine. I like being on my own."

Viana just raised her eyebrows at me. "No one likes being alone, Avalon Halhed. We aren't made for that. But if you aren't ready to admit you need a badass bestie, I'll be waiting." She waggled her eyebrows. "Or maybe you're getting it on the regular from Hayle Taeme, so you really aren't lonely. If that's the case, though, you definitely need a girls' night to tell me if the rumors are true."

"Rumors?"

"That Hayle Taeme is hung like a horse. I've heard it hangs between his thighs like a third leg. Peony heard that he had to get special undergarments made to keep it contained, so people don't accidentally clip it during hand-to-hand combat training."

The hound beside me grunted, his eyes sparkling, and I wondered if he was keeping track of my conversations. He was a dog, though; there was no way he could inform his master that we were talking about his cock, right?

Looking at Braxus, I wasn't entirely sure that was true. "I'm not sleeping with Hayle," I told Viana softly. "I'm not sleeping with anyone."

I'd never slept with anyone. No one would dare to defile the daughter of the Baron of the Ninth Line, and I'd never had any suitors, the way my sister Lenora did. Everyone knew of my father's hatred—it was infamous up north. Ignoring my existence was a better way to get into his good books than asking for my hand.

"Yet I've seen how he looks at you," Viana told me with a devious chuckle. "He's imagining what you taste like between your thighs."

I gasped, my face flooding pink. "Viana!"

The girl opposite me cackled even louder, drawing stares. "You Upper Elevens are such prudes. So caught up in your alliances and chastity and arranged marriages, you don't know how to *live*." She looked at me with pity. "When life is a struggle, you find your happiness where you can," she said seriously, before her smirk reemerged. "Especially if it's in an orgy, and you're the meat in a Polus and Link sandwich." She looked over her shoulder at two Twelfth Line guys.

They were looking better too; regular food had filled out their muscles, and their faces were less gaunt. Water that they could use bathing instead of just surviving meant that they were clean and handsome. And they were looking over at Viana like they wanted her to consume her pleasured screams.

I felt myself flushing just being in the proximity of that much sexual tension. "Good for you." I wasn't even being my usual sarcastic self. "Won't one get jealous?"

She shook her head. "In Eelrood, between death and malnutrition, birth rates are down. It's quite common to create family groups. Several men to tend to one family, one farm"—she gave me an exaggerated wink—"one woman."

"And the Twelfth are all just… what? Having orgies down in the bowels of Boellium?"

Viana just smirked. "You're always welcome to come down to the Twelfth and find out."

My cheeks pinkened, and I was trying to think of a way to say *thanks, but no thanks*, but I had the distinct impression that Viana was teasing me, especially as she continued eating with a stupidly large grin on her face.

A moment later, her face went slack at something over my shoulder, and I looked, almost unsurprised to see Hayle standing there. "Viana." His voice was smooth and cool, like marble.

The girl from the Twelfth looked up at Hayle like he was some kind of avenging angel. "Mr. Taeme."

I snorted, and he turned his gaze on me, his eyes sparkling with mirth. "Just Hayle is fine. I'm about to steal your dinner companion, so I suggest you move along."

It was a clear dismissal, but I knew from experience, she wasn't easily deterred. She looked back at me and raised an eyebrow. "I'll see you later?" she asked lightly, and Hayle actually growled in the back of his throat.

He couldn't know what we'd been talking about, right? He hadn't even been in the food hall with us.

"Avalon won't be going to the bowels with you, Viana," he said with so much certainty that I knew without a doubt, he'd been informed of our conversation.

I looked at the hound at my feet. Any doubt I might've had that he was sentient and aware, could follow along with conversations and was reporting back to his master, disappeared. *Traitor,* I mouthed, and Braxus just huffed and laid on his side, like he was exhausted by my humanness. I still reached down and scratched the fur at the base of his tail, so he knew I wasn't really angry at him.

Looking up at Hayle, I narrowed my eyes. "Hayle isn't the boss of me, Viana, so I'll do what I like."

Viana looked between us and stood. "I'll leave you two to decide. Uh, it was good to see you, Hayle." She stepped away, and behind Hayle's back, she tapped the middle of her thigh, mouthing the word, *Horse.*

My cheeks were on fire. It took every ounce of etiquette training I'd ever had to wipe the horror from my expression and look up at Hayle dispassionately. "Is there something I can help you with, Hayle? Perhaps you're here to reclaim your furry snitch?"

He threw his head back and laughed, the sound

drawing the eyes of everyone in the room. *Oh, for fuck's sake.*

"Will you *stop?*" I hissed.

He continued to look amused. "Why are you avoiding me?"

I screwed my nose up at him. "I'm not avoiding you." *Lies.*

"I haven't seen you in two weeks."

"Classes are busy, I guess." I stood, moving around him, carefully not meeting his eyes. Let everyone around us think it was deference, not that I was embarrassed that I'd been caught talking about his cock.

After taking my tray to the return spot, I almost sprinted from the food hall, Braxus on my heels. Not far behind him was Hayle, eating up the distance with his damn long-legged stride, even though he wasn't moving faster than a swagger.

Spinning on my heel, I waited for him to catch up. "Fine, I was avoiding you. I'd like it if you could respect my wishes and leave me alone." I spun back around and strode toward the main building and the library. I had a reading list a mile long, but at least Instructor Perot had stopped calling on me in class. Our little heart-to-heart had obviously traumatized us both, because now, his eyes just skipped over me like I wasn't even there.

That hurt too, in its own way, but at least I understood it.

Hayle appeared back at my side, the two hounds

walking behind us. Sighing, I looked over at him. "I should have saved my breath."

Shrugging, he kept up easily. "Probably. My mother always said I must have an affinity for a donkey, because I was a stubborn ass." His smile was fond, and it didn't take a genius to know that he loved his mom, and that she probably loved him.

I snorted a laugh. Man, what would it be like to have parents who loved you? "She sounds like a smart woman."

"Doesn't hurt that she's where I inherited my stubbornness from, so if I'm an ass, so is she. I wouldn't say that to her face, though. She could probably put me down without breaking a sweat." Hayle reached out and grabbed my hand. "Wait a second. Look, Avalon, we can forget the beach ever happened, if that's what you want. I won't push you about it, though I think talking to someone about it might be helpful."

He went on before I could tell him to mind his own business. "Do you know what I really want, though?" he murmured, stepping close until he was towering over me, his sparkling eyes hot with something I didn't want to name. "What I really want is to invite you to a party."

I knew the Upper Six partied hard. Sometimes, if I was at the base of the stairs that ascended from the atrium, I could feel the steady thump of drums, even if magic muted the sounds. But that wasn't for the Lower Six, which included me.

"I'm not allowed at your parties," I whispered.

"Who says? Vox Vylan? Fuck him. I'm inviting you, and I want you to come." He said those last five words as a purr, and I could imagine him saying them, in a different time, a different place, making heat pool in my lower belly. "What do you say, Avalon? You can even bring your friend from the Twelfth."

I wanted to say that Viana wasn't my friend, that I barely knew her, but admitting to this man that I had no friends was just too embarrassing. "Uh, I'll think about it?"

His grin made me lose my breath. It was bright and wide and heartstopping. "I'll pick you up from your floor at ten."

Before I could argue more, he was gone. I looked down at Braxus, whose tongue was hanging from the side of his mouth, as if he found this whole thing hilarious. "Don't you laugh, buddy. You're on my shit list."

Turning from the library doors, I moved back to the stairs down to the dorms. Studying would have to wait. I had to find something to wear.

chapter ten

Avalon

DESPITE HAYLE'S insistence that I never go down to the bowels of Boellium, I found myself descending past my own floor and down three more flights to the home of the Twelfth. My first impression was that it was loud. There were people laughing, music was playing, and conversations were being yelled over the top of one another. The smell of food cooking permeated the landing. The whole floor felt like a living, breathing creature.

I knocked on the door, but no one answered. I knocked again, but I doubted anyone could hear me over the noise. I pushed it open slowly, unsure of what I was about to see. Viana had suggested that it was an all-day orgy, but when I stepped in, everyone was wearing pants. Most of the guys were without shirts, though, and I felt a flush climb my cheeks.

I had brothers. I'd seen my fair share of man nipples in my life. But there was something about being surrounded by so many unrelated-to-me man nipples that was freaking me out. Why did I keep thinking about their nipples? That was odd, right?

Fuck, I should just go.

"Are you okay there?" A girl shorter than Viana, with shockingly orange hair, appeared in front of me.

"Uh, I'm looking for Viana?"

The girl rolled her eyes and smirked. "She disappeared to her rooms with Polus and Link ten minutes ago, so if you want to talk to her before tomorrow, we better interrupt now. Wait here." She strode down a short hall and slammed her fist against a random door. "Viana! Avalon Halhed is here to see you!" Thumping once more for good measure, she walked back toward me. "They'll probably need a minute. Are you hungry? Sit down; we'll grab you something to eat. Clancy, get Avalon a bowl of the stew that's on the back burner."

She pushed me toward the couch, where two other people were sitting, eyeing Braxus like he was about to pounce and tear them to shreds. I'd say that was preposterous, except he'd done that very thing the day I'd arrived. I gave the hound a raised eyebrow, and he huffed, wandering over to sit by the door.

The people on the couch scooted to the left, giving me a spot, their smiling faces welcoming. Clancy appeared with a deep bowl of thick stew that was golden in color. It smelled amazing, spicy and aromatic, and my mouth watered, despite the fact that I'd eaten less than an hour ago. He also edged toward Braxus with a large lamb bone in his hand, placing it on the ground a good four feet in front of the hound and scurrying away. Braxus just yawned and stretched toward the bone, picking it up and gnawing on it like it was the very least of the tributes he deserved.

Chuckling at the hound's antics, I lifted a spoonful of stew to my mouth, and despite a soft burn, let out a moan of appreciation. "This is amazing," I mumbled. We didn't eat many spices in the Ninth Line lands; they didn't grow easily in the high-altitude cold weather, and we were too far away to trade with the Eleventh and Twelfth lines, who had the right climate to grow such things. So whatever this stew was, it was a damn revelation. "I've never tasted anything like it."

Clancy looked wildly pleased. "We brought the spices with us. We all know the Upper Six are allergic to flavor, so anything served in the food hall will be tailored to their tastes. We stockpile what food we can from scheduled mealtimes and make dishes from home down here." He handed me a plate with some kind of fluffy bread resting on top like a cloud. "We do tasks for the kitchen staff to get the leftovers as well."

I was wondering how I could get a permanent invitation to dinner when Viana appeared, her hair mussed but smiling. Two guys stumbled out after her, giving me a wave, but heading over to a large vat in the corner. They poured what looked like wine into wooden cups.

"Hey, Avalon. I can't believe you're here. If Hayle Taeme told me to do anything, I'd say, 'Yes, sir.'"

"Is this before or after he spanked you and told you that you're a good girl?" the redhead quipped.

Viana threw back her head and laughed. "Hopefully both." She looked back at me. "Are you here for the orgy?"

My face was physically on fire at this point. I was just waiting to smell the smoke. "Uh. No. Hayle invited me to a party, and said you could come too, if you want. No pressure."

Viana actually squealed. It was ear-piercing, and I was fairly sure had damaged my eardrum. "Oh my fucking Goddess. An Upper Six party. I bet they have the good booze, Acacia."

The redhead, Acacia, screwed up her nose. "Yeah, but it comes with a heavy dose of condescension, and guys who are hot but probably couldn't find the clit if you gave them a road map and step-by-step instructions." She gave me an apologetic expression. "Hayle Taeme excluded, of course."

I shrugged. "I don't sleep with Hayle. He could be shit."

Viana snorted. "I've heard rumors, girl. I think if your dick is that big, you're good by default."

"Unless he's a two-pump pony," Clancy offered.

"A three-stroke joker," someone shouted from the other side of the room.

"A preemer-creamer," Acacia added.

I wasn't sure if you could die from the embarrassment of being a prude, but I was testing the theory right now.

Viana giggled with delight. "Avalon is going to have to save the poor man's reputation now." She looked at the group of people in the room with so much love. What would it be like to grow up in such a close community, bonded by hardship and laughter? "I'd love to attend your stuffy Upper Six party. Goddess knows, you'll need the backup up there with those sea dragons." She looked at my tattered pants and over-sized shirt. "Is that what you're wearing?"

I shrugged. "I don't have anything else."

Viana looked at Acacia, who was aghast. Glancing over her shoulder at the rest of the room, she clapped loudly. "You know what to do!"

I wasn't sure how it had happened, but two hours later, I stood in front of the mirror in Viana's room. I was in a deep yellow dress that Acacia had informed me was dyed with the pods of some of the spices I'd eaten. It was a rough fabric that had been treated with love and respect until it created something beautiful and unique. There was beautiful stitching on the bodice and the hem, and the skirt flowed around my body in a swirl when I walked. It laced up at the back, hugging all my curves in a way that made me look like a siren.

"You guys, it's *beautiful*. I promise I'll take care of it and give it back to you tomorrow."

Acacia waved me away. "No, keep it. It was always a little long on me, and I'm too lazy to hem it. Besides, I'd never be able to wear it now, because I could never look as amazing as you do in it." She sighed heavily, but her eyes were shining with mirth.

I spun from the mirror, the fabric swishing with me. "I… I can't pay you for it. I don't even have anything to offer you in return."

Acacia waved a hand. "It is a gift from the Twelfth. We don't believe in tit for tat. We know that one day if you're in a situation to help another person, you'll remember this kindness and how it felt, and you'll aid the other person." She sat me down on the chair, pulling out what I assumed was makeup. "Do you know the Twelfth believes that while we are the furthest from the First Line, we are the closest to the Goddess herself? That we survive by honoring her every day— not through pointless dogmatic rituals that make the Upper Six feel vindicated for their cruelty. I mean, we celebrate the small things every day. Helping people, sharing our food, our shelter, our clothing. We thank the Goddess when the seeds take root in our crops, when a baby is born, when we light a bonfire and celebrate life with friends and family. We honor her by living and loving and giving freely."

Emotion clogged my throat. I might not be close to the First Line, but apparently, I wasn't close to the Twelfth either. My life had been as cold as our climate, as barren as the mountains that towered around my home.

Choking back the lump in my throat, I murmured, "That's a good way to live."

Acacia squeezed my arm. "My mama always said a great tree can't grow in a desert."

I wanted to say something, to thank her again, but

Viana reappeared, looking beautiful. Her dress was a muted orange that bled down into a deep purple. It should look like too much, but somehow, it was art. "Come on, Avalon! We'll be late."

Polus and Link appeared behind her, both dressed for the party. I raised an eyebrow, and the taller one—I was pretty sure he was Link—shrugged. "No offense, but we aren't letting you go to a party with the Upper Six with only Taeme as protection. The Upper Six can be…" He trailed off, like he was trying to think of a non-insulting thing to call them, his eyes slipping to Braxus.

"Entitled cunts?" Viana supplied.

Link leaned over and kissed the top of her head. "Exactly."

Having met Vox Vylan on several occasions, I couldn't even disagree. Hayle seemed different, though.

Viana grabbed my arm, and we ran out of the room, Braxus leading us up the stairs. My thighs were burning by the time we got to my floor. "How do you guys climb from down there to the atrium after training every day?"

Snorting, Viana held out a hand. "We've always worked hard. Starving might rob the meat from our bones, but that didn't mean we got to stop."

Braxus let out a short bark, announcing that Hayle was already there. Hayle's eyes went wide as he looked at me, and I realized I hadn't checked my makeup before we left. Hopefully, I didn't look like a court jester. But the more Hayle stared, the more I worried.

"Sorry we're late," I said warily.

Shaking his head, Hayle grinned. "Right on time. Brought a few extras?" he asked lightly, nodding at Polus and Link.

"Didn't want to walk into the lion's den without backup." I wasn't going to be apologetic about it.

Hayle, however, just laughed. "Fair. Well then, let's go." He held out his elbow. "My lady?"

Placing my fingers in the crook of his arm, I told my thundering heart to behave itself. No ties. No waves. That was the goal.

Who was I kidding? I'd failed miserably already.

chapter eleven

Vox

EACH OF THE Upper Six Lines took it in turns to host a party. I didn't usually attend, unless I thought it was beneficial to whatever alliance I needed to create, or I needed to get my dick wet, or it was held by the Third Line.

Which was why I was here today. I couldn't let the Third Line get too out of hand, couldn't let Hayle Taeme win more people to his side. So I came to the Third Line parties, and I held court like I was royalty. I invited people to sit with me. I engaged. I was personable and friendly, sociable to a degree that I wanted to vomit at the shallowness of it all.

Looking around the room, I was surprised that Taeme wasn't here; I could see his cousin and a few of his inner circle mingling, as well as people from every one of the other Six Lines that mattered, most of them already well on the way to being black-out levels of inebriated. Before the end of the night, Lines and alliances wouldn't matter as they all got drunk off their faces and fucked like the Lower Lines. Like animals.

A murmur flowed through the crowd, and I tuned out what Ephily from the Fifth was droning on about on my lap, because Taeme had arrived, but not alone.

No, he'd brought three dirt scrabblers from the Twelfth, and *her*.

I clenched my back teeth, grinding them together, as Avalon Halhed looked around the room with wide eyes. She looked unsure of herself, but fuck, she was beautiful. She was in a dress in the style of the Twelfth Line, which might explain the other guests, but with her soft, creamy skin and her full breasts, she looked like a goddess.

I fucking hated her. Or perhaps more correctly, I hated that I wasn't fucking her.

"What the hell, Taeme?" Eugene from the Fourth Line muttered. "These parties aren't for them."

Audacious of him to say that to the host of the party.

I made a mental note to talk to Eugene, especially if he got on Taeme's bad side. The enemy of my enemy was my friend, or whatever the saying was. I dreaded it already, though, because Eugene was a boring, pretentious asshole.

Taeme's eyes snapped to Eugene, his vicious smirk just shy of a snarl. Eugene was an idiot; he wouldn't be able to sense the pure threat in Taeme's stance. "What floor are you on right now, Eugene? Is it yours? No?"

Eugene just stared.

"Then shut the fuck up. I'm the Heir to the Third

Line, this whole domain is mine, and I'll invite whoever the fuck I want. Or uninvite anyone who I want. Get the fuck out."

Eugene blustered, stuttering over his words, but Lucio Taeme just picked him up, walked him to the door of the dorm, and threw him out.

Hayle spun in a circle, meeting the gaze of every person in the room who was staring at the small group. "If anyone else has a problem, get the fuck out." His eyes met mine, a challenge in them once more. I could fight him over this, but why bother? Having her here would just give me a better chance to fuck with Hayle.

And I didn't give a shit about the dirt scrabblers either. I didn't need to jockey for power like the rest of them. So I shrugged, like it meant nothing to me.

With Taeme and I in agreement, the party had no choice but to restart, and Lucio Taeme turned the music back up. "Shots!" he yelled, receiving some half-hearted cheers, and the night went on. Taeme directed the girl to the other side of the room from me, and pointed out the bar to the Twelfth Line conscripts.

Ephily crawled back into my lap. "What is Hayle thinking, inviting this trash to our parties? Look at their clothes, their hair. They don't fit in here at all," she tittered, and I resisted the urge to shove her off my lap. Ephily sometimes forgot she was Fifth Line, so to me— and my parents—she may as well be Twelfth. She wouldn't be suitable for the Heir of the First Line. I was probably going to end up with someone from Fourth, or if my parents wanted to appease Third, someone from there. If they wanted to cement our place among our own people, I'd probably marry the daughter of one of the Capital diplomats.

What Ephily seemed to fail to understand as she "accidentally" ground on my dick with her ass, was that she could warm my bed, but I had little to no choice in who I married. She was still yammering on, and it was beginning to give me a headache.

Time to distract her. "I'd like a drink."

As predicted, Ephily leapt off my lap like this one act of service was going to secure her a ring.

I watched Avalon Halhed until she was shifting around, and just to fuck with her, I wrapped a small thread of wind around her ankle, then up her calf muscle. Her eyes snapped to mine, and I hated how much I enjoyed the fire in them as she glared. I wondered how she'd look at me if I ran the wind thread a little higher.

Holding her gaze, I curled it further up her dress, twisting it around her knee, then her thigh. Her jaw clenched, her eyes turning furious. I should stop, but something about her reaction was almost addictive. The dislike in her expression that she didn't even try to mask. Her complete lack of social etiquette. So I didn't stop. I moved the wind thread higher, at her very upper thigh, a mere inch from her pussy.

She leapt to her feet, marching toward me. I leaned back in my chair, giving her a crooked grin. I liked her flushed cheeks, even if it was with anger. I liked the way her eyes flashed at mine.

"They really are letting anyone into these parties." I echoed the words of Eugene. "Is there something I can help you with, Ninth?"

She glared at me. "My name is Avalon."

I arched my brow. "I know. And you are infecting the air around me with the scent of mountain sheep shit. So I repeat, what can I help you with, Ninth?"

"You can keep your magic to your goddamn self," she snapped.

I tilted my head and ran a small tendril of air across the seam of her panties. They were damp. "Seems to me you might like it."

Predictably, her eyes went wide. Unpredictably, her fist snapped out and cracked me in the nose.

I roared as pain shot through my face. I could feel the splash of blood on my hands as I jumped to my feet. "You little…"

Taeme was immediately there, his eyes flashing with his beast that he kept leashed inside. At his feet were his hounds, growling with their teeth bared and saliva dripping from their maws. He stepped between me and the girl. "Make a move, Vylan," he rumbled. "We'll see which one of us is more powerful, once and for all."

I scoffed, which made blood fly between us. "That isn't even a question, Taeme." The rest of his Line were behind him, and I didn't even need to look behind me to know that my own Line was prepared to retaliate on my behalf. I waved a hand behind me, telling them to stand down. I'd gone too far. "Apologies, Avalon. I will keep my magic to myself until you beg me to share it." I winked, though it hurt my face to do so.

Taeme hissed an angry noise at me, and I rolled my eyes. *Fucking Third Line. Little better than animals.*

Shaking my head, I looked around the crowd of people all staring at the three of us with varying levels of horror and glee at the thought of me and Hayle throwing down. Turning my back on him, I looked at Shay, my cousin and the next most powerful person in this school after Taeme and I. She was glaring at him, but gave me an equally annoyed look.

"Relax. Just a misunderstanding." Someone handed me a pocket square, and I squeezed my nose to stop the flow of blood. It had been a decent punch, so I guess Avalon Halhed was learning something at Boellium after all. "Isn't that right, Ninth? You wouldn't purposefully commit treason by hurting your superior?"

Avalon's eyes were still flashing, but she turned on her heel and moved back across the room to her Twelfth Line friends. I found her lack of bootlicking refreshing. How long had it been since someone other than Hayle Taeme and the rest of the Third Line disrespected me so thoroughly?

I grinned, and when Ephily shied away, I knew I must look like a mess. Taking the drink from where it dangled in her hand, I gulped it down. My nose stung, but I pressed a finger to the bridge, icing it so it didn't bruise too badly. It didn't feel broken, and I didn't want to leave the party just yet.

The altercation had changed the vibe of the party,

adrenaline now running high, and I noticed more and more people coupling up. One of the Third Line couples was already fucking against the wall, the steady thump of music muffling the girl's moans. As if permission had been granted, the party kicked into gear, devolving into the debaucherous sexfest that it normally did.

It was inevitable, really. We worked hard, and we partied harder. Most of us would never get the choice later to choose our marital partners, and it was an unspoken agreement through the Lines that what happened at these parties stayed here. The price for running your mouth was ostracization, and I knew that in previous years, there'd been more than a few "accidents" in the training ring for those who'd opened their mouths to people they shouldn't.

Hayle was sitting with Avalon, and whatever he was saying to her was making her laugh. But her eyes kept shifting around to couples fucking, the room getting hazy and filled with pheromones. The music was low and sensuous, made for fucking and dancing, and more than a few people were doing both right there on the makeshift dancefloor. Third Line parties always ended here faster than any other Line. *Animals.*

Avalon's eyes met mine, and I grinned. I reached for Ephily, and she came willingly. "My nose hurts. Make me feel better?" Her eyes sparkled with glee as she began to kiss her way down my body, unbuttoning my shirt as she went. Her fingers scraped down my skin, and I gave myself over to the sensations.

Ephily slowly kissed her way down my abs, and I

resisted the urge to push her head where I wanted it. I didn't want or need foreplay. She undid my pants, dropping to her knees between my thighs. So pliable and eager to submit. Tedious, really.

I hated the idea that Ephily was blowing the Heir and not the man. However, she served a purpose for stress relief, and when she took my semi-hard cock in her mouth, I closed my eyes and buried my fingers in her hair. Avalon Halhed's face popped into my mind, and despite the fact it was unfair to Ephily, I imagined it was Avalon's mouth on my cock right now. Imagined her defiant eyes looking up at me as I fucked her face. I was suddenly rock hard and fucking Ephily's mouth, her saliva dripping down my shaft.

"Good girl," I growled at imaginary Avalon. She would be a good girl as she took everything I gave her.

My eyes snapped open, and I looked straight into Avalon's, feeling them burning against my skin. I held her gaze as I blew inside Ephily's mouth, and when Avalon dragged her eyes back to Hayle, I realized he'd been staring at me too. His expression was harder to read.

Ephily tugged on the ends of my shirt, and guilt swept through me. I looked down at her, staring up at me with stars in her eyes. She might have been using me to get a better position in society, but I'd always promised myself I wouldn't use women the way my brothers did, the way my father did with his mistresses.

So despite the fact that I'd just imagined she was a stubborn girl from the Ninth Line—and I'd just blown in her mouth while Avalon was hatefucking me with her eyes—I pulled Ephily up onto my lap and spoke to her softly for the rest of the night, like she mattered to me. Like that blowjob had meant anything more than a quick release.

I ignored the woman across the room, ignored the way she was laughing huskily at Hayle Taeme, ignored how much I still wanted her. Because she wasn't for me, and never could be.

If I was honest with myself, that was the real reason why I hated her so much.

chapter twelve

Avalon

I WATCHED some girl give Vox Vylan a blowjob and tried not to examine my feelings on the matter. I didn't look too long at the burning in my gut that felt a little like lust. I hated that prick; if some little sycophant wanted to take his microdick in her mouth, so be it.

I sighed, not prone to lying to myself, especially when his cock was so obviously not a microdick. The girl was gagging as it hit the back of her throat, and it wasn't even halfway past her lips.

Turning away, I looked back at Hayle, who was watching me with dark eyes. "You okay?"

I shrugged. I was okay. Honestly, I could have stood up and demanded he stop teasing me with his air a lot earlier, but the feel of the breeze gently caressing my leg had been... erotic. Even if the manipulator of the element was a psycho.

"I'm fine. He was just being an asshole."

Hayle laughed. "That's his default." The silence

settled back between us, and the mirth slowly left his face. "He's powerful, though. Stay out of his way if you can."

Shaking my head, I gave him a sad smile. "You're all dangerous to me, Hayle. I shouldn't even be here." I was breaking my own rules, and this was my karmic justice. I looked around for Viana and her guys, but they seemed to be joining an orgy in the corner of the dorm.

Ah, sex. The only time Lines didn't matter.

I wouldn't drag them away, but I still stood. "Tell Viana I've gone home?"

Hayle reached up and grabbed my hand. "Don't let him chase you out," he said softly, and I stared down at our connected hands. His skin was so hot, almost like he was running a fever, and his eyes were imploring. He wanted me to stay, but I didn't know why. I didn't want to be the plaything for a powerful man. If I wanted that, I could have stayed in the wilds of the Ninth Line lands and married some rugged mountain lord.

The warmth of Hayle's skin on mine seemed to be running through my veins, heating my body, or maybe it was the desire in his gaze. It was muddling my thoughts, flaying my willpower so that I was helpless to resist his next words.

"Stay, Avalon. For me?"

This was dangerous; nothing good could come from forming an attachment to the man in front of me. "Why?"

The tilt of Hayle's head at my question was undeniably animalistic. The Master of Beasts. "I thought that was obvious?" he rumbled, his deep voice like a caress.

I laughed, a crazed, almost demented sound. "Nothing about this place, or you and these people, is obvious, Hayle." I waved a hand around the room as I leaned closer. "I have no idea why Vox keeps seeking me out to torment me. No idea why this place even exists if we aren't at war." Closer I went, until we were almost nose to nose. "I definitely have no idea why you gave me a hound bodyguard, or why you invited me to this party, or what your interest in me even is. None of it is obvious." I went to move away, but Hayle captured my face between his palms.

"I want you to stay because you've captivated me since the day you stared down Lucio's war cat in the atrium to save a stolt. Something inside my chest knows you, wants you, and while I don't fully understand it either, I trust my instincts above all else. My hounds might actually like you more than me."

Braxus gave a short yip from somewhere, but I couldn't turn to look. Because Hayle was holding me tightly, not with his hands, but with the heat of his gaze.

"So sit back down and get to know me. I'll help you make sense of all this."

"I'm not going to sleep with you, Hayle Taeme, so if this is an elaborate ruse to get the poor little Ninth Line country mouse into bed, you're out of luck." I gave him a hard look. "And if you're thinking of pressing your obvious advantage over me, you should know I've castrated a lot of barn cats in my life, and I'm pretty sure the concept is the same with people."

Hayle threw back his head and laughed, dropping one hand to cover his dick. "Duly noted, Avalon Halhed. I won't even suggest taking you to bed until you climb onto my lap and ask me so prettily for what you want."

It didn't escape me that both powerful Heirs had suggested I would beg for their attention eventually, but with Hayle, the temptation was too real.

Someone was making pornographic noises, and I couldn't help but look. The girl kneeling in front of Vox was making a show of it, either for the crowd at the party or for Vox himself. But the Heir had his eyes screwed tightly shut, his head tipped back, and his lips parted in pleasure. His fingers flexed in the girl's hair as his body tensed. I'd learned enough about sex from books and stable boys that I knew he was about to blow, and I couldn't look away.

When his eyes snapped open and met mine, there was something burning hot in them. I didn't have time to look away and pretend I wasn't staring at him.

No, he held my gaze as he came in someone else's mouth, and I should've felt disgusted, but instead I felt... hot. Aroused. Disgusted with myself. My pussy clenched—that traitor—and when he looked down at the girl slipping off his cock, I dragged my eyes back to the man beside me.

Hayle was also watching Vox get off, his face unreadable. However, when he turned back to me, he gave me a lopsided grin. "I knew the Heir to the Throne was a one-touch fuck," he murmured against my ear, and I couldn't help but laugh.

I purposefully didn't look at Vox Vylan the rest of the night, or at the girl on his lap. Instead, I concentrated on Hayle, and he made it so easy. He was like a sun the entire party revolved around. He was warm and engaging, and funny. He got me drinks, asked me questions, told me stories until I was sure I was going to wet myself with laughter. People came and went from his stratosphere like moths to a flame.

As the night went on, I forgot more and more why it was a bad idea to fall for Hayle Taeme. He loved his hounds, his home, and most of all, he loved his family. It was right there in every anecdote, every dream, every funny story he shared.

Right now, he was telling me about the time that Lucio had wanted them to prove themselves against their older brothers by doing some ancient ritual that involved a bonfire and being shirtless with mud smeared on their chests. But when they couldn't get the fire started, Lucio had tried pouring his father's home-distilled alcohol on the flames and got third-degree burns to his nipples.

"To this day, he can't grow chest hair," Hayle said conspiratorially, pointing over at Lucio, who'd lost his shirt at some point during the night. He was indeed hairless. I couldn't draw breath through my laughter.

Braxus and Alucius looked relaxed, but both were

clearly keeping an eye on the people in the dorm, and it felt nice to just let go. To be happy.

I was pressing closer and closer to Hayle, and the drinks were definitely helping me feel warm and free and a little light-headed. I needed to get out of here before I made stupid decisions and begged him to kiss me already.

As I stood, Hayle stood with me. He was so warm and alive, and for a moment, nothing mattered. Not my past, not my future. It was a heady feeling. "I should go," I murmured, and he nodded.

"Dance with me, just once, then I'll walk you home?"

Logically, I knew I should tell him that I didn't want to dance, that I could find my own way down a couple of flights of stairs, but I didn't. Instead, I took his outstretched hand and allowed him to lead me to the living room, which was currently doubling as a dancefloor.

The song playing was slow and undulating, a song made for sex and hedonistic pleasures. Hayle's hands landed on my hips, and he pulled me closer. This wasn't like the polite waltzes I'd been taught by etiquette tutors. This was something else entirely, something that would make Madam Proctor, my dance instructor, have a stroke.

His leg went between mine, and he hooked my hands around his neck. "I'm so out of my depth," I muttered beneath my breath, but Hayle just chuckled, moving me to the music.

"Don't you dance up there in the Ninth?"

I could feel the hard press of his body, including his dick, and I was desperately trying not to think about it. Had I mentioned his cock was hard too? "Not like this."

His hands wandered up my spine, and he smiled down at me. That smile should be illegal. Maybe that was his magic really; getting girls to lift their skirts with just a smile. I knew I was helpless to resist.

"Relax, Avalon," he whispered against my ear. "Feel the music. Let it flow through you into me." I was so close to him now that if my father could see me, he would have had me thrown in a temple to devote myself to the Goddess quicker than you could say *whore*. But Father wasn't here. He would never know that Hayle was almost fucking me with our clothes on, and that I wanted more. So, so much more.

I wanted to *feel*. I wanted someone to look at me like Hayle was right now, every day and forever.

Shaking away the dangerous thoughts, I stepped back slowly, and Hayle let me go. His eyes were burning with desire. He could have had any person here, and he was undressing *me* with his eyes. He let me put space between us, but his fingertips remained on my body, like he was finding it difficult. Wishful thinking on my behalf.

He let out a shuddering breath, before a self-deprecating smile crossed his face. "Give me a minute, then I'll walk you back to your dorm," he said softly, and I made the mistake of looking down between us. At the hard line of his cock.

Holy shit, Viana was right. Definitely a horse shifter.

"Avalon, if you don't stop looking at my cock like that..." The gentle threat was there, but the threat was sounding more like a promise of pleasure. With willpower I didn't know I possessed, I lifted my focus back to his forehead, then down to his laughing eyes. My face felt like it was on fire, and he chuckled deep in his chest; I could almost feel the sound against my skin. "I'm not sure the doe-eyed look is much better. Come, let's go."

He led me off the dancefloor, and I couldn't help but look over at Vox Vylan one more time. He raised an eyebrow at me, and I gave him a rude gesture in return. My etiquette tutor would have been horrified that I'd given the two-fingered salute to the Heir of the Goddess-damned First Line.

More surprising was the fact that Vox threw back his head and laughed, making everyone in the room turn toward him. Hayle looked between us, but shuffled me out of the Third Line dorms and into the stairwell.

Shaking his head at me, he wrapped an arm around my shoulders, his fingers brushing over my bare skin, making goosebumps of pleasure rise in their wake. "I bet you were the kind of kid who stuck their head in a beehive just to see how it worked, weren't you, Avalon Halhed? Just beware that it doesn't come back to bite you."

"Lucky I'm friends with the Prince of Beasts then, isn't it? A predator with even bigger teeth," I said haughtily, though it was hard to hold back my grin.

"A Prince, am I? Or was it a predator?" he growled, picking me up and walking down the stairs as sure-footed as one of the wild mountain goats near my home. Still, I squealed and wiggled to get down.

"Hayle, if you drop me down these stairs, I'll kick your ass," I warned, making him laugh again. He shifted me in his arms and looked down at me. I realized we were already at the atrium—the halfway point between us and them.

"I'd really like to kiss you," he whispered, and my heart stopped beating.

It was so foolish, but my tongue darted out, wetting my lips. "I'd like that too," I whispered, like the silly little idiot I was.

He lowered me slightly, until my feet barely touched the ground, and then he kissed me softly. Just a brush of his lips against mine. He sighed, or maybe it was me, and brushed another kiss across my lower lip once more.

"I knew it would be perfect," he whispered. Then he scooped me back up in his arms and all but ran down the rest of the stairs. I hung on tight, and when we stopped outside my floor, I looked up at him.

He backed me up against the door to my dorm and kissed me again, but there was nothing soft about this kiss. Nothing delicate. He plundered my mouth with his own, his tongue stroking along mine, tempting me to throw caution to the wind and invite him in. To have a night of something I would remember forever, even if I left it all behind in two years.

Suddenly, I wanted nothing more than that. Nothing more than to see a gloriously naked Hayle. To feel every inch of his skin. To taste him intimately. Fuck the consequences and my goals and Boellium and the Lines.

But Hayle dragged his lips from mine and took a small step away. His lips curled at the edges in a grin that set my soul on fire. "You're going to ruin me, Avalon Halhed, and I can't wait." One more brush of his lips, and then he was climbing the stairs.

I watched him go, forever changed.

chapter thirteen

Avalon

SOMETHING HAD CHANGED since the party with Hayle. Before last week, the other conscripts of Boellium had been happy to let me live on the periphery. An anomaly, sure, but ultimately uninteresting. Now? Now they knew I was firmly Team Hayle, and the divide in the college was all the more pronounced.

People who'd never spoken to me before went out of their way to converse with me. I'd said hello to more people in the last week than I had in the month I'd been at Boellium. And it wasn't just the Lower Six Lines, either. Even some of the Upper Six acknowledged my existence, especially the Third Line. Their Heir had all but announced that he was interested in me, and they let it subtly be known that they had my back.

However, the people who were loyalists to the First Line had decided to curry favor with Vox Vylan by making my life as miserable as they could. They aimed to maim me in battle practice. They tried to trip me down the stairs of the auditorium. They talked about me behind my back and sometimes to my face.

The ringleader of the new Avalon Halhed Hate Club was none other than the girl who probably still had cock breath from Vox's dick. She was definitely trying to get in Vox's good books by being an almighty bitch, and I even understood, kind of. There weren't a lot of places for women to go in our society, especially if you were of noble blood. Other than being bartered through marriage or being good enough at Boellium to become some kind of high-ranking officer, you were pretty screwed. Literally. Just there to make Heirs.

What a conquest the second son of the First Line would be, the best thing outside the actual Heir, I guess. I'd heard rumors that Vox's older brother, Yaron, was an utter manwhore and already betrothed to some powerful First Line daughter. I'd also heard that he cheated on her as often as he bathed, as was often the trade-off for a life of luxury and power.

So while I felt sorry for Ephily, she was still a raging asshole. As she tripped me once more by using the Fifth Line's terraforma powers to create a divot in the training ring, I contemplated punching her in that cute button nose and burying her in one of her own potholes. I glared at the woman, then continued back to the large barrels that held the swords. It was hand-to-hand combat day, and she was making it all the more miserable.

Viana appeared at my shoulder, giving Ephily a death glare of her own. Between us, we had almost zero magic, but I was pretty sure we could beat the crap out of her if it came down to it.

"That woman needs to pull the stick out of her ass and have some self-respect before Hayle's hounds take a chunk out of her," Viana said loudly. "Vox isn't going to want to put his dick in you more, just because you can put some holes in the ground." She wasn't talking to Ephily directly, but there was no doubt she wanted her to overhear, as well as everyone else in the training ring.

I laid my hand on my friend's arm. "Don't. I don't want you to become a target too."

Viana crossed her arms over her chest. "I'm not scared of them, Avie. They're so full of themselves and their magic, they forget they're just as susceptible to a knife to the throat as the rest of us."

Before I could even comprehend her movements, she spun and threw a dagger. *Where the hell did that even come from?* It thunked into the tall fence right beside Ephily's cheek. An inch to the left, and it would have been in her rapidly widening eye.

Hell, my eyes were just as wide. "Holy Goddess, Viana. That was *incredible.* How?"

She grinned at me, dragging me toward the swords. "Comes from starvation. Not a lot of food or money in Eelrood, so a lot of us became excellent hunters. You should see me with a slingshot."

"You never cease to amaze me, Viana of the Twelfth Line." Shaking my head, I pulled a sword out of the barrel, which Viana quickly grabbed from me and discarded. She pulled a smaller, thinner sword from the selection.

"That one was too heavy. Try this one." As I swung it, she watched me intently. "They use it like a crutch. The magic, I mean. It makes them overly confident. They could do with a reminder every now and then that the rest of us exist."

Someone appeared with her throwing knife, and I realized it was Lucio, Hayle's cousin. "I believe this is yours?" he asked lightly, and I didn't need to have psychic abilities to see the interest in his eyes as he looked at Viana.

She stared back at him, absolutely zero fear in her eyes. "Thank you," she purred.

"That throw was amazing. I saw it from across the ring."

She chewed her lip, and I leaned in close. "I verified the rumors about the Taeme family attributes. One hundred percent true," I whispered to her, and winked at Lucio before disappearing back into the crowd of conscripts. One of us should be getting laid by a guy with a huge... personality.

Hayle and I hadn't been alone since the party; he'd been called back to Hamor, the seat of the Third Line, for some kind of political business. In fact, Vox had disappeared too. I wondered if they'd caught the same ferry back to the mainland.

Lucio had remained here, and so had Vox's cousin, Shay, to maintain the status quo. The two glared daggers at each other, and I would've thought it was sexual tension, except Shay seemed to throw possessive looks at Ephily. Honestly, it was almost insane, the relationships in this place. One would need a full season and a blessed amount of patience to unravel it all.

"Avalon," someone called, and I turned to see Eugene from the Fourth Line.

What the hell does he want? I frowned, suddenly missing Braxus and Alucius. I hadn't realized how much of a security blanket Hayle's hounds had become; they always seemed to know more about the people near me than I did, and they had far bigger teeth.

But the hounds had returned to Hamor with Hayle, because they were meant to be his bodyguards, not mine. Hayle hadn't left me without a guard, though, as there was a raven who sat on the fence post even now, watching me with a disconcerting amount of intelligence. Quarry the raven seemed to watch everything, and even though roosting at night underground in my dorm must have been uncomfortable for the bird, he didn't seem to mind.

Epsy, my stolt, loved him. I swear, he curled around Quarry's feet like he was offering to be his very own living nest. So freaking weird. I'd already established Epsy had no survival instincts.

I realized I'd been staring silently at Eugene for too long, and he was looking a little annoyed. "It *is* Avalon, right?" It might have been posed as a question, but his tone suggested that he was checking I didn't have some kind of brain damage.

"Uh, yeah. What can I do for you?"

"Would you like to spar?"

Fuck no. From memory, Eugene was from the Fourth Line, and if he wanted to spar with me, it was because he wanted something. I bet he'd been practicing sword-work since he could walk. I didn't feel like getting my ass kicked today.

"Uh, no, thank you."

He lifted his sword and swiped half-heartedly at me, forcing me to block his sword with mine. "It wasn't a request, Ninth."

"Yet you posed it as a question, fuckface. How about you work on your language skills?" I snarled back, pushing off his blade and parrying into a strike of my own. He wanted to spar? So be it. He sneered at me, and I rolled my eyes. "We're sparring now, so how about you get to the point, *Fourth?*" I used his Line instead of his name, because I could be a disrespectful ass too.

He lazily adjusted his grip and advanced, forcing me backwards. "I just wanted to see what was special about you to have both the First and Third Heirs panting after you. Whatever it is, I can't see it. You're magicless. You're unskilled. You're uneducated and have no etiquette. You're fat and averagely pretty." He swung at me, one after another, making me scramble backwards until I tripped over my feet and landed my ass. He stood over me, his sword to my throat. "You're nothing. I don't get it."

A shadow blazed across my vision, and then Quarry was there, slicing at Eugene with his talons, his loud caws sounding like a death knell. Eugene swiped at the bird with his sword, clipping Quarry.

A giant war cat was there then, and so were Lucio and Viana. The war cat launched itself at Eugene and had his throat between giant fangs faster than should be physically possible. Lucio looked furious. He stomped on Eugene's wrist that was holding the sword, and an audible snap echoed around the training ring.

He glared down at the man from the Fourth Line. "You were warned," was all he said, as Viana helped me to my feet.

Hatred mixed with the pain and fear in Eugene's eyes as Lucio whistled, calling away his war cat. There were divots on Eugene's throat, proof that it had just been a fraction of force away from killing the man.

A soft noise had me searching for Quarry, and I found the raven near the fence, his wing hanging loosely by his side. I fell to my knees in the sand, his soft caws filled with pain. "Oh, sweet boy, did he get you?" I stroked Quarry's head, holding my breath. Blood dripped from his wing, and I hoped Eugene hadn't done irreparable damage. "Does anything else hurt?"

"He says that it's just his wing. But he'll need to go to the healer," Lucio informed me softly over my shoulder. "He also said don't cry."

I hadn't even realized I'd been crying, but when I swiped at my cheeks, they were indeed wet. I looked up at Lucio. "He said don't cry, or was that you?"

Lucio grinned down at me. "A little of both. Reach down, and he'll hop on your arm. Or I can take him if…"

I was already shaking my head. "No. He got hurt protecting me. I'll take him; I owe him that and much more." The war cat huffed, and I smiled down at her. "You too. Thank you for defending me."

The war cat just sat on her haunches, giving me an imperious glare as she cleaned the fur that was ruffled on her shoulder. I'd find a way to thank her later.

I leaned down and Quarry hopped onto my arm, his wing still hanging limply. "Come on, handsome." I looked over at Lucio and Viana. "Thank you both too. I…"

Viana waved me away. "It's what friends do. We have your back."

I raised an eyebrow at Lucio, who shrugged. "Hayle told me to look after you. You're important to him, so you're important to all the Third Line here at Boellium." He grimaced. "He's going to kick my ass when he realizes how close you came to losing your head on my watch. I won't let it happen again. I swear it."

None of this made sense to me. Not why Eugene was so pissed at me, or why Hayle was making his Line look out for me. We had a barely casual friendship and a few kisses between us, that was it.

Those were questions for my insomnia demon tonight.

Sighing, I excused myself from battle training and went to the healer. The trainers didn't even blink; they'd likely seen the whole thing and hadn't lifted a finger.

For the first time since I arrived, I seriously wondered if I'd even survive Boellium.

chapter fourteen

Hayle

IT WAS standard practice that when a Conclave was called, the current Barons brought their spare Heir. The official Heir to the Lines stayed in their seat of power, out of harm's way, and acting as an underlying threat in case of betrayal from one of the other Lines.

Any Line could call a meeting of the Conclave, and we'd all have to journey to Fortaare and hear their grievances. Most of the time, it was tedious shit: taxes, land disputes, tariffs, that kind of thing. However, the Eleventh and Twelfth Lines had called this Conclave in conjunction with each other, and it was already proving more exciting than the sixteen other Conclaves I'd had to attend over the last six years.

Feodore Vylan waved a hand. "I understand that you're facing hardships, Baron Abaster, but we govern our own Baronies. It has been that way since long before my time, and the times before my father. It is not the responsibility of the rest of the Lines to save you from poor planning."

Jacob Abaster bared his teeth at the Baron of the First Line, our ruler, and if I hadn't been able to scent the rage coming off him in waves, I'd almost think it was a smile. "I understand, Baron Vylan, but our people are starving. This drought is a once-in-a-hundred-year weather event. We need aid from the Capital."

"A once-in-a-hundred-year event would insinuate that this has happened before. What did you do a hundred years ago?" Roderick Rovan asked haughtily, his nose scrunched as he took in the Lower Lines across from him.

Ingrid Ulsen glared at the man across the table. She was the only female Baroness at the table. "We *died*, Baron Rovan. The Eleventh Line barely survived the Great Drought 163 years ago, and we did it by seeking aid with the Eaglehoth, who graciously allowed the survivors refuge until the drought broke. Our numbers dropped into the hundreds, and it has taken a hundred years for our population to recover."

Baron Rovan, of the Fourth Line, shrugged. "Can't Eaglehoth come to your aid again then?" He looked at the Baron of the Eighth Line, like it was his fault he was sitting at the Council table with the rest of us plebeians.

If Ingrid Ulsen was the only female Baron at the table, then Zier Tarrin was the only Baron under the age of fifty. Zier had come into his Baronacy three years ago at the age of twenty-seven, when his father died in a hunting accident. The new Baron was a lot less patient with the bureaucracy of these events, and I couldn't fault him.

"We would, as we don't believe that we could just sit by and watch as our neighbors starve to death. However, we can't take this many drought refugees without sending our own people into a famine."

There was a not-so-subtle censure in his words, and honestly, I agreed. Having spoken to the Twelfth Line conscripts now, I was a little more sympathetic to their plight than if I'd been living it up over here close to the mainland, with bountiful access to hunting, the ocean and farm land. The food on the table at last night's welcome dinner must have felt like a slap in the face to the Lower Line Barons.

I looked at my father. *We should offer assistance. There's power in the Lower Six Lines, despite what Vylan and Rovan think. I'd rather have six friends at my back than enemies all around.*

My father inclined his head slightly to tell me he'd heard me and agreed. The fact that our family could speak mind to mind was a well-kept secret and had been the ace up our sleeve in many of these negotiations. "I believe that no matter our Lines, we have a duty to Ebrus to care for all its people. The Third Line will send what aid we can to the Eleventh and Twelfth Lines."

"As will the Eighth," Zier Tarrin agreed, and I saw some relief in his expression. I had a feeling that no matter what decision was made today at the Conclave,

Tarrin would have provided aid to the Eleventh and Twelfth Lines.

I'd suggest to my brothers that perhaps a visit to Eaglehoth might be advantageous soon. My father was already talking about retiring to spend more time with family, and Remy and Lyle would step up sooner rather than later. Having good relations with a younger Baron would definitely ease the tension of these things.

Lunderov, of the Seventh Line—a small island Barony that sat in the middle of the Alutian Sea, almost directly between my home of Hamor and the western parts of Ebrus—offered to transport the goods from the eastern side of the country to the west, cutting weeks off the transport times. The Seventh Line had seafaring magic, and you could get from Hamor to the seaports of Teneby in four days.

Not everyone offered assistance—most notably the Fourth Line, whose very magic was the weather and could break the drought in a week, and the First Line, who were just asshats. However, almost everyone from Fifth Line down offered aid.

Vox Vylan looked tense as he left, which gave me a little satisfaction. If Vox was an asshole, then his father was a power-hungry megalomaniac. But he was powerful in magic, and no one could stand against him or his Line.

Baron Abaster came over and shook my father's hand. "We appreciate you speaking up. Your position definitely influenced the outcome of today."

Father's eyes slipped to mine, and I could see pride

there. "Of course. We are all one country; divisions help no one."

They began talking about trades and logistics, and I wanted to shed my human skin and run. We would head back to Hamor tonight, and then I'd be on the ferry back to Boellium War College by the end of the week. I'd run all the way there if I had to; it had been a long time since I'd run with my hounds.

The more I thought about it, the more the idea excited me. That freedom to run and hunt had been denied to me for far too long. There were no good places to flex my skills on the tiny island of Boemouthe. If I didn't want all the Lines knowing our powers, I had to stay constrained in my human skin.

I transmitted the idea to Alucius and Braxus, getting their enthusiastic approval, if the tail wagging was anything to go by. Decision made, I waited until my father was done with politics and we were in our carriage home.

We both sat in silence for a moment, lost in our thoughts, before my father broke it. "You're heading back to Boellium in the morning then?"

I was no longer surprised about what my father knew. He'd been this way my whole life, always far more knowledgeable than he should be.

"Yes. I thought I might run back with my hounds. It's been too long since the beast has been able to stretch its legs."

My father arched a brow at me. "And it has nothing

to do with the girl from the Ninth Line back at the college?"

I clenched my back teeth and shot a glare at my hounds. Braxus huffed, and Alucius glared right back. They both protested in my mind that it wasn't them, and I reached out and scratched their heads in apology. I shouldn't have doubted them. They were loyal to our family, but to me first and foremost.

My father had his own animal spies. It could have been a mouse in the kitchen, or a kestrel from above who'd seen me mooning over Avalon Halhed.

Taking in a deep breath, I steeled my spine, then raised my eyes to meet my father's piercing gaze. "Avalon is my Soul Tie. My other half. She calls to me in a way I don't understand, but she's *mine*."

My father stared at me for a long time, his eyes a blazing gold. His gaze had disconcerted many men before, but it was the same gaze that had watched me learn to shift forms, to ride a horse, to wield a sword. I knew beneath it was a love so deep that he'd lay down his life for me.

Finally, he nodded once. "When you choose to bring her home, we'll be excited to meet your Tie."

And that was it. No censure. No edict that she wasn't good enough.

It was what separated us from the other Lines, what made our people so loyal. Family came first, and the honor of the Line came second. And every single person who was the Third Line was family to the Taemes.

We were as loyal as we were fierce.

I knew politically, this was a setback for the family. We couldn't create bonds through my marriage anymore, and allying with the northerners was not beneficial to us at all. Besides, I'd barely held myself back from ripping off Baron Halhed's skull already, after what Avalon had told me of him. I couldn't make myself ally with him if I tried. So Avalon would bring nothing to the strength of the Third Line, not politically at least.

But to me, and to my family, it wouldn't matter. A Soul Tie was something greater than marriage, something greater than even magic. It was the very hands of fate that made us for one another, and it was so rare that the last Tie had been my grandparents. It was respected and revered. The Line would cope without marrying me off to some Fifth Line golden child or First Line debutante.

A sea falcon slammed into our carriage with uncanny precision, coming to rest on the bench seat beside my father. Zephyr was my father's eye in the sky. The sea falcon was as familiar to me as my own beasts and had been a constant in our household for as long as I could remember.

Whatever Zephyr was telling my father had him frowning, before he looked at me. My heart stilled in my chest. He flicked his fingers, and the horses slowed. There was no groom or driver. The horses pulled the carriage out of loyalty to my father.

"There has been an issue at Boellium. Someone

attacked your Soul Tie, although Lucio was there to stop it. Quarry was injured." I was already jumping from the carriage before my father had even finished. He leaned out the door, shouting at my retreating back, "*Do not change* until you reach the Mistwoods, Hayle. I mean it."

The Mistwoods were the edge of the Third Line lands, and the dense forest meant we could shift unseen. I held up my hand in acknowledgement, and took off through the trees. My hounds were already running alongside me. It would take me an hour to make it to the Mistwoods on human feet, then an entire day to get to Ovl if I ran as a beast.

I didn't care. I'd swim the whole way to Boemouthe if I had to, and if anyone in that forsaken place had hurt my Soul Tie, I would burn the place to the fucking ground in retribution.

"MY POOR, sweet hero. Do you want some more steak?"

Quarry squawked pitifully, opening his little mouth like he was a baby bird, and I popped some of the meat into his beak. He had a wooden box filled with the softest fabrics the healers would let me have, and was positioned in a prime spot in front of the fire in my dorm room. My stolt Epsy was curled around him, looking at him lovingly.

Lucio had left his war cat with me, just in case someone else got murderous thoughts toward me before Hayle returned. Honestly, I thought Eugene might have been an anomaly. With both Hayle and Vox away for the time being, the buzz around me had died off.

Well, until Eugene had tried to chop my head off, and then it picked back up again.

"I swear, I just wanted to get through these two

years without drama. What the heck happened?" I said to Leviat, the war cat, who looked at me like I was stupid. I didn't know how she managed to convey her thoughts so clearly, but I knew she was here begrudgingly, that she thought I was as useless as a cub, and she only remained in case there was a chance to eat someone.

Epsy had remained by Quarry's side, perhaps a little because the war cat still looked at him like she wanted to eat him. Lucio had promised me she wouldn't, but there was some serious longing in the predator's eyes.

Suddenly, the war cat was on her feet, ears pricked as she looked at the door to the dorm. I stood too, palming the knife I'd been using to cut up Quarry's food. The bird seemed unperturbed, but maybe he was just full and sleepy?

Blink. The door to my dorm slammed open, and Hayle was there, his hounds on his heels.

Blink. He was in front of me, picking me up in his arms and holding me in a hug so tight, I couldn't take a deep breath in.

"Hayle!" He nuzzled his face into my neck, inhaling me into his lungs. Well, at least one of us could inhale. "You're suffocating me."

He finally loosened his arms and dropped me to my feet, but didn't release me entirely. He looked down at my face, and when he saw the slight cut on my throat, his eyes turned murderous. "I'm going to destroy him."

He spun, but I grabbed his hands just in time to halt him. "Hayle, stop. It's fine. Calm down."

"Calm down? Calm down?!" He was definitely losing it. "Eugene almost *killed* you."

I dragged him to the couch, my free hand dropping down to reassure the hounds that were snuffling at my palm. I scratched their coarse fur, and they licked my fingers. They were filthy, with a twig even caught in Braxus's coat. "You guys look rough."

Leviat licked her paw, like even being in the room with the hounds was making her dirty, and then slunk out of the room, her need to watch over me done now that Hayle and the hounds were back. "Thank you, Leviat!" I called after her, and she swished her tail in my direction.

Hayle watched the cat go. "Lucio has a lot of explaining to do. How he let anyone get close enough to —" He cut off, like the idea of me getting injured actually physically hurt him too. He sat down on the couch, but pulled me onto his lap. I hadn't realized we'd progressed this far in our friendship, but it was obvious that Hayle needed this, and there were worse places to be than snuggled into the chest of a very hot man.

I held his neck as he stroked his cheek against mine, marking me in an animalistic display of possession. "It wasn't Lucio's fault. Who could have predicted Eugene becoming a fucking lunatic? Besides, Quarry was there to protect me."

The raven cooed happily, drawing Hayle's attention. He was silent for a time, and I wondered if perhaps they were conversing. Finally, he drew his eyes back to mine. "I owe Quarry a life debt."

Braxus huffed and laid down at my feet, his head knocking against my ankles. Alucius laid by the door, rolling onto her back, sticking all four feet in the air and falling asleep immediately.

Hayle chuckled low in his chest. "They're exhausted. We ran."

I gaped at him. "From Hamor?" He nodded, and I blinked at him. "Why? Lucio said you wouldn't be back until the weekend."

Instead of answering my question, he kissed me. No, it wasn't a kiss. That seemed too mild for the way his lips devoured me, his tongue pushing into my mouth, stroking mine like he was tongue fucking me, like he couldn't get enough of the taste of my lips. I kissed him back, because *holy shit*, and his hands slid to my hips, pulling me tight against his body and the hard ridge of his cock.

"You're mine, Avalon Halhed. Mine to protect." He squeezed my hips. "Mine to kiss. Mine to pleasure."

Uh, yes please. I slipped my legs either side of his thighs, and then his cock was there, rubbing on the rough fabric of my conscript uniform, barely anything between us. We let our bodies speak for us as he ground up into my core, making me moan.

He dragged his mouth from mine, panting hard. "Avalon, please," he begged.

He wanted to fuck. I had enough clarity of mind to know that. And I also knew that I wanted him to do it. I wanted him to be my first. The connection between us was almost undeniable as his fingers stroked fire over my skin.

When he shifted my shirt upward, feeling the lack of breast bindings, he groaned like he was in physical pain. "Let me taste these glorious tits."

In answer, I dragged my shirt over my head and threw it across the room. Hayle stared at my breasts like he was moonstruck, his eyes glued to them like they were a target. Then he stood, still holding me to his chest as he walked me into my room, shutting the door with his foot.

"Don't need a four-legged audience for what I want to do to you," he rumbled, then took my nipple in his mouth, sucking hard.

Holy shit.

I arched toward him, my fingers threading through his hair, holding him tightly to my chest. Given the moans that were vibrating my nipple, I didn't think he was going anywhere, but just in case. He pulled off and moved to the other nipple, not before breathing, "Gorgeous," at my boobs like they were artwork.

As he sucked, he laid me on the bed, his fingers on the buttons of my pants. He stilled, his eyes begging for permission. Was this it? The moment I lost my virginity? Was Hayle the right person?

There was no doubt in my mind that the answer was yes. Absolutely yes. "Fuck me, Hayle. Make me feel good."

He let out a pained groan and dropped to his knees. He dragged my pants off roughly, grunting with annoyance as they got caught on my feet. "I can't wait to taste you, Avalon. I can't wait to commit the flavor of you to memory. I can already smell that you'll be the sweetest thing I'll ever taste on my tongue." He tore my underwear off, and I squeaked a protest. He looked up at me completely unapologetically, any words of chastisement halting on my tongue as he sucked my clit into his mouth.

Oh Goddess. "Hayle!" I shouted, and his happy hum almost shot me into the stratosphere.

"Fuck, I love the way you shout my name. Do it again."

I raised an eyebrow at him. "Make me."

"Didn't you ever learn not to challenge a member of the Third Line? We are extremely competitive. Hold on, Avalon Halhed, because I'm about to make you scream until your throat hurts and your body is mine."

His firm tongue slid up and down my slit, before he began thrusting it inside me. *Holy shit.* I gripped his hair tightly, and he moaned, doubling down his efforts. He licked and sucked and scraped his teeth along every part of my sensitive core. Before I could even contemplate what was happening, what that feeling building in my belly was, I was coming in an avalanche of pleasure, the sensation flooding through my veins like I was dying. I slammed my thighs around his head, stopping his movements, because any more and I was going to be completely eviscerated. I would be an Avalon stain on the bed.

Despite the power of my thighs, Hayle managed a

gentle nudge of his nose through my folds, like he wanted to collect as much of my release on his face as he could. He was making soft groaning noises, and as I came back down, I knew I wanted him *right now*. I wanted him to fuck me. I wanted him inside me.

"Hayle…" I begged.

"What, baby? What do you need? Tell me," he crooned, and my vagina wept tears of joy.

I tugged on his hair, making him climb my body. "I want you to be naked and inside me in ten seconds, Hayle Taeme, or so help me…"

He grinned down at me. "So help me what?"

"I'll go join the orgy in the Twelfth dorm."

Mirth slipped from Hayle's face, and he growled, his eyes intense. "Never, baby. After this, when I take you, you'll be mine and mine alone forever, do you understand? I'll fuck you so good, you won't even look at another man. I'll make love to you so thoroughly, you'll see only me. I'll protect you so well, you'll never have to be scared again. I swear it."

This seemed intense, but something deep in my chest cried tears of relief. Like it had been waiting for this moment, for this man. So I found myself nodding, and he breathed a sigh of relief. It only took him four seconds to get naked and line his cock up at my entrance.

But then he paused. "This means something to me, Avalon. You understand, right?"

I was so dick-dazed, I would have agreed to

anything to have him inside me at that moment. My soul knew, though. "It means something to me too."

Relief washed over his face as he pushed inside me, and my eyes watered at the sting of his intrusion. Hayle threw his head back, his jaw tense. "So tight, baby. You feel like bliss on my cock. It's taking everything in me not to slam myself deep inside you right now."

I let out a choked noise. "Considering I've never done this before, we should probably leave the slamming until the second round."

His eyes went comically wide. "You're a virgin?" My cheeks pinkened with embarrassment as I nodded, but his lips were quickly on my cheekbones, kissing away the heat. "*Fuck.* You don't know how wild that makes me. How honored..." He choked on the words, dropping his forehead to mine. "I'll make this so good that you won't ever regret giving me this gift. Lie back and be my pillow princess, because I'm going to ruin even the thought of other men for you now. Only my hands will ever touch this body; only my cock will find its home in this pussy. Fuck... I'm going to blow just at the thought."

He sucked in a few deep breaths, and then resumed his movements, more tentative now. He rocked into me, making me see stars as he slowly got deeper and deeper inside me. So deep, I was sure I could feel him in my stomach.

"Hayle..." I breathed. "*More.* Fuck me harder."

"Anything you want is yours, Avalon. My Avalon."

Be careful what you wish for, because he fucked me

like an animal. He pounded into me as he sucked my nipples, his body curled like a contortionist so he could touch and taste me everywhere.

I *loved* it.

"Come for me, baby. Goddess, I need to feel you clench around me. I need you so badly." The authority in his voice was like a blanket over my body, and I was helpless to resist. My limbs seized with pleasure, my muscles contracting and my breath stilling in my lungs as wave after wave of my orgasm rocked me.

I feared that Hayle was right. He had ruined me for any other man ever.

chapter sixteen

Vox

I SIGHED as I disembarked from the ferry. As much as this island was almost primitive, it was blissfully free of Line politics. Well, sort of. On a much smaller, less treacherous level, politics was still played at Boellium War College. It was more fun than it was dangerous. The same couldn't be said for Fortaare.

The Conclave had been interesting, for several reasons. One, it was interesting to see where the Third Line was placing its pawns. I didn't think that the Taemes gave a single fuck about the Lower Lines, no more than we did anyway. Although maybe Hayle Taeme was going soft, hanging around with the dirt scrabblers all the time. Maybe that was rubbing off on his father.

The other interesting part of the Conclave had been meeting the Baron of the Ninth Line. Roman Halhed was an average-looking man, with a craggy face and a full beard. He was short and muscled, like most of the men of the northern mountains. There was nothing of his daughter in his face or coloring. If I hadn't known Avalon was his daughter, I wouldn't have been able to pick her as a relation at all.

More than that, he had none of her spark. He seemed flat and gray, nothing interesting or useful coming from his attendance at the Conclave. He hadn't offered aid to the Twelfth Line, despite his daughter's friendship, and I wondered if they even conversed. He hadn't asked me or Hayle about how she fared at Boellium, which even my father might have been inclined to do.

No, the only color I saw from the man was when he was deep in the liquor at the banquet, and dwindling our alcohol stores was the only thing he contributed to the meeting at all.

He was a disappointment.

My cousin Shay met me on the dock in Boemouthe. She picked at her nails with impatience, but she could wait. We would take this moment to discuss matters of importance, while we were outside the walls of Boellium, which always seemed to be listening.

"Cousin," she greeted cooly. She might have the emotional range of a rock, but I trusted her nearly more than any other member of my family. Shay and I had grown up together, and there were very few secrets between us. It had always been that way.

I liked to think she was more loyal to me than my father, but that might be wishful thinking. "Hello, Shay. Make anyone cry while I was away?"

She raised an eyebrow. "No, but you're not technically back at the college yet. I could race ahead and remedy that."

I smirked at her and indicated we should start walking. It was about a twenty-minute walk to the walls of Boellium War College, and it wasn't worth getting our own mode of transportation to make the distance.

"What did I miss?" I asked, lowering my voice, swirling us in a dome of air to keep our conversation private.

"Not a lot. There's rumors of the Lower Six starting their own networking parties, but so far, nothing has happened. Taeme was away with you, so the Third Line were also quiet. Lucio is far more relaxed than Hayle, so they were more of a disorganised rabble than usual. Hayle's new girlfriend almost lost her head to Eugene, though, which was possibly the most exciting thing that happened while you were gone."

My feet stuttered on the well-worn path, and it was only decades of training that kept my face neutral. "The girl from the Ninth Line?"

Shay nodded. "They were sparring, and Eugene lost it. Had her on the ground with a sword at her throat before Lucio had even stopped flirting with some girl from the Lower Lines. If I was Taeme, I'd be asking for a new Second."

"Was she injured?" My tone was bored, but my heart felt like it was pounding, for reasons I didn't want to understand.

Shrugging, Shay glared at a conscript who was

walking down the path toward us, making the soldier move onto the grass and hustle a little faster. "Barely a scratch. That damn bird of Taeme's swooped in to save the day, and got injured in the process, but the girl from the Ninth managed to escape any real harm."

Some of the tension released from my shoulders. "Is that why I didn't see Taeme on the ferry today?"

"He got back yesterday. I heard that the noises coming from the Ninth Dorm have sounded like a brothel on the dockside in Ovl. Taeme was obviously very worried about his mistress. I even saw one of the Third Line conscripts packing them food to take down. Have to keep up your strength to do it doggy style." She chuckled at her own joke.

I gritted my back teeth, but the idea of Taeme fucking Avalon made rage burn in my stomach. It wasn't jealousy, though. Why would I be jealous of the fact he was fucking a whore from the Lower Lines?

I was silent as we walked the last little way to the walls of Boellium War College. It was impressive, I'd give it that. It had stood here for centuries. A pillar of strength, or maybe a subtle threat.

Stone walls ran around the whole college, and the atrium shot from the center like a jewel in its setting, a taunt made of glass. It was impenetrable; whoever had built the main building of Boellium had powers that were lost to us now, because it was stronger than stone or steel. We hadn't been able to replicate the material, and it had frustrated Father to no end.

Stepping through the large iron gates of Boellium, I

relaxed a little more. I knew what to expect here. I was the king of this domain, and the people within it were predictable.

Except for her.

Avalon Halhed had been an anomaly since she arrived. I didn't like people who stepped out of their expected roles, and it was hard to deny that she'd had some effect on the social structure of the college. The mingling between the Upper and Lower Lines had always been frowned upon, but the girl didn't seem to care.

Add Eugene from the Fourth stepping out of line like that, and something was off in Boellium. People needed to be reminded of their standing, their place in the power structure of the college, and moreso, in the structure of Ebrus itself.

I looked over at Shay. "I think it's time we had a little healthy competition. What do you say?"

She grinned. It reminded me why she was here with me, rather than being someone's diplomatic bride. It wasn't just that she was strong, and that we'd been similar ages. She'd been raised with me as a sibling, far more so than my actual siblings.

It was also because Shay was bloodthirsty. She loved to fight; she'd fight the stable boys, her brothers, our cousins, and as she got older, the younger soldiers and bodyguards. She was fast and strong, but more than that, she was mean.

No, not mean. She was *angry*. Simmering rage had flowed just below her skin since we hit ten years of age, and it had stayed there. No matter how badly her mother had tried to beat it out of her, had tried to turn her into a lady, Shay stubbornly remained the person she was.

She'd told me once she did like the stilettos beneath the ballgowns, though—all the better to stab a man with.

No, it wasn't that Shay was a psycho, despite the rumors.

Shay just didn't want to be some diplomat's wife, because she had no interest in men. Shay was only interested in women, and that didn't fit with our family's agenda. So when I left for Boellium, I'd convinced my family that I trusted no one else to have my back, and gave her a reprieve from her family duty. It wasn't untrue; I didn't trust anyone with my back the way I trusted Shay.

I couldn't help her forever, though. Eventually, my father would put his foot down, and she would be forced into a political marriage, unless I could keep her out of his reach until one of my brothers took the mantle of Baron. They were more sympathetic to her predicament than Father.

Shay twirled her favorite dagger over her fingers. "What are you thinking?"

"A battle of strength, no powers. Just a nice fair fight where people remember why I sit on top of this fucking shit heap, and that my word is law."

"A tournament?" She looked at me imperiously. "You know, you could always just fight Taeme for the girl, if you want to fuck her so bad. Or maybe you can just ask nicely. He's an animal; they've been known to share."

I glared at her as we headed toward the stairs that led to our penthouse dorm. "It's got nothing to do with Taeme, or Avalon Halhed. It has everything to do with the fact I'm not sure I like the unrest and the boldness of the conscripts this year. They need to respect their betters, and what more perfect way is there than handing them their asses without my superior magic?"

I was highly trained, as was Shay, and I'd been learning the art of war since I could hold a sword. I could comfortably beat any man, or woman, in this college, including most of the instructors. It was time they remembered.

"Let me guess, you want to be paired in the first battle with Taeme?"

I snorted. "No, cousin. I want you to pair Eugene and Taeme in the first fight."

Shay quirked an eyebrow at me, but shook her head. "Eugene's funeral, I guess."

It would be bad if the Lower Lines rose up, but honestly, they could only do it through full-scale revolution, and even then, it would be hit or miss. With the current drought, they had neither the manpower nor the resources for such actions.

No, the real threat to the current status quo weren't the Lower Lines, but the ones with just enough power to think they could stand with the big boys. Eugene had been getting a little too cocky, a little too power-hungry, and it was certainly time for him to remember he was the Fourth Line for a reason.

And Taeme would eat that slimy fucker for lunch without ever having to lift a finger, especially if what Shay had said regarding Taeme and the Ninth conscript was correct.

That was the reason I wanted them paired. It had nothing to do with Avalon Halhed.

She shook her head at me. "Sometimes I wonder if you missed that Vylan cruelty gene, then you do shit like this, and I remember that you're still your father's son."

The words were meant to be a slap in the face, and Shay was the only person I'd allow to deliver these verbal barbs.

"I might not respect the man, but not all his notions are incorrect." A flash of hurt in her eyes told me she thought I meant the sexuality thing. I didn't. So I squeezed her arm gently. "Most of them are bullshit, though." Straightening before we both became uncomfortable with the contact, I added, "Arrange the tournament for the weekend. Tell them I'll give fifty gold coins to the winner."

Shay whistled low, striding off. I put my bags on my bed and didn't think too hard about what the fuck I was doing this for.

chapter seventeen

Avalon

FOUR DAYS after Hayle returned home, we emerged from my dorm. Lucio had covered for us both, and none of the teachers would contradict the Third Line's claim that we'd both gotten food poisoning from bad clams.

The Third Line had also been bringing us food and leaving it in my dorm's kitchen, though more often than not, by the time we dragged ourselves from the bedroom, either one of the hounds or Epsy had nibbled at the edges.

It was blissful, this connection to Hayle. He worshipped me for hours on end, until I thought I'd go insane from the pleasure of it all. A little voice in the back of my head told me that he'd get bored of me eventually, that I was just new, and he was a predator who enjoyed the chase. That eventually he'd get bored, and I'd be back to being alone, only it would be worse. I would know what it was like to be as close as humanly possible to another person, and the loneliness would be unfathomable. Unbearable.

When those thoughts entered my brain—usually late at night while I was awake and Hayle was snoring softly beside me—I tried to remember his face when he'd burst into my room. That panic wasn't the response of a man who was merely playing with his food before he moved onto something more tasty.

I didn't understand it, but I knew deep in my gut that what was happening between us meant something.

Grabbing my hand, he pulled me closer on the stairwell. "You're thinking awfully hard over there. World domination plans? Because I can help."

I snorted a laugh, and didn't even try to resist the urge to stand up on my toes and brush my lips over his. "Not today. You just focus on your battle."

Lucio had brought word that Vox Vylan had returned and was bored enough to set up a tournament for the conscripts. The prize was fifty gold coins, basically a generational wealth to the Lower Lines, and had made the rules of battle magicless. Everyone would fight with the same amount of magic as the Twelfth Line, evening the playing field. The buzz around the tournament had found us, even though we'd been buried deep in the haze of lust.

Viana had marched into my dorm last night and declared that the entire Twelfth Line was going to participate, and the fact that Hayle's name wasn't on the signup sheet had been noted and whispered about.

Hayle had left to sign up immediately, though he did apologize by bringing me back an entire cake and then eating it off my naked body.

Like they'd been waiting for him, the First Line had closed the signup and announced the rounds would start the following day.

Now, he kissed my temple. "I was born for battle. Unless they put me against Vylan in the first round, there's no one else in this school who's even close to my skill level."

I wouldn't put it past Vox to put himself against Hayle in the very beginning. Maybe that's what this whole thing was—a giant dick-measuring contest.

We reached the atrium level, and Hayle stepped away, putting distance between us for the first time in days. I pushed down the hurt in my chest. He was Hayle Taeme of the Third Line. I was a Ninth Line nobody. Of course we could have sex, but he couldn't be seen with me up here, in the cold light of day. I knew enough about politics for that.

Inhaling deeply, Hayle turned to look at me, frowning down at my expression. "What's wrong?"

Shaking my head, I pasted a smile on my face. I'd just had countless orgasms, so maybe my hormones were all over the place. Logically, I knew I should be so blissed out that none of the negativity could touch me.

Logic and emotion rarely saw eye to eye.

"Nothing, just hungry. You better go before people talk." I shoved him gently in the other direction.

Understanding dawned on his face. "You think I

don't want people to know?" He was back in front of me in a single movement, picking me up with his hands under my ass and walking me backwards toward one of the large stone pillars that held up the atrium. He pressed my back against the smooth stone and fucked my mouth with his tongue in a way that was definitely indecent. "I want every fucking person in this college to know you're *mine*, Avalon Halhed. I will shout it from the rooftops, if that would reassure you. I told you that you're mine, and that means I'm yours too."

He kissed me hard once more, branding me as his. Whistles and laughter and the hushed chatter of dozens of people whispering at once drowned from my hearing slowly until there was no one and nothing but Hayle.

He pulled back, letting my feet slide to the floor. Turning, he faced everyone in the atrium: conscripts, tutors, college staff. "Listen up. Avalon Halhed is mine. I claim her, and I will fuck up any single person who says something to her about it. Am I clear?"

No one said a single thing, but it was clear from their expressions that they understood and *definitely* would be gossiping about this later in their own Line dorms.

Grinning, Hayle turned back to me. "You aren't my dirty little secret, Avalon. This is deeper than that." He kissed my forehead. "Go get some breakfast. I have to race up to my dorm and get my weapons and armor. I'll meet you back downstairs?"

I felt like I was in a daze, but I must have nodded,

because he was bounding up the stairs toward his own dorm room. I hoped he remembered the way after all this time.

A self-satisfied smirk curled my lips as I headed toward the food hall, and I tried not to enjoy the fact that people got out of the way for me now. Blending in was a dream that was long gone—might as well enjoy it while I could.

Walking into the food hall, I had a feeling that Hayle's declaration was only just reaching ahead of me, because heads still turned. Viana waved me over to the Twelfth table, and I held up a finger so I could grab a piece of fruit first. I needed sustenance after the last few days. I couldn't even feel my thighs, and it felt like I'd been riding a horse across all of Ebrus.

Acacia moved over so I could sit between her and Viana. "Good to see you've left your den of ill-repute down there on the Ninth Level," she quipped, grinning.

Viana hummed her agreement. "Did you see her waddle from the food line? She's got dicked all the way to the dungeon, I think. Don't worry girl, I've got an oil that will clear that right up." She winked at me and laughed at the flush in my cheeks. "I heard in the breakfast line that Hayle just fucked you in the atrium in an animalistic mating ritual."

I frowned. Okay, so the declaration had gotten a little skewed between the atrium and here. "Uh, he kissed me, but we were both fully clothed?"

Viana actually pouted. "Boo. But regardless, way to

go, girl. Bagging a Taeme is like finding a chest of gold buried in your lavatory."

I wasn't sure exactly what response that visual was meant to produce, but ew. "Thanks?"

Deciding it was a good time to change the subject, I bit into my apple. "Are you guys all going to the tournament?" I looked at the rest of the Twelfth conscripts.

Acacia ate another piece of bread slathered in honey. "That amount of money is life changing. We could save our entire village with that much coin."

"We could save ten villages with that much coin," someone interjected, and I shook my head. Vox was dropping that amount on some random tournament to keep himself entertained, and he could literally feed the whole of Eelrood with that money. That was the difference between the Upper and Lower Lines in a nutshell.

Not Hayle, though. He'd told me that he'd encouraged his father, the Baron of the Third Line, to support the drought efforts of the Eleventh and Twelfth Lines at the Conclave meeting he'd been forced to go to. Something in my chest had fluttered, but I didn't want to think about that feeling just yet.

Viana shrugged. "I don't think we could beat any of the First Line, or the Third Line even, but it's worth the risk. They're doing it magicless; we've trained without magic forever, so maybe we have a small advantage. Maybe they'll knock each other out, and the Goddess will be on our side."

Acacia nodded. "We've all agreed to send the prize

home if we win. So we have the numbers too." The Twelfth did that often—operated as one entity. "Plus, the college tutors have suspended lessons so we can have this tournament, and personally, I'm going to enjoy the lack of theory work and nine-hour drills, even if I get knocked out in the first round. It's almost a holiday."

We all laughed, but just as suddenly as it started, the mirth around the table died off, their eyes over my shoulder. I knew who was behind me before I even turned to look.

Vox Vylan stood at the table of the Twelfth Line, probably for the first time ever. He didn't look at them. Didn't acknowledge them in any way. "Ninth. I see you didn't sign up for my little tournament."

I raised an eyebrow. "I don't feel the urge to perform for you, my liege," I mocked gently, but I couldn't keep my lips from curling. He enjoyed our bickering as much as I did; I was sure of it. "Are you participating in your own tournament?"

He gave me an imperious look. "Of course. I need to show the masses that I do not need my magic to be the most powerful person here." I wondered how long he'd been listening to our conversation as he glanced behind me at the Twelfth table.

Rolling my eyes, I cleared my throat. "Of course. What was I thinking? Is there something I can help you with, Vox?"

He opened and closed his mouth several times, before he shook his head. "No. Just wanted you to know that you are a disappointment to me yet again, Ninth."

Yeah, I didn't think that was it, but I didn't want to dig around in Vox Vylan's words for his hidden meaning today. I inclined my head. "I'll be sure to cry myself to sleep tonight over your words."

Had his lips just twitched? Before I could confirm, his face was once again the royal, pompous mask.

"Be sure you do. Enjoy the first round."

Then he was gone. I didn't have time to wonder what the fuck that was all about, because Hayle was bounding over, a grin on his face as he scooped me from my spot. "Hey, guys," he said quickly to the Twelfth conscripts. "Just going to steal my girl." He didn't wait for anyone's response, just carried me like a sack of potatoes to the Third Line section. "Guess what?" he said as he dumped me on the table beside Lucio's plate.

I smiled apologetically at Hayle's second-in-command. We'd bonded over my almost death. "Hey, Lucio." I turned back to Hayle, and my heart beat faster in my chest. Why was he so damn beautiful? Surely this feeling in my chest should have disappeared by now. "What am I guessing?"

"They put out the rounds. My first battle is against Eugene from the Fourth." His grin was purely predatory. "I'm going to make him wish he was never born."

I frowned, my eyes drifting to Vox, but his back was to me as he talked to his own second, Shay. Had he done that on purpose? Did he know about Eugene trying to kill me? Why would he even care?

The mysteries of Vox Vylan's actions were far outside any mere mortal's ability to comprehend, that much was clear. But maybe, just maybe, he gave a shit about me?

I snorted at the ridiculousness of the thought. But he'd been right; I really would enjoy the first round.

chapter eighteen

Hayle

THE INSTRUCTORS HAD OPENED up the training ring for the tournament, splitting it into six different rings. People sat on the post-and-rail fence that ran right around the edge, including Avalon. I was glad she wasn't fighting. I would've laid down my sword and let her win if we'd ended up against each other, and if she'd been hurt?

Blood would've been spilled.

Besides, I kind of liked the idea of her watching me from the sidelines, making Eugene remember that he was nothing more than a shitstain on my boot. I looked around the rest of the ring, at all the other people prepping for their fights, stretching and warming up their muscles so they were limber.

Except Shay Vylan, who sat behind a table, looking annoyed. She'd gotten stuck hosting this thing rather than fighting too, and I knew she'd be annoyed by that. Strutting over, I smirked down at her. I liked Shay far better than her fuck of a cousin—she was mean as a war cat with its tail on fire, and she hated everyone equally, regardless of Line. I could get down with that.

"Shay, pushing pens for Vylan today, I see?"

She glared at me. "Fuck off, Taeme, before I have you neutered."

I laughed, drawing the glare of others around the table. "I would just like to see the battle bracket, if I could." It wasn't a question, but she was a haughty bitch, so she might make me beg.

The other thing I liked about Shay was that she never hit on me at the Upper Six parties. I'd fucked my way through most of the Upper Line conscripts, where social standing and politics didn't matter. But Shay was the only female in the First Line dorms, because unlike my Line who had warriors from all genders, the Vylans were patriarchal. They believed the daughters of the First Line were only good for marrying off and for political alliances. Boys got trained in the art of war at Boellium War College, and the girls got trained how to lie on their backs and produce Heirs. It had been that way forever—until Shay. I had a feeling Vox had something to do with that, given how close they were.

Not to aggrandize my own desirability, but I was fairly sure that Shay wasn't interested in me, not due to Line loyalty, but because she wasn't interested in dick at all.

Some of the other conscripts had suggested that she and Vox fucked to keep the Line pure, but those were just rumors, and I highly doubted they were true. Vox and Shay were close, in the same way Lucio and I were close. I trusted that man with my back, but I didn't want to fuck him.

"Do you want me to read it to you like a fairytale your mama would tell you at night, or are you going to fucking take it and read it like you have two braincells to knock together? You *can* read, right?" Shay snarked while I was lost in my thoughts.

"I think so. Does this word here say boobies?" I pointed to the word *battle* at the top of the handwritten sheet. Shay actually picked up her dagger, and I danced away, laughing. "Sorry, sorry!"

Looking over the sheet, I noticed that Vox was against Lucio in the second round. That would be a good match to watch; I hoped my own battle was done by then. I'd duelled Vylan a few times since we were both conscripted, and while I wanted to blame his powers for his battle prowess, it wasn't true. He was highly trained in several different weapons, as well as hand-to-hand combat.

But the Third Line was made for battle. We were warriors by blood and by code.

Yeah, Lucio and Vylan would definitely be a good battle to watch.

Handing back the schedule to Shay, I winked and sauntered back to my Soul Tie. I'd wanted so badly to bond her during our sexfest. I wanted to explain to her that she was mine, that my life was hers, why we felt what we did.

But I couldn't, not yet. She needed time to learn that

my feelings for her were genuine. That I wasn't going anywhere, and she never needed to go back to those mountains to that drunk old fuck she called a father. I would introduce her to my family, to my Line, and they'd accept her. She'd have a family who loved her, who would have her back at all times against any foe.

Avalon smiled down at me from the top rail of the fence, and at that height, my shoulders fit perfectly between her thighs. "You know, this is quite a good height," I mumbled and bit the inside of her thigh.

"Hayle!" she squealed, her cheeks flushing that pretty shade of pink that I adored. She slammed her thighs around my shoulders, burying her fingers in my hair and pulling my head up until I climbed the rails, making us face to face.

I kissed her lips gently. "You ready to see me avenge your honor?"

She snorted. "I can avenge my own honor, Hayle Taeme. But I will enjoy watching you bloody up that smug asshole. Show him he just doesn't get to pick on those lower than him."

I tilted my face toward her. "Kiss me again for good luck?"

She wrapped her arms around my neck and leaned forward to kiss me in a way that I felt in my soul. Fuck, she was everything. Four days of insanely amazing sex could make anyone smitten, but it had reinforced what I already knew. She was my Soul Tie. The constant connection had just reinforced the bond.

She pulled out the ribbon that was holding her hair

back. "In the old days, you'd give a token to your champion, so if you're going to avenge my honor, I guess I better pay you in fake lace ribbons." She tied it around my wrist, tucking in the ends so they didn't get caught during the fight.

Ha, little did she know she was never getting this back. I'd tell her later that in the Third Line, this basically made us married. It wasn't true, but I'd enjoy watching her sweat about it for a bit.

Someone whistled. "A-Side, to your rings!" The shout was amplified by magic, and I kissed her once more with a bit of tongue, before jumping down.

"Cheer for me," I said with a wink and swaggered to my ring. Eugene sneered at me, and I just smirked in his direction. I hoped he was about to piss his pants.

"You fuckers know the rules," Shay yelled. "To first blood. If you aim to maim, I will personally shove an icicle up your ass until you get a brain freeze." I laughed, swallowing it down as she glared in my direction. "If you aren't in your ring when I let up the starting flare, you forfeit, so don't be fucking late."

Someone raised their hand, and she turned her eyes on them in a hard glare. It was one of the Tenth Line kids. He must have been all of seventeen. "The Upper Lines are all wearing armor, which is disadvantageous to the rest of us. If this is until first blood and based on skill, shouldn't we be all equally armored?"

Shay raised a brow at him, then looked over at Vox. He shrugged and took off his armor. "Sounds fair."

Whatever, I doubted Eugene was going to get the

point of his sword anywhere near me, let alone draw blood. I tossed my armor over the rope designating our ring.

Holding her finger in the air, Shay gave us all the stink eye one more time. "Remember, *no magic.* Anyone using magic will instantly forfeit, so keep it in your pants, fuckers. Ready?"

I twirled my sword in my hand, and Eugene lifted his own. The point shook a little, making me grin at him maniacally. "I'm going to make this hurt, you fuck. You'll never even look at my girl again without pissing your pants."

He sneered at me. "Whatever you want to dip your disgusting dick in is between you and the rest of your flea-infested Line," he snarked back.

"GO!" Shay yelled, shooting an explosion of ice in the air that probably would've been beautiful, if I could see it.

Instead, I advanced on Eugene immediately. He was the cerebral type of fighter, all memorized forms and patterns. I fought with my instincts and my senses, by reading body language and relying on muscle memory from years of sparring and fighting.

He was already on the back foot, but he recovered quickly, swinging his sword in a solid counterattack. Solid wasn't going to win him this battle.

I parried again and again, pushing him around the ring like I was playing with him. A cat and a mouse. A wolf and its prey. He was going to know what pain was like before the end of this. There were a hundred ways I could make him hurt without drawing blood and ending the round.

First, I got close, blocking his swing with mine and kicking him in the knee. His yell echoed around the training ring, but there was no blood, just a lot of fucking hurt.

I smirked down at him. "Want to forfeit? No shame in being a little bitch."

"The only bitch here is that whore from the Ninth."

I shook my head and tsked. "If you liked pain so much, Eugene, you should have just gotten someone to spank you and call you a naughty boy. This is a little extreme." I put my foot into his gut, sending him sprawling backwards across the ring. The instructor watching us for first blood raised an eyebrow, but didn't stop the round. "Come on, Eugene. You're Fourth Line, remember? Stop embarrassing the Upper Lines and get back on your feet to fight. Look, I'll even go over here first." I shuffled back toward the ropes.

Eugene, to his credit, struggled back to his feet, his face so red that it was almost purple. He charged at me then, his sword whirling in a wild and messy set of twirls that must have been hell to hold onto, but they were quite difficult to block. He was coming for my head now; shit had just gotten interesting.

I parried each blow, one after the other. He telegraphed his next move like he was shouting them at me, and it was easy enough to get him on the back foot again. One, two, three, and then I hooked my foot around his ankle, unbalancing him completely. He landed on his back, and I swung my sword down to point at his throat. The same place that Avalon had a small, pink mark from a healing wound that this asshole had put there.

I let all of the lighthearted fuckboy leave my face until he could see the monster underneath. "You hurt her, and that is unforgivable. Your days are numbered, Eugene Rovan." I pressed down harder, until blood trickled and pooled into the indentation.

He snarled at me, his face full of hatred and malice. "Fuck you."

Magic surged from him in a hot wave.

A deafening bang.

A blinding flash.

Searing pain.

Nothing.

chapter nineteen

Avalon

NO.

Lightning struck at the ring where Hayle had stood. Three bolts in rapid succession.

Boom. Boom. Boom.

My ears rang, and my eyes burned, making seeing anything but black spots almost impossible, but still, I jumped down from the fence and ran. Bodies were strewn around, people covering their ears as blood leaked from their lobes like teardrop rubies.

Hayle.

No.

The hounds were yowling, and someone was screaming. I ran, hurtling people and bodies. I was there. So close. "Hayle!"

Eugene lay on the ground, uninjured. Beside him was scorched earth from the thunderous crack of lightning that had reverberated around the training ring.

The earth was still smoking. No, not the earth. Something.

Someone.

No.

"Hayle!" I screamed. I could hear it now, my voice echoing around my head. My pain spread down my limbs. I climbed under the rope, but others were arriving.

It wasn't him. It couldn't be him. I refused to believe it.

The charred lump was a person, I had to acknowledge that. It had arms and legs and a head, but everything else was black. But it couldn't be Hayle. The smell of burned flesh made me want to vomit but still, I went closer. A flash of white on the charred wrist was like a razor blade to my heart. Burned at the edges, but achingly familiar.

"Hayle..." Pain ruptured in my chest. Pain like nothing I'd ever felt, or maybe I had. It felt like an old friend, but also like my mortal enemy.

Loneliness and pain. My heart splintering into a billion pieces.

Someone scooped me up and walked me away, but I was screaming, searching the crowd. Looking for Hayle, because that couldn't be him. Maybe he'd be okay. I should have checked if he was still alive.

I looked up into the pale face of Vox Vylan. "Take me back!" I screamed in his face, spittle flying from my lips. "This is your fault. *Your fault.*" I slammed my hands against his chest, but he didn't put me down. "Your fault."

"I know." I felt the words more than heard them.

My scream got louder and louder until the world was spinning. I screamed until the man in front of me, his mouth wide with shock, flashed in and out of my vision. I screamed until shooting stars of burning light spun around me, like a cyclone of fire. The world was on fire. My chest was on fire. My heart was a charred, burning lump in the middle of the training ring.

No, there was no world without Hayle. No world in which I lost him so soon.

I screamed at the Goddess. I screamed at Vox Vylan. I screamed at fate and fear, and as I fell to my knees, I screamed even as the world disappeared.

I screamed myself and everyone around me into oblivion.

chapter twenty

Avalon

conscription day - the first day of spring

THERE WAS blood pooling on the cobblestone entrance of the Boellium War College. I shouldn't be surprised, given the baying of the crowd jammed into the front courtyard, and the man suspended in the air, bleeding steadily from his nose. The ruby liquid fell in huge drops, splashing on the ground beneath him with a gruesome dripping sound. Once the puddle of blood became too much, someone with water abilities seemed to wash it away.

That would definitely explain the pink stones.

The guy in the air, bound with invisible ropes, looked at me imploringly. "Help me," he gasped weakly.

I met his eyes, keeping my face shuttered and neutral, then timed my steps to walk under his blood droplets so they didn't splatter on me.

Someone huffed a laugh, and someone else muttered, "That's cold," but I ignored them all. I wasn't here to be someone's savior. I wasn't here to change the status quo.

I was here because I was *the useless daughter*.

Every one of the Twelve Lines had to enrol a child into the Boellium War College every year, and once a decade, it had to send a young person from the leading family of that Line. If I had to guess at their reasoning, I'd say it was so they didn't all send simple farmer's sons and create an army of uneducated cannon fodder.

Some Lines sent their most gifted children, either physically or mentally, in the hopes they could make advantageous connections or better still, marriages.

But that was for the Upper Six Lines. I was the youngest daughter of the current Baron of the Ninth Line. I was barely better than pond scum to these people. The only thing worse would be if I was from the Twelfth.

So I didn't care who was hanging up there, dripping blood for the cause; I couldn't help them. I didn't want to help them. I wanted to learn to fight, then go home to where there were fewer people and smaller egos.

I'd spent hours reading journal accounts of prestigious Ninth Line warriors, who talked about coming to Boellium War College like it was the best and worst time of their life, so I knew what to expect. I knew this was part of the hazing, helping to sift the weak of stomach and will from the strong contenders.

I knew that a little blood was going to become an

everyday occurrence for me. That was why I kept walking. It's why I avoided the eyes of the milling crowd, and closed my ears to their muttered commentary.

I wasn't cold. I was realistic. A tender heart in Boellium would soon bleed out, and then it would be their blood painting the courtyard's cobblestones red. That wouldn't be me.

I'd walked here all the way from my home in Rewill, and I was exhausted. As the conscript for the Ninth Line, I wasn't given any aid; even the clothes on my back had been stolen from my brothers. This hazing was the final hurdle before I could sign myself into the college's ledgers, then collapse on a bed somewhere and sleep for a week.

Eyes on my face had me looking across the courtyard, and when I met some glacial blue irises, I quickly turned my sights back to Boellium War College's fabled atrium.

I knew who it was. I might have lived in the mountains, far away from the glittering courts, but I knew Vox Vylan. The second son of the current Baron of the First Line. I'd heard he was powerful, but the way he held that person suspended in the air effortlessly was definitely a telling example. I didn't want to meet the Heir. I didn't want to be in his sights at all. I wanted to do my time and leave again.

Walking through the atrium quickly, I knew this was the part where the Third Line hazed the incoming conscripts. It was a madhouse of screams and animal sounds so loud that it hurt my ears. Known for their beast magic, the Third Line were as scary as the First. Their hazing wouldn't be as easy to ignore as the First Line.

As if to prove my point, two giant hounds leapt in front of me, their eyes intent on my face, like they were contemplating what I tasted like.

I stared them down, my heart hammering. You weren't supposed to run from predators; that's what I told myself over and over as I held my ground. Finally, someone whistled, and the hounds retreated.

Unable to stop myself, I turned toward the sound, meeting a pair of forest-green orbs so transfixing that they stole the air from my lungs. I knew enough about current affairs to know this was Hayle Taeme, third son of the Taeme family, leaders of the Third Line.

Staring in those eyes made my heart beat so hard, it felt like it was seizing in my chest. Pain spread down through my limbs, and I urged myself to move. Whatever he was doing to me was dangerous. I knew they had beast powers, but what if he could literally reach into my chest and crush my heart as well?

We all had powers we had to keep a secret. Something tickled in the back of my brain, a secret that I denied even to myself, but I shut it down. I wasn't here to uncover any secrets about myself or anyone else.

I vowed to myself I would stay far, far away from Hayle Taeme. I would also stay away from Vox Vylan.

I was going to do my time and get the hell out of Boellium War College, safe and whole, and I would never look back.

Seeing the future is the curse of our Line. I hope to the Goddess that our magic weakens until we can find happiness instead.

–Ellanora Halhed, First Daughter of the Ninth Line

chapter twenty-one

Avalon

GETTING out of the atrium was harder than I thought. Beside the door was a giant war cat that had something pinned in the corner. It looked like a small purple stolt, and the sight of its pitiful, shaking body pulled at my heartstrings.

I felt some kind of kinship to the pathetic creature, and despite my thoughts only moments earlier, I couldn't let it be eaten.

But getting between a war cat and its prey was a recipe for a mauling that I was in no hurry to experience. I looked at the door behind the big cat, then back at the stolt. You weren't supposed to run from predators, but right now, I wasn't its prey.

Tightening the straps of my pack on my arms, I sucked in several deep breaths. If I died on the first day of my conscription at Boellium War College, so be it. It would hardly be a record for the school, or for my Line.

If I was lucky, the door would open outwards. If I

167

was unlucky, I'd be eaten. Surely Boellium wouldn't let its conscripts be eaten by the animals of the Third Line? There had to be rules and order of some kind here.

Before I could talk myself out of it, I sucked in one last long breath and sprinted toward the door. I raced around the groups of people, other conscripts and members of the other Lines, heading straight for the purple stolt. I kept my eyes on it, leaning down and grabbing it by the scruff of its neck as I darted past the war cat and straight at the door. I hit it with all the force of my full body weight, and it flung open, slamming backwards against the wall in a way that would have smashed the glass of a normal door. Spinning quickly, I grabbed the handle and slammed it shut in the face of an annoyed war cat.

Fuck, that was *not* something I wanted to do again. Leaning back against the door, I dropped the stolt on the ground. "Off you go. You're on your own now."

It looked up at me, blinking slowly, then ran up my leg and into the pocket of my oversized skirt. I tried to empty it, but the angry call of, "Next!" from the office in front of me had me giving up.

"Uh, okay. I guess you're coming with me." I pushed into the administration office, where the woman behind the desk was glaring up at me.

"About fucking time. You must be from the Ninth Line?" She had one arm and a wicked scar that ran across her upper lip, making her look fierce. Her head was also shaved close to the scalp, but somehow, none of those things detracted from her femininity. It was like looking at a warrior elf from one of my childhood storybooks. "Name?"

"Oh, Avalon Halhed, fifth child of the Baron of the Ninth Line."

She eyed me sternly, her gaze too knowing. Did she know of me? Had she heard the rumors too? "Fancy fucking title. Your dorm is three floors down. There's no one else from your Line here, so it might be a bit quiet." She handed me a folder of paperwork. "Your timetable. Be early." *Or else* hung between us.

I stepped out of the office and straight into someone. Looking up, and up again, I found myself nose to chest with Hayle Taeme. My breath caught in my lungs until they felt like they were on fire. I scooted backwards, away from him as fast as I could. "Sorry."

His hand snapped out and gripped my arm. "Who are you?"

My eyes felt like they might pop out of my skull. "No one." When he didn't let me go, I swallowed down the lump in my throat that threatened to choke me. Why was I reacting this way? Was it the sheer power that emanated from him? Finally, I found my voice. "Avalon Halhed, from the Ninth Line."

Listening to the warnings banging around inside my skull, I dragged my arm from his grasp and sprinted to the stairs, barrelling down them so fast that if I'd tripped, I'd be dead. My head was screaming at me to stay as far away from Hayle Taeme and the Third Line as I could. That in that direction lay only incredible pain.

Could I sense that he was a predator? Was it my hindbrain taking over due to my obvious lack of self-preservation?

Stepping into the Ninth Line dorm, I noted that dust covered *everything*. Someone had stacked a bunch of chairs in the room, which looked like it had been long uninhabited. There were still dirty plates in the sink, and I tried not to think about why. Tried not to think about the fact that most of my Line had died here before they could graduate.

You only had to be a conscript for two years, and then if we went to war, you got called up to fight. But we hadn't been to war in so long that I doubted there were people alive who remembered the last time. Even longer since we'd been to war with anyone but the other Lines of Ebrus.

I moved some boxes and chairs to the far wall and picked the furthest dorm room from the entrance. Putting my bag down, I worked at stripping the sheets and blankets. Who knew what was living in these things after all this time? Piling the linens on the floor, I was surprised when the stolt leapt from my pocket and curled up on top.

Laughing at the small purple animal, I nudged the nest of linen with my foot. "You aren't very smart. Are you someone's pet? Someone from the Third Line, maybe?" It just yawned and blinked jewel-colored purple eyes at me. "Well, if someone comes to beat me up for stealing their pet, I'll tell them I tried to get rid of you twice. Stubborn creature." I reached down and scratched its head, and it leaned into the touch. Definitely tamed. "Should I name you? Calling you Stupid seems a little counterproductive."

His color reminded me of the purple epsirialle flowers at home. That was a long name for such a tiny creature, though.

"What about Epsy? Do you like that?" It booped my hand with his face, either agreeing or asking for more head scratches. Or both. "Epsy it is." I didn't know why; it just felt *right*.

My stomach rumbled angrily, reminding me I hadn't eaten in twenty-four hours. I wanted to change out of my traveling clothes, but I was a little worried that I might pass out from hunger in the shower. Food, then a bath. And then sleep for at least twelve hours.

Walking to the dorm entrance, I looked up at the stairs and rethought my plan, but I'd thrown up the whole way over to Boemouthe on the ferry, and I was *starving*. I'd start stockpiling food down here as soon as I could, because although the trek down here might've been hard, Boellium War College wasn't going to be any easier. If the accounts I'd read were correct, it would be the most difficult training of my life.

So I grabbed the handrail and pulled myself up to the main floor of the atrium. I looked around for Hayle Taeme, because if he was up here, I would be tempted to head back down to my dorm. But there were just crowds of people milling around, most of them heading in one direction. The sun was setting, and I'd bet my non-existent dowry that they were heading to the food hall.

I walked behind them, just going with the crowd. There weren't as many people in all of my hometown of Rewill as there were in the atrium right now. Not even in our Keep, at least not outside celebrations. Father hadn't had any celebrations in the Keep, however, since I'd murdered my mother.

Pushing the thought away, I stepped into the huge stone building. I noticed immediately that the long dining tables were segregated by Line, which meant finding mine was easy. It sat toward the back, like a desolate tribute to the fact this whole place was a death trap.

I headed over to the food line and grabbed a plate. I really was starving, with my head now beginning to throb. Still, I straightened my spine and slowly loaded my plate. The only thing more embarrassing than inhaling a mountain of food would be eating so much that I puked all over the table.

The other tables were filled to capacity with people, and while most of the Lines were hard to distinguish from one another, one table was so overfilled that there were people sitting on the tabletop, as well as squished down the long benches.

"Twelfth Line. They're having a famine, so they're sending as many teens as they can to Boellium," the girl behind me murmured, probably because I was staring. She nudged me further down the row, and I ladled a heaping spoonful of some kind of stew into the deep well of my Falain plate. I placed two bread rolls in another section, with some form of dried meat in the third. In the last section, I placed an apple.

A little foil-wrapped packet was at the end of the row of food, and my eyes went wide. It couldn't be, right? Picking it up, I found it was heavy in my hand. It *was*.

Chocolate.

Just sitting there at the end of a buffet, like it was nothing. I forced myself to only take one packet, not even putting it on my tray, in case it somehow fell in my stew. Not that it would stop me from eating it.

We never had chocolate in Rewill. My father had banned its import, stating that it was a luxury our Line couldn't afford. But Kian said it was because it had been Mother's favorite food. It had been Kian who'd gotten me some for my twelfth birthday and who, along with my siblings, had sat around and shared it with me, hidden in the turret at the top of the fort so Father couldn't find us.

Suppressing the thoughts of my father, of my life before this moment, I walked toward the back of the room. I'd made it halfway there when a giant hound appeared in front of me, its head cocked to the side. I knew this hound from my arrival earlier, so I knew it was from the Third Line. It was looking at me with large, intelligent eyes, the tilt of its head making it look like it was trying to figure out if I was edible or not.

When it curled its lip up, I realized I was frozen. I stared at it, not looking away, making myself bigger, like they'd taught me back home. We had huge mountain wolves, but even they weren't as big as this hound. I stared it down until it turned away with a huff.

Sidestepping it with caution, I didn't take my eyes from its face. Which only meant that I wasn't watching what I was doing and tripped over the edge of my skirt. Falling backwards, I watched in depressingly slow motion as my tray went up, while I went down.

Fuck. This was almost more embarrassing than throwing up my food across the table. I braced myself for impact, but it never came.

Instead, I felt myself wrapped in ropes of air, my tray equally as suspended mid-motion. Not even a drop of stew had overflowed.

I turned my head and realized I was right beside the First Line table. Holding my breath, my eyes connected immediately with the sparkling blue ones of Vox Vylan. I'd almost thrown my food all over the Heir to the First Line.

So much for lying low.

The sheer strength of his magic had me dumbfounded, especially as his air pushed me back to my feet. I reached up and grabbed my tray from midair, feeling the moment that it was once again subject to the laws of gravity.

Clearing my throat, I turned and nodded my head respectfully. "Thank you."

He flicked his fingers, a clear dismissal, and I took that one small gesture for the escape it was.

chapter twenty-two

THE CONSCRIPT from the Ninth Line stuck out like a fly in the soup. It was more than the near-ethereal paleness of her skin, indicative of her Line, or the fact she scowled at everyone who moved. I couldn't put my finger on what it was yet, but the fact that one of Taeme's damn hounds had cornered her last night had to mean something. I trusted my instincts, and whatever was bugging me about the girl from the Ninth needed investigating.

I turned to Shay, my cousin, who was also my second. "What do we know about the Ninth Line conscript?"

We were walking into the training ring, even though I had more swordwork experience than most of the instructors here. Back home, I'd been given a sword as soon as I could be trusted not to poke myself in the eye with it, and sent to train for at least an hour a day.

Shay shrugged, loosening up her muscles so she

could do her formwork. "No more than you; only what's in the ledgers. Avalon Halhed, fifth child, and youngest daughter of the Baron of the Ninth Line."

I rifled through my memory, trying to pinpoint what I knew of the Baron of the Ninth Line, and mentally thanked my tutors for drilling this bullshit into my brain along with my ABCs. Roman Halhed was in his mid-sixties, a craggy-looking figure who spent far too often in the drink—to the detriment of his Line's coffers, if my father's sources were to be believed. It had made the whole Line weak, though there wasn't a lot they could have offered the rest of Ebrus anyway. They had weak foresight magic, barely more than a gut feeling. They had no good farmland to barter with—nothing but inhospitable mountains and livestock as tough as the people who tended them.

"Find out more," I instructed Shay.

She raised an eyebrow at me, but didn't negate the order. She just disappeared, and I knew she'd know everything there was to know about the Halhed girl and her whole Goddess-forsaken Line before the end of the day.

"Lift your fucking sword higher, Ninth, or your enemy will chop off your fucking head!" Instructor Yarlow yelled at her. He was right; her form was sloppy. She wouldn't last a day walking through Fortaare like that, let alone on the front lines of a war. I could see her arm shaking and knew she'd hit muscle fatigue. But the punishment for dropping your sword was missing three full meals in the food hall, and that was a powerful motivator.

She was gaunt, but not as bad as the Twelfth Line conscripts, who looked like too-tight flesh walking around on a skeleton when they arrived, especially if they were from villages on the outer rims of Ebrus. No, she looked like she'd missed more than a few meals, but wasn't starved. Nothing that wouldn't be solved by the regular meals offered at Boellium.

But her muscles were obviously weak, and for reasons I didn't understand, I slipped a small cushion of air beneath the point of her sword. Barely more than a whisper, and only those highly skilled in elemental magic would even know it was there.

When Instructor Yarlow blew the whistle to signify the end of the session, I allowed the air to dissipate and watched her sword tip lurch to the sand. She glared at her hand, and I realized she'd locked her muscles around the hilt.

Unable to help myself, I walked over to her. "Do you need assistance?"

Her eyes flew to mine, wide and worried. I watched as she swallowed hard, shaking her head. She met my gaze with her own darker blue ones. "I'm fine, thank you."

I couldn't remember the last time anyone who wasn't in my inner circle had met my eyes. Usually, it was beaten out of them by etiquette instructors and courtly manners. Guess they didn't have either of those things up in the wilds. *Or maybe...*

"Do you know who I am?" I asked her, my voice in its usual bored superiority.

She nodded, something like defiance edging back into her expression.

"Then why do you meet my eyes so freely?" I took the bite out of the words, softening my tone from the harsh one I'd usually employ to ensure people knew their place.

She dropped her eyes to her feet. "Would you believe insanity runs in my family?" she said softly, and I laughed. It was almost involuntary, and several eyes turned toward me. I pushed the sound away, folding my face back into its proper mask.

Reaching out, I tilted her chin up so her eyes were back on me. "Yes, I would."

I could feel the intensity of someone's stare on my face, and I turned, knowing who it would be before my eyes even met his forest-green ones. Hayle Taeme was glaring at me and the way my hands rested on this girl from the Ninth.

"What's your name?" I asked her softly. I already knew it, but wanted to hear it from her own lips.

"Avalon Halhed."

"And how do you know Hayle Taeme?" Was she a little spy? It was a good ruse; I'd never expect her.

But the incredulity on her face scrapped that idea almost immediately. "I don't know anyone from the Third Line, let alone an Heir."

I believed her. "Then why is he staring at me

touching you, like he wants to rip each of my fingers off and shove them up my a—nose?" I corrected myself.

She shrugged, switching her sword to the other hand. "I don't know. I think perhaps I might have accidentally stolen one of his animal familiars."

I raised an eyebrow, because I doubted that. If Hayle's hounds were anything to go by, they would rather tear you to pieces than be kept from their master. In fact, they'd shredded a conscript yesterday. The Third Line were wild and uncouth, but their pets were loyal.

Whatever it was, Taeme's interest in her just made her even more of an enigma. A mystery I was going to solve. I leaned forward, and she stared up at me.

Where was her self-preservation? Maybe she was like all the rest, just here to make a good impression on one of the Upper Lines and marry out of the hellhole she called her Line's territory.

Disappointment flowed through me. That was all this was. A tale I was all too familiar with.

But that didn't mean I couldn't play with her a little. Leaning even further forward, I watched her stop breathing. Our lips were close, and I was almost excited to kiss her. How long had it been since I'd been excited about anything, let alone some little Line jumper?

A low growl beside me had me stiffening. I looked down at the hound baring its teeth at me, or perhaps at Avalon Halhed. "Fuck off, Taeme, or I'll make a rug out of your pet," I growled back. I knew he could see through the eyes of that fucking mutt, and he'd get the message loud and clear.

It was pure politics that I didn't strangle the thing with my air right now. Perhaps one day I would, just to prove a point. My father would have, without hesitation.

"Maybe it can smell its little stolt friend on me," Avalon murmured, seemingly frozen in fear. She looked down at the hound, and her body slowly relaxed. "I swear, I keep setting him free, but he keeps coming back. Have you ever tried to keep a stolt out of a room? It turns into a freaking liquid and just slides back under the door. Tell your master I didn't mean it." As if she'd come to her senses and realized how close we were, she stepped back, hefting her sword to her chest like it was a shield. "I should…" She turned and ran, and I watched her go.

What the fuck *was* it about that girl? I wasn't like the men in my family. I didn't fuck everything that moved, just because I could. Not that I was a monk, obviously, but this was odd even for me.

I needed a shower; sweat was making my skin itch. I strode toward the atrium, people immediately moving out of my way, as if I was a single moment from losing it and exsanguinating them all. Yesterday's little exhibition probably hadn't helped that notion, but the kid from the Eighth Line had been seen stealing from my dorm. If you were stupid enough to steal from the First Line, you could suffer the consequences. He was lucky I hadn't taken his hands with my sword.

When I was finally back in my dorm, I moved through the space that housed the rest of the First Line conscripts, and over to a set of private stairs. Climbing them slowly, I emerged into what was known as the Dome.

My suite was made of the same glass that enclosed the atrium, glass that had been made impenetrable by magic that was long lost to us. It also protected from the harsh sun of the Ebrus summers, and blocked out the chill of the sea breeze in the winter. I wished I knew what magic had created this place, so I could learn to replicate it. From the Dome, I could see 360 degrees around the college.

I could see Hayle watching the girl, who was now standing by a tree with her face tilted to the sun. I could see the Upper Lines surrounding a person, and judging by the slight build, it was probably someone from the Eleventh or Twelfth Lines. I could see Headmaster Proxius talking to Svenna, who'd once been a feared warrior, but had been demoted to administrator of Boellium after the battle that took her arm. Whatever they were talking about, Svenna was gesturing angrily with her remaining limb. I wondered if I could get some ears down there to listen in on that conversation.

My eyes drifted back to Avalon Halhed. She looked almost ethereal, with her pale skin glowing in the hot Southern sun. She would burn if she wasn't careful. Once again, I tried to figure out why I even cared.

Sighing, I stepped into my private bathroom and turned on the large shower. Using my elemental abilities, I swirled the water around me until it cleaned and caressed every inch of my dirty skin. I could control all four elements, unlike most of the people in the First Line outside my immediate family. Most were Goddess-blessed with one or two elemental affinities, but the men in my family controlled all four, and my mother controlled three, which was why she'd been chosen to wed my father.

I'd also have to wed someone with at least two elemental powers, preferably three.

My eyes stayed fixed to the conscript from the Ninth Line. Girls from the Lower Six weren't even well-bred enough to fuck. Yet, even knowing that, I had still wanted to kiss Avalon Halhed.

chapter twenty-three

Avalon

I'D NEVER KNOWN exhaustion like this. All of my limbs ached in a way that made me want to vomit, but still, I had to keep going. They'd been testing our skills and fitness for the last two days, and it became blindingly obvious that I lacked both.

I was becoming helpless, and I hated it. Struggling with the tongs in the lunch line, my fingers lacked the strength needed to close them after pulling back a bowstring for seven solid hours. I couldn't even feel my fingertips, and there was a place on my cheek that was burned raw from the amount of times the fletching had hit my cheek as I loosed the arrow.

I was seriously contemplating using my fingers, but a girl behind me from the Twelfth Line came to my rescue. "If you grab the meat with your hands, the Upper Six will cry. Goddess forbid you sully their food with your watered-down bloodline," she muttered, picking up a slab of meat easily and putting it on my plate. "What else do you want?" She nudged me down the line, since we were blocking the flow of the dinner service.

I wanted to protest. No connections. No friends. In and out—that was the aim. But starvation *wasn't* the aim, and that was a very real possibility right now.

"Vegetables, please?" I asked pathetically, and the girl smiled. Her cheeks were little round apples, and her clothes fit her well, those bright, ornate colors associated with the Twelfth Line. Clearly, she wasn't a new conscript, because she'd had time to fill out after starvation.

"Yes, good choice. Filled with nutrients. You'll need those to survive." She put some on my tray, followed by her own. Then she grabbed a couple of pieces of dried meat and dropped them into my pocket. "For later. More than vegetables, you'll need meat. Otherwise, your muscles will ache something fierce tomorrow." She did the same with bread rolls. One went on each of our trays and one into my pocket, though it bulged a bit more than the jerky.

Finally, we reached the fruit and some kind of frozen dessert. We both stared at it, like it was something poisonous.

"The Upper Lines call it ice cream. They have a special elemental-magicked container to keep it like that."

I grabbed a little bowl of it for my tray. It looked like snow.

"Look at them, staring at ice cream like it's going to

attack them," someone snickered, and I looked over my shoulder to see a girl from the Fifth Line—Effie or Emilee or something. I ignored her, but the girl beside me turned and glared.

"When they told me it was kept in cold storage, no one told me it was your frigid vagina, Ephily. It does smell a little sour. Better put it back," she quipped, pulling it from my tray and putting it back on the table. I mourned the ice cream, but I could appreciate the stand.

The girl from the Twelfth hustled me to the back of the room, where their table sat, packed with smiling, laughing people from her Line. I went to veer off toward my table, but she shoved me in their direction.

"It's unhealthy to be alone." That's all she said, the only warning I'd get that I was about to be adopted into the Twelfth Line.

There was a pretty girl sandwiched between two large guys. "Acacia, who did you find?"

"This is the Ninth conscript. She's sitting with us," Acacia said easily, like I'd had any choice whatsoever in the matter.

The sitting girl waved. "Viana."

I gave her a tight smile. "Avalon."

Viana gave me a big smile before looking down at the table. "Shove along, guys. We have a guest."

No one seemed particularly perturbed that they were being squished to make way for an interloper. Viana climbed into the lap of the guy beside her, making room for both me and Acacia to slide onto the bench. They looked very friendly, and my cheeks flushed. The way his hand rested on her thigh, too high to be considered appropriate, let me know these two were clearly having sex.

Casual touching was definitely not allowed at home in Rewill. Not amongst spouses or lovers—hell, Father even discouraged hugging amongst his children. If he could have banned it altogether, he probably would have. If he was miserable, *everyone* had to be miserable.

I tried to act like I was unfazed by it, but I could feel how pink my cheeks were. I'd just blame sunstroke.

"So, what's it like living up on the Ninth Line floor by yourself?" Viana asked. It was weird to consider it *up*. It felt like I had to descend into the depths of Hell every night to sleep.

"Uh, quiet?" I stabbed at my meat, resisting the urge to wince as I curled my fingers around my cutlery. With a tsk, Viana took my cutlery from me and cut my meat into tiny pieces like I was a toddler. The gesture was bossy, but undeniably sweet.

My throat felt thick with emotion, and when she handed me my fork back, I swallowed it down to say, "Thank you." She waved a hand as if it was nothing, and maybe to her, it was.

When was the last time a person had ever helped me like that? My brothers, maybe, when they could get away with showing me any kind of softness.

"Sounds lonely." My eyes shot to Viana, like she could read my mind, but I realized she was still talking about living alone in my dorm.

I shrugged. "I'm kind of used to it."

Shaking her head, Acacia was chewing her food with relish beside me. "That would be miserable for someone from the Twelfth. We were made to be many parts of a whole. We like to say that our community, our family, is our magic."

The Twelfth Line was magicless, the reason they were ridiculed amongst the other Lines of Ebrus. But there were a lot of them, and they stuck together. It made them fearsome fighters, I thought.

I cleared my throat. "That sounds nice."

Viana laughed. "I'm glad you think so, because I've decided to honorarily make you one of us, Avalon. The idea of you rattling around your dorm by yourself just breaks my heart." She raised a perfect eyebrow. "Unless being seen with the Twelfth is too embarrassing for you?"

There was a challenge in her tone, but honestly, there was very little magic in the Ninth Line. It wasn't like I was out here predicting horse races or visions of legendary battles. I wasn't being invited to Upper Line soirées either, and I wasn't here to make politically advantageous connections.

"Not to me. Have you seen me swing a sword? *That's* embarrassing."

The guy beneath Viana laughed, and got a whack on the chest for his effort. They fell back into conversation about people and things I was clueless about, but they filled me in like I was going to get a pop quiz on who was getting laid, who was going to need to work more with Acacia to get their battle knowledge up, whose grandmother made the best rock cakes, and why it was Viana's grandmother and no other answer was acceptable.

It was... nice. This feeling of family that flowed so easily up and down the table, regardless of who came and went. They *belonged*, and it was such a foreign concept to me that I sat in awe long after my food was done.

Once Ephily and her cronies from the Fifth Line left, Acacia got up and got us two bowls of the ice cream. If I thought chocolate was a luxury, this frozen dessert was beyond my imagination. I knew the kitchen here had a magicked box to keep things fresh, but wasting magic to keep something cold enough to be frozen seemed like an insane misuse of power.

I spooned some into my mouth and moaned. *Holy Goddess.* "Oh my," I breathed, spooning in another mouthful. "This is..." It was smooth, cold, and creamy, sweetened by vanilla beans and sugar, neither of which were in abundant supply in our territory by the mountains.

Acacia was already on her fourth bite. "Fucking amazing."

I laughed, but I was already putting another spoonful in my mouth. It was starting to melt a little, and I ate faster. Then I got a shooting pain in my forehead. I clenched my fingers on my temples, wincing against the ache. It was like a terrible headache, but as suddenly as it came, it disappeared.

Viana was laughing. "I heard the Upper Lines call it an iced headache; it happens when you eat it too fast."

I frowned down at my bowl, betrayed by this deliciousness. Narrowing my eyes at it, I knew it was too good to throw out. So I ate slowly, giving it no chance to attack me again.

When I was done, I took my tray and Acacia's over to the table where it would be collected by the kitchen staff. I slipped a small, foil-wrapped square of chocolate into my pocket as well. I was getting quite a sweet tooth.

Several of the Twelfth Line had stood by the time I returned to the table, including Viana and Acacia. "Why is Vox Vylan looking at you like he wants to split open your insides and see what makes you tick?" Acacia whispered, and I looked over at Vox. He was watching me and raised an eyebrow as our eyes met.

I whipped back around to the girls. "No idea."

I definitely didn't say I'd thought he was going to kiss me earlier. I didn't tell them that I'd really wanted him to, which was so, so wrong. He was not for me. He was not for anyone, except one of the beautiful girls in the First Line.

"More to the point, why is Hayle Taeme looking at you like he wants to make the beast with two backs with you?"

The beast with two ba… Oh.

Oh.

Shaking my head, I didn't turn to look at those forest-green eyes that sent panic and pain spiraling through my veins. "No idea. I've never even spoken to him. Maybe he doesn't like my Line?" I wouldn't put it past my father to have short-changed them out of something important.

"A man doesn't look like that at a person he hates, Avalon." Viana shook her head, throwing her arm around my shoulders. "You're an interesting one. I don't think being your friend will ever be boring."

Was that what I was doing? Making friends? I hadn't had any of those before.

It felt kinda nice.

chapter twenty-four

Hayle

FOR THE LAST THREE NIGHTS, she'd haunted my dreams. I dreamed about kissing her, tasting her, the way she would moan my name beneath me. It felt so real that I would wake up in a sweat, hard and aching, and have to head to the showers to cool off.

I didn't understand why she plagued me, and it was driving me crazy.

What was also driving me mad was the fact that if she saw me in the halls, she'd run the other way. The scent of her fear in my nose was like a knife to the heart. Lots of people smelled of fear when they were near me, and I'd be lying if I said I didn't enjoy it.

But not her.

I needed to know more, and I found myself sneaking into Svenna's office after the dinner service, when I knew she'd be down in town, getting the cream for the scars on her arm. Easily unlocking the door, I made Braxus keep watch. The hounds had also been slightly poutier than normal since this last round of conscripts, and although they couldn't express to me why, I had a feeling it had something to do with the girl from the Ninth.

Was she related to the Third Line? Did she have latent Third Line magic that I was reacting to? I needed more information. Slipping inside, I walked to the shelf where the admission ledgers were kept. I didn't need to turn on a light—the ability to see well at night was one of the boons of my Line.

Flipping it open on the table, I wondered if Svenna would know I'd been here. I wouldn't be surprised. She'd been both wily and fierce when she was in the Dawn Army, and if she hadn't lost her arm in a skirmish, then I had no doubt she'd have been high up the ranks.

Flipping open the ledger, I slid my finger down until I found the right entry. *Avalon Halhed.* Youngest child of the Baron Halhed of the Ninth Line, so nobility. Who sent their daughter to be a conscript when they had so many sons? Not that I didn't think women could be amazing warriors; Svenna and my mother were both proof of that. But I'd seen Avalon in training, and it was very obvious the only sharp instrument she'd ever held was probably an embroidery needle. Who sent a barely trained girl to be their Line's conscript, especially the daughter of the Baron? Was it because she was a spinster at the ripe old age of twenty-three?

I stalled on a brief line about her being present at her

mother's death as a toddler, but I couldn't imagine why that would warrant an entry under physical fitness.

Closing the book, I sat back in Svenna's chair. That really hadn't shed any light on the mystery of Avalon Halhed, other than filling in a few small gaps. It didn't explain why I was so drawn to her. It didn't explain why she was tormenting me in my dreams.

With a sigh, I hefted the tome back onto its place on the shelf and slipped out of the office. Walking toward the stairs that led to the Upper Six dorms, I paused on the landing, seeing Svenna there, leaning against the wall.

"Find anything interesting?" she asked lightly.

Braxus weaved in front of my legs, but unlike most people, Svenna didn't seem perturbed by his presence. It could be because she had at least six daggers on her body, despite only having one arm.

"I'm sure I don't know what you're talking about," I said, pasting my usual charming grin on my face. It was the one my mother said could disarm even a burly warrior on the battlefield.

Svenna snorted. "Keep your charm for someone who gives a shit, Taeme. You were in my office, and I want to know why."

Glancing down at Braxus, I sent him up the stairs to make sure no one was eavesdropping on our conversation. When he let out a short, subdued yip from the top of the stairs, I knew it was safe to talk.

"Nothing wild, Svenna. I just like to know who the new conscripts are."

"Horseshit." She stepped closer. "What were you looking for, Taeme?" There was something fervent in her gaze, the intensity making goosebumps spread across my skin. I didn't know if I should tell her or not.

Hell, maybe she'd know more. I had a reputation, and hopefully, she'd just assume I wanted information because I wanted to screw Avalon Halhed.

So, clearing my throat, I gave her my best bashful *aw gosh, you caught me* expression. "I was looking into the new girl from the Ninth Line. She won't give me the time of day, and I wondered if she was already married, or you know, didn't like men?"

Svenna continued to eye me, her hand on her hip. "You think those are the only reasons a girl wouldn't want to climb into bed with you—if she was gay or married? You have quite the opinion of yourself."

I smirked. "The theory hasn't been disproven yet."

Her eyes searched my face, but I'd been playing spy for a long time. I could hold my own under an appraising gaze. Finally, she straightened. "Well, I hope she holds out as long as possible, just to give you a taste of humility." She stepped back and lifted her chin. "Back to your dorm before curfew." She walked down several more steps before looking back up at me. "And Taeme, for future reference? If you want information about people, there is a thing called a library. Stay out of my damn office."

I watched her go, then walked the rest of the way up the stairs. There was silence on the landing outside the Third Line dorm, but that wasn't a surprise. Walking into the place was a madhouse. Animals and people littered every surface, and it had been so noisy in years gone by that someone had eventually forged a sound-proof barrier around our dorm.

It was loud, but it felt like home. Lucio was having an arm wrestle with Oleg, and someone was cooking in the small kitchen, judging by the smell of it. We couldn't be sustained by the three meals served in the food hall. We needed twice as much food as every other Line, because our inner beast just burned through energy way too fast. It meant that someone was always cooking something, and we usually managed to snag extra rations from the kitchen.

I came to stand near Lucio, turning over the problem that was Avalon Halhed in my head. Honestly, I prob-ably would have written it off completely, but some-thing about her put my animals offside too. Not because they disliked her; quite the opposite. They'd all instantly liked the girl, and that was unusual. They didn't like anyone but me most of the time.

Maybe she did have some Third Line blood in her somewhere. Maybe Svenna's quip about heading to the library was actually helpful. I'd check it out tomorrow.

Vox Vylan was watching the girl with nearly as much intensity as I was, which made the beast inside me bris-tle. The First Line was filled to the brim with the worst type of people in Ebrus: power-hungry and corrupt. The Baron of the First Line held control of Ebrus with immense power and more than a little ruthlessness—a trait passed down to his Heirs.

My interactions with Vox had been few and far between this year, which I appreciated, but perhaps it was time to ensure he knew that I was here, ready to be a thorn in his damn side.

Instructor Perot was also giving the girl a death glare, and I didn't understand that either. I really needed to know more about her. I put up a call, and a mouse ran up my pants leg. "Follow her."

Mice had small minds, mostly preoccupied with finding food, warmth and a warm female mouse to reproduce with before they were eaten either by Lucio's war cat or the castle cats. But they responded well enough to requests for information, and unlike Braxus and Alucis—who could almost analyse what they were seeing and decide what was relevant—a mouse just sent me snapshot after snapshot of what it saw. It wasn't efficient, and sometimes it could be exhausting, but mice went places larger animals couldn't.

Like the Ninth Floor dorm.

The mouse scurried down the stairs, until it froze, lifting in the air like a balloon. I climbed to my feet and glared at Vox, the only person who could use their elemental magic with that amount of precision. "Put him down."

Vox raised an eyebrow. "No."

My hounds came to my side as I stepped forward. "Now, Vylan, or else."

"Or else what, Taeme? You'll send your puppies

after me? They can't take me. *You* can't take me. And I'm sick of your little spies everywhere listening to fuck knows what. Maybe I should just take all this one's air? It's just a dirty mouse."

A hand reached up and plucked the mouse from where it was suspended in ropes of air. I watched as Avalon Halhed put the mouse in her pocket and went back to looking at the instructor, like that hadn't just happened.

She couldn't have just stolen the mouse from Vox's power unless he let her. What the fuck did that mean?

I stared Vox down once more, until Instructor Perot cleared his throat. "If you're done, keep your squabbles out of my damn classroom. Inside is for learning, outside is for posturing. There's an entire ring for you to flex at each other, and it's a lot easier to clean blood from sand than from thousand-year-old parquetry."

Sitting back down, I didn't relax until the class was declared complete, then I walked out of the room with my head held high and my back turned to Vox Vylan, completely unbothered that he'd come for me like the coward he was.

I reached a room where the college staff kept cleaning products and stepped into it. Getting Quarry, my raven, to keep an eye out for the girl, I waited until she was in front of the door before I grabbed her and yanked her in.

The girl squeaked out a scream that I muffled with my palm. "We need to talk."

chapter twenty-five

Avalon

I BREATHED HEAVILY against the palm of Hayle Taeme. This close, the ache in my gut, that primal feeling of fear and pain, was nearly overwhelming. He removed his hand, and I glared at him.

"What is *wrong* with you? You don't drag women into dark closets, you animal," I hissed. All the while, my hand was searching for the doorknob behind me.

He leaned closer, inhaling deeply. "You're right. I am an animal." His tone strongly suggested that I was the prey.

Reaching into my pocket, I pulled out the mouse. I hadn't wanted to get between powerful Heirs, but I wasn't going to let a defenseless mouse be hurt, just because they couldn't keep their egos in check. I thrust the tiny creature out at him. It was curled in my palm, obviously having been napping in my pocket.

"Take better care of your pets. I can't keep saving them for you."

He glared at me, and honestly, the expression was terrifying. But he took the mouse with gentle fingers, releasing it up into the collar of his shirt. "I take excellent care of my animal companions, as do my whole Line. Their trust is our magic."

I scoffed. "Yeah, well, what about the stolt that you keep stink-eyeing me about?"

Now it was his turn to look incredulous. "None of the Third Line here at Boellium have a stolt. I certainly don't." He raised an eyebrow. "That one is all you."

Impossible, because Epsy was super tame. Last night, I'd caught him sleeping in my boot and chewing on the leather like it was his favorite pastime. Those were not the actions of a wild animal.

"Whatever," I coughed out, because the scent of his skin was starting to whisper into my nose, and he smelled amazing. "What do you want, exactly?"

He looked down at me, his eyes stern. "Who *are* you, Avalon Halhed?"

Had this guy been dropped on his head as a baby? "You literally just said my name. Avalon Halhed. And in case you've been living under a rock and haven't heard the whispers that echo around the hall, I'm the only conscript in the place from the Ninth Line. That's all there is to know."

He growled, and the noise was equal parts terrifying and arousing. Well, that was awkward.

"And your connection to the First Line?"

I frowned. I didn't want to be some chew toy in

inter-Line politics, but still, who did he think he was? "None of your fucking business."

He leaned forward until his nose was brushing mine, those green eyes arresting. "What if I make it my business?"

I wanted to run away, or fall to my knees, and I didn't like either option. Instead, I showed a little bit of spine. "Then I guess we're both bound for disappointment."

Finally finding the doorknob, I twisted it open and escaped before he could grab me and hold me hostage in that tiny room any longer. If anyone thought it was weird that I was in a cleaning closet, they minded their own business for once.

In the next class, we were scheduled for hand-to-hand combat, and the instructor was a hard-ass. He'd punish me just because I looked soft. My brother, Kian, had taught me a little self-defense, enough to escape my father if he ever managed to corner me drunk and tried to beat me to death... again.

But being able to escape a drunk old man was very different to being able to best a trained soldier in combat. Or an untrained soldier, as I would later discover.

"Halhed, you are so weak and uncoordinated, I'm amazed you've never tripped over your own feet and been eaten by chickens. You're that Goddess-cursed slow. Move. Jab, jab, turn, sweep. It's not that hard.

Think of it like a dance, if that helps with your courtly attitude."

I gritted my teeth. I'd never been to court in my life, and didn't know how to dance either. I didn't correct the instructor, though. Instead, I did what he said.

Jab. Jab. Turn. Sweep. Catch your own ankle. Fall on face in dirt.

This was ridiculous.

Viana from the Twelfth Line reached down and pulled me back to my feet. "I feel like I should apologize, but that was all you."

I huffed. "How are you so good at this?"

She shrugged and got back into a fighting stance. "Practice?"

I squinted at her. "I hate you a little right now."

Eugene from the Fourth Line, who I'd met a couple of times but avoided, strode over to me, a sneer on his face. "Lower Line scum. You're making us all look bad."

Viana pushed her shoulders back, stepping forward to make him eat his words, but I'd seen Eugene fight—he fought well, and he fought dirty. A bad combination. My hatred for Eugene was almost visceral, an on-sight loathing that I didn't really understand, but I trusted my gut. If it said that Eugene was a snake, I'd treat him as such.

Putting my hand out to stop Viana from taking a swing at him, I cocked my head like I was appraising him and found him wanting. "You make yourself look bad without any assistance from us," I told him coolly, then turned my back.

The crackle of the air around us told me that this was a poor decision, that turning your back on someone as powerful as a Fourth Line Heir was a good way to get dead quickly, but I didn't let myself quake.

The sky went dark, the winds whipped up, and the fact that the Fourth Line power was weather control came flooding back into my brain from my tutoring. Extremely powerful Fourth Liners could target an enemy with a well-aimed hailstone, drown them in a flash flood, or strike them down with lightning.

Fear had me glancing up just in time to see hailstones hurtling toward me and Viana. "Look out!" I pushed her to the ground, covering her head with my body and protecting my own with my arms. Several small hailstones hit me before the storm just... stopped.

Glancing up, I realized it hadn't stopped at all. Rather, an umbrella of air was flowing above my head. Vox Vylan walked toward me, his face impassive, but I could see his hand clenched into a fist by his side. Looking up, I watched the hail bouncing off the air canopy he'd created around Viana and I.

Vox didn't even look at me as he walked over to Eugene. "What are you doing?"

Eugene smirked. "Teaching a lesson about the social hierarchy."

Throwing back his head with a laugh, Vox slapped him on the back. "I didn't realise they'd made you an instructor here. Should we start calling you Instructor Rovan, instead of Eugene?"

I wanted to get out of here, but only the air umbrella was protecting me from getting pummeled. Everyone else was on the edge of the training ring, unable to move through the hail toward us. We were trapped. Well, except for Vox.

All the Twelfth Line conscripts—including the guy whose lap Viana had been sitting on earlier in the week —looked terrified for their friend. No one would be terrified for me, which was a depressing thought.

Eugene was still laughing with Vox. "Maybe you should. It's time the Lower Six learned that we're their betters, don't you think?" His eyes sparkled with the feverish shine of a zealot.

Vox's expression was condescending before something shifted, his eyes reflecting pure danger. If Eugene had any sense, he'd run. But apparently, the pompous Heir didn't.

"Maybe I should put all the Lower Lines in their place," Vox murmured. "I'll start with you." His hand whipped out, and suddenly, Eugene was on his knees, gasping. "You need to learn your place, Eugene, and it isn't tormenting the Lower Lines. It's right here, on your knees, swearing fealty to your betters. To *me*. You're little better than the Twelfth Line with no magic. Weak. At least they find some nobility in it. You wouldn't know nobility if it bit you in the ass, or in this case, was presented to you on a silver platter."

Vox's lip curled in disgust. "So while you're down

there, coming up with ways to make yourself feel larger, remember that there's always someone stronger, who'll relish doing the same to you."

Eugene shouted, gritting his teeth as hail as big as cannonballs pelted against Vox's air shield. The other members of the First Line stood just outside the fenced arena, and their faces looked stressed, but they were being held back by the instructors. There were rules in Boellium, of conduct and combat. Once you were in the middle of a battle, you couldn't leave until one of you was declared the victor. No one else in your Line could interfere either, not without great shame.

Viana screamed as hail pounded against the dome of protection, and we huddled together close to the ground. Thunder and lightning cracked the sky, and terror I hadn't ever felt before ran through my veins. Like an old fear that I couldn't quite remember.

Another flash, another crack, and I screamed. I'd never been scared of storms before, but something was whispering at the back of my brain. The echo of a nightmare.

One of the huge rounds of hail finally punctured the air dome, and I screeched as it barely missed me. Scrabbling away from the hole, I unfortunately crawled straight into the path of another chunk of hail piercing the veil. The ball of ice barrelled toward my face, and its icy kiss of pain was the last thing I felt before blackness swamped me.

chapter twenty-six

Avalon

"MAYBE WE SHOULD TAKE her to the healer again?"

"He said she just needed to rest."

"He was here, in our dorm. I almost pissed myself."

The voices in the room were hushed, but frantic. I felt like my brain was mush in my skull, and the pain of it sloshing around in there was astronomical. I tried to drag my eyelids open, but they refused to cooperate.

"An Heir to the First Line, *here*, in the bowels of Boellium. I doubt that's happened in a hundred years," a familiar voice said, and the mention of the First Line had my eyes opening. There were five people in the room, all talking softly. They may as well have been shouting with a big brass band as background music, because it would make no difference to the pain in my head.

"Where am I?" I croaked out.

Viana was there immediately, staring down at me with worried eyes. "Hey there. You're down in the Twelfth Line dorm. The healer said you had a concussion and had to be watched, but there was no one else on your floor, so we said we'd watch you. You know, because we unofficially adopted you." Her face was smiling, but her eyes were worried. "How do you feel?"

I groaned. "Like someone dropped an anvil on my head."

Someone snorted, "Close enough," in the darkness of the room, but I couldn't tell who it was. My vision felt off, and my thoughts were slow.

Someone appeared with a small bottle. Acacia. "A spoonful of this should help with the pain. The healer gave you something and said you'd be fine, but honestly, I'm fairly sure the guy learned to heal on horses or something. Even in your sleep, I could tell you were in pain. That's what happens when you get your job through nepotism and not actual skill," she muttered angrily, then held up the bottle. "This will definitely help."

Fuck it. What did I have to lose? I opened my mouth, letting her spoon some foul-tasting elixir between my lips. I swallowed it down, and it tasted like an asshole, stuffed with rotten fruit and rancid meat. Someone poured a chaser of strong fruit juice down my throat directly after it, but still, I could taste the medicine on the back of my tongue. "Ugh, that's fucking disg—" Almost instantly, the pain went away. "Ohhh…"

Someone laughed, but I didn't care, because I didn't even feel my body any more. I was a discombobulated consciousness, floating through the air. *Huh.* "I take it back. This is nice."

Viana fixed something over my left eye, and I realized it was a bandage. "Yeah, I bet you do. We have a lot of good medicine out in the Twelfth Line. Acacia is learning from one of the elder healers, and she'll continue to learn more when she goes back. We take care of our own out there."

It felt nice, this care from other people. Foreign, like so many things, but the fact there were so many of them tending to me like I mattered? It made something ache in my chest.

Viana sat down beside me and grabbed my hand. "That was scary," she whispered. "I thought we were going to die today." I could see how pale she was, her eyes tight and worried.

Flashes of what had happened echoed in my brain. The hail. Eugene and Vox. But it was just that. Flashes. Any real memories seemed to have been knocked from my head and lost in the swirling darkness of pain. But I remembered the lightning. The fear.

No, that felt wrong too. That hadn't happened, had it? It had been hail. And thunder.

Only one person could tell me for sure. "What happened?" I asked Viana, and her jaw went tight.

Face solemn, she cleared her throat. "Eugene was trying to make a statement, I guess, really throwing everything he had at Vox Vylan's defenses. The hail coming down was bigger than my head, Avalon! Vox must have lost concentration or something, because right at the end, they were piercing through the air veil. We dodged what we could, but it was too much. You shoved me out of the way, and one got you in the head and half your shoulder. Your collarbone is broken."

I looked down, and sure enough, my arm was strapped to my side. I just hadn't felt the pain of it over the absolute agony of my skull. I wiggled my fingers, relieved they were fine. However, it was like now that I could see the bandages, it unlocked the far-away ache in my shoulder. Damn, that was going to hurt later too.

Viana continued. "After you were injured, Vox stopped trying to flex, and instead kicked Eugene in the face and knocked him out. The hail dried up almost immediately, and the Heir himself scooped you up to take you to the healer, though I thought he and Hayle were going to throw down about it. Their argument looked intense." Her eyes glinted with intrigue. Viana loved to gossip. "Anyway, the rest of my Line brought me back down here to patch up my war wounds." She pointed to some scrapes of her own that were bandaged up. "And an hour later, Vylan reappeared with you still in his arms. He ordered us to take care of you, threw in a few threats about how painful our deaths would be if we let you die, then left again. Honestly, it was kind of hot. Terrifying, but hot."

I didn't know why he would do any of that. Maybe he felt guilty or something. I was kind of glad I didn't remember being cradled in his arms, though. How embarrassing.

"And Eugene?"

"Being punished for allowing his battle to spread outside the designated battle zone. He'll get a slap on the wrist, even though you almost died," she muttered angrily. "If it had been one of the Upper Lines getting clobbered with hailstones, he'd be expelled in disgrace or sent to the dungeon or something. But not someone from the Ninth and Twelfth."

Yeah, I'd probably be pissed about that later too, but right now, I didn't have it in me to do anything. The echo of the pain was there, but almost like it was happening to someone else.

I'd never been more thankful for Viana and Acacia. "I'm sorry you got caught up in this," I told Viana softly, and she just shook her head.

"The vanity of the Upper Lines isn't your fault, Avalon. We were just in the wrong place at the wrong time, and he's a petty little man who has to use his magic, because he has a tiny little dick." She huffed. "I think Eugene might be a psychopath. There's something definitely wrong with him. My money's on too much inbreeding. Some of those Lines like to keep them pure, you know?"

Ew.

Was that what I was picking up from Eugene that made me hate him so thoroughly, without any real cause? Could I sense that he had some kind of mental malady? Well, I guess I had a real reason to hate him now, but I'd still do my best to avoid him for the next two years.

Viana stroked my head in an almost maternal way, and I sighed. No one had touched me with care in so long. Maybe not since my sister was shipped off to be wed, back when I was a child? My brothers had been there for me, but displays of affection weren't permitted by the Ninth Line Baron.

It was… nice.

"You should rest now," she said softly. "You need sleep to heal." She left, softly closing the door behind her.

I noticed that this room had two beds and was bursting with stuff, and I wondered who I'd displaced from their room. But I'd worry about that later, along with every other problem that seemed to be cropping up during my conscription. This was why I should've kept my head down and faded into the background. I'd forgotten what my purpose was: to be completely unremarkable.

But no one was going to forget what had happened today. Being in the gravitational pull of Vox wasn't going to help my cause either.

A sudden scratching noise on the floor had me opening an eye. What was that?

I opened the other eye and watched a fuzzy blob appear in my vision. Shit, I'd forgotten about Epsy. Had he tracked me down because he was hungry? I wondered if I could push my friendship with Acacia and send her to feed him.

As the fuzzy blob got closer, I realized it was significantly smaller than my stolt. I mean, *the* stolt. He wasn't *my* stolt.

Instead, it was a tiny mouse. Recognizing its speckled white-and-black coat, I gave him a sleepy smile. "Oh, it's you."

It came right up to my face, its whiskers twitching as it sniffed softly. I couldn't even feel the weight of it on my chest, it was so small.

"Have you been sent to check up on me?" Its tiny ears swiveled around, listening. "You're pretty cute, actually. You can tell your master I'm okay." I scratched the little mouse between its ears with the hand strapped to my chest. "Actually, could you get him to feed my stolt?"

How much did a mouse understand? Could it understand my words, or could it just transmit images? I wished I knew how the Third Line's powers worked. So I did my best stolt impression with one arm; I held up a hand like it was an ear, and maybe I cleaned myself with an imaginary paw while I mimed eating.

Hopefully, he got the point. Otherwise, the stolt was just going to have to wait until I was up and around tomorrow to eat. He'd be pissed, but I'd bring him some of the jerky he loved.

The little mouse scurried away. I hoped he'd gotten everything he needed, because my eyes felt like they were being dragged down by heavy weights. I was glad to be falling into the darkness, where I didn't have to think about why Vox Vylan had personally carried me to the healers and stayed with me. Or why he'd ordered people to take care of me. Or why Hayle Taeme had sent one of his tiny, furred minions to check on me.

Just blissful silence, where I didn't have to think how close I came to dying.

chapter twenty-seven

Vox

I DRUMMED my fingers on my desk, trying to shake the girl from my head. My powers had failed against Eugene, of all people, and the shame was entirely consuming. The fact that the girl was hurt was disconcerting. The fear I'd felt when she was injured was… perplexing.

I didn't know what to do about any of it.

Well, that was untrue. I knew what I was going to do about Eugene.

A small smirk curled my cheeks. He was a dead man and didn't even know it yet. No one defied me, especially not some Fourth Line weakling. If it had been anyone under my air shield but Avalon Halhed—

No. If it had been anyone other than Avalon being tormented by Eugene, I wouldn't have even stepped in. I didn't interfere with the squabbles of the Lower Lines. However, when I'd stumbled on her and the girl from the Twelfth being pelted with hailstones, I hadn't even thought before acting. I'd protected her like she mattered, but she didn't. Not to me, not to Ebrus.

See. Perplexing. Even now, I had the urge to go and check on her wellbeing.

Sighing, I leaned back in my desk chair. I had to write a missive to my father about today's events, and I needed to get my shit together. Weakness was not something that I could let my father see. I might be his flesh and blood, but he wasn't above exploiting my emotions in the name of teaching me how to be a leader, despite the fact it was unlikely that I'd ever be the ruler. The title of Baron of the First Line would go to my brother, and I'd always been ecstatic to be the backup. May my brother live a long, miserable life.

Shay slid into my room silently, her brows drawn together. I wiped my expression from my face automatically, even though I trusted Shay with my life. She was my closest friend, advisor, and more of a sibling to me than my own. But she'd never had to stand against my father, and I would rather her be blissfully unaware of potential secrets, should that ever happen.

"Is it done?"

She nodded, her face twisting into a malicious grin. "Yep. It's so cold in the dungeon tonight that if Eugene doesn't have frostbitten balls by the morning, it would be a Goddess-granted miracle."

It was just the first of many small ways I was going to make that fucker's life a misery. He'd soon learn how insignificant he was in the hierarchy of true power, and he'd remember exactly who was in charge at Boellium.

I kept my voice light and my expression neutral. "And the injured conscripts?"

Shay gave me a look that said I was full of shit. "Both resting in the bowels of Boellium under the watchful eye of the Twelfth Line." She sat on the edge of my desk. "What was that about, Vox? And before you give me some bullshit answer, remember I've known you since before you could shit in a toilet. I can tell when something's more than a passing amusement to you. You carried that girl from the Ninth Line all the way to the infirmary. You sat with her while the healer tended to her, then you carried her down to the lower level dorms. Have you ever even been below the atrium before today?" I shook my head, and she gave me a hard look. "People will have noticed, Vox."

The underlying warning was that if people had noticed, the information was bound to make its way back to my father, probably my brother too. Hell, I'd be surprised if my mother didn't also have spies in Boellium.

"I was just angry that someone as insignificant as Eugene had bested me. Carrying the girl was my punishment."

"Oh, your punishment?" Shay sat back casually, uncaring that her hands were scattering my paperwork. She knew I hated that shit. "Is that why you stepped into their disagreement in the first place? Were you punishing yourself when you had me looking into her history?" Shay glared at me. "Is it a punishment to look at her with moon eyes all the time, watch her wherever she walks, when she eats, when she trains? Don't insult my intelligence, Vox. We're past all this. Your secrets are safe with me, cousin. They always have been." She dropped her voice low. "My loyalty has always been—and always will be—to you. Not our Line, or our Baron, or even my own family. To you."

I looked around, because her words were dangerous at best, treasonous at worst, and these walls had ears.

There was no love lost between Shay and the men in my family. They'd tried to force her into a political marriage with someone truly fucking awful but incredibly influential, and it was only my insistence that she needed to come to Boellium with me that had saved her from being married and probably pregnant right now. Completely against her will.

In my family, the will of women wasn't something to be considered. They were property, something to be bartered with, used, discarded. Not to me, though. Shay was worth a thousand of my brother. A million of my father. I would always protect her to the best of my abilities.

"I know, Shay," I told her softly. "I don't know what's going on yet or what it is about her, but it's *something* and it's tormenting me. It's like a song you hear in your mind, but you just can't quite remember the whole tune."

Jaw tensing, she nodded. "Fine. But I'm getting you a *tal* that wards against psychic manipulation. She's Ninth Line, after all."

I snorted. "They have basic precognition, Shay, not

mind control. Even then, there hasn't been someone in their Line that could predict the future in nearly two hundred years. My thoughts are my own." I slumped back. "Maybe it's my dick being led astray. Maybe I just need to get laid. I'm sure Ephily would happily warm my bed. She's been hinting at it for six months."

"Probably. Want me to tell her that all her dreams have come true?" Shay's voice was light as she slid from my desk, but something that looked like resentment flitted through her expression. A normal person might have missed it, but I'd been trained since I was a child to read micro-changes in body language.

"What?" I asked softly. She shook her head as she turned to leave, but I gripped her wrist. "Shay, after all that talk of honesty and trust, you don't get to stomp out of here like the injured party. What is it?"

She sucked her teeth. "Ephily and I hooked up at one of the Line parties a few months ago."

I blinked, a little shocked. Not that Shay had slept with a woman; I'd known she was gay since… forever. No, the real shock was that Ephily was her type. "Ephily from the Fifth Line, *that* Ephily? The one who offered to blow me on her first day?"

Scowling in my direction, she snapped, "Yes. There's only one Ephily in this Goddess-forsaken shithole, Vox. It was only once, and when she got out of my bed the following morning, she told me that she'd had fun, but I was the wrong Vylan."

My lip curled in anger on my cousin's behalf. "Shay…" She'd suffered so much by being the wrong

Vylan. The wrong gender. The wrong branch of the family tree. The wrong orientation.

Shay shook her head. "Sometimes, I think perhaps the Twelfth Line has it right. A life of love and community, not this political backstabbing bullshit where everyone's trying to climb over your corpse to the top. When you're at the bottom and you can't see the pinnacle for the clouds, you can just convince yourself that life on the ground is better. There's something simple in it."

She tugged lightly, and I let her arm go. "It won't always be like this, Shay," I promised.

The pity on her face made my chest feel tight. "Won't it?" She strode toward my door, but paused at the threshold. "You should know that while I was in the library looking for information about Avalon Halhed, I wasn't the only one."

I stilled, my eyes snapping to hers. "Who?"

"Hayle Taeme."

What the hell did Taeme want with a girl from the Ninth Line? He was no more likely to pursue her as anything more than a bedmate than I was; we were both manacled by our Line.

I thought about how he'd gotten in my face when I was carrying the girl to the infirmary, and while his words had been the normal goading bullshit, if I thought back on the moment, looked past my panic that the girl in my arms was maybe dying, he'd looked just as frantic. His eyes had drifted to her repeatedly, like he cared if she lived or died.

What the hell did that mean? Was she a spy?

So many fucking questions without answers.

Pulling out a sheet of the official First Line mono-grammed paper, I wrote a brief account of the events of today for my father, from Eugene's insubordination to my plans for his comeuppance. I only put a brief note about two conscripts from the Lower Lines being injured, as dismissive of them as I could make it, without not mentioning them altogether. I put in a little lament for my failure, in case anyone else snitched about how I'd carried the injured girl to the infirmary personally. A throwaway sentence about good optics to build better bonds with the Lower Lines, should I need them.

Anything but the truth I couldn't face. There was something about Avalon Halhed that spoke to my soul. She was a weakness that I had to exorcise immediately for both of our sakes. There was one sure way to do that, and it would kill two birds with one hailstone.

"Elliott!" I yelled, and the most personable of the First Line conscripts appeared. He wasn't from the Vylan line, merely a kid with big ambitions who'd volunteered so he could raise his station through the Dawn Army. He didn't have a lot of magic, but enough to enhance some pretty impressive weaponry skills.

"Yes, sir?" he said.

"We're going to have the first Upper Line party of the new conscript year. I want to have it tomorrow night. Make it happen."

He grinned at me. Fucking kid hadn't had the joy

beaten out of him yet, but I found him kind of endearing, like a big, dumb dog who just wanted to please. "Yes, sir!"

A party would help two-fold. I could fuck away some of this tension that was riding my body and clouding my mind, and I could corner Hayle Taeme. He was overly interested in someone who should be an inconsequential conscript, and I wanted to know why.

chapter twenty-eight

Avalon

IT WAS NOT ALL that uncommon to see a conscript walking around with their arm in a sling. We were training to be soldiers, after all. However, the amount of stares I was garnering had little to do with the sling and everything to do with the Heir to the First Line having carried me through the halls of the War College like a damsel.

That was it—the only reason the event was worth the gossip. There was no mention of Eugene and his hissy fit. No talk of how I'd almost died. My only value to these people was as a focal point for speculation. There were two prevailing rumors.

One, which seemed to be the most obvious, was that Vox Vylan was fucking me and had grown attached. I almost snorted at this one. *Unlikely.*

The second rumor was that I was the Baron of the First Line's ill-begotten love child and that's why Vox—the normally cold-as-ice prince—gave a crap about me.

Again, equally preposterous. Though, given the rumors I'd heard about the Baron of the First Line, it was likely that he did actually have more than a few affair children roaming around, but I wasn't one of them, for which I was eternally grateful. My father had made my life a misery, but I couldn't imagine having to live out that nightmare beneath the collective gaze of the Court of Fortaare and all the leeches who hung around Ebrus's seat of power.

No, the preposterous part of that rumor was that the Baron would give a fuck about the wellbeing of any of his illegitimate children.

In all of the speculation, however, no one had suggested that perhaps it was just because Vox was a kind person. That he'd carried me to the healer out of the goodness of his heart. That made me kind of sad for the Heir to the First Line.

On the plus side, my instructors had excused me from combat training for a whole week. I felt like I should send Eugene a thank-you card for that unexpected boon. It was like a holiday from life. I still had to attend Battle Strategy and History lectures, though, attempting to make notes with my left hand. I'd have to commit most of it to memory, because the notes were illegible.

At the moment, I was trying not to fall asleep as Instructor Tryelle told us about the history of Ebrus before the Line segregation, back when we'd been warring tribe factions rather than a united country.

The feeling of tiny nails against my socks was all too

familiar now. Dropping my pen as an excuse, I reached down and held out my hand for my little black-and–white mouse friend. It had been my almost constant companion since I was injured, hanging out in either my collar beneath my hair, or in one of my pockets, unless it was off doing… whatever mice did.

Epsy liked the mouse too, which was a relief. I was fairly sure rodents were Epsy's main food source, though the other day I'd caught him eating a head of lettuce, so maybe I knew nothing about what stolts ate.

But the mouse in my collar and the stolt in my pocket seemed to have an understanding. Although I was fairly sure that Epsy would've eaten at least a hundred of the mouse's family line, they seemed to have come to some kind of truce.

Or maybe it was just wishful thinking, and Epsy would feel like a midnight snack one day and I'd wake up to no more mouse friend.

No, not a friend. A spy. I had to remember that this mouse was one of Hayle Taeme's animal companions. However, as far as spies went, this one was freaking adorable.

Instructor Tryelle was looking at us with something that might be aggrieved disappointment. "I know you're out here living your best life, swinging your swords like the past doesn't matter, but just know that we do have a library where you could do your own research. There is a lot to learn from the past that could help you well into your future."

I was probably guilty of this. I knew we had a

library here in Boellium, and normally, that would be the first place I'd go, but I hadn't managed to do anything except eat, sleep and train in the few weeks since I'd arrived. I'd barely gained my footing, and I expected that until I was a lot stronger, I wouldn't feel anything but perpetually exhausted. Maybe my forced combat training hiatus meant I could check out the rest of the campus, including the library.

The instructor excused us, and it was time for my favorite part of the day: dinner. I'd never been so hungry as I had in my time at Boellium, the extra physical exertion making me constantly starving. But that was only a small part of why I loved the food here.

The college didn't differentiate between the different Lines when serving the meals, and the tastes of the Upper Lines were far more finicky than the Lower Lines, which meant I was trying foods I would never have tasted back home. Like ice cream and pistachios. Like cuts of venison so tender, they melted as they hit my tongue.

The spoiled Upper Line conscripts complained if the same thing was served more than twice in the space of a month, so it was also varied. I wasn't the only person who enjoyed the easy access to food, even if it did come with a side of snide humiliation from the Upper Liners like Ephily.

I was disheartened to see that today's meal was some kind of soup; not the easiest thing to eat with my non-dominant hand, but I'd just get an extra bread roll and soak it up.

As soon as I stood in the food line, Epsy disappeared into the kitchen. "Epsy!" I hissed, but the damn stolt didn't even look back. He was going to end up at the business end of a cleaver, if the cooks caught him. He wasn't a very smart creature, and I could only hope that the kitchen staff thought he was part of the Third Line and would be too scared to throw him in tomorrow night's stew.

The mouse in my collar had more sense, just burrowing in deeper so no one could see it. I slid my tray along the smooth bench, using my good hand to shakily ladle soup into the deep well carved into it. I would be glad when the sling came off, even if my collarbone still ached. Tonight's dinner was going to be messy; I could predict it now.

None of my Twelfth Line friends had appeared at their table yet, since they were probably still at combat training. Putting two bread rolls onto my tray, I ignored the jibes of the girl from the Sixth Line, calling me a fat ass. I doubted they'd say that to the guy in front of me, who had two bowls of soup and three damn bread rolls, even though we were all working just as hard in battle training.

No, the real reason was that a fraction of the women in the college weren't here to be soldiers—they were here to create alliances, preferably of the marital variety. Where better to get close to the Heirs and Upper Lines than in this microcosm of our society?

Those conscripts were all thin, svelte, ball ready at any moment. *Fuck that.* I wanted to not pass out during training, which meant I was going to eat two bread rolls and probably come back for some of that cake sitting at the end of the long benches.

I looked over my shoulder and smiled at the Sixth Line girl with far more teeth than would be considered polite as I added a third bread roll to my tray. I would just take it down to my dorm later if I didn't eat it. Making the point was more important.

Heading over to my empty table, I balanced the tray precariously with one hand and breathed a sigh of relief when I didn't drop it all over myself. My good arm was now aching from taking on the bulk of today's tasks, and as I lifted my spoon to my lips, I shook, spilling most of it off the side.

Dammit. This was going to be slow.

Scooping up another spoonful, I lifted it again to my lips, but this time, I felt something cool wrap around my wrist, a band of air that I felt as physically as if someone had grabbed me with their hand. The air gently maneuvered my wrist toward my mouth, and the spoon sat there at my lips, waiting for me to sip the soup from it.

I didn't spill a single drop.

I slurped it down, and the air on my wrist pulled my hand back down, back to my bowl. I scooped up more, and this time, it merely steadied my hand as I ate my soup. Who had that kind of precision—and would give a damn—if I could eat my soup without making a mess?

There was only one person I knew for a fact who

had that skill. My eyes wandered across the room, but Vox Vylan wasn't paying attention to me. The spoon tapped gently against my lips, and I opened them almost on instinct. It had to be him, right? No one else was that powerful.

Again and again, he fed me, or at least aided me in feeding myself. It was oddly caring, and what the hell did I make of that?

Vox continued to carry on conversation with the others at his table, and I noticed Shay, his second-in-command, watching me closely. Maybe it wasn't Vox doing it, but Shay? However, judging by the way her lips tightened as she turned away, probably not.

Finally, the soup was done, and the air around my wrist loosened, sliding down my arm and off the tips of my fingers in almost a sucking motion. I gasped in a breath as the sensation went straight to my core. My eyes flew back across the room, and this time, they clashed with Vox's icy blue ones.

But they weren't so icy right now. No, they were filled with heat, like he could sense my thoughts, or taste the desire that had shot through my veins. I was trapped in the snare of his gaze, helpless to escape.

Not when the sucking air trailed down my throat like hungry kisses. Not when it slipped below the billowing V of my shirt and between my breasts. Not when it brushed across the curve of my flesh, wrapped around my nipple, and sucked.

"Fuck!" I squawked loudly, making everyone in the room turn in my direction. My cheeks flushed hot and red as I dragged my gaze up to the ceiling. If I wasn't looking at him, he wouldn't be able to see the sheer *need* in my expression. I scrambled from my table, not even bussing my tray as I hightailed it out of the room.

But not before I met Vox's blue eyes once more, finding them filled with molten desire, the small smirk on his face promising access to untold secrets, untold pleasure. My feet tripped over themselves, but I kept going, out of the food hall, across the courtyard, down to the beach.

I need to climb into the waves and cool down my overheated skin. Needed the water to wash away the visions of Vox Vylan doing even more depraved things to me with his elemental abilities.

I was all the way to the shoreline when I realized I wasn't alone on the beach. Hayle Taeme was sitting on a large, flat stone, his hounds at his feet, his intense gaze watching me as I stood with the waves splashing up to my knees.

The last thing I wanted was to be in the path of another powerful man who made me feel things I didn't understand. Turning, I sprinted back up the rocky path toward the walls of Boellium, but the hounds blocked my way.

"Stay," Hayle commanded, and I wasn't sure if he was talking to me or the hounds, at least until he tacked on, "Please."

I turned slowly, my heart thundering in my chest, and tried not to feel as if I was walking to my doom as my feet moved toward Hayle.

I DIDN'T KNOW what I was doing. Braxus heaved an annoyed sigh and lay down at my feet, but I ignored him and his insinuation that I found Avalon Halhed to be a tempting rutting partner. Alucius had snapped her teeth at him about it, but I didn't understand that either. Some of their conversations were just for them, not meant for human understanding.

Avalon walked over to me slowly, almost like she was worried I'd tear her throat out. Had I given her any reason to believe that was something I wanted?

I shuffled over on the flat rock, inviting her to sit beside me. She perched right on the edge, like she was ready to sprint at any moment. She should know better than to run from a hunter. It just invited us to chase.

A mouse peeked out from her collar, and I found myself smiling as I put out my hand and he launched himself off her shoulder, into my palm.

"Such a traitor," Avalon mumbled, and the mouse's

whiskers twitched. He bombarded me with images of everything that had happened since I'd last seen him, including the taste of magic while she'd been trying to eat earlier. Vox was more than interested in her; that was becoming obvious. In all the years I'd known him, he'd never shown softness toward anyone, except maybe his cousin, Shay.

I stroked the mouse's head in thanks and fed him one of the nuts I kept in my pocket for Quarry. "It's not his fault. It's nice to be seen, especially when you're so small," I told her softly. Once the nut was clenched firmly between his teeth, I lifted him back up to Avalon's shoulder, where he returned to his place under her collar. "Besides, he likes you. I relieved him of his duties days ago, and he chooses to stay with you."

She gave me a crooked grin. "I have a way with rodents, I guess."

"Must be why Vox Vylan is so enamored with you then."

She slid her eyes to me, but said nothing. I watched the waves again, the seabirds swirling, sending me images of a great school of fish just off the shore.

"I've been looking into you and your family," I said casually, and I didn't imagine the way her body froze. I wanted to know her secrets. "There's a lot of literature about them in the library."

"Oh?" she asked with forced lightness. "Must have been a pretty boring read. Besides, you don't really strike me as the studious library type."

I gave her a toothy grin. "Are you saying I look stupid?"

Her cheeks flushed pink, and she shook her head so vigorously, it was a wonder she didn't knock off the mouse in her collar. "No? I mean, definitely not."

Probing a little more, I tuned into her scent. She smelled… stressed. *Interesting.* Was she a spy? There was always a chance here, and I had no doubt that more than one of the Lines had installed people in Boellium just to see the way the winds of power were turning.

"As I was saying, there was a lot of literature about your family. They were once revered seers, did you know that?"

Now she was looking at me like I was stupid. "Of course I knew that. I lived up north, not in a cave on the side of a mountain. I can even read," she said with mock amazement. I tried not to grin at her sarcasm. She was kind of cute when her heart wasn't beating out of her chest like a scared bunny.

"As I was saying, people would come from all over Ebrus, putting aside decades of feuds, to talk to members of your family. To get their predictions." I sucked on my back teeth thoughtfully. "Then somewhere around ten generations ago, the power started to dwindle."

She rolled her eyes at me. "Really? Do tell me more about my own family history."

I smirked. "Don't you wonder why?"

She shook her head. "No. Every Line's power has been dwindling over the last few centuries, and I wonder how much of the original reports of our powers were just exaggerations for the history books anyway."

I didn't tell her that the Third Line's powers hadn't dwindled at all. That perhaps my brothers and I were the strongest direct descendents of the Line in… well, ever. I also didn't mention that Vox's abilities were just as impressive, and if my brothers were to be believed, Yaron Vylan's powers were equally as strong.

No, it seemed only the powers of the Lower Lines were dwindling, and I was neither the researcher nor the historian needed to figure out the whys and hows of that. That was for minds more academic than my own.

Turning to face her, I stared into her eyes. "Why are you here, Avalon Halhed?"

She raised an eyebrow at me like I was stupid. With any other person, I would've flexed my powers until they cowered under my domination, but I found the bravado hiding under Avalon's soft exterior kind of endearing.

"The same reason we're all here, Hayle Taeme." Was she mocking me right now? "Ebrus's conscription laws mean each Line has to send at least one conscript every year."

That was true, but what made a man send his youngest daughter to Boellium War College? "But why you? If it was about training a fighter or garnering political influence, I know you have several older brothers. If it was just about sending a warm body to fulfil the conscript quota, I assume you have several dozen farm boys up in the wilds who'd like a chance to prove themselves in the Dawn Army. So why you? Why the youngest daughter of the Baron?"

Her jaw was tense, and I knew I'd struck a nerve. "What you don't know—and can't discover in the library's history books—is that my father hates me. Sending me to Boellium was probably the happiest he's been in decades."

I hadn't spent much time with Avalon, but even I knew that she was a kind person. She'd saved my damn mouse, after all. "I'm sure that's not true. Maybe it feels like it right now because he sent you here, but I can't imagine anyone hating you for no reason."

She frowned at me, pain in her eyes. "Is murdering my mother a good enough reason?" she snapped, and with that, she slid from the rock beside me and marched back toward the college while I stared after her, dumbfounded.

She'd murdered her mother?

There had to be more to it than that, because unless she had an evil twin, there was a better chance of me being one of Baron Vylan's illegitimate children than her being a murderer. Standing, I brushed the sand from my trousers. Something was not right with the Ninth Line, and I was going to figure out what it was.

The last thing I wanted to do tonight was go up to the First Line dorm for an Upper Lines party, but I was basically duty-bound to attend. If I didn't go, the delicate balance of power in Boellium could shift.

Right now, Vox and I stood almost at an equilibrium. We both had enough people on our sides that we could go about our days without any kind of power struggle. But an entire party, this early in the year, with no Third Line representation? Well, Vox Vylan could whisper all sorts of lies in the ears of the new Upper Six conscripts, and the hierarchy could be redrawn overnight. It was an exhausting, petty juggling act that I loathed with my entire being.

Lucio was already dressed like he was planning to get laid and was waiting by the door when I emerged from my own room, proof of how long I'd been dragging my feet getting ready. Lucio tended to take forever to get his hair perfect in the mirror.

"Brother, we're going to a party, not your execution. Cheer up," he teased, slapping me on the back. I rolled my eyes and whistled for Braxus. While it was generally accepted that we wouldn't bring our creature familiars to parties, no one was stopping me from bringing at least one of my hounds. They were as much a part of me as my own hand.

Braxus groaned, and I caught a smug emotion from Alucius, who was still curled up in front of the fireplace. "Sorry, Brax. If they weren't such fucks, you could stay home and snuggle in front of the fire too. Unfortunately, I need you to watch my back."

He sighed heavily, plodding toward the dorm door before me. However, as soon as he crossed the threshold, he was immediately on alert. Forever my bodyguard.

We walked up the stairs to the top floor, past the permanently locked and barred Second Line dorm. Even from the landing, I could tell the party was already in full swing. While the First Line dorm didn't have the same level of soundproofing as ours, the pounding music was still muffled pretty well.

It was the first party of the new conscript year, so the First Line appeared to have gone all out. There was alcohol flowing freely, and Lines mingling, and already, there were people fucking in the corners of the room.

The party had only been going for an hour.

The conscripts of Boellium worked hard, but they also played hard. For some, it was the first time they'd ever been outside their Line's territory. I guess there was something to be said for extensive "networking," especially the naked kind.

Lucio sniffed the drink he was handed by someone in the Fourth Line before handing it to me. I sniffed it too, our heightened senses able to pick up any note that wasn't meant to be in the burning liquor.

"I'm going to see if I can convince Shay to dance with me." Lucio wandered toward the enigmatic second-in-command for the First Line. He liked trying his luck with her, because for each other, they were both safe.

The Third Line had enough spies to know that Shay had absolutely no interest in Lucio romantically. He did not possess the right parts. But no one said it out loud, and Lucio didn't want to get caught in the sticky tendrils of some scheming Upper Line female who wanted to marry their way into clout. So he made it known that he was only interested in Shay, and she played along, for whatever her reasons were.

I sipped my drink, enjoying the burn, with Braxus sitting in front of my legs giving enough of a *fuck-off* vibe that I didn't have to worry about dealing with pandering or political manuevering.

At least, I didn't, until Vylan appeared in my personal bubble. "Taeme."

"Vylan."

"I would like to talk." He always sounded like he had a stick up his ass. Like he hadn't felt a single moment of passion in his short, obnoxious life.

"Perhaps you should try one of the healers. They'll give a shit about your problems."

Rolling his eyes at me, he didn't leave, nor rise to the bait. He must be serious. "It's about the girl."

I stiffened. There was only one girl who'd piqued our collective interest, and I had no urge to share what I knew with this pompous douchebag. "Which girl?" I said lazily, sipping my drink like we weren't seconds from throwing down.

He gave me his normal bored, impassive expression, but I saw the subtle tightening of his jaw. "Avalon Halhed, the one from the Ninth Line."

I shrugged. "What about her?"

Vox stepped into my space, making Braxus bare his teeth. I sent him a reassurance through our bond that I had this, and to stand down, but he didn't like it.

"Stay away from her. If you have an interest in her, I suggest you forget it. She's mine."

Well, fuck me. I hadn't seen that coming. Was Avalon thawing the ice prince? I'd believe it when I saw it. It was more likely that he just didn't want me playing with his toys.

"Says who? I think that's for Avalon to decide, don't you?" I buried my fingers in Braxus's fur. "A little healthy competition might be just what the healer ordered. May the best man win, Vylan." I laughed at the sour expression on his face. "And no one would ever consider you the best man."

He straightened, his eyes turning frigid. "At least I'm a man and not a beast. Stay away from her, Taeme. I won't warn you again."

He may as well have put a giant X on her head, because now she was a treasure at the end of a hunt, and I was going to have her for myself.

chapter thirty

Avalon

SOMETHING HAD CHANGED, and it felt big. I didn't notice for a week or two, just going about my days in blissful ignorance until Shay from the First Line appeared in front of me on a random Wednesday. I was finally out of my sling and back on the training field, swinging a slightly lighter sword.

"I'm Shay." That was all she said, like it should explain everything. And in her defense, it kind of did. She was the second-in-command of the First Line here at Boellium War College. Everyone knew that.

"Uh, I'm Avalon." I wasn't sure why we were doing introductions, but I was polite, if nothing else.

She looked at me as if I were a bug under a looking glass. She eyed me a little longer, then turned on her heel and left. That was it.

I looked over at Viana and Acacia. "What the fuck was *that*?"

Viana snorted a laugh. "That was Vox Vylan's cousin

trying to work out why her Heir is panting after some nobody from the Ninth Line. No offense."

I rolled my eyes. "None taken." I truly meant it, because it had been really weird. An anomaly. "And Vox is *not* panting after me."

Acacia and Viana did that annoying silent conversation thing that came from knowing someone inside and out for a long period of time. Finally, Acacia shook her head. "She must know."

Viana raised an eyebrow. "How could she? You know what she's like." They both turned toward me, so there was no doubt I was the "she" to which they were referring.

"You *know*, right?" Acacia asked.

Quite frankly, they were talking in riddles and giving me a headache. "Know what?" I shouted a little louder than necessary.

Viana looked triumphant. "I told you she had no idea." She gripped my hands. "Vox Vylan wants to fuck the brains right out of your head. He wants to use his dick to reshape your insides until they're cock-embossed. He wants you to ride him like a magic carpet."

Magic carpets didn't exist anymore, since the First Line had evolved beyond using them as transportation. That wasn't important, though.

I blinked at Viana. "No, he doesn't."

She gripped my chin and turned my face toward the other side of the training ring where Vox was shirtless, his pale skin flashing under the harsh sun as he downed water from a glass bottle. He'd been training one-on-one with one of the instructors. Not that he needed any instruction, as his fluid movements were graceful and mesmerizing.

Though, at this moment, he was watching me with eyes that made my skin tingle and my body feel hot. I tried to intellectualize the sensation away; it was probably the sun, combined with the fact that I was out of shape after resting for two weeks. It definitely didn't have anything to do with the way his piercing blue gaze was burning against my skin.

Viana let go of my chin, but she stayed close. "See that expression? That is the look of a man who wants to lay you down in the sand right here, and fuck you where everyone can see. That's the expression of a man who desperately wants to know what you look like as you orgasm."

My mouth suddenly felt bone dry, and I wet my lips without dragging my eyes from his.

Acacia snorted. "He's eyefucking you like you're the last pussy on earth, Avalon Halhed, and I can't believe you've never noticed. I bet you don't even realize that him and Hayle Taeme are about to come to blows, because Taeme also wants to make the beast with two backs with you. I don't know what kind of vagina magic you possess, but I'm here for it. It's about time that some of the Upper Lines realize the quality of partners available in the Lower Six."

At her words, my gaze shot to Hayle, who was

lazily sparring with his cousin, Lucio, but mostly watching the intense interaction between Vox and I.

"What the fuck?" I breathed again, but I didn't get a chance to think about it too hard because Vox was striding across the training ring toward me. I wanted to run away, like he was a mountain lion and not an Heir to the First Line. Honestly, I might be better off taking my chances with the mountain lion.

He stopped in front of me, and my two friends took up positions behind me. They had my back, and honestly, it felt kind of nice to know that someone would be there to witness my inevitable destruction at the hands of Vox Vylan.

"Your arm is better." It was a statement, not a question, so I just stared up at him dumbly. "Your presence is required tonight in the First Line dorm."

Honestly, I'd have been less surprised if he'd asked me to strip down and do a traditional Ebrian moon dance with him right out here in the open. "What?"

He didn't repeat himself, just raised an eyebrow.

I cleared my throat, Viana's words echoing around in my brain. The audacity of this guy to just order me to his dorm room, as if I was some kind of cheap prostitute. He hadn't even tried to word it like it was a request. So I held his eyes as I said, "No, thank you."

The look of shock on Vox's face would have been amusing in any other situation. "Excuse me?"

"No." I mimicked his eyebrow raise. "You do know the meaning of the word, right? It's like the opposite of 'Yes, Sir.' I don't like being ordered up to your ivory tower, Vox Vylan." His incredulity was making me feel even more irate.

I heard Acacia gasp, and I suddenly remembered the guy who'd been hanging suspended in the courtyard of Boellium the day I arrived. I wondered what he'd done, and if it was remotely as bad as insulting the second in line to Ebrus's throne of power.

He stepped closer, bending down until his nose was mere inches from mine. "My apologies, Avalon. Would you please accompany me in my dorm room on the First floor tonight? There is a meteor shower predicted, and I would like to share it with you, if you are at all interested?" How could he make such an innocent invitation sound like an all-access pass to a First Line orgy?

Did I want to go and see a meteor shower? Yes. It was common knowledge that Vox's room was in the glass dome at the very top of the atrium's tower.

Did I also want to have sex with Vox Vylan? Well, that was a secret I was even keeping from myself.

I licked my lips again, and he followed the action with his eyes. "Just the meteor shower? No sex?"

Viana snorted, but held her tongue. Vox's gaze briefly flicked to the two women behind me, then back down to my face. "Your virtue is safe with me, Ninth." He leaned closer, which seemed impossible, considering his breath was already misting against my lips. "But is my virtue safe with you?" he asked lightly. Straightening, he turned away and strode back across the practice ring, falling into the fighter's stance opposite the instructor once more.

I sucked in oxygen like he'd stolen it all. Looking over at Acacia and Viana, I gave them a wide-eyed look of panic. "That just happened, right? I didn't have a fever dream?"

Acacia shook her head. "No, girl. You didn't." She tugged at my arm. "When we're done here, we need to head down to the bowels. I have a sneaking suspicion that there's not a single thing in your wardrobe that's appropriate to wear 'star watching' with an Heir to the First Line." She said "star watching" the way some people would say "flying pigs." With a heavy dose of skepticism.

She was right, of course. I had my brother's pants and my traveling skirt, which had as many holes as pockets. I needed to mend it, but there really hadn't been time. Neither of those were respectable enough to even be in the First Line dorm, let alone Vox Vylan's living quarters.

"I'd be grateful. Thank you."

I'd been to the bowels of Boellium—the colloquial name for the Twelfth Line dorm, as it was at the very bottom of the main building—a few times now, and I envied the camaraderie they all had together. The community they'd somehow adopted me into.

When Acacia and Viana arrived with me in tow, I was greeted like a long-lost sibling. Someone thrust a bowl of stew in my hand, someone else grilled me about how my collarbone was healing, and others asked after my stolt. They all cared. It was like a bandage around my stone-cold heart, and I didn't know what to do with the emotions it evoked.

"Our friend from the Ninth has a date with none other than Vox Vylan, and has a truly abysmal wardrobe. Does anyone have anything they'd think is appropriate?" Viana asked.

Someone whistled low, and there was a lot of elbow nudging and banter, but at least six people ran off into their dorm rooms, including Acacia. I sat in the middle of their common room, eating stew like a fool, while Viana gave them all a blow-by-blow of what had happened in the training ring.

"Then he leaned in, and I swear, I thought he was going to either headbutt her or kiss her, but instead, he said please. Vox Vylan said *please*." They all went wide-eyed, like he'd fought and defeated a three-headed dragon, instead of using good manners.

Acacia rushed out of her room holding a red dress, roughly the same color as the sun-scorched earth of her home territory. "Come on, Avalon. We only have four hours until you have to meet Vox Vylan in his bedroom, and you smell like the ass end of a beast of burden."

I sniffed my armpit and winced. She wasn't wrong. She herded me into the big copper bathtub, filled with some kind of fragrant herbs and murky white water. I didn't even have time to be embarrassed as she undressed me, and three of them scrubbed me down, even cleaning the dirt beneath my fingernails.

By the end, I was in fact several shades lighter. Here

I thought I'd been getting a tan in the harsher Southern sun. Turns out, it was just caked-on dirt.

They preened me until the clock read 8:55pm, and I was standing at the door of the bowels, the whole floor hovering around, as if I was off to my first ball rather than some guy's dorm room. Viana had her arms wrapped around the waists of both Polus and Link—her boyfriends—and they were all looking at me like I was a miracle.

Acacia chewed her lip. "You should see if you can get him to do something about the famine in the Eleventh and Twelfth Baronies while he's buried between your thighs."

Viana hushed her. "We aren't pimping her out for humanitarian aid, Acacia. The Upper Lines don't care, and we shouldn't ruin Avalon's chances of a better future by making her a political spy." She grinned and hugged me tightly. "You look beautiful, though, so if anyone could make a man like Vox Vylan spontaneously grow a heart, it'd be you. Remember, if you start to gag, just force yourself to swallow." She pushed me out onto the dorm landing.

I frowned at her parting words, and the way Polus was laughing. "What?"

"She means have fun," Acacia answered, then closed the door.

Sucking in a deep breath, I made the climb to the top floor of Boellium, and the elite of all of Ebrus's Lines.

chapter thirty-one

Vox

I'D CLEARED out the dorm, because I could. Not because I was embarrassed that I'd invited her here, but because I didn't think she'd enjoy being stared at like some sort of freak. Ridiculous, really. I hadn't been living like a monk in this hellhole for the last year; I'd had lovers. Many, in fact, because I couldn't fuck anyone twice without them getting stars in their eyes and dreaming of crowns on their heads. Figurative crowns, of course. Ebrus didn't actually have royalty.

Though the First Line would be as close as you could get. At least, that's how everyone had always treated us, and my father would be the first to expect their reverence. I hated it. Always had, even when I was a child. The stares and expectations were the heaviest mantle.

Displacement in my air barrier told me that Avalon had arrived. I stood and straightened my clothes, still unsure why I was doing this.

There'd been a small seed of feeling that had been sown upon seeing her, and it compelled me to dig at it, whether I understood it or not.

Walking down the spiral staircase to the common room, I strode confidently toward the door. Straightening my face into its normal stately mask, I opened it. And my jaw immediately slackened.

With the lights of the landing behind her, she looked almost ethereal. I cleared my throat. "You look nice."

That was bullshit. She looked more than nice. She looked *beautiful.* Her skin was glowing, her hair falling in beautiful waves over her shoulders. She was in a dress that I knew was of the Twelfth Line style, a fitted bodice that hugged her curves right down over her hips, before flaring into a full skirt.

She looked like a goddess. That small seed of feeling began to sprout into something else. Something that I wasn't sure would get enough light to bloom into anything more.

Mentally shaking myself, I stood to the side and indicated she should enter. She gave me a tight smile, stepping across the threshold. She was possibly the first Ninth Line conscript to step foot on this floor in a hundred years.

"Where is everyone?" she asked softly, like she was worried about being shushed by a librarian. I shut the door behind her, and she briefly looked panicked.

Well, that was good sense, I guess. I hadn't thought about how it would seem, just her and I in a deserted dorm, with the door locked.

"Everyone is out, but if you're uncomfortable, I could get Shay or someone else to come back?"

I was a fool. When was the last time I'd made an effort with a woman? Normally, they crawled into my lap with little effort on my part. I didn't do anything as basic as *trying*.

Shay, while she didn't pretend to understand my fascination with the girl from the Ninth Line, had insisted this kind of effort was good for me, even if it couldn't go anywhere. That I should consider it training for whatever bride my father inevitably picked out for me. Or my mother, I guess. I wasn't sure which option was more terrifying.

Shay might've been right. I knew that I didn't want a loveless, messy marriage—the kind my parents had, fuelled by rage, gossip, and illicit affairs. It was the most toxic environment I'd ever witnessed… and I'd grown up in court.

Avalon canted her head toward me appraisingly, then shook it. "No, it's fine. I can always stab you if you get too handsy."

I choked back the laugh that threatened to burst out. "That's treasonous talk, Ninth. Don't you know the walls have ears?" Not in here, though. This dorm was my domain, and there were no spies here right now. Nothing but the sphere of silence that I meticulously maintained and the girl across from me. "Let's go up to my suite. The meteor shower is estimated to begin within the next hour."

She followed me obediently up the spiral stairs, and

when we stepped into the Dome, she sucked in a small gasp. I resisted the urge to preen, like I'd had anything to do with the beauty of this room. It had been here for longer than I could comprehend. The large diamond panes of glass managed to be both beautiful and unobtrusive, a frame for a breathtaking view of the stars. The moon was thin and dark, making it the perfect night for the meteor shower.

She spun around, taking in my suite with wide eyes. I tried to see it the way she did: the large bed covered in the finest blankets, the ornate desk and chair that overlooked the courtyard. Intricate rugs, sculptures, and swords all sat side by side. A low bookshelf ran right around the room, filled with numerous tomes that varied in rarity and boringness.

Along the wall that faced back to the vast openness of the sea was my telescope. My one little vice. My father thought it made me a dreamer, looking for answers out among the stars, but my mother—for the first and only time in her life—had argued that it was an educated field of study that would be well respected by the other Lines.

You know, because I was the spare Heir. The one they didn't really need, unless my brother got himself stabbed by the husband of one of the many married women he debauched.

Finally, Avalon looked at the soft couch in the middle of the room and moved toward it, a confidence in the sway of her hips that hadn't been there before, though I could still see the wariness in her face. She paused, looking around her once more. "This is weird. I should go," she said quietly.

"I swear, my intentions are honorable." And they had been, until I'd seen her in that dress. Now, I just wanted to peel it off her and taste every inch of milky skin that was glowing warmly in the soft lights dotted around my room.

This had started out as a point of interest, and maybe Taeme had turned it into a competition, but something about Avalon Halhed was dangerous. My interest in her was walking a knife's edge between curiosity and obsession.

She looked away, and I could've sworn I heard her mutter, "Maybe mine are not."

My mind had wandered so far that it took me a moment to realize she meant her intentions. I must have misheard, but her cheeks were pink, though even that might have been a trick of the light.

"Would you like a drink? To calm whatever thoughts are obviously racing through your mind right now."

She rolled her eyes, but eventually nodded. I went to the small tray of liquor that I kept off to the side of the room, pouring us both a small glass. It was strong, especially if you weren't used to it.

She took a small sip, and her eyes went comically wide. "Holy Goddess, are you sure you aren't trying to get me drunk, so you can take advantage of me?"

I almost laughed. "No, Miss Halhed. When I take you to bed, it will be because you're on your knees, begging me to please you. Not because you're three cups deep in the honey wine the Seventh Line makes down in their dorm room."

There was no doubting the pink cheeks this time. Grabbing the ice cream from the small cabinet I kept frozen, I transferred it to a bowl that wouldn't give her frostbite and stuck a spoon in it. "This might be so I can get you into bed, though."

"It's brown." She frowned at the bowl, like I'd just handed her spoiled food.

"It's chocolate flavored, and now for my next trick," I muttered, as I grabbed a small chocolate from the pile on the side table and hovered it over the bowl of ice cream. Drawing warm air from around the fireplace, I gently melted the chocolate until it poured over the ice cream.

Avalon Halhed looked at me, then the ice cream that was now covered in melted chocolate, then back at me. Her amazement was like a balm on my soul.

She handed me the bowl back and stood. I frowned. Had I read her wrong? She'd seemed to enjoy ice cream when it was served the other day, and I often saw her pocketing little pieces of foil-wrapped chocolate left out as a treat for the conscripts.

"Do you not like it?"

Shaking her head, she stared down at me, her eyes sparkling in the soft lights. "I'm taking off my clothes. If you were trying to get under my skirts, ice cream coated in chocolate is a surefire way to do it. Congratulations."

I looked up at her, shocked, and she burst out laughing, sitting back beside me and taking the bowl back, shoveling a mouthful past her lips and sighing happily.

"Goddess, I don't think anything else in all of Ebrus could taste this good." She smiled, and there was a smear of chocolate on her lip. "You should see your face right now. You look like the Heir to the Fish Kingdom or something."

I snapped my jaw closed as I realized she was teasing me. Me, of all people. And instead of irritating me, I found it was refreshing. Fuck me, they mustn't have taught her any etiquette up there in the wilds of the Ninth Line, but I was enjoying it. I gave her a mock-annoyed look, which made her giggle into her bowl a little more, before she single-mindedly devoured the dessert with soft little moans I wasn't sure she even knew she was making.

She didn't eat it demurely, or make polite conversation, though she thanked me at least twice. "Would you like some?" she asked softly, and I couldn't tell if she was hoping I'd say yes or no. I couldn't resist the urge to share something she enjoyed so much, though.

"Yes."

Instead of handing me the bowl and the spoon, she scooped up the perfect mouthful and held it out to me, like I was a child she had to feed. I found myself leaning forward, snagging her eyes as I did, wrapping my lips around the spoon. It was delicious, but I wanted to taste it from her tongue.

I pushed down the thought. For now, at least. "Very nice. The cooks did an excellent job."

She finished off the bowl and leaned back with a sigh. "I didn't realize it came in flavors. I thought it was just cream that had been frozen into ice. Like the name suggests."

I licked my lips and pushed down the urge to get ice cream made in every flavor imaginable, just so I could watch her joyful wonder.

Someone would definitely report that to my parents.

"There are no limitations to the flavorings, though some would be terrible. I imagine a meat-flavored ice cream would be fairly unpleasant," I informed her.

She grinned. "I bet the Third Line would love it, though."

I lifted an eyebrow and left it at that. She was right; they probably would, but I didn't want to give Taeme and his band of feral animals any more enjoyment than they deserved. Which was none.

I stood and went to the telescope, adjusting it to point at the darkest part of the sky. The air around her seemed to shimmer as she stood, setting the bowl on the side table and walking toward me. "It surprises me that you're a stargazer, Vox."

"Oh? Why is that?"

She shrugged, her warmth beside mine as we stood shoulder to shoulder. "Why would you be searching the stars when you have everything you need right here?"

I almost laughed at her words. She would see it like that, I guess. I couldn't blame her for believing the visage I projected to everyone. "The sky shows us that there is more than Ebrus, more than the Lines. More to the Goddess's plan than this. It's humbling."

I waited for her to quip something back, but instead, she tipped her head back and watched the sky. "Do you ever feel like there's something planned for you out there, and you aren't sure what it is yet, and all the trials are just leading you to where you have to go?"

Every single day. There had to be more to life than what I'd experienced so far: political jockeying, familial expectations, and finally, death. That couldn't be the sum total of our lives, right? Sometimes, when I looked at the stars, I wondered if we'd done all this before. That yearning in my chest had to be for something.

Instead of telling her all that, I simply said, "Yes."

She sighed softly. "Me too."

We were silent for a long time, and then a flash of light across the sky heralded something special. Something that was as rare as the woman beside me. Wrapping my hand in hers, I tugged her over to the telescope, where she stood on her tiptoes to see in the eyepiece. She let out soft, sweet noises as she saw shooting star after shooting star, pieces of meteor raining down.

As I stared at her while she watched the sky, I was suddenly very aware that she hadn't let go of my hand.

chapter thirty-two

Avalon

THIS HAD BEEN the most confusing night of my life, but also one of the best. Vox Vylan was surprisingly good company, once we'd settled on how we were supposed to act around each other. If he wanted me to fawn over him like his biggest fan, he was probably going to be disappointed, but he seemed happy with comfortable silence.

Was it depressing that I could be so easily won over with ice cream and chocolate? Absolutely. Even now, I could remember the creaminess on my tongue, the sweetness still clinging to my lips. The pure pleasure of a mouthful. Fickle I might be, but I had no regrets.

He was a surprisingly knowledgeable guide about the stars. Passionate, even. His face lit up as he explained that this meteor shower was caused by debris left behind by a larger comet, which had been a huge rock hurtling across the stars last week. What we'd see were tiny bits of rock caught in the sky and burning up, making it look like it was showering shooting stars.

The comet that had left behind this meteor shower was called Sucreid, and it moved across the sky only once every hundred and seventy-three years. Some of the Lines' magic users believed that the comet itself heralded a time of great change, and a lot of superstitions were born from its appearance in the sky.

I didn't think we had any superstitions about them up in the Ninth Line, though our library was depressingly grim. There was very little about anyone further back than my father's grandfather. The histories of my ancestors before that were all gone, lost in a fire long before I was born.

Now, I lay on Vox Vylan's bed, watching the stars streak across the sky through the giant glass dome that he had instead of a ceiling. There were so many shooting stars now that we didn't even need his telescope to see. It was magical.

He lay beside me, on the other side of the bed, an appropriate amount of mattress between us, and watched it just as intently. We didn't need to speak. Words would ruin the moment.

Finally, the meteor shower lessened, and my eyelids began to droop. It was time to leave, even though I was almost sad to do so. Last week, I would've been desperate to get out of a space occupied by Vox. Now, I found myself dragging my feet.

I raised myself up on my elbows. "I should go. It's

late, and I'm sure your dorm mates would like to return to their beds."

He shrugged. "They'll return when I tell them they can." His nonchalance really was abrasive sometimes, and I wondered if he knew how pompous that sounded.

I chewed my lip. "Even so, it's time for me to go."

He rolled onto his side and watched me with those ice-blue eyes. I felt their weight on my face like a physical touch. His shoulders were broad, and his chest was muscular from the amount of swordwork he did. He might be a rich, bored Heir, but I couldn't say he didn't work as hard as the rest of us—harder than some, even —though there was never any chance of him failing. Of going home in disgrace, broken and useless. Or worse, dead.

His dark hair fell across his forehead, and I wanted to reach out and rub the silky-looking tresses between my fingertips. Wanted to bury my fingertips against his scalp. And more.

So, so, so much more.

They were dangerous thoughts that couldn't lead anywhere good, but my brain and my lady parts were very much in disagreement about what we should do right now. My brain said to get up, walk to the door, and thank him for a very pleasant evening. Then run all the way back to my dorm room, like the coward that I was.

My lower parts—the ones that clenched when he spoke in that deep, husky voice close to my ear while explaining about the meteor shower—said I should push him onto his back, throw a leg over his hips, pin him to his bed, and kiss the hell out of him. Then fuck him. They were pretty adamant about that last part.

"Your words say one thing, Avalon, but your body is saying something very different."

Ugh, those husky words again. I sucked in a calming breath, trying not to pant, and clinging to my higher reasoning by my fingernails. I shook my head. "My body doesn't know what's good for me."

He smiled at me. A wide, beautiful smile that lit up his whole face and made my own go slack. Had I ever seen him smile? I mustn't have, because it would have been burned onto my retinas.

"Maybe your body knows exactly what you need." He sat up. "But don't worry. I can wait for your mind to catch up." He rolled off the bed and got to his feet in a lithe manner that I could only dream of replicating. I climbed off his bed like a drunken fawn and followed him to the stairs that led down to the dorms.

I couldn't believe I'd been in Vox Vylan's bed. I took one last look around, committing everything to memory so I could tell Viana and Acacia about it.

Vox looked amused. "Don't worry, Avalon, you can come back and climb into my bed as often as you like. I promise you an enjoyable time." He leaned closer so his breath feathered across my cheek. "I'll make you scream my name so loudly, even the stars will hear it."

My breath stuttered in my throat, and I turned toward him. His face was so close to mine, his lips just there, tilted down toward me. Unable to resist, I lifted up on my toes and brushed my lips across his. They were softer than I'd imagined, and tasted a little like the chocolate we'd shared. He remained still, and I lowered myself back to my heels, sucking in a breath and fixating on the top button of his shirt so I didn't have to meet his eyes.

A finger tucked under my chin, tilting my head back. His hands gripped my hips, then he *kissed* me. Not a peck, like I'd given him.

No, he owned my mouth, taking and taking and taking until I was breathless and my whole body tingled. Only his strong hands on my hips, holding me close to his torso, kept me from falling down the stairs on rubber legs. He pressed himself closer, and I chased his warmth like he was an inferno I wanted to perish within.

When he finally pulled away, my heart was thundering so loudly, it was like I'd just run a hundred laps of the training ring. My eyes felt too wide, and my hands were trembling softly where they hung at my sides. His normally icy eyes were simmering with desire, and it felt warmer in the Dome than it had all night. Even the fire looked larger.

"Goddess," I muttered beneath my breath, my brain synapses glitching inside my skull. I needed a healer, or maybe some serious alone time in the dorm showers.

Vox grinned, making my knees go weak once more.

"Put that away," I mock chastised.

"Put what away?"

"That smile. It's dangerous. Represses every single responsible thought I've ever had."

He laughed and wrapped a band of air around my ribs, holding me steady as he led me down the spiral staircase. It was still as quiet in the common room as it had been when I arrived, even though it was close to midnight.

"I'll walk you back to your dorm," he told me softly.

My first instinct was to tell him no. He didn't need to trouble himself by walking me through the perfectly safe halls of the college. But I stilled my tongue, because despite my earlier statement, I wasn't really ready for the night to end.

He led me out of the dorm and onto the landing, and once again, I felt the subtle brush of whatever element he used to keep the dorm secure. Air, I guessed, but it felt more charged.

Almost as charged as whatever was happening between the two of us. It could all be in my head, though. What experience did I have with flirting and sex and making moves on Heirs?

The silence stretched between us as we made our way down the six flights of stairs. It had never occurred to me that it took the same amount of effort to get to the Dome as it did to the bowels.

We hit the atrium, and Vox moved toward the stairs that went down to the Lower Line levels. "Have you ever been down here?" I asked, and he shook his head.

"Only once. There hasn't been any other good reason to visit."

He meant when he'd carried me down to the Twelfth Line dorm. I'd forgotten, with all the healing and crap that came afterwards. I didn't know how to feel about that. On one hand, I preened, because apparently I was a good enough reason, but on the other, it made it blindingly clear that we were from two separate worlds that could never meet in the middle.

Was that something that mattered to me, though? I didn't have dreams of power and privilege. I'd hate living in Fortaare, always under the eyes of others. I wanted a quiet life somewhere out of the way, preferably by myself. I guess I'd take Epsy, my stolt, with me too now, but that was it. A simple life for a simple person, away from my father and politics, Heirs and the war college.

"What are you thinking about?" Vox asked quietly as we descended past the Sixth, then Seventh Line floors.

I chewed my lip, trying to decide how honest to be. *Fuck it.* I hadn't made it this far by being a sycophant who spared his feelings. "I was thinking how terrible it would be to be your wife."

His feet stilled, and he stared down at me, shock written all over his face. "I don't disagree, but I'm not going to lie and say that doesn't prick at my pride."

I raised an eyebrow at him. "I think your ego will be fine, Vox Vylan."

We moved past the Eighth Line's landing, until finally, we were standing outside my door. He paused, and I turned toward him. He was looking down at me as if I was a problem he couldn't quite solve. Some part of me knew that if he ever did solve the riddle of me, he would move onto the next puzzle or woman or problem.

"Out of interest, why would it be so terrible to be my wife? I promise, my wife will have all the pleasures I could offer her."

I gave him a crooked smile. "I bet." There was something about the way Vox carried himself that told me he knew what to do between the bedsheets. But that wasn't the aspect of being his wife that I meant. "Your life is right there under the spotlight, all light and heat and eyes on you. That's the exact opposite of the person I am. I'd melt under that kind of scrutiny."

He was silent for a long time, and I wondered once again if I'd offended him. Finally, he sighed. "I don't like it either. But it is the life the Goddess gifted me, even if sometimes it feels more like a prison than a present." He lifted a hand and stroked a thumb across my bottom lip. "It's a shame, though. Tonight has been surprisingly not tedious. I would have liked to do it again sometime."

Snorting, I shook my head. "High praise from Your Highness," I mocked. "I said I didn't want to be your wife, Vox. Not that I didn't want to do… other things."

That cocky smirk was back. "What things?"

Instead of telling him, I launched myself at him, kissing him hard on the lips with more enthusiasm than finesse. He kissed me back, holding me easily against his body. Despite the fact the skirts of my dress kept me hogtied, my legs were desperate to wrap around his hips.

He took easy control of the kiss, and soon enough, I was pressed against my door. His hands hiked up my dress, and he hissed into my mouth when his calloused palms reached the warm skin of my thigh. He squeezed the flesh hard, then dragged himself away.

"Fuck, you feel and taste too tempting, Avalon Halhed." He looked disheveled. I wasn't sure I'd ever seen him look anything but calmly in control. "I have to go to Fortaare for a few days. When I get back…" He trailed off, like he was trying to find the words to explain all the terrible, debauched things he'd like to do to me. "Think about where you would like this to progress, because Avalon?" He leaned closer to me, until our lips were almost touching again. "I can't wait to taste your pleasure on my tongue. Can't wait until you're screaming my name so every single person in Boellium will know that I am fucking you so good, I'll be branded on your soul forever." He brushed his lips lightly across mine. "See you in a few days."

Then he turned and began the long climb back to his glass tower, while I was left panting at the door to my abandoned dorm.

Goddess, what have I done?

chapter thirty-three

Hayle

IT WAS good to be back with my father. My Line. My clan. Someone with more dominance than me, so I could just relax for once and hand off the mantle of responsibility to him, even if it was only for the duration of this tedious Conclave.

It was custom for the Barons of the Lines to bring their spare Heirs to these things. Firstly, to preserve the Lines, should anything underhanded happen, and secondly, in case something happened to the first Heir and we were stuck in the position of taking over the Barony of our Line.

The only silver lining to this was that if I had to be here, so did Vox Vylan, so he wasn't back at Boellium, making moon eyes at Avalon Halhed.

"How is Boellium?" Father asked, leading me through the ostentatious walkways of the Hall of Ebrus in Fortaare. It had been completed by Vox's forefathers and was as cold and barren as its creators.

I shrugged. "It's the same as ever, I guess. Political ass-kissing and Vylan being an asshole."

A small smile quirked his lips. "That does sound about right."

Up ahead, I could see a small gathering of the other Barons and Heirs. "Who called the meeting today?" I asked quietly.

Father's jaw flexed. "A joint request by the Eleventh and Twelfth Lines."

Interesting. Joint requests were unusual, but it didn't take a genius to figure out what the purpose of the meeting was. The record high number of Lower Line conscripts, especially from the Eleventh and Twelfth Lines, due to the drought, spoke volumes of what was happening over there in the Western parts of Ebrus.

Standing in front of the doorway was someone who was far more interesting to me than he'd been at the previous sixteen of these tedious Conclaves I'd had to attend. The Baron of the Ninth Line looked nothing like his daughter. He held none of her light; instead, he seemed almost drab in comparison. It could be because Avalon shone brightly, or it could be because Baron Halhed was famously a drunkard and had the gray pallor to match. His hair was unkempt, and although he held himself tall—perhaps a throwback to the man he'd once been—his clothes hung off him in an ill-fitting way, the smell of stale liquor making my nose scrunch.

Beneath even that scent was the taint of illness. Probably something from drinking himself into a grave, but if he did die soon, I could only imagine his Barony would benefit from his Heir stepping into his shoes.

Hell, the Conclave as a whole would benefit from some younger blood in its ranks. So far, only Baron Zier Tarrin of the Eighth Line was younger than fifty.

My father greeted the other Barons, and I watched Roman Halhed out of the corner of my eye. The way he moved, the way he spoke, the things he said were all more interesting to me this time.

It irked me that Vox Vylan seemed to be watching him intently too.

Finally, Feodore Vylan, the Baron of the First Line and our official ruler, appeared. "Barons, thank you for gathering. Shall we begin? There is a feast to be had after this."

The subtle jibe at the Eleventh and Twelfth Lines landed squarely, and I watched the way their jaws tensed.

My father hated Feodore Vylan, and I understood why. Vox was a high-handed, pompous asshole, but there was something truly predatory about the Baron of the First Line. A power that was insidious and unchecked, because there was no one in Ebrus who could stand against him outside of his own children, and they weren't about to give up their power anytime soon.

Once everyone was seated at the long table—with Vylan at the head, of course—Baron Abaster of the Eleventh Line stood. "The Eleventh and Twelfth Lines request aid from the Capital. Our people are starving, due to consecutive years of drought conditions. We have reached a crisis point, and if nothing is done within the next six months, our people will begin to perish. Our numbers will dwindle, and those who remain will become environmental refugees."

Feodore Vylan waved a hand. "I understand you're facing hardships, Baron Abaster, but we govern our own Baronies..." I watched the faces of the rest of the Barons firm up at his words, and I knew that was it for the Eleventh and Twelfth Lines. Vylan had just declared it not their problem, absolving them of any need to concern themselves with the Lower Lines.

The Eleventh and Twelfth Lines would not get their aid. As we stood at the end of the meeting, I watched Ingrid Ulsen—the only Baroness in the Conclave and leader of the Twelfth Line—storm out of the room, closely followed by Baron Abaster. I raged inside at the weakness of the Barons. My father had argued for official aid, but he'd been voted against pretty quickly.

Feodore Vylan leaned back in his chair at the head of the table. "Women. This is why they shouldn't lead Baronies. Too emotional."

Too emotional? Her people were *dying*. He wouldn't understand, though; I doubted the Vylans cared if their own people lived or died, as long as they remained at the top of the power structure.

My father rose, not even hiding his sneer, and I stood with him. Vox looked... uncomfortable. There was something in the way his eyes were shuttered, the way he was holding himself stiff, the way the blood rushed through his veins as his heart thumped hard in his chest that told me that perhaps he didn't agree with his father.

My father turned. "If you'll excuse us, we must freshen up before the banquet." His tone was disdainful, and we left. I heard the footsteps of Zier Tarrin behind us, and the door slammed closed with a little more force than necessary.

"Baron Taeme," Baron Tarrin called softly, and my father slowed his steps. "Can we speak?" Nodding once, my father waited until he caught up. "Thank you for your cooperation. It's unfortunate that more of the Upper Lines didn't follow suit."

"Let's walk. This building has ears and eyes, and it is harder to catch a moving target." We walked in silence for a little longer, until my father was happy there were no other ears listening. "Unfortunately, not many of the others have the balls to go against the First Line. Preservation of their own power is the first in their minds."

Tarrin shook his head. "The Eleventh and Twelfth Lines will not survive another year, unless something is done. I'm doing what I can, but my Line is also feeling the strain of consecutive droughts. At this rate, the only survivors of the Lowest Lines will be the ones that they've shipped off to Boellium War College."

Father nodded. "I understand. I will try to talk to Lunderov and see if he's open to at least assisting us with passage through his island, rather than sending it all the way down through Boemouthe. If we can figure out a quicker passage so the food doesn't spoil on the way, the Third Line will send aid to the West."

Tarrin's face flashed briefly with relief. "Thank you, Taeme. It's hard to watch them wither and die on our doorstep, but so many see them as expendable."

Father clapped him on the shoulder. "Not the Third Line, son. We'll do what we can."

Tarrin's face got solemn. "I fear the very foundations of Ebrus rest on it. We are a tinderbox, ready to explode."

I tilted my head at him. When his eyes met mine, I saw a very real fire there. I couldn't help but wonder if he would be the one to strike the match.

Excusing myself from my father as he talked to another one of the Barons, I slipped out of the banquet room and moved down the darkened hallway toward the library. You'd be excused for thinking I'd all of a sudden become a studious pupil, but in reality, there was something niggling at my brain, a mystery I needed to solve, and I knew it centered around Avalon and the Ninth Line.

The library here at the Hall of Ebrus was second to no other. It contained generations of knowledge. Pushing open the large, ornate doors, I stepped inside. It was quiet, but lights still burned in the sconces.

"Hello?"

A small woman, younger than I imagined the Librarian to be, appeared. "Hello there, Heir Taeme. Can I help you?" She was kind of plain, with a deep line between her eyebrows that told me that she spent a lot of time reading small, indecipherable text. She would have been in her thirties, maybe a little older, but not by much.

"Librarian, I'm after books on—"

"The Ninth Line. I'm aware, Mr. Taeme. We librarians have quite the network all over Ebrus. Knowing the Conclave was being called, I gathered all the information we had on the shelves regarding the Line and their powers. That was what Librarian Enora suggested you were looking into?"

I hadn't even realized that was the Librarian's name at Boellium. I'd just kind of thought of all Librarians as, well, Librarian.

My mouth was hanging open, and I snapped it shut. "Uh, yeah. I am. Thank you, Librarian."

She waved a hand, like it was nothing. "Come, I've placed them all in the reading room. If you're going to look at all the material tonight, you might need to get started now. I expected you earlier." Was there light censure in her tone?

"Apologies for keeping you from your bed."

"I'm the night Librarian, Heir Taeme. I would have been here among the books, whether you arrived or not." She stepped up to a door and unlocked it. "I don't need to tell you that some of these books are very old and need to be handled with care. Also, none of them may leave this room."

"Of course, Librarian."

Her eyes were knowledgeable, like I was just a babe in the woods who needed to learn to find my own way home. "You're welcome here. The library holds the answers to many questions, if you just know where to look."

With that, she was gone, and I dived into the huge pile of books in front of me. It was going to be a long night.

chapter thirty-four

Avalon

BOELLIUM without both Vox and Hayle was a different beast. Simultaneously more volatile and relaxed. No matter what happened while the cats were away, the mice could never rise up and change the system in which they lived. But there were more parties, and more fights, and nothing felt as serious.

To me, however, it felt wrong. I wouldn't tell anyone else, but I was looking forward to them returning. I was excited to see Vox again. The memory of his kiss was never far from my mind, and I found myself daydreaming in class about the taste of his lips. I'd thought of hardly anything else, because I knew even if nothing else could come of it, I wanted more. I wanted to taste his skin, feel his lips on mine again, watch his eyelids close heavily in pleasure. I just *wanted*.

I wasn't a fool. It couldn't go anywhere, and I couldn't be more than a notch in what I was sure was an impressive bedpost, but I didn't care. I was so tired of being alone. If I could have him even for a moment, I was going to take it.

He'd been gone five days, and I found myself watching the horizon for the ferry from the mainland. I chastised myself for acting like a lovesick cat. I needed to cultivate a more worldly persona. Mature. Aloof, even. The last thing I wanted to do was throw myself into his arms like some desperate clinger.

It didn't help that every night I was having filthy fantasies. The dirty dreams were getting intense, and I felt needy. Those dreams sometimes featured more than Vox, though.

Last night, I'd dreamt of making love to Hayle, and it had felt so real, I'd woken up sweaty and aching. It was like I could smell his woodsy scent, taste the salt of his sweat on my tongue. It was the most vivid dream I'd ever had, and left me feeling riled up.

Hayle Taeme was off limits. There was no way I could trust the way my heart raced like it was going to beat out of my chest, or the panic in my veins whenever I was near him. I didn't understand it, but I trusted my gut. Hayle Taeme meant pain. I knew that in my soul.

So I'd wait for Vox to arrive, then I'd tell him exactly what I wanted.

Someone whacked me in the shoulder with one of the training blades. "Girl, you better concentrate, or Instructor Wallred is going to beat your ass," Shay hissed, and I looked over at the First Line's second-in-command. She was beautiful, in the same haughty, cold way as Vox. It left very little doubt that they were related.

"Uh, thanks." I went back to forms, hoping not to draw the ire of the instructor. They said his last name came from the time he'd taken on a battalion of rebels and painted the walls red with their blood. It sounded like a rumor you'd perpetuate just to ensure new conscripts were terrified of you, but I applauded the creativity.

Another whack to my shoulder. "*Fucking hell*, Ninth. You have to be the most addle-brained conscript I've ever had the misfortune to meet. It's like you *want* to get the shit beaten out of you." She grumbled something about Vox and duty.

I frowned at her. "Why do you care?" I remembered her from the first day here at Boellium, and now that I had a better handle on the strength of people, I knew it had to have been either her or Vox suspending that guy, letting him bleed out on the cobblestones.

Shay ran her tongue over her teeth. "Because my Heir told me to watch you. He's never asked that of me before, and I'm not about to fuck it up." She paused, stepping closer. "Because he's never looked at anyone the way he looks at you. He deserves this small taste of happiness, before the rest of his life becomes a jail cell. You wouldn't understand, but his life isn't gilded thrones and grand banquets."

I raised an eyebrow at her. "You know jack shit about my life."

She shrugged. "And I don't want to. He deserves his happiness, but anyone with half a brain knows that this will end in disaster. I don't want to get attached to you, but I can ensure that you keep your head on your shoulders until Vox returns to do it himself—or he gets sick of you, whichever comes first."

Damn. She didn't hold back, but I could respect that. In Boellium, the cloying fakeness was everywhere. "Fair enough."

I returned to my forms, Shay continuing her own beside me. She moved like liquid, and I was so jealous, I could actually spit. She must've had the same tutor as Vox, because they had that same smooth style. I could only dream of being that lithe and deadly.

Huffing an annoyed sigh, she turned to me. "He returns on today's ferry. I'll be glad to be off babysitting duty."

Honestly, I hadn't known she was *on* babysitting duty, so either she was a terrible babysitter or a scarily good spy. Nodding, I tried to concentrate on the rest of the forms, and not what I'd do once Vox was back in the grounds of Boellium.

I'd wait for him to find me—that much was clear, because there was always the chance that I was reading too much into this. Maybe he'd gone back to Fortaare and realized that I was some rough-hewn rock next to all those glittering diamonds.

Yeah, I'd wait for him to track me down first.

· · ·

It wasn't Vox who found me first, though. It was Hayle Taeme's hounds. Everyone was scared of those giant dogs, but not me. I felt we had an understanding, and whenever they came up to me, I always gave them a little bit of my pilfered jerky.

I wasn't above bribing them to like me.

However, it was odd for me to see both of them at the same time. Usually, one was always with Hayle. Braxus came over, and I squatted down on my haunches. "Hey, handsome, how was Fortaare?"

Braxus huffed a disgruntled noise, and I laughed. Yeah, that was pretty clear.

"I think I'd feel the same way about that place. Give me wide-open spaces and clear blue skies any day." I stood and went to walk away, but Braxus gripped my fingers in his mouth. Not hard, but he definitely wasn't letting go. "Uh, I don't have any more jerky, big guy."

The other hound, Alucius, nudged my butt with her snout, and I realized they wanted me to go with them.

"I get the point. You can stop slobbering on my hand now," I said to Braxus, who gave me an unamused glare, but let go of my fingers and trotted ahead of me. Following him through the halls, I ignored the wary looks of the other conscripts. They looked at me like I was walking to the gallows.

We ended up in the library, and I was embarrassed that I still hadn't been here in the months that I'd been in Boellium. In a past life, it would have been the first place I'd have visited. Even now, the sweet smell of old books and leather was like a warm hug.

I saw Hayle over in the corner of the reading room and walked toward him. The hounds stopped by the door, taking up guard positions. That seemed kind of ominous.

"You know how weird it is to be fetched like a stick?" I asked Hayle, who grinned at me. Fuck, he was so handsome, it was like a punch in the gut.

"The Third Line are beastmasters. I absolutely know what it's like to be fetched like a stick." He snorted loudly, and it echoed around the library. "My father has a lion companion, and once, when I went out in the woods without telling my mother, Lazlo came and collected me, carrying me by the scruff of my neck like an errant cub."

I shuddered. That would've been horrifying. "Fair." I looked over at the hounds. "You guys are terrifying enough, but I'm glad you aren't lions." I pulled out a chair and sat across from him. "What can I do for you, Hayle?"

His lids dropped, and he looked at me with so much heat, my body flushed. It was the exact same expression as he'd had on his face in my dream last night. My mouth went dry, and I crossed my legs, pressing my thighs together.

Sucking in a deep breath, he closed his eyes. When he opened them again, the heat was gone, and he cleared his throat. "While I was in Fortaare, I found myself in the library at the Hall of Ebrus."

I'd heard about the library at the Hall of Ebrus. It was a giant, cavernous space, with shelves that went right to the ceiling and endless rooms of knowledge. I dreamed of going there one day, just to soak in the knowledge, right down into my bones. "Well, I'm jealous, but I'm not sure what that has to do with me."

Hayle's jaw clenched. "While I was researching, I found the account about your mother's death."

My blood froze in my veins. I waited for the disdain, the hatred, that had poured from my father all these years to spill out from between Hayle's lips. I tried not to flinch as he covered my hand with his own.

"Avalon, you were three. There is no way that was your fault. It was a terrible accident, and the word of a distraught lady's maid trying to save her own skin shouldn't cloak you with such sadness. You were a baby. It was *not* your fault. Do you hear me? No matter what anyone else has told you, it was not your fault."

I was shaking my head, but he squeezed my hand. She'd just fallen off the cliff. My brother Kian had told me that over and over as I'd grown up, but the insidious words of my father were strong. When your only remaining parent hated you so much that he did terrible things to you, you tended to believe his words.

I cleared my throat. "Thank you for your kind words—"

Hayle shook his head. "Not kind words. The truth. Not the venom of a grieving family, or a distraught husband, or a scared servant. The words of an impartial party. It was not your fault."

Nodding, I stood. "Thank you. I should go." My words were rushed, but my heart was pounding.

But Hayle didn't let me go. "We aren't done, Avalon. Sit down." He tugged my hand, but his voice softened. "Please. I won't mention your mother again."

Sucking in oxygen until my lungs felt like they'd explode, I sat down again.

Hayle didn't wait, nor apologize. "I'd been thinking about your words, about the powers of the Lower Lines dwindling. Did you know that until five generations ago, your family never gave birth to female children? They were notoriously all males, and it was a sign of a strong bloodline. Then Ellanora Halhed was born. They treated her like a jewel in their crown, and by all accounts, she was beautiful."

I snorted. Apparently, it wasn't only our powers that had dwindled then.

Hayle continued. "She was also extremely powerful. She saw visions—more than just immediate futures, far into the unknown. She was revered and coveted. She had requests for her hand in marriage from the First Line all the way down to the Twelfth. Everyone wanted her in their Line."

Ellanora was barely a scratched name in our family bible. I'd never heard all this before.

"Then she disappeared. They investigated, assuming a spurned consort captured her and murdered her in a fit of jealousy, or that her visions sent her crazy and she threw herself from a cliff." He winced. "Her body was never found. A month later, there was the First Line uprising, and they killed off the

Second Line, and a missing woman from the Ninth Line got lost in the insanity that followed."

What did that even *mean?* This was centuries ago—what did it even matter anymore?

Hayle grabbed a folder from in front of him. "From that point on, the Ninth Line continued to have sons, but they were interspersed with daughters. Their powers dwindled, but as you said, so did a lot of the Lower Lines, and it was so gradual, no one really noticed. They likely believed the old accounts were exaggerated, until your magic is as it stands now."

He meant almost non-existent.

"But while I was researching, I found this. It had been sent directly to the Hall of Ebrus library, and they figured it had gotten caught up in the uprising chaos and was sent before Ellanora went missing. I'm not so sure."

He pushed a piece of parchment over to me. On it was beautiful, flowing handwriting.

The Ninth. The Ninth. The Ninth.

Well, that made no sense. "So she did actually go insane?"

Hayle shrugged. "Perhaps. But look at the date."

Up in the corner, in a tiny, neat script, was the very date of the uprising. She'd sent this letter on the day that the First Line murdered the Second Line and secured their power. She had to have been alive then.

I shook my head. "It's nonsense, Hayle. It means nothing. She could have just picked that day and dated it wrong."

He grabbed another book and dragged it between us. "This is your official Ancestral Lineage. This is Ellanora Halhed." He pointed to the middle of the parchment. "Let's call her the First Daughter of the Ninth Line." He pointed down to the next row. "Her brother's daughter would be the Second."

He pointed down, down, down. Third, Fourth, Fifth were all in one family. My great-grandfather had a bastard, also a daughter, who was Sixth. My aunt, who'd died when she was twelve from the fever, would be the Seventh. My sister was Eighth.

Lastly, Hayle pointed to my name. "Avalon Halhed, Ninth Daughter of the Ninth Line." He looked at me like I was suddenly meant to sprout another head and start breathing fire or something.

"It means nothing, Hayle. She'd obviously lost her grasp on reality." Even as I said the words, something niggled in my chest. "Thank you for researching this. It's more than I've ever known about my Line. But it means nothing to me."

I stood and moved away from the table before he said anything else, backing toward the door of the library. Past the hounds. Past the Librarian, who was looking at me with a blank face behind thick glasses.

"Avalon!" Hayle called, and I paused. "I think it means something."

I fled the room before he could say anything else that would alter my life.

The Ninth. The Ninth. The Ninth.

chapter thirty-five

Vox

I WAS LOOKING for Avalon's face in the crowd, even as I half-listened to Shay's updates. Apparently, much of a nothingness had occurred while I was away—the same jockeying for power, just on a different day. We walked back from the docks, and the others who'd been on the ferry with me gave us a wide berth. I had a small dome of silence around us, because Boellium had eyes and ears everywhere.

Taeme and those damn hounds raced in front of us, and I scowled at his retreating back. I hated the derision in his expression when he looked at my father, but worse than that, I hated the pity in his eyes when he looked at me and compared our relationships with our respective paternal figures.

Feodore Vylan ruled with absolute authority; his family was no exception. I was to be seen and not heard, especially as the spare Heir. Here, at Boellium, I had the semblance of control, even if it was just in this tiny microcosm. Taeme and I were not equals anywhere, but least of all here. I didn't need or want his pity, even if I did slightly envy the way his father looked at him with pride.

Pathetic.

"Are you even listening to me right now, or should I just go and shout my update at the sea? Maybe the mermaids will give a fuck what I have to say," Shay grumbled.

I tightened my lips, giving her an apologetic nudge with my shoulder. "Sorry, Shay. I know you took care of business while I was away. I have absolute faith you could organize this rabble like a General in the Dawn Army, with or without my presence." It was entirely true. "The Conclave is playing on my mind. It was called because of the drought over in the West of Ebrus. The Eleventh and Twelfth Lines are going to face mass starvation if something isn't done, and my father wasn't interested in my opinion on the matter."

My back still ached from the air-lashes he'd given me for talking out of turn. I was a figurehead, and that was the box I should stay in. It didn't help that my brother didn't give a damn about anyone but himself and his own power, much like Father. All of Ebrus could starve, as long as they took the knee before us as they died.

Shay gritted her teeth. "He would rather they were gone. In fact, I'm fairly sure he'd be content if everyone below the Sixth no longer existed." Her voice was pitched low, so even if my privacy dome fell, people would struggle to hear her words. Because what she said was inflammatory at best, treasonous at worst. "What was the Conclave's verdict?"

I snorted. We were a false democracy, and once my father declared it not their problem, the spineless Barons had been all too happy to wash their hands of the whole problem.

"They're on their own. I overheard Baron Taeme conversing with the Tenth Line to send aid, though, so perhaps they'll circumvent the Conclave altogether."

Shay raised a brow. "Will you tell your father?" Working outside the Conclave was frowned upon.

"And stray outside my predetermined role of seen and not heard? No. My father made my role clear before the banquet—it's to be an example of his virility and not much more. The humanitarian efforts of the Third Line are outside my purview." Frowning hard, my cousin checked me over, patting me down until I moved away. "What are you *doing?*"

"Checking for a *tal* that might have stolen all your common sense." We both knew there was no talisman that could do that. She was just ribbing me.

I shooed her hands away. "I care about the people of Ebrus, Shay. That's not a new thing."

"But defying your father is," she hissed. "It's the girl, isn't it?"

I kept my face blank. "What girl?"

The droll look she gave me was perfectly Shay. "You know who. Does your sudden interest in the welfare of the Lower Lines have something to do with Avalon

Halhed, who happens to be an Heir of the Ninth Line, as well as have great boobs?"

Now it was my turn to frown. "Don't look at her boobs."

"Why? Do you have a vested interest in her chest?"

I ignored her completely as we stepped into the atrium, feeling satisfied as people scurried away. I wanted to find Avalon and not get dragged down into social bullshit. I just had to drop my bags in my rooms, then I'd head down to see if she was in her dorm, or perhaps the food hall.

"She missed you, you know." Shay sounded way too smug, like she knew that would make me stop and give up the pretense.

Sighing heavily, because she wasn't going to let this go, I looked over at her. "What makes you say that?"

"She watched the ocean horizon like a married fisherwoman waiting for her husband to return." She snorted derisively. "Honestly, I'm surprised she didn't lose her head during some of the combat classes." The mirth left her face, consumed by something more solemn. "It's a dangerous game you're playing, Vox. It can't go anywhere, and you might have everyone else convinced you have a lump of ice in your chest rather than a heart, but I know better. You have to guard yourself."

I strode through the dorm room, inexplicably happy that most of my Line brethren were either in class or in the food hall. I didn't want them here for this conversation, even if they couldn't hear me. Shay was the one person who I could be open and honest with, and I knew, even under the penalty of torture, she would hold my secrets close to her chest the way I held so many of hers.

"Something about her speaks to my soul," I mumbled, frightened of the words, as if speaking them out loud would make them even more true. "I can't help but be drawn to her, even if logic tells me that this can't be anything more than a fleeting pleasure."

Shay stared at me, her gaze roaming over my face, like she could see the truth written on my skin. Finally, she sighed. "I told her as much. Here, give me your bag and go find her. Maybe get laid. It's been too damn long."

I screwed up my nose. "Stop thinking about my sex life; it's weird." But I still handed her my bag and kissed her temple. "Thanks, Shay. You're the best thing ever produced by the First Line."

She muttered something that was probably an agreement, but I was already out the door on my way down the stairs. I made myself walk slowly, nodding but being unapproachable to the rest of the college. When I reached the atrium, I straightened my spine, ignoring the stares of the other conscripts as I descended the stairs to the lower levels. I didn't even get offended when the Lower Lines stared, rather than offering the respectful acknowledgement they were supposed to give me. I just didn't care.

Finally, I made it to the Ninth Line dorm. I sent a tendril of air under the door, searching for life inside the room, and I smiled as it found the displacement of air indicating a person was wandering around in there.

Knocking softly, I waited. There was stomping, and then Avalon was there, wrenching open the door. "Look, Hayle, I don't want to— Oh, Vox. You're back!"

She seemed genuinely happy to see *me*. Not the Heir of the First Line. Not someone who could help them climb the social ladder. Me.

"I am. Is Taeme giving you a hard time?"

She stepped back, inviting me into her dorm, and fuck, she smelled so good. She must've just showered, because her hair was damp, and the scent of flowers and sunshine curled around her. "No, he's fine. He was just trying to give me a family history lesson that I don't want or need. The less I have to do with my Line once this is all over, the better."

I knew so little about her, and she knew so little about me, but I didn't care. I had time to learn. "I want to know more about that," I promised her. "But first, I need to kiss you again, because I haven't been able to get the feel of your lips from my mind. Have you decided, Avalon?"

Her tongue dipped out to wet her lips, the same lips that I was desperate to taste. "Decided what?"

"Where you want this to go," I murmured, stepping closer to her, crowding her back toward the wall of her dorm room.

"Yes," she breathed.

Finally, her delicious ass hit the wall, and I lifted my hands so they rested on either side of her head. She was caged between my body and the stone walls of this ancient fortress. "And where is that?" I asked, so close to her lips.

"To my bedroom." The husky sound of her voice undid me, and I couldn't take it anymore. I leaned down and captured her lips with mine, sucking them between my teeth and scraping them gently, desperate to hear her tiny gasps of shocked pleasure. I was going to ruin her in the best possible way.

Sliding my hands down her hips, I grabbed a handful of her ass and lifted her into my arms. "Your bedroom it is." I traced the line of her neck with my tongue. "And then your shower, the dorm couch, the kitchen, the floor in front of the fireplace." She held my hair tightly as I bit the soft curve at the top of her breast. "There is no place in all of Boellium that I don't want to fuck you senseless, just so every soul in the college knows you're mine."

I was dying, because all the blood in my body was now in my cock, and when her thighs tightened around my hips, rubbing the hot center of her body against me, I mentally cursed. I needed to be inside her, or I was going to come before I even got my pants off.

I strode into the first dorm room, immediately knowing it wasn't her room. It was barren and empty, but that was okay. We were going to fill it so full of life that every conscript who entered the room afterward would get inexplicably hard as the stone walls of the college itself.

chapter thirty-six

Avalon

THERE WASN'T a single atom in my soul that didn't feel the effects of Vox's kiss. It tingled in my fingertips, burned through my blood, and clouded my brain. He was everywhere, yet not where I wanted him. My body ached for him, and it was such a foreign feeling—like I was being possessed by some sex-obsessed demoness— that it was momentarily disconcerting.

Not disconcerting enough to stop, though. Not even the college itself falling in around our heads could make me tell him to stop. He continued to kiss me as he laid me down on the bed, his body poised between my thighs, and I hooked my ankles around his hips, trapping him to me.

I didn't have to worry about him leaving, because his mouth devoured me, kissing and nibbling his way over my skin as he peeled my shirt from my body. He kissed down my neck, then further south, between the valley of my breasts and over to one of my pink nipples.

When he sucked it hard, I moaned. When he blew a freezing cold breath across the peaked bud, I squealed and wiggled beneath him, pleasure shooting straight to my clit.

A little voice in the back of my head told me I was far too out of my depth to be doing this with Vox, a man who'd probably had more lovers than I'd had hot meals, but again, I didn't care. We had nothing but this moment. I wasn't trying to woo him; we were just two souls, coming together to find pleasure where we could.

He tugged at the waistband of my pants, and I used my legs to lift myself so he could tug them down over my ample ass. Time at Boellium, with its unlimited rich food and rigorous exercise, had given me curves that weren't soft, but were definitely a little too steep to be considered fashionably beautiful. Especially not in the Court of Fortaare, and the women Vox must have slept with before.

As he moved down my body, over the soft round-ness of my stomach and the harsh curve of my hips, I tried to drag him back up to my face. Away from the parts of me that made me feel insecure.

I should have known better, though, because Vox Vylan didn't do anything he didn't want to do. Air curled around my wrists and dragged my arms upwards until they were above my head, my fingertips touching the cool bars of the metal bedframe.

"I've been dreaming about this for too long, Ninth, to half-ass it just because you can't get out of your head. Lie back and let me feast," he murmured. I should've been pissed at him calling me Ninth, but the way he crooned it, like a pet name and not a curse, made me keep my mouth closed.

Well, for a moment anyway, because my lips parted as his mouth found my core, and he sucked my clit between his lips without warning.

"Goddess!" I yelled, my abs contracting. I would have jack-knifed into a sitting position if those bands of air hadn't been holding me still. Vox chuckled around the sensitive bud, making my eyes roll back in my head. No wonder people were sex-obsessed. Nothing I'd ever done to myself had ever felt this good. This kind of pleasure was only ever felt in my dreams. I hadn't thought it could be real.

"Such a pretty pussy, all hot and wet just for me," he groaned, and I tightened my thighs around his shoulders. More air captured my ankles, holding them still. His power was immense, and to be honest, hot as hell. "Maybe I need to cool it down a little, hmm?" he breathed. As he pushed a finger inside my aching core, it was so cold that I gasped.

Fucking Goddess, his fingers were like icicles. The combination of the heat of his mouth and tongue, and the coldness of his fingers sliding in and out of my body, had me coming so hard, the edges of my vision went spotty.

"Vox!"

He hummed a happy noise around my clit again, pulling away as he stroked me through my orgasm.

"That's it. Scream my name. I want everyone to hear it and know you're mine."

He didn't stop thrusting his fingers in and out of me, but he warmed them back up, and the heat of them after the chill was… I had no words. I climbed higher and higher, and he watched my face, like he was collecting my orgasms, stacking them together like blocks until I was so high, I had nowhere to go but down into the messy abyss of mindless pleasure.

I gave him another orgasm, his crooned words senseless to me. But when he stood and removed his clothes, my breath stilled in my chest. Clarity crashed down around me like a bucket of ice water.

He was fucking beautiful, a work of art so glorious, it took my breath away. Strong and broad, he reminded me of the white marble cliffs near my home, hard and cutting and breathtaking. His cock jutted out from his body, and my eyes bulged.

Holy shit. Was that supposed to go inside me? Because it looked big and unyielding, and I wasn't sure there was enough space in my body to take that without perforating something important.

He chuckled low. "I don't know if I should be honored or insulted that you're looking at my cock like it's a deadly weapon."

I didn't know either. "I feel like this is probably the time to tell you that I'm a virgin and I've never done this before and that thing is scary."

His whole body went still, looking like the marble statue I'd just imagined him as. "Never?"

I shook my head, my face probably as red as a beet. "If you want to change your mind, it's okay. I probably should have told you earlier."

"Fuck," he breathed softly, coming back down between my thighs, his whole body pressed tightly to mine. "A better man would stop. Your first time should be with someone who can give you a future," he mumbled against the skin of my shoulder. "Not the stolen moments I can give you."

Wrapping my fingers in his dark hair, I pulled his head back so he was forced to look at me. "Lucky for us both that this isn't just your decision to make. I choose you, Vox Vylan. Now, fuck me—gently—until I can't help but remember the feel of you inside me for the rest of my life."

He groaned, but palmed his cock, lining it up with my entrance. "I'll go slow." Then he was pushing inside me, with calm precision that was in direct contrast to the tenseness of his jaw. He felt too big, too much, too painful. His cock was as cold as ice, numbing the pain until he was seated all the way inside me.

I felt like I could feel him everywhere. "Handy trick," I breathed, and he grunted, his eyes closed like he was physically in pain. Slowly, his cock returned to normal temperature again. Pulling out excruciatingly slowly, he was gentle as he pushed back in again, and every thought I'd ever had about anything at all disappeared from my head.

There was just Vox, and me, and this moment.

"You feel so fucking perfect." He kissed the corner

of my mouth and down my throat, his body trembling from holding himself so tightly. "You fit around me like we were made for each other by some divine fate." Raising himself up on his arms, he looked down at my expression. "Are you okay?"

"Yes!" I gasped out. "Please, Vox. *More.*"

He grinned, and it was a devastating expression. One I knew would be imprinted on my heart forever. It left me feeling dazed, but I didn't have time to focus on it, because he was pushing himself up on his knees. Holding me by my hips, he pulled back and snapped them forward again, and a whole new type of pleasure made my skin feel too hot, too tight, too much as it coursed through my muscles and bones.

He made love to me. We could call it fucking, I guess, but the care he showed, the tenderness, it was something more. I knew it deep in my chest.

"You don't know…" He shook his head, like he was as lost in this moment as I was. "Anything you want is yours. Avalon, my Avalon," he groaned, and an echo of the words rang around my head. A different voice. A whisper from my dreams.

I didn't have time to dwell on the sensation of déjà vu, because pleasure was hurtling through me. I clenched around Vox, my whole body arching upwards as I was consumed.

"Fuck," he cursed, gripping me even harder until I knew I'd have fingertip-shaped bruises on my flesh. He fucked me with single-minded focus, riding out my orgasm before he pounded into me like a man possessed. He came hard, and I felt the hot splash inside me. It was a sensation that I wouldn't forget anytime soon.

He collapsed against me, his body a heavy blanket over mine. I ran my hands up his spine, then out over the hard lines of his shoulders, until my fingers grazed large, raised welts. Had I done that with my nails? It was almost impossible, given that my nails were little more than chewed-down nubs. Having long nails and doing sword work didn't really go hand in hand, not without a lot of time and energy, or a heavy dose of magic.

So what were those welts on his back?

I looked up into his face and noticed his eyes had gone blank, his body tense. "I didn't do that, did I?" I asked softly, and he shook his head.

There were only two people in all of Ebrus capable of inflicting harm on Vox, and I could stand against neither of them. Moving my fingers away from the painful, raised skin, I wrapped my arms around his waist and held him tightly to me. I didn't say I was sorry, didn't offer him empty platitudes.

I'd been where he had, at the hands of a man who shared my blood and was meant to love and protect me, but didn't. "I know this feeling," I told him simply. "It's their failing, not yours."

Vox's body went taut again, his eyes running over my face, finding the secrets that I was laying bare before him but was too cowardly to say out loud. He knew, though. I could see his understanding in the way his jaw tensed. "I'll kill him," he growled.

I couldn't help but laugh. He absolutely could, but not today. "Okay, my Ice Prince. But do it later. I want to cuddle first."

Huffing a small laugh, he rolled onto his back and gathered me up against his chest. That had to hurt the lash wounds on his back, but he didn't seem to mind. Acacia had given me a poultice to put on my injuries after the Eugene incident, so later, I'd use some of that on Vox's lashes to help ease the pain. Hopefully by tomorrow, they'd be gone.

But right now? I would just lay here and hope that this moment was enough to heal the wounds that no one else could see.

chapter thirty-seven

Hayle

SHE SMELLED LIKE HIM. It riled the beast that lived inside me, until I swore he was about to rip out of my skin. They weren't even trying to hide it, not really. Anyone with eyes could see the way their gazes lingered on each other, the small touches, the way he was protective of the Ninth Line conscript.

It meant people gave her a wide berth, almost as wide as the one she gave me. If she saw me coming, she turned and went the other way. If I was in the same class as her, she'd sit on the other side of the room. She was avoiding me, and it made me both angry and despondent—a completely unreasonable response. She didn't owe me anything. I barely knew her. I knew more about her family history than I did about Avalon herself.

Braxus growled beside me, but it wasn't an alert to tell me of a threat. It was the kind of growl he aimed at pups who were doing stupid things that were going to get them hurt, or who needed to be corrected. It was his annoyed sound.

"*What?*" I snapped at him, and he clacked his teeth back at me. He might be considered *my* hound, but no one owned Braxus. We were partners, up until the time he decided he was done with me. "Sorry, Braxus."

Sighing heavily, he cast an annoyed expression at Alucius, which was how I knew the message they wanted to impart was going to be about feelings. Braxus tore apart my enemies, but Alucius helped me navigate the beast within.

She sent me an image of her and Braxus snuggling. They were a mated pair; it's why they were so good at their job. Then she sent me an image of me and Avalon snuggling too.

I looked down at her. "I know that I want her, but I can't just steal her from the First Line Heir. She has free will."

Alucius huffed and looked at Braxus, who nipped my fingers, no doubt on her command.

"Ouch. That was out of line," I grumbled down at them both. It didn't really hurt, but I was beginning to get the impression that they were frustrated.

Alucius sent me another image, this time of her and Braxus standing side by side, strong and united, followed by a similar image of Avalon and I, shoulder to shoulder, with me looking down at her adoringly. That had definitely never happened, so she wasn't sending me something she'd seen in the past.

Walking around me, Alucius licked at Braxus's muzzle. They were mates.

Oh.

Ohhh.

"You think she's my mate?"

Alucius nudged my hand anxiously.

More? I blinked down at my loyal companion, and she gave a look that very clearly expressed that I was being a silly pup. "No, I understand, but also, it can't be. You think she's my soulmate? My Soul Tie?"

She licked my hand with her long tongue, the same way she'd congratulated her puppies when they learned a new trick.

I shook my head. "I can't be her Soul Tie." I thought about the pulling in my chest that had almost been instantaneous. Like my soul *knew* hers and wanted her more than anything. "She basically runs the other way anytime she sees me. Also, she's with Vox, and while I find that aggravating, I don't want to rip his face off the way a soulmate would, if they saw another male with his hands all over his Soul Tie."

I mean, I'd been tempted to tear his face off more than a time or two, and since Avalon had arrived, that impulse had basically doubled. But not enough. I'd heard stories about Soul Ties, about the way their bodies had found each other in each life—sometimes as lovers, sometimes as adversaries, but forever twined together. My grandparents had been a Soul Tie, and my grandfather had once ripped the arms of a man who'd thought to touch my grandmother without her permission.

Braxus tilted his head, the universal hound gesture for *I don't know* or possibly *did someone drop you on your head as a pup?*

I shrugged. "She would make a fine mate; no one's arguing that. She's beautiful, and like..." I struggled to explain how my heart felt when I was near her. "Like that feeling you get after a long run in woods you know like the back of your hand." Like home.

Alucius huffed and trotted away, her tail high, so I knew just how annoyed she was with me. Braxus stayed by my side as I made my way toward our Battle History class, thinking about what the hounds believed. I trusted them in all things. Well, almost all things— Braxus had once let me chase a polecat as a kid, knowing I'd get sprayed. It had been a valuable lesson, I guess, but I'd stunk for a week afterwards.

The hounds had been with me so long that I could hardly remember a time when they weren't by my side. If they believed that Avalon was my Soul Tie, I owed it to them to try, right? Owed it to myself?

I stepped into the auditorium and looked around at the other seated conscripts. This was my last year, as well as Vox's, and eventually, there would be a new wave of conscripts, who'd take over the mantle of the Kings of Boellium. It was a quirk of fate that both Vox and I—Heirs to the two most powerful Lines in Ebrus— were both in attendance at the same time, starting in the same year. When we left, there would be a power vacuum that I didn't envy, and I hated the idea that Avalon would be caught up in it. That she would be unprotected.

She didn't realize that the closer she got to the Heir of the First Line, the more jealousy and political bullshit would put her life in jeopardy. And she'd be alone.

Lucio had one more year, and I trusted him to watch her. My other cousin, Carell, would arrive next year, but she wasn't as strong as Lucio, let alone me. There was a chance that the First Line conscripts would walk all over them. Hell, there was a chance that someone truly powerful from the Fourth Line would rise up and take control of the whole school. Unlikely, but still a possibility.

"Take a seat already," the instructor snapped, and I moved toward my family, my Line. I searched the rest of the room for Avalon, though, but she didn't seem to be here yet.

The instructor stood behind the lectern to start his presentation, when she stumbled in, her face red and her lips puffy, her hair looking freshly fucked.

When Vox walked in moments after her with a smirk on his face, it didn't take a genius to know that they'd been together, fucking, only moments earlier. It didn't matter that they pointedly didn't look at each other. It didn't matter that they sat on opposite sides of the room. If I sucked in a lungful of air, I could pick up her scent, and it contained traces of Vox's. He'd come inside her, and his seed was still leaking out down her thighs.

I growled long and low, and it echoed around the room. I could swallow it back, but I didn't want to. I wanted to howl in pain at the fact that she was with someone else. Braxus eyeballed me, before his gaze landed on Vox, like he was contemplating ripping his throat out for me.

He must be communicating with Alucius too, because I suddenly got an image of her looking insanely self-satisfied. She'd been right. Avalon Halhed was my Soul Tie, but she also wanted nothing to do with me.

So what the fuck did I do with that?

I felt her eyes on my face, and I could almost hear her heartbeat from across the room. I stared at my feet, trying to calm my raging beast. This wasn't the time or the place to lay bare my Line's secrets. Breathing out through my nose, I waited until I had a firm hold on myself to look back up.

Vox Vylan was looking at me, and the triumph on his face made me want to rip his throat out. It was going to be a long class.

Two torturous hours later, Lucio followed me out of the auditorium. He had a frown on his face that meant he was going to try and have a heart to heart, but honestly, I had no idea what to say to him. How did I tell him that I'd found something so revered by our people, but that my Soul Tie was fucking someone else? That she didn't feel the same pull as I did?

So I didn't say anything. I gave orders. "I want to have a party. Make it bigger than the First Line's. Actually, let's have it on the beach. I don't want it restricted to the Upper Lines either. Invite everyone." I didn't want to have to be in close quarters and smell his scent on her skin. It had been fine when she'd just hated me and felt nothing for Vox, but I wasn't sure I could cope with the idea of them having sex now. Of him fucking my Soul Tie.

Shaking my head, I pushed the thought down. "Make it a party no one will forget."

"Fuck yeah," Lucio hooted and ran off, properly distracted. If there was anything Lucio loved more than fighting and fucking, it was a good party. It would keep the whole Line distracted, and that meant no one would be looking too closely at the fact I was about to have a meltdown.

Why would the Goddess give me a Soul Tie from another Line? Someone who had no chance of understanding that for me, she was it. She was the only person I would ever love, the only person I could ever fuck again, without the beast inside me trying to rip out from my flesh?

I needed to run. I needed to let the beast free and speed through the woods of my home. I needed to talk to my mother.

Instead of any of those things, I turned back toward Boellium's library. I couldn't have the girl—not yet, anyway, though I wasn't about to give up—but I could get to the bottom of the mystery of her family. The mystery of her.

The Ninth Daughter of the Ninth Line. She didn't think it meant anything, but in my soul, I knew it was important. I didn't know how, and I didn't know why, but I would.

chapter thirty-eight

Avalon

THE BUZZ around the Third Line's party consumed most of Boellium for the next week. Viana and Acacia were giddy with excitement, as were the rest of the Twelfth Line. From what I could gather, the Upper Lines held parties regularly, but the Lower Lines were never invited. Forever separated by not just the social divide, but the main landing of the atrium.

I'd been down in the bowels at least three times this week, just so they could try and dress me up like a child's doll. Not just Viana and Acacia either—the whole Twelfth Line seemed to be invested in what I should wear. However, the party was tonight, so it was decision time.

"The blue. It brings out her eyes," Elkie insisted, holding a dress up in front of her. Not for my approval, despite the fact I would be wearing it, though I definitely had a vote. They were a democracy through and through, especially once they'd decided I was a helpless lamb when it came to fashion. Honestly, they might be right.

"The purple—it's the color of royalty, which she might eventually be if she gets it on with Vox Vylan," someone called from behind me, I flushed red. I was already getting it on with Vox Vylan, but there was very little chance of me ever becoming his wife.

"We're just friends," I told them all for the thousandth time, but Elkie just gave me a knowing look and patted me on the head like I was some sweet summer child.

Someone was holding the purple dress in front of me, switching between that and the blue, when there was a knock at the door. Acacia strode over to answer it, then took a quick step back.

Standing stiffly at the door was Vox's cousin, Shay. There was something inherently edgy, maybe a little wary about Shay, like she was always waiting for the next attack. She looked around the dorm room, but waited patiently over the threshold.

"May I come in?" she asked, unable to keep the haughtiness from her voice. There was no doubt that in every way, the First Line and the Twelfth Line were different. Their social standing, their hold on their magic, their community—it was all in stark contrast.

But while a conscript from the Twelfth Line at the door of the First Line dorm would have been turned away immediately, maybe even ridiculed, Acacia welcomed Shay into the dorm. "Sure. Want a drink?"

Acacia's voice was warm, almost a purr, and I frowned at her. That was weird.

"Thank you. I'd appreciate that." The rigid formality in Shay's tone sounded wrong down here.

Acacia laughed. "No worries." As my friend walked toward the kitchen, I noted the way that Shay's gaze ran over the other woman's curves, before they shot back to my face.

I raised an eyebrow, but didn't say anything. Instead, I gave her a warm smile. "I don't want to be presumptuous, but I assume you're down here for me?"

It was then that I noticed the black cardboard box suspended in the air beside her. Shay heaved an annoyed groan. "I've been sent as an errand girl, yet again. This is from Vox." She floated the box to me, and as I took it from the air, she dropped her magic's hold on it. It fell lightly into my arms.

I placed it on the long, communal table, and the rest of the Twelfth gathered around, like this was a present for us all, rather than just for me. Instead of feeling annoyed, I felt... loved.

Shifting off the lid, I separated the folds of tissue paper. Inside was a dress. Not just any dress, though. It was the most beautiful dress I'd ever seen. A midnight-blue gown in a fabric so light, it felt almost unreal. It had a bodice that threaded at the back with silky ribbon, and a knee-length skirt that defied gravity, pooling like mist.

"Wow," I breathed, and Viana gripped my arm.

"Do you know what that *is?*"

I slid my eyes to her. "A dress?"

She shook me gently. "Not just any dress. That's a Liliana Ingmire original. She creates the fabric herself from some plant that's a giant secret. That dress is so expensive, it could feed my entire village for a year." She fingered the skirt, her eyes wide. "Maybe two years. It's so beautiful."

Acacia snorted. "Did I just watch Viana fall in love?" she teased, coming to stand beside Shay and handing her a glass of their homebrewed liquor. It was so strong that it put me on my ass every time I drank a single glass. "It is very pretty." She seemed almost disapproving, with none of the awe that was in Viana's expression. I understood her reaction; it was a flagrant excess when they could barely eat, which was a little tone-deaf.

"Liliana is a bitch, but she makes pretty clothes, I guess," Shay agreed. "I'd rather a set of daggers from the metalsmiths of the Eleventh Line, though."

Acacia raised a brow. "You don't think the First Line smiths could do better?"

The staring match between them was intense. "It has nothing to do with Line and everything to do with skill. Metalworking is in the bones of the Eleventh Line."

They continued to stare at each other, and I realized that they weren't antagonizing each other at all. They were… flirting? I mean, it was a weird form of flirting, but it seemed to work for them.

Viana smirked in their direction, but then her eyes caught on the dress again. "Go and try it on! I need to see how it looks on you before I go crazy." She shoved me toward her room, and I went, carefully carrying the dress. It was the nicest thing I'd ever owned, but what did it mean?

Quickly shedding my own clothes, I held my breath as I pulled the dress up over my ass and hips. It seemed to defy gravity, floating around me. There were no sleeves, but I couldn't pull the ribbons tight at the back.

"Viana?" I called, and she burst in before I'd even finished her name. She'd definitely been standing just on the other side of the door. She slammed it as she strode into the room, a gasp on her lips.

"You look like a *queen*," she breathed, then came around behind me, gripping the ribbon laces. "Now breathe in, Your Majesty, because you're about to bring the entire kingdom to their knees with this waistline."

An hour later, Viana had strapped me into the dress and used little rods warmed on the stovetop to curl my hair. Acacia had dragged me out to the main room and done my makeup with an artful hand, and I'd been surprised to see Shay still there. Her eyes ran over me, and she gave a satisfied nod.

"Okay, maybe I see it. You look good, Ninth." High praise from the surly First Liner indeed.

I grinned at her. "Thanks, Shay."

She climbed from the couch, walking over to place her glass in the sink like she'd been to the bowels a hundred times before. "Thank you for your hospitality," she said politely, but she wasn't looking at Viana or the others. Her eyes were snagged on Acacia.

"Visit anytime," Acacia purred.

Shay dipped her chin. "I'll see you on the beach." Her gaze was on me now, but she was clearly talking to Acacia.

Oh, yeah. Definitely flirting.

Shay's departure was like a kicked ant nest. People were running around everywhere. Acacia finished my makeup, then disappeared into her room to change. At some point during my grand makeover, the rest of the Twelfth Line had gotten ready for our first ever Line party and they looked festive in their brightly colored clothes, dyed with plants native to their region. Viana had told me what plants they used to make each color, but honestly, I had no clue what any of them were. Botany hadn't been my forte during my tutelage back home.

I smiled at my new friends, these people who'd accepted me so easily. "You guys look great."

Viana slung an arm around my shoulders, careful not to muss my hair. "Not as great as you do. Let's go stun the heck out of a Heir or two, shall we?" She led us from the room, and as we climbed the stairs, more and more of the Lower Line conscripts joined us.

The atrium was overflowing with people making their way down to the beach, and I could already hear music in the wind. Something smelled amazing, and I wondered if the Third Line had managed to convince the cooks to serve dinner down on the rocks. If anyone could convince the curmudgeonly kitchen staff to do something against the rules, it'd be Hayle.

"I can't wait to dance," Viana said, shimmying her way between her two boyfriends. I was beginning to think her boyfriends were also boyfriends with each other. I mean, it made sense, in a weird kind of way. At least then no one felt left out then, right?

As we walked, people's eyes lingered on me. I pushed my shoulders back, like wearing this beautiful dress was an everyday occurrence for me. I was the Heir to the Ninth Line. They couldn't know that our Barony was dirt poor from my father's excessive drinking and bad choices.

The dress itself floated around me like a midnight storm cloud, and I was truly in love. I mean, not as in love as Viana, but definitely in love.

There was a small line down to the beach as we all hurried, and we had the unfortunate luck to be behind Ephily from the Fifth Line. She took one look at my dress, her eyes narrowing. "I wonder if my cousin Liliana knows her creations are being put on a pig?"

That would have hurt once upon a time, but now, I just smiled at her with too many teeth. "Give her my compliments. This dress is beautiful."

She opened her mouth to say something cutting and cruel in return, but Vox appeared, and his eyes were filled with equal amounts of wonder and lust. "Avalon, you look like a dream." He leaned closer, until his lips were beside my ear. "A wet dream." Standing back to his full height, he nodded respectfully to Viana and

Acacia, then glared at the girl from the Fifth Line. "Ephily."

Then he surprised the fuck out of me by gripping me around the waist and pulling me tightly to his body, kissing me with so much authority, there was no doubt it was a claiming. I kissed him back, clinging to his shoulders as warmth consumed me. It ran through my veins and burned in my chest.

Finally, when my lungs were on fire and my thighs felt like they were made of pudding, he pulled back. "The image of you in this dress is going to be etched in my mind forever. Every time I close my eyes, I'll picture you this way," he murmured against my lips. Then he uncurled to his full height and moved his hand down to grip mine.

As he dragged me down to the beach, I realized I was a fool of the worst kind.

I'd gone and fallen in love with Vox Vylan.

I was in love with the one person in this world I couldn't ever have.

chapter thirty-nine

Avalon

I'D NEVER BEEN to a real party before. When Father had banquets or balls, I'd been confined to my rooms. Sometimes, I'd sneak out to watch the men drink and the women flirt. No one danced in the North—it was a frivolity that we didn't really ascribe to—but people knew how to get drunk and fuck in dark corners.

That seemed to be the version of partying that Boellium was fond of too, because in the short walk down the beach with Vox, Shay, Acacia, and Viana, I saw at least four couples fucking. Well, three couples and one quad. My feet stuttered as I watched the group have sex behind a large boulder that wasn't quite private enough, especially considering the sun had barely dipped below the horizon.

"Would you like a drink?" Vox asked, and I nodded as I dragged my eyes away. We walked to where a kid I vaguely recognized as being part of the Third Line was playing bartender. He was having a good time at least, mixing drinks and pouring them down someone's throat with a funnel.

Shay snorted. "Fucking Lucio."

The person drinking through the funnel was indeed Hayle's second-in-command. I snorted a laugh, but instinctively looked for the Heir of the Third Line. There were at least a hundred people on the beach, though I couldn't see him anywhere. Maybe he was in the shadows with someone else too?

The thought of Hayle with his body wrapped around some random Upper Sixer made my blood turn to ice in my veins, but I pushed the jealousy away. Who Hayle fucked, married, or loved had nothing to do with me. I had Vox, and he was all I needed.

Hell, he was *more* than I needed. And if I was honest with myself, Hayle was as out of reach to me as Vox was. No, I should be happy with what I had, and when it was all over, I'd be glad that I got to experience this freedom at all.

"What would you like?" Vox asked close to my ear so he could be heard over the band, which was playing something heavy and melodic and made me wish I really did dance.

I shrugged. "Whatever you suggest." I knew even less about fancy Upper Six alcohol than I did about dancing.

Lucio slid close to Shay, already swaying slightly with a goofy grin on his face. "If it isn't my favorite ball-crusher," he teased, and she rolled her eyes.

"I stood on your balls once, Lucio. Get over it." Her

eyes shifted quickly to Acacia, then back to him, and Lucio tilted his head, his alcohol-hazed mind picking up the vibes of the group quickly. His grin got even wider, if possible, and something nearly imperceptible passed between them. An understanding, maybe.

He slung an arm around Shay's shoulders. "You know, I'm okay if we make our little duo into a ménage, Shay-Shay." I wished I understood the dynamic between those two, because his words were more teasing than lecherous. Almost like a performance, he seemed to be saying what he knew the people around him expected to hear, but didn't actually want to follow through. Shay also didn't move his arm from her shoulder, and Acacia was watching them shrewdly.

Finally, Acacia shrugged. "You'd both be so lucky," she said snarkily, throwing them a wink and flouncing off into the crowd. Soon after, both Shay and Lucio disappeared, and Viana and her guys left to dance.

"Then there were two," Vox murmured softly, leading me away from the bulk of the crowd. The liquor was sweet and high quality, and strong. So fucking strong. "Fuck, you look so beautiful tonight, Avalon."

He stepped closer to me, out here in the open where anyone could see. While he'd never outright said we should keep our rendezvous secret, he hadn't exactly walked me into the middle of the the atrium and announced he was fucking the nobody from the Ninth Line.

Right now, though, he may as well be shouting it to the rooftops. Especially when he leaned down and kissed me softly, reverently, in front of hundreds of eyes.

It was impossible not to lean into the kiss, not to kiss him back with the burning desire in my gut. I wrapped my arms around his neck, and he gripped my hips with firm hands, holding me close enough that I could feel the hardening of his cock behind the laces of his pants.

I tore myself away before I lost all good sense and moved us toward one of the rocky crevices and demanded he fuck me. "You make me crazy," I whispered against his lips, and he chuckled low.

"Not as crazy as you make me. Giving you up is going to be the hardest thing I'll ever have to do." The pain in his voice reflected the ache in my chest. But that was a problem for another day. A heartache for a future Avalon.

The drink was making me brave, and I leaned back so I could look at him properly. "Do you dance?"

He snorted, dropping his hands and leading me toward the dance floor. "Do I dance? Ninth, I was waltzing around a grand ballroom with vapid nobility before I could even piss standing up."

I laughed, even though that was a little sad. "I don't really know..." I trailed off, because I didn't want to admit that I was so uncultured, I couldn't even do the casual swaying dance they were doing on the sand, let alone a waltz.

Vox grinned at me over his shoulder, and my heart stuttered in my chest. I memorized that expression, that moment, like I would one day try to recreate it in a painting. The light of torches stuck in the sand behind him bouncing off his dark locks like a golden halo, those blue eyes darkened by the shadows, the glint of his white teeth, and his full lips stretched wide.

He was so perfect, so mesmerizing, that it took me a moment to realize he was saying something. "Don't worry, I'll teach you. It's as natural as fucking, and I can promise you, you're perfect at that."

I slapped his shoulder, but followed him onto the dance floor and let him pull me closer. His knee slipped between my thighs, and I was so close to his body, it would be impossible to see the firelight between us.

He bent his head down toward mine. "You let me lead, sweetheart, and just enjoy yourself. Feel the music. Feel my body. Feel how connected we are." Then he began to sway, and my body moved with his. It really did kind of feel like sex. The same connection, the same primal understanding of the rhythm and movement. He pulled me even closer, and the way his hard thigh rubbed my core made me wet.

Goddess, I wasn't going to last an entire song at this rate.

"Why the change of heart?" I mumbled against his chest, and he dipped his face low.

"Hmm?" He rubbed his cheek on mine, making me sigh at the soft scrape.

"Why are you suddenly dancing with me in public? Kissing me in public?"

"I was standing at the end of the path as you walked toward the beach, and I saw the way everyone watched you. I knew they were seeing you as I do, rather than how they think you should be."

I raised an eyebrow at him. "What does that even mean?"

"It means you walked down here looking like a wet dream, and *everyone* noticed you. Desired you. Wanted to be you, or just worship at your feet. I'm a petty, jealous man. I don't want to share you with these fuckers. I want everyone to know that you're mine." He leaned down and kissed me again, never stopping the gentle sway of our dance. "I want them to know that you're only mine to kiss. To touch. To tease. To claim." He bit my lip, dragging it through his teeth with an erotically painful scrape. "To fuck."

"You're a very bad influence, Vox Vylan," I grumbled, lifting my face for more kisses. If he was claiming me, then I was going to claim him right back.

The night went on like that, with more songs, more drinks, more of… what could only be described as foreplay.

Sometime late in the night, Vox was dragged away by Shay, and I walked over to the bar again. I needed water; my body was overly warm from the dancing and the liquor. I watched all the Lines dancing and laughing, partying together like the divide between us and them didn't exist. At least for tonight, anyway.

I was surprised to see Hayle beside the bar, Alucius at his feet. I reached down and scratched her ears, and she allowed it. She wasn't so easily affectionate as her mate, but she sure was beautiful. And regal.

"Alucius. You're looking radiant tonight," I told her softly, and she turned her face to lick my hand softly. I tried not to melt on the spot, but I'd swear my heart grew three sizes in my chest.

"She thinks you look lovely too," Hayle told me. His smile was soft, but something else tinged the edges. Something I couldn't name. "I have to say, I agree. That dress is beautiful." Pausing, his eyes meet mine. "*You* look beautiful."

I blew out a quick breath, my heart thudding hard. It always felt like this, like something inside me was too big and was trying to break through the bones of my chest. I swallowed the lump that lodged in my throat. "Thank you. This is a great party. You should invite all the Lines more often. It's good for Boellium."

It would be good for Ebrus too, but I kept that to myself. My thoughts on the Upper Six and Lower Six divide bordered on treasonous.

"I think you're right. Definitely better than some of the other Line parties, that's for sure. Do you want another drink?"

For some reason, as he spoke, I was drifting closer. I couldn't stop myself. "Just water, please. I think I've had enough of your expensive alcohol, though I've built up quite the tolerance after drinking the Twelfth Line's moon water for a month. That stuff will melt your insides."

Hayle laughed, grabbing me a jug of water from behind the bar. "I've heard of it. I should ask your friends for a sample. It's very hard for the Third Line to get drunk, which is why we funnel-chug most of our drinks."

I laughed. "Well, see Eliot over there?" I pointed across at a Twelfth Line conscript sipping from a secret flask he kept on his hip. "The still in the bowels is his baby. If you ask about it, he'll talk to you for hours about batches and vintages and all sorts of stuff I don't understand. Just don't talk about his eyebrows... or lack thereof."

Hayle chuckled. "What happened to his eyebrows?"

I leaned toward him. I'd missed the sound of his laugh. "Word is that the alcohol percentage of the last batch was too high, and a small spark from the burner set it alight like a fireball. Blew off his eyebrows and his mustache. Well, his former mustache."

Hayle snorted, until he looked past me and frowned. I spun to see what he was frowning at. Maybe people had stopped trying to hide their fucking in dark corners and were just screwing on the dance floor now?

Instead, it was a man in a uniform walking in our direction. I was so surprised when he stopped in front of me, I didn't think to do anything but gape. I didn't recognize him, and he wasn't in the Boellium guard uniform.

The uniformed man looked me over once. "Avalon Halhed?"

I nodded. "Yes?"

He raised a gun I hadn't even seen and pointed it at my head. "The Baron sends his regards."

chapter forty

Vox

SHAY'S WHISPERED, "STANLUS IS HERE", in my ear had me moving away from Avalon and excusing myself to disappear into the shadows of the party. My stomach soured at the thought of Stanlus here. He was my father's right-hand man, as brutal and apathetic as his commander.

Him being here, at Boellium and at this party particularly, was bad news.

"Did he say what he was doing here?" I whispered to Shay, and she shook her head. Her jaw was tight, and while her face was neutral, there was fear in her eyes. Few people scared Shay; our fathers, of course, and Stanlus. Not even my brother scared Shay. But Stanlus was... cruel. Needlessly so.

He'd been given a free hand to ensure the kingdom ran smoothly on my father's behalf, with an army at his disposal, and he'd decided to do it in the most brutal way possible. There were rumors that he kept traitors alive in the dungeons of the Hall of Ebrus, going back periodically to torture them and then disappearing until they'd healed, only to return and start the cycle again.

The man was a monster in a uniform.

I straightened my shoulders, becoming the imperious Heir I was meant to be. He wouldn't hurt me, of that I was sure, but I didn't want Shay anywhere close to him. And I wanted him an entire continent from Avalon.

I leaned down closer to Shay, keeping the barrier around us so unwanted ears couldn't hear. "Leave. Go and keep an eye on Avalon from a distance. Be discreet."

She hesitated, loath to leave me alone with him, but I shoved her back in the direction of the party. She went, but her shoulders were tense.

I steeled my spine and walked around the rocks to see Stanlus perched on a boulder, cleaning dirt from beneath his nails with his knife. At least, I hoped it was dirt. There were three other soldiers around him, each decked out in the uniform of the Baron's personal guard.

"Stanlus. This is an unfortunate surprise," I said coolly. He might have strength, but magically speaking, I walked all over the older man. I was more powerful than him, and my brother too. I suspected I was even more powerful than my father, though I would never suggest that out loud. It would be a death sentence.

Stanlus's shrewd gaze suggested he knew it, though.

"Vox. Your father has sent me down here to investigate rumors of dissension."

I actually raised my eyebrows at him. "Dissension? Here in Boellium?" The idea was impossible. Boellium War College was a tool of indoctrination. A gentle fist around the throats of the citizens of Ebrus. "I haven't seen any behavior that would suggest anything but an adherence to the status quo."

Stanlus snorted, like my opinion meant nothing. He walked toward me. "Haven't you? No whispers? No little Lower Liners sneaking their way into your bed to infect your mind?"

My body went cold. That was a pointed barb. He knew about Avalon, which meant Father knew about Avalon. I didn't let any of that show on my face; I had years of practice at this little push-and-pull routine.

I rolled my eyes at him and scoffed. "Please, Stanlus. We both know that if I fuck the Upper Line women, they get big ideas that they'll be the next Heiress of the First Line. I find it cleaner to fuck among the Lower Lines—they know their place and they're just so happy to get my dick, they spread their thighs. You need to stop listening to rumors." I hated speaking of Avalon that way, but the last thing I wanted was for her to be on Stanlus's radar, let alone my father's. "Besides, the only thing they could infect me with is the pox, and luckily, the healer gave me medicine to fix that, should the need arise." I gave him a lecherous wink straight from my brother's playbook. Fuckboy extraordinaire.

Stanlus eyed me critically, and I kept my face imperious and cocky. It had been my former weapons master who'd told me quietly one day never to let Stanlus see your fear, because once he knew what you feared, he would have you forever. I'd taken that to heart.

The silence stretched on between us, and I knew he was waiting for me to break. Finally, he smiled, and it was the most unnerving expression on his harsh, craggy face. His many battles had left him scarred and ugly, though perhaps it had less to do with his war wounds and more to do with his inner ugliness seeping out onto his skin.

When he smiled, it turned your guts to water.

I almost collapsed with relief when Svenna appeared from the darkness. Her hair was gelled back, and she was wearing tight leather pants and a breast-plate, like she was prepared for war. She always dressed like that. Even with one arm, she was one of the fiercest warriors Boellium had. She probably could have still been a Captain in the Dawn Army, even with one arm. But the Dawn Army accepted only perfection, and for the first and probably only time in my life, I was thankful that was the case, because it meant she was here.

She didn't seem surprised to see Stanlus or the other members of Father's guard. "Master Proxius is a little miffed you didn't stop and say hello before joining the party, Stanlus. Poor etiquette," she quipped, as if a monster such as Stanlus would give a shit about etiquette.

He snarled at Svenna. "Just here to talk to the Heir."

His tone was dismissive, but Svenna had huge brass balls. If there was anyone in the world who wasn't scared of Stanlus, it was Svenna. "You mean the conscript from the First Line? All conscripts are the same within the walls of Boellium, Stanlus. You remember that, right?"

Judging by the way his face went a puce color, he did indeed remember, and whatever she was referring to wasn't a nostalgic memory. "It's so good to see you, Svenna. I'd forgotten you existed since you disappeared behind the walls of Boellium, nothing more than a useless cripple."

I didn't even see her move, but she had a knife under his chin before my eyes caught up. *Holy fuck.*

"Not so useless. Even with one arm, I'm a better warrior than you'll ever be. You're just a small man, with an even smaller dick, blessed with a big army."

I touched her elbow gently, a warning. I didn't want her to die just because she'd gotten into a pissing match with this psychopath.

Someone shouted down the beach, the partygoers oblivious to the battle of wills happening in the shadows.

Stanlus snorted at her, his eyes moving back to me, dismissing her like she hadn't nearly slit his throat. "Don't stress yourself. I've taken care of the problem that brought us here. We'll be on our way."

Svenna's head whipped down toward the beach, and I realized the shouting wasn't drunken conscripts. It was something more.

Every ounce of training I had disappeared, and I turned and started to run, ignoring Stanlus's cold laughter echoing behind me. The crowds were thick between me and the place I'd left Avalon. I tried to see her, my eyes running through groups of people. I couldn't see her, or Shay, or even her friends from the Twelfth Line.

Where was she?

I wanted to shout for her. Call her back to me so I could see with my own eyes she was safe, but I couldn't. If Stanlus was full of shit, he would know for sure that she meant something to me and her life would be forfeit.

"Shay?" I shouted instead. She was meant to be watching her. "*Shay!*"

People were starting to run up the beach, back toward the dorms and away from whatever was causing their terror. I created a buffer of air around me and pushed through them. I needed to find Avalon; I needed to make sure she was okay.

When I broke through the crowd, my heart stopped beating in my chest. One of my father's guards stood there, his gun raised and pointed at Avalon as she stood, wide-eyed beside Hayle Taeme.

Guns were something used only by the First Line. Even the weakest of our Line could use air magic to propel a bullet from the chamber, aided by the mechanics of the weapon. It was how we'd held our power for so long against the other Lines, who didn't have elemental abilities and relied on swords and hand-to-hand combat.

Guns were effective killing devices from far away. As close as the guard was standing to Avalon? There would be nothing left of her head if he pulled the trigger.

"No!" I shouted, running, thrusting my power out, but I was too slow. The whistle of sound, the scrape of the bullet propelling through the chamber, the clap of its release echoing around the rocky outcropping, all screamed that I was too late.

I spotted Shay on the other side of the clearing, her own hand out to use her powers to divert the bullet or create a barrier or something, but she stood even less of a chance of being fast enough.

What happened next occurred so slowly, it was like torture, even though in reality it was between one frantic beat of my heart and the next.

Hayle pushing Avalon.

The bullet lodging in his chest, exploding his flesh outwards like crushed fruit.

A knife lodging in the back of the guard's neck, severing his spine.

My air catching Hayle and lowering him gently to the ground.

Hayle's hounds tearing the guard to pieces as he lay paralyzed and helpless.

The wailing sound of Avalon's cries as she climbed over Hayle's body.

He'd saved her. He'd saved her, and now he was dead.

chapter forty-one

Avalon

NO.

Not again.

"Hayle!" I screamed, the world around me going hazy as I scrambled through the sand to him, my hands buried in the mess of bone and flesh in his chest, trying to hold him together. Trying to hold him here with me.

Blood trickled down his face. "Glad you won't know…" he gurgled. His eyes were trying to tell me something as they went blank. Lifeless.

My screams echoed around me. A memory flashed into my mind. Hayle charred on the sand.

Not again. Not again. Not again.

Arms wrapped around me, and I knew it was Vox. Knew the feel of his arms like my own. "I'm sorry. I owe him everything. I'm sorry. I love you." He repeated the words over and over, but it couldn't matter right now.

I screamed and screamed, hands grabbing at me, but

it was too late. Too late for Hayle. Too late for them. For me.

I screamed and screamed as the burning torches flared and spread, as people melted into the darkness, fire and light swirling around me like a tornado, my hands buried in what remained of Hayle's chest.

I felt the hands on my arms tighten, and I looked over at the disappearing face of Vox, like he was being erased, like the world around me was being erased. I felt sadness as he disappeared, but there was no universe that existed without Hayle. No universe that could exist without both of them.

I would accept nothing else. I would burn it all to the ground every single time if I had to.

As reality faded, I could hear the soft voice of a woman, so familiar, whispering on the swirling tornado of emotion.

The Ninth. The Ninth. The Ninth.

chapter forty-two

Avalon

conscription day - the first day of spring

THERE WAS blood pooling on the cobblestone entrance of the Boellium War College. I shouldn't be surprised, given the baying of the crowd jammed into the front courtyard, and the man suspended in the air, bleeding steadily from his nose. The ruby liquid fell in huge drops, splashing on the ground beneath him with a gruesome dripping sound. Once the puddle of blood became too much, someone with water abilities seemed to wash it away.

That would definitely explain the pink stones.

The guy in the air, bound with invisible ropes, looked at me imploringly. "Help me," he gasped weakly.

I met his eyes, keeping my face shuttered and neutral, then timed my steps to walk under his blood droplets so they didn't splatter on me.

Someone huffed a laugh, and someone else muttered, "That's cold."

My steps faltered. I spun back around. I couldn't just leave him there, could I?

"Why are you up there?" I asked softly, and the whole courtyard held its breath.

The guy suspended in the air gurgled on his own blood. "I pissed off the wrong person."

I looked past him, to a pair of ice-blue eyes that I had no trouble identifying. Vox Vylan, Heir to the First Line. I'd seen the portraits, and even if I hadn't, I could feel his magic swirling around the courtyard even now. There were very few people in all of Ebrus who had that kind of power.

I was a bug to this man, insignificant in every way, but the way he watched me was unnerving. A shiver ran down my spine. I stood up on my toes and looked at the guy suspended upside-down in the eye. "I can't help you, but even I know you need to watch yourself. We mean nothing to men as powerful as the Vylans. It's a lesson you need to learn if you want to survive."

I touched his arm, then leapt back as the guy fell from the air. He landed heavily on the ground, but I kept my eyes on Vox Vylan. *Shit, is he going to think I did that?*

Fuck him. Let him think I had a *tal* to break his elemental magic. I didn't, of course, because talismans that powerful would cost more than all the money in the small coffers of my Line.

But I hadn't come from being beaten down every

day of my life to stand by and watch someone else bully those weaker than them. As soon as I'd stepped over the threshold of this college, the unwanted daughter of a heartless Baron, I knew this was my chance to change my fate. I would get what I wanted—my freedom—and if I had to go toe to toe with the Heir of the First Line to do it, I would.

I held his gaze, fully expecting to be the next person to be hung up in the courtyard as an example, but instead, the Heir to the First Line smiled at me. Or maybe he stole my air, because I forgot how to breathe.

"I'll be seeing you, little dirt scrabbler." It sounded like both a threat and a promise. "Run along now."

I didn't need to be told twice. As I opened the door of the atrium, my ears were immediately assaulted by a cacophony of animal sounds and the yelling of a rabble of conscripts. Two hounds had a man cornered, and I was watching them so intently, I didn't even see the man in front of me until I ran straight into his chest.

My heart climbed up my throat as he stared down at me, his wild green eyes and square jaw so familiar to me. I knew his face like my own, even though I'd never met him before in my life.

"Excuse me," I whispered, my bravado from the courtyard suddenly disappearing. I dipped around him, but he reached out insanely fast and grabbed my arm.

"Who are you?" he breathed, and my mind went blank. I had a name; I knew I did, I just couldn't remember it right at this particular moment.

He gave me a little shake, and words returned to my brain. "Avalon Halhed of the Ninth Line."

"You," he growled.

Oh fuck. I was dead.

Some people are destined to die, no matter how much we wish it weren't so.

–Ellanora Halhed, First Daughter of the Ninth Line

chapter forty-three

Avalon

Some people are destined to die, no matter how much we wish it weren't so.

— Ellanora Halhed, First Daughter of the
Ninth Line

"DO I KNOW YOU?"

The guy had a weird expression on his face. "No. You don't." One corner of his mouth curled up. "Not yet, but you will."

Not if I had anything to do with it. His expression was predatory, like he'd scented his prey, and that unfortunate creature was me.

I said nothing, just backed away toward the door that sat off to the side of the atrium. The animals throughout the tall, glassed entryway made it feel more like a zoo than a war college, but I didn't fool myself that they were normal animals. No, they were tools of battle, just as much as the humans in the room.

One look at those huge hounds told me everything I needed to know. They were watching me with the same careful expression as the man they'd come to stand beside.

No, not a man. An Heir.

Hayle Taeme.

Rumor had it, he was as vicious as the beasts he commanded, and given that they were licking someone's blood from their muzzles, I should have been terrified.

Yet, I wasn't. Not really. Carefully cautious and apparently stupid were better adjectives.

As I backed carefully away, never taking my eyes from the Heir to the Third Line, I paused beside the door, almost tripping over the large war cat that was licking its lips and cleaning something—which I didn't want to think about too hard—from its paws.

I needed to get out of this atrium *right now*. Slipping through the door, I breathed a sigh of relief. Just down the hall, I found the admissions office and knocked quietly.

"Come in," a woman's voice grumbled.

I hesitantly opened the door, surprised to see there were two people in the room. A scarred woman with a shaved head and only one arm, and an older man with a solid jaw and wispy white hair combed straight back. He would've been a hell of a looker once upon a time, but now, he was probably a little older than my father, although three times as fit. He was leaning close to the woman, both of them looking down at an old ledger that they snapped closed as I entered.

"Ah, the conscript from the Ninth Line. Avalon Halhed, I believe?" the man asked quietly, but didn't wait for an answer. "I'm Master Proxius, the director of this institution. Welcome to Boellium War College."

Well, that was off-putting. Had Father sent a message ahead, indicating I would be this year's conscript? Maybe he'd wanted to insist that I be killed in the first training session, so he could kill two birds with one stone: fulfill the Line's conscription quota and get rid of me at the same time.

As if he could read the question on my face, the man gave me a kind smile. "You look like your mother. We were friends, once upon a time."

I froze, the blood in my veins turning to ice. My eyes felt too wide in my face as I waited for the derision, the accusations that I was a murderer, or at least a cursed child. However, Master Proxius's face didn't change from the gentle expression.

I cleared my throat. "I, uh, didn't really get to know her, and we don't really speak of her."

Sadness flashed across his face. "Indeed. Fate can be cruel sometimes. Her cousin is an instructor here, if you have questions about her." He looked down at the woman sitting at the large desk. "I will leave you in the capable hands of Svenna." He patted her shoulder, and they shared a look I wasn't even going to try and decipher. "Enjoy your training here, Avalon." He left quietly, while my eyes lingered on the door.

Svenna stood, grabbing another large ledger from the shelf with her good arm. She flicked it open to the Ninth Line page, and in long columns, written in deceptively neat script, was a list of the conscripts who'd come before me.

Avalon Halhed, Daughter of the Ninth Line, she wrote in the same blocky writing. "Your dorm is the third sublevel. There's no one in there at the moment. Enjoy the serenity. Don't be late to your classes, or you won't like the consequences the instructors will concoct for tardiness." She pushed a timetable across the desk toward me, then looked back down at her ledger, making it clear that I was dismissed.

Opening the door, I hurried back through the atrium, over to the staircase that I assumed would take me to the subfloors. I could feel eyes on me, but I ignored them as best I could. It didn't help that someone was screaming, or that the scent of blood and sweat perfumed the air, or that I viscerally *knew* it was Hayle watching me. I wanted to flick my gaze around like a scared rabbit, trying to find an escape route.

Instead, I straightened my spine and walked toward the stairs with my chin up. You didn't run from a predator. Everyone knew that.

And I refused to be prey.

But once I made it three floors down, I finally let out the breath burning my lungs. How had I managed to catch the ire of two of the most powerful Heirs in the country? My bad luck knew no limits.

Pushing open the door, I found the air smelled stale and empty, the communal space cluttered with discarded furniture. There was still a bowl in the sink, like the conscript who'd been here before me had just gone to class and not been killed in a training accident.

I'd clean when I wasn't so exhausted. Picking the furthest room from the door, I placed my pack on the bed. It felt so heavy after all the days I'd carried it from my home in Rewill, all the way down here to Boellium.

However, when I flicked open the flap of my bag, I realized that perhaps it wasn't just exhaustion making my pack heavy. Hiding beneath my clothes and the solitary book was a light purple stolt, the same shade as the epsirialle flowers that had been my favorite in the garden at home.

I shook out my bag, and the stolt fell onto the bed, shaking out its fur. It was odd that it was even inside the college—they were forest dwellers—and I wondered if the Third Line had brought it into the atrium for bloodsport.

"You're safe now. Off you go. Back to your home," I murmured, hoping it could find its way back to the surface. There weren't any windows down here for it to escape from.

I expected the stolt to be terrified, but instead of skittering away, it walked up to my pillow, curled into a ball and went to sleep.

Well. Okay then.

Honestly, I could use the company down here. I briefly wondered if it wasn't some kind of Third Line sacrifice, and instead an animal companion for one of the beastmasters. It seemed pretty tame, after all. It was either a pet or stupid.

I needed to shower, but my stomach was gnawing at itself. Food first, then hygiene; otherwise, there was a chance that I'd just pass out beneath the water. Then I would rot here in this empty dorm, until I either decomposed and oozed down the drain, or the stolt ate me.

On that depressing thought, I reached out and grabbed the little rodent. "Come on. You must have an owner somewhere. I need to give you back before the Third Line thinks I stole you and feeds me to those hounds."

The small purple creature looked like it rolled its eyes as it yawned, but it let me pick it up, not even trying to bite me. Definitely not a wild animal. It ran up my shoulders, then wrapped itself around my neck.

I scoffed. "Make yourself home there. Don't mind me."

Shutting the door to the dorm, I slowly climbed the stairs, the muscles in my thighs screaming at me. As I willed my legs to lift, I could hear the voices of people climbing the stairs behind me. They were laughing, and I wondered what Line they were from.

I was halfway between the first and second subfloors when my head began to spin from either hunger or exhaustion, or maybe both. I clutched at the neck of my shirt, pulling it away as it began to suddenly feel like a noose. Black dots edged through my vision, and I swallowed back the bile threatening to claw up my throat.

The room spun, making me moan a pitiful sound, as my thighs turned to liquid and I made a grab at empty air.

Fuck.

Well, I guess I was going to go down in the family histories after all—as the conscript with the shortest stay at Boellium War College. Father would probably be happy.

My legs stopped working entirely, and no matter how hard I clutched at the rough stone walls, I couldn't grip them. I fell backwards, and fortunately, hit my head on the step below, knocking me out so I didn't have to feel every stone step all the way back down to the bowels of Boellium.

Darkness was a pleasant escape from my reality.

I dreamed of Hayle Taeme. His overheated skin against mine, his strong body between my thighs. He kissed me and called me his Soul Tie, whispering the sweetest things against my lips.

Lights swirled, and then he was Vox Vylan, who held me still with bands of air as he buried his face in my core before grinning up at me with an expression that made my heart pound in my chest.

More swirling, and it was Hayle again, dancing with me at a party.

Vox once more, holding me as we looked at the stars.

Back and forth and back and forth, their faces morphing one after another, until they blurred together and light threatened to blind me.

No, shit, that was actually a light trying to burn my retinas straight out of my eyeballs. *Ugh.*

"She doesn't have uneven pupils, despite the large bump on her head. We should probably still take her to the healer, though," a stern voice said.

"Of *course* she needs to go to the healer. Can you imagine if one of the conscripts died because of our 'primitive healing'?" another voice replied with a huff. "Like they don't just use magic to do what we do with skill and knowledge. Polus, lift her?"

I felt myself being lifted weightlessly. "Fuck, she's skin and bones, Viana," a male voice murmured, and I tensed.

"She's the Ninth Line conscript," another male voice said. "She probably walked down from the mountains."

There was a murmur of conversation I couldn't quite grasp, and I pulled open an eyelid. My head was pounding as I looked up into the face of a man, who smiled down at me.

"Hey, she's awake. You fell down the stairs, so we're taking you to the healer," he told me quietly.

A girl dressed entirely in eye-searingly bright blue peered over his shoulder. "Any pain, other than your head? Arms, shoulders, ankles?"

I shook my head and immediately winced.

"Leave her, Acacia. The healers will ask her those questions." Another girl appeared in my line of sight, and I realized she was dressed just as vividly, though her dress was more of a deep ochre color. They were the Twelfth Line.

I'd always envied their vibrant fabrics. In the Ninth Line Barony, we all wore black. Unending black. But the Twelfth Line dyed their clothes with the plants and minerals that ran through their Barony, giving them a bright, happy wardrobe.

The girl smiled gently at me. "I'm Viana. The big guy holding you is Polus, and that's Acacia." She indicated the girl in blue. "Link is behind us, but don't look for him, in case you've hurt your neck." She squeezed my hand comfortingly, and I tried to think of the last time someone had comforted me.

Ten years? Fifteen?

Viana didn't seem fazed by my silence. "We're from the Twelfth Line. We were just behind you when you fell."

"Avalon," I croaked out. "From the Ninth."

She smiled once more. "It's a pleasure to meet you, Avalon."

She didn't let go of my hand, and her fingers were warm. Giving in for just a moment, I closed my eyes and just basked in their sunshine.

chapter forty-four

Hayle

MY SOUL TIE was here at Boellium. I still couldn't believe it, but I'd known instantly that she was the one. She was the other half of me. My mate. It had hit me like a bolt of lightning to my chest, a deep knowing that was indescribable.

I hadn't known it could happen that way; from what my grandparents had told me, it wasn't an instantaneous thing. It was like two magnets moving toward each other, pulled by invisible strings until it grew into a longing to be in their presence, to know everything about them. Eventually, when the time was right, the Soul Tie snapped into place, and you were helpless to resist.

Maybe it was different because she wasn't from the Third Line. Avalon Halhed of the Ninth Line, that's what she'd said. I needed to know more about her. I needed to know everything.

My first stop was Svenna's office. She'd have the

basic information, and from there, I'd have my own sources look into her.

I was just stepping up to the door when I scented blood. Not unusual in a war college, but still, I paused. When some conscripts from the Twelfth Line emerged from the stairs, one was holding some girl in his arms.

No, not *some* girl. My girl.

A growl rumbled up my throat, and I was striding across the atrium before the thought even took hold in my mind. "What happened?" I snapped at the wide-eyed Twelfth Line conscripts.

These ones had arrived last year, but the Twelfth Line had sent triple the amount of conscripts this conscription day. The drought in their Barony was brutal, and I didn't blame them for sending their half-starved teens to Boellium to be fed and trained for a couple of years. Hopefully, by the time they were done, the drought would have broken.

The guy holding Avalon stared at me, but didn't move to put her down. My Soul Tie turned her head, groaning, but conscious and kind of pissed. She tapped at the guy's chest, and he placed her gently on her feet. They were all still staring at me mutely.

That's when I saw the bleeding gash on her head, and all reasonableness left me, subsumed by rage. "I asked *what happened?*"

The guys stiffened their spines, stepping in front of the women, including Avalon. The urge to protect through violence rose up in me, and I worked hard to keep it tamped down.

What the hell was wrong with me?

They were all saved from serious injury by Avalon stepping out from behind them, back into my line of sight. She was frowning at me, her expression somewhere between confused and annoyed. "I fell down the stairs, and they were taking me to the healer. Well, they *were*, until you came over here growling like a rabid bear."

Someone gasped, tugging at her sleeve in warning, but I had to admire her audacity. No one outside my Line spoke to me like that—fear and a healthy dose of self-preservation made them watch their tone.

Either Avalon Halhed had no idea who I was, or she was brave. Or perhaps stupid. I couldn't wait to see which it was.

"I'll take you to the healer," I told her, stepping into her space to scoop her into my arms.

She stepped back, batting away my hands. "Whoa. I don't need or want your help," she said, holding out both hands like she was trying to ward off the aforementioned rabid bear. "I'm more than capable of getting myself to the healer. I just had a little moment of dizziness." She turned to the people behind her. "I'm fine. Thank you again for the rescue."

One of the Twelfth Line girls eyeballed me, like it was my fault she was sending them away. "Fine. But if the healer says someone needs to watch you due to a possible concussion, you're welcome down on our floor. I have some healing experience." She glared at me again, and I tried to remember her name. I didn't have much to do with the Lower Six, so I had no idea, but I'd get Lucio to find out.

Avalon gave her a genuine smile. "Thank you again for your help. I appreciate the rescue."

The other female narrowed her eyes at me and opened her mouth to argue, but the guys bundled them away. Avalon watched them go, then stepped around me to walk down the hall. The wrong hall.

I realized she had no idea where the healer was.

I trailed along behind her, ignoring her annoyed huffs, until she was so turned around, I was fairly sure she wouldn't even know how to make it back to the atrium, let alone the healer or the food hall.

Eventually, she reached a dead end and was forced to turn and face me. I leaned against the wall, grinning at the enraged expression on her face.

"Lost, Avalon?"

She ground her teeth and winced. I straightened, moving toward her. I gently touched the lump on her head, and she hissed. It was a bad contusion, but she looked okay. I was a shit Soul Tie, chasing around after her, rather than getting her medical attention.

"Are you okay?"

"Apart from a massive headache and a giant pain in my ass?" she asked pointedly, and I smiled. Man, she was fiery. And beautiful. So fucking beautiful. I stared at her a little longer, until she let out another aggravated noise and went to move around me.

I gripped her arm and pulled her to a stop, staring in awe at the place where my skin touched hers. It was like a current passing between us. I wanted to get her naked and feel every inch of her skin until I was electrified.

I looked down at her solemnly. She was kind of tiny. "Please let me escort you to the healer's rooms."

She closed her eyes slowly, in obvious pain. I resisted the urge to lean down and lift her into my arms. "Fine," she ground out.

I slipped my palm from her forearm to her hand, lacing our fingers together like it was the most natural thing in the world. When she didn't pull away, I smiled. We were making progress already.

Sighing, she followed along behind me, and I slowed my pace to match hers. "You know, there has to be an easier option," she informed me lightly.

"Easier?" Easier than the healer? Not that I was aware of. The healers had magic on their side. The kind of slow medicine the people down in the Twelfth used would have taken her days to heal.

"An easier way to get laid. I'm not interested in being your conquest, Heir Taeme." Ah, so she did know who I was.

My jaw tensed. How did I explain to her that there would be no other ways to get laid—no other conquests, no one else but her from now on—without scaring the shit out of her?

I squeezed her palm in mine, relishing the contact. "I'm not looking to fuck you, Avalon." Lie, lie, lie, but it wasn't the reason I was doing what I was doing. "I'm just being a good member of Boellium War College, helping you find your way to some of our important facilities."

She snorted, like she knew I was full of shit, then fell silent. It was okay; with the warmth of her palm in mine, I knew everything would be fine.

"Why did you fall down the stairs?"

She shrugged. "Exhaustion, probably? I should have slept, but there was no food in the dorm, and I was hungry. It's been a while since I've eaten."

I looked down at her. "You missed breakfast?"

Staring at me like I was stupid, she tried to yank her hand away, but I held it tightly. She glared at me instead. "The last three breakfasts. And midday meals. Though I've had some nut bread for dinner the last few nights, so that's something, right?"

I slowed. My mate hadn't eaten in three days? The beast inside me howled its outrage, and I worked hard to keep it from my face. "I'll take you to the food hall after the healers. And I'll get someone to stock your dormitory."

She side-eyed me. "No, thank you."

I stared down at her, letting her see how serious I was. My Soul Tie would never go hungry again. She'd never have to choose between rest and food. She'd never have to exhaust herself to the point that she could be hurt.

I refused to think about the fact that she'd gotten lucky. The stairs to the dormitories were steep, and if she'd fallen wrong, my mate could've been dead within hours of me meeting her. Braxus howled somewhere in the building where he was keeping watch, affected by my devastation at just the thought.

Taking her chin in my fingers, I tilted her face up so I could see those pretty midnight-blue eyes. "I wasn't offering, Avalon. You better get used to seeing my face, because I'm going to be your shadow for as long as I live and breathe."

Shaking her head, she just blinked up at me. "I don't understand."

I resisted the urge to lean down and rub my face along hers, marking her as mine in the way of beasts. "I know."

We were almost to the healers when she gasped, grabbing at her neck. "Oh no."

Terror made my heart thunder in my chest. *Fuck.* Was she more injured than I'd first thought? Had I let her wander the halls with a broken neck? "What is it? Where does it hurt?"

She patted at the hood of her long jacket. "Is it okay?" Her voice shook lightly.

Looking into the deep hood, I saw a stolt, curled up in a ball. Poking him gently, I let out a relieved sigh when he blinked one eye open. *Are you injured?* I asked him mentally. The ability to speak to animals was the generally accepted power of our Line.

He showed me an image of him leaping off her shoulder as she fell, then hiding in her hood as she was scooped up by the guy from the Twelfth Line.

Name? I asked, and he showed me a picture of a

purple flower, a bird known for making a distinctive "ep ep ep" noise and the ocean.

Your name is Ep-Ocean?

He bared its teeth at me. Okay, not Ep-Ocean. He showed me an image of a seed in the grass.

Oh, Ep-sea.

He licked my fingers happily, then went back to sleep. He'ddefinitely chosen Avalon as its person.

"The stolt is fine. He abandoned you as you fell and climbed back into your jacket afterwards. His name is Epsy, apparently."

She grinned at me. "Like the epsirialle flowers." Ah, those were what the purple flowers were. Maybe she'd named the little beast.

"I didn't realize you had an animal companion. Do you have Third Line genes somewhere in your family history?" It would explain the instant Soul Tie.

She shook her head. "Oh, he's not mine. I just found him. I thought he belonged to one of you?"

I laughed, scratching the little stolt's head. "I know every animal companion in my Line, and he's not one of ours." Grabbing her hand again and tugging gently, I continued down the hall. "He's yours now. He claimed you. It happens like that sometimes, that instant connection." I sounded intense, even to my own ears, but was saved by further questions by our arrival at the healer's rooms. "Let's go in and get you checked out."

chapter forty-five

Avalon

THE HEALER WAS PROBABLY MORE attentive than he normally would have been, since Hayle was there, glaring at him with an intensity I didn't really understand. I didn't understand anything about any of our interactions so far, but Hayle Taeme was a force of nature, and I was swept up in his storm.

When the healer suggested I had a mild concussion and that someone should monitor me during the night, Hayle had automatically volunteered for the job. Yeah, that was definitely not happening. There was no way that this near-perfect stranger was sleeping in the same dormitory as me, let alone the same room.

Despite the almost unnatural comfortableness I felt around him, I wasn't an idiot. He was powerful, both physically and socially. He could murder me in my sleep, and the responses from the authorities would range from perplexed to confident that I was the one in the wrong. No one would avenge my death. Definitely not my father. He'd probably send Hayle a fruit basket in thanks.

Hayle was leading me toward the food hall, though, so I'd worry about all that later, once I had a full belly and an entire jug of water flowing through my system. The healer had said I was suffering from severe dehydration and the beginnings of malnutrition, though he couldn't understand how that had happened so quickly.

I didn't tell him that food had been scarce long before I'd been selected to be the Boellium War College conscript for the Ninth Line. It had begun when I was only allowed to eat table scraps, since food was for leaders, soldiers, and the farmers who kept the coffers of the Ninth Line full. Well, as full as they could be when my father drank a large portion of it and gambled the rest. Food wasn't for girls who murdered their mothers, and who were completely worthless.

The cooks and my brothers probably would have gotten in trouble for the food they snuck me, but they'd been stealthy, and honestly, my father didn't care enough about anyone but himself to police it too closely.

Luckily, I wasn't the only conscript who'd come with malnutrition and dehydration, given the amount of Twelfth Line conscripts who'd enrolled this year. So the healer had everything he needed on hand to help me regain some of my lost strength. He shot me full of some kind of liquid with a big metal needle, gave me some green paste that he said I should eat every day, and sent me on my way.

The sounds coming from the food hall were cacophonous. Conscription day meant there'd be new faces as well as the old coming together after the small break they'd had over the solstice.

Hayle gripped me tightly, like he was worried I was about to keel over and die on the spot. He'd actually offered to carry me, which I'd refused immediately. It had been bad enough when I was unconscious. I wouldn't start my time at this war college like some damsel. I mightn't be a bloodthirsty killer, or particularly coordinated, but I would try my hardest to do what I was asked and fly under the radar here at Boellium.

However, I probably should have committed to that ideal before walking into the most populated area of the college beside one of the most powerful Heirs in all of Ebrus. The chatter in the room dulled until it eventually stopped, everyone's eyes on me and Hayle.

Yeah, no thank you.

I scurried away from Hayle, but his hand snapped out and grabbed my wrist. "Where are you going?" he asked softly, his eyes filled with concern.

Dammit. "To get food and sit at my allocated seat." It didn't take an oracle to determine that the room was segmented by Line, and that mine was the empty one toward the back. "I don't want... I just want to get through the next few years, Hayle. That's all."

He looked down at where his hand gripped my

wrist, frowning. Slowly, like it hurt, he released me. "If it would be okay with you, I'd like one of my hounds to stay with you tonight. They'll monitor you and make sure you're okay." I blinked as one of the hounds from earlier appeared at his side. The male one. "This is Braxus."

I chewed my lip as I stood almost eye to eye with the huge beast. He had a dark gray coat, with piercing yellow eyes that seemed to see into my soul. His head reached my shoulder, and I noticed that everyone seemed to lean away from him when he walked across the room, an urge I completely understood. Braxus seemed… intelligent in a way that was kind of unnerving in a creature with so many sharp teeth.

As he leaned forward to sniff my hand, I held completely still. The hound sniffed my fingertips, then my palm, before finally brushing his wet nose over my wrist, at the spot where Hayle had held me. Then he licked me, his tail wagging softly.

I let out a huffed laugh. I didn't want to die in my sleep, but I also didn't particularly want Hayle in my dorm, or to thrust my wellbeing onto the conscripts from the Twelfth Line, despite the fact they'd offered. "Okay. He can stay."

Hayle looked down at the hound, and the canine gave a quick yip before herding me toward the dinner line. I guess it was decided then.

I could feel dozens of eyes on me as I walked down the line, inconspicuously trying to get the layout of the college and the people in it. The Twelfth Line had the most conscripts here, with them all jammed around their table, some even sitting on the tabletop itself.

My Line obviously had the least. But there definitely seemed to be a lot of Third Line conscripts, and a healthy amount of First Line conscripts too.

As my eyes passed over the First Line table, they were ensnared by a set of icy blue ones. I felt like a spider, caught in a web, staring directly into the eyes of a creature that would be the end of me, but I was help-less to resist. I couldn't understand the reaction of my limbs, which were aching to move toward him, even as my brain screamed to drag my gaze away—or better yet, run out the door.

Braxus nipped my fingers, pulling me from the hold Vox Vylan had on me. He was the third most powerful person in Ebrus, and definitely someone I should avoid. I concentrated on the back of the girl in front of me, the scent of hot food making me salivate. It had been too long since I'd eaten, and I was trying my best not to fall on it like a savage. When the girl in front didn't move fast enough, Braxus growled low, and she hurried out of the line, her plate only half full.

The smile on my face felt like it had been put there almost against my will. "Thanks." I loaded my plate high, even as my mind told me to be cautious. I was hungry, and I was going to fill my stomach, regardless of what people thought.

When I was done, I moved toward the end, where a bowl of bread sat ready to grab. Beyond it were squares of something wrapped in little pieces of wax paper.

It couldn't be... right? Chocolate? Just sitting out there, to be taken by anyone, even those in the Lower Lines?

I looked down at my already overflowing plate, then back at the chocolate. It had been something forbidden in the Ninth Line Barony. The only time we got to eat it was when my brother snuck me some for my birthday. There were hundreds of people back in Rewill who'd never have the opportunity to taste it, because of an accident that had happened when I was a child. Because of me.

I dragged my eyes from the chocolate and walked toward the empty table, sitting down and ignoring the curious gazes on my back. I finger waved to my accidental heroes from the Twelfth, pointing to the bandage on my head, then set about eating with a single-minded focus usually only possessed by a dog on the hunt or teenage boys looking at boobs.

The heavy, gnawing hunger disappeared almost immediately, and I slowed down, not wanting to make myself sick. I picked up a piece of meat and put it in my hood for Epsy. Hesitating only slightly, I shared another slice with Braxus, who took it gently from my fingers as if I were made of glass.

He was kind of cute, considering I'd watched him lick blood from his muzzle earlier that day.

By the time I'd finished demolishing the small mountain of food, half the hall had cleared out, and I had a pain in my stomach. My limbs all felt heavy, my eyelids struggling to stay open. I needed to sleep for an entire week to recover my strength, but my classes started tomorrow, so I didn't have that luxury.

Braxus let out a low, rumbling noise, somewhere between a growl and a grumble. I looked down at him, and by the time I looked back up, there was a small pile of wrapped chocolates beside my tray.

Looking around at the nearly empty tables, I couldn't see anyone close by who could've put them there without me noticing. I didn't think teleportation was magic anyone possessed.

Feeling eyes on my face, I turned to the side and watched Vox Vylan swagger from the room, total confidence oozing from every pore of his body.

He wouldn't have done it, would he?

No, it had to be someone else. It didn't matter, though. I'd take my gift and return to my dormitory, where things were silent and made sense. Stuffing the chocolates into my coat pocket, I stood.

"Let's go, Braxus," I murmured, as I tried to emulate the enigmatic First Line Heir, walking like I didn't give a fuck that everyone was staring at me as I left the food hall.

chapter forty-six

Vox

"DO YOU HAVE A BRAIN TUMOR?"

Shay's voice pulled me from my thoughts. "Excuse me?"

She was staring at me, like she could see inside my skull. "I'm trying to find an explanation why you're acting like… this." She waved a hand, indicating my entire body. Rolling my eyes, I continued up the stairs to my room.

If I thought that would stop my cousin from following me, I was sadly mistaken. She trudged up the stairs behind me to my dorm room, though calling the Dome something as mundane as a dorm room was a serious injustice to the magic and architecture that had gone into creating the giant glass half-sphere that made up the walls and ceiling of my bedroom.

Sighing, I turned toward her. "I'm not sure what you're even talking about, Shay." In this room, with my cousin, I could shed the ego that I had to wear like a constant heavy cloak.

"I saw you give the girl from the Ninth Line chocolate. You couldn't drag your eyes from her the whole time we were in the food hall. She wasn't especially pretty, or magical, or anything that I can tell would attract the spare Heir of the whole country. She's not even your normal type."

I didn't really have a type, unless my type was available and willing to keep our trysts casual. If I was honest, I had no answer for Shay. I'd noticed the girl in the courtyard when she stopped to talk to Jackus, who'd been suspended as a warning to the new conscripts not to fuck with the First Line.

Someone from the Eighth Line stealing from my dorm was unacceptable, but killing someone so far below me was almost considered unsporting at Boellium. Jackus would get my leniency once, and after that, he'd be hanging by his intestines rather than threads of air. He was lucky it was me he'd tried to steal from and not my brother, who would have killed him, college rules be damned.

The girl was dirty and skinny, yet somehow braver than most of the other conscripts who entered through the gates of Boellium. I wondered if Jackus's answer had been something different, whether she'd have helped him. If she'd have gone against *me*, in the defence of a stranger. There was something about her that spoke to my soul, an airy concept that I hadn't believed until I saw her today.

When she'd walked into the food hall with a bandage on her head and Hayle Taeme by her side, my interest had been drawn, whether I wanted it to be or not. I hadn't been alone; every person in the room had turned to watch them. She'd skittered away from Taeme like she couldn't escape fast enough, but seemed happy to be trailed by those untreated furs he called companions.

That should have been the end of my interest. Anyone with a connection to the Third Line was an automatic threat. But when I'd seen her stare at those chocolates, her face twisted with both longing and guilt, that had pulled at a muscle in my body that I'd long thought calcified.

No one except Shay would have been able to pick up the residual energy of me bundling something as small as those chocolates across the room, high over everyone's heads until they landed in front of the girl from the Ninth. Obviously, I'd kind of hoped Shay had also been oblivious.

Still, I had to maintain my nonchalance. "I think she's kind of pretty, and it's been a while since we've had any new blood here worthy of sticking my dick in. You're overthinking it, Shay." I paused. "She was with Taeme, though, so find out more about her. I want to know their connection."

Giving me a droll look that said she wasn't going to just let it go, she turned and perched on the edge of my couch. "Whatever you say, Vox." She cleared her throat.

"Your mother reached out to me with another suitable pairing today. Ephily's brother, Caden."

I screwed up my nose. Ephily was a persistent annoyance who'd warmed my bed once or twice and now had visions of being Queen of Ebrus. Like that would ever happen. Caden was worse, by all accounts. A social climber who would kiss your ass, then stab you in the back.

"Did you tell her that I need you here, unwed and not burdened down by some barely connected halfwit for at least another year?"

I was hoping that by then either I'd have a solution, or my mother would have moved on to trying to marry off my brother rather than me and Shay. Perhaps if Mother acknowledged that Shay wasn't going to be interested in any *male* suitors and tried to marry her off to Ephily instead of her brother, she'd have better success.

But the First Line was nothing if not closed-minded and hellbent on using the women of our Line to spread both our control and genetics.

"Did I suggest that reproducing with Caden would weaken the intellectual integrity of the First Line? Yes. Your mother isn't nearly as terrifying as the Baron."

Nearly as were the prudent words there, because whilst my mother wasn't as violent in her retribution, she was still powerful in her magic and prone to forcing people to her will, whether they liked it or not.

"How'd she take that?"

Shay shrugged, and while she pretended as if she

didn't care, I knew it played on her mind. "She agreed in the end. She suggested that they got their dim-wittedness from their mother. No love lost there."

The backstabbing and rivalries among the Court in Fortaare was legendary. "Another reprieve then?"

Sighing, Shay stood. "For now. I better head to bed." She patted me on the shoulder. "Night, Vox."

I lifted my chin, my smile coming easily for her. I hated that I couldn't save her from her fate, any more than I could save myself from mine. "Night."

Turning off my lamps, I lay down in my bed and stared up at the stars. When I finally drifted off to sleep, it was to dream of the girl. Of holding her in this room, in my arms, and staring at those same stars as they burned across the sky.

Should Ebrus ever go to war, it would be over in minutes, if this was the quality of citizens we were trying to turn into soldiers. Father insisted that every child in the First Line begin training in hand-to-hand combat as soon as they entered the schooling system, silently building his own little army, should the other Lines ever turn on him. I knew that the Third Line did this too, evidenced by the smooth way Hayle Taeme fought, both hand to hand, and with long-range weapons.

But from the Fourth Line downwards, the reliance the conscripts had on their magic for defense was abysmal. One well-stocked army with enough talismans to go around, and they'd be as helpless as civilians.

I knew the conscripts from the Upper Lines; most had come to see me last night in the food hall and metaphorically kissed the ring, and my ass. Watching them try to swing a sword at each other now was both humorous and disheartening. Some were already vomiting over the rail of the training ring from exhaustion and the hot summer sun.

Surprisingly—or perhaps not, considering they had no magic to speak of—the Lower Lines were proficient in mid to long-range attacks. Throwing knives, bows, and crossbows were all handled with practiced precision rather than magic. They relied on their bodies to survive, and that was never clearer than in the practice ring right now.

The Eleventh and Twelfth Line conscripts seemed to deal best with the exertion, despite being half starved. It was obvious that they toiled away in the overbearing heat of Western Ebrus every day, just to survive. They went through the simple forms with ease, not even breaking a sweat. No wonder Master Proxius was accepting them all without complaint. They probably would make good soldiers, as long as they never had to go anywhere too cold.

My eyes kept drifting to the girl, though.

Shay stood next to me, her expression mocking. "No, Shay," she said in a faux-baritone. "My interest in the girl isn't unusual. I just want to fuck her." She was definitely mocking me. "You're full of horse shit, Vox Vylan."

Huffing a sigh, I dragged my eyes from the girl, back to my cousin and second-in-command. "What do you want, Shay?"

She crossed her arms over her chest and looked over the training ring with me. "Just providing the information you asked for, my Heir."

Oof. She'd used my title, which meant she was annoyed. Squeezing her arm, I apologized with my eyes. I couldn't do it out loud, not here, where anyone could hear. A Vylan never apologized, because we were never wrong. It was basically our family motto.

"And what did you find?"

Lowering her voice, her eyes drifted to the girl. "Avalon Halhed, youngest daughter of the Baron of the Ninth Line. I guess that explains her ladyballs—she's some pampered little heiress from the middle of fucking nowhere."

"What else?"

"No connection to the Third Line that I can find. Other than Hayle, none of the Third Line conscripts know who she is, at least according to Lucio."

I didn't understand the relationship Shay and Lucio had, but it worked in our favor. They shared intel, so Hayle and I could be outwardly antagonistic.

"And you believe Lucio?" She nodded, and I left it at that. I trusted Shay's gut. "Anything more?"

She hesitated. "This isn't a fact, more of a rumor that I

picked up in the hallways. One of the new conscripts from the Fifth Line was telling Ephily that Avalon Halhed murdered her mother in cold blood. Rumor has it that her own father sent her here because he feared for the lives of his other children and the people of his Barony."

My eyes flashed back to the girl in question, who was staring at the tip of her sword like it was personally betraying her as she tried to drag her arm up and complete her forms. She was talking to a conscript from the Twelfth Line; their colorful clothes made them easy to distinguish from the rest. Swinging too hard and overbalancing, she landed on her face in the dirt.

"You want me to believe that girl committed matricide?" I snorted my disbelief. "Look into it, and see if it's more than a rumor. We both know how quickly these things can spiral out of control."

I watched as the girl dragged herself to her feet, her arms shaking with the effort. Hoping that Shay didn't notice, I sent a small pulse of air to sit beneath the tip of her sword, taking some of the weight from her straining muscles.

But Shay was not an idiot. "You should go over and say hello. Getting women into bed happens to be my specialty, and I have it on very good authority that the first step is talking to the person you want to fuck."

Shaking my head, I turned away from Avalon Halhed and went through my own forms quickly. But I continued to help her hold up her sword, at least until she could hold it high enough herself.

chapter forty-seven

Avalon

I **FELT** like a bug under a microscope for the entire first week at Boellium. No matter where I was, there were eyes sitting heavily on my skin. Most of the other conscripts seemed to look at me like a sideshow, but the really searing gazes were those of Hayle Taeme and Vox Vylan.

It took the Heir of the First Line eight days to finally corner me. I wouldn't say I'd been avoiding him, but I wasn't actively trying to hang around in the spaces he occupied.

Okay, I was avoiding him.

But as I came out of Battle History class, he stepped up beside me. "Are you avoiding me, little dirt scrabbler?"

Shit, he'd read my mind. I wouldn't have known he was even talking to me, except for that pleasant nickname. He wasn't looking at me and was walking at least a foot away. To outside eyes, it appeared as if we were just both walking down the same hallway at the same time.

"Uh, not intentionally?" Lie. Definitely intentionally.

The quick flick of his eyes in my direction told me that he didn't believe me, and I started to walk a little quicker, hoping to lose him in the mass of people.

But any thought of that escaped when he reached out and gripped my wrist. My skin prickled, like I'd just stepped into a snowstorm. We both stared down at the place where our skin touched, and Vox Vylan quickly withdrew his hand.

I kept referring to him in my head by his full name to reinforce the fact that he was a *Vylan*. Dangerous. Attractive. But wildly out of my league.

"You're an Heir?" His words were haughty, imperious even, and although it was phrased as a question, his expression told me it really wasn't. That he knew everything there was to know about me, about my life, right down to my favorite color.

"Yes. Of the Ninth Line, though an Heir is a bit of a stretch. I have a lot of siblings who'd have to die for me to take the mantle of Baroness."

He frowned at me, like I was plotting something. Little did he know there was nothing I wanted less than to be Baroness of the Ninth Line. I'd rather flay my own flesh from my bones.

"Is that something you plan to do?"

My blood froze in my veins, because while his words were light, there was a knowing in them. A hint at a secret. He *knew* about my mother's death.

I stopped and turned to him, making him halt. No one passing by would wonder if we were talking to each other now; our bodies were close, and he stared down at me with an intensity that made my bones feel like jello. His eyes were like shards of glass, cutting along the curves of my face as they wandered across my skin. I couldn't see Braxus, but experience told me that he'd be here somewhere, watching and waiting.

Clearing my throat, I straightened my spine. "No," I said with so much conviction, there would be no doubt that I was speaking the truth. "I have no interest in killing my siblings—the only people in Ebrus who love me—or becoming a Baroness. If I can help it, I don't even want to return to Rewill, or the Ninth Line Barony." I licked my lower lip, nervousness making my skin itch and my mouth dry. What if I was just being sensitive? What if he didn't know about my mother, and I was projecting my insecurities onto his words?

Because even if I hadn't directly murdered her, I knew deep down that I was the cause of her death.

He put a hand on my arm, leaning down close to me, so no one around us would hear his words. "I've lived around enough cold-blooded killers to know that you aren't one, Ninth." His jaw tense, he straightened. With one last incline of his chin, he strode off like we hadn't been conversing at all. His black hair glinted in the sunlight, so dark it almost shone with a blue gleam, like the swans who migrated to the lakes around Rewill.

Something wet touched my fingers, and I looked down to see that Braxus had appeared at my side.

Burying my fingers deep in his coat, I leaned into his warm strength. "Hey, Brax, there you are." His tongue licked my palm, making me laugh, even as I wiped the doggy drool on my pants. "Don't tell your owner, but I'm glad you're here. I think I would've been lonely without you."

Although the loneliness might've been because as soon as people saw Braxus, they turned around and went the other way. It was like having a fluffy body-guard. I'd miss him when he returned to Hayle. Pulling some jerky from my pocket, I ate a strip, reaching down to feed one to Braxus as well.

My dorm kitchen was fully stocked now, the shelves brimming with more shelf-stable food than I could possibly eat in a year. Hayle had even managed to get me a spelled icebox, which was filled with meat.

I didn't know what to make of the gift, or what to make of the gifter. Hayle Taeme was a riddle that I wasn't sure my heart was ready to solve. If I was honest enough with myself to admit that I was avoiding Vox, then I had to admit I was kind of avoiding Hayle too.

I hadn't even gone up to the food hall last night, letting my exhausted muscles relax rather than climb the stairs on legs that could barely stand without quiv-ering. If it had the added benefit of avoiding the stares and the too-intense gazes of Hayle and Vox, all the better.

But today, we hadn't had anything but basic train-ing, and I could actually still feel my thighs. I wanted to explore a little more of Boellium before I grew some ladyballs and went to the food hall, and I knew just where to start.

The library.

Looking down at Braxus once more, I scratched him behind the ear. "Do you know where the library is, Brax?"

He wagged his tail once and trotted off in the direction of the atrium. I followed, appreciating my scary hound privileges as he cut a path through the bustling crowds of people. The atrium was truly beautiful when it wasn't filled with people and creatures, all baying for the blood of unsuspecting conscripts.

The dome of the atrium was glass and steel and magic. It almost hummed with the residual power that was so old, the methods of creation were lost to time. Some historians said that Boellium had stood before there was even a Line system in Ebrus.

Others suggested that Boellium had stood before there was even an Ebrus.

Walking down the halls, the only sounds I could hear were my own heavy footsteps and the light click of Braxus's nails on the stone floors. After a confusing number of turns, he stopped outside grand wooden doors, though calling them merely doors was an injustice.

They were beautiful, at least twelve feet tall, with each door made from a single slab of some kind of ancient redwood. Each one was intricately carved with a multitude of reliefs, depicting a forest scene filled with animals and hunters, towering trees and swirls of magic. I could have stood at those doors and looked at them for hours, tracing the tiny faces of people hiding within the patterns, but as if they recognized that someone was waiting to enter, the doors slid open slowly.

Inside was paradise.

The room was as cavernous as the atrium, the same glass roof making filtered light shine down on the patterned wooden floors. Rows upon rows of books lined the walls from floor to ceiling, which had to be at least three stories high. Ornate metal railings wrapped around each level, and I could see one or two people perusing those high shelves.

And then there was magic. I could feel the hum of power as soon as I stepped across the threshold.

"Avalon Halhed. I wondered when you'd darken my doorway." A woman who could have been an old thirty or a youthful seventy stepped into the entrance of the library. I had no doubt in my mind she was the Librarian.

"Uh, my apologies for taking so long, Librarian." I felt guilty, even though none of my lessons or classes had even suggested I come here.

She looked down at Braxus fondly, who was gazing up at the woman with a doggy grin. "I see you had a guide. It's okay, Miss Halhed. Every conscript makes it to the library when the Goddess feels it's right." She gazed at me with eyes that saw far too much. "What is it you wish to find?"

I blinked at the intense woman, my brain struggling

to find a good reason to be in the library. Or *any* reason to be in the library. "I just came from Battle History and wondered if you had any texts on recent battles?" I squeaked out, grasping the first idea that popped into my mind with both hands.

Something flashed across her face, something akin to disappointment, before it was once again fixed in that studious glare. "Of course. Are you interested in the general history of battles, or of those that include your own Line?"

Once she figured out what I needed, she quickly checked the books out to me. I wanted to linger amongst the shelves for a little longer, but being in the presence of the Librarian was unsettling. The feeling was only reinforced when I stepped toward the door, and her voice seemed to echo toward me unnaturally.

"Life is full of questions, Miss Halhed. I believe that this library contains all the answers you might require."

I nodded, mumbling my thanks and rushing out those large, ornate doors as fast as my legs could carry me and my absolute cache of books.

chapter forty-eight

Hayle

BRAXUS WAS DEBRIEFING me on everything that was happening with my Soul Tie, and it made me grind my teeth in frustration, even if I did sit there and listen with rapt attention. I wanted to be the one experiencing all these moments with Avalon, especially when Vox Vylan was trying to dig his manipulative claws into her.

Alucius had cautioned me to go slowly. Actually, she'd sent me an image of a pup running headlong into a bush and getting bitten on the ass by a swarm of bees. But I knew what she meant.

I could do slow and steady. I could woo my mate, until she felt the same aching draw that I felt. "Maybe I should ask her on a date?" Alucius nodded her approval of the idea. "First, I have to get her to stop avoiding me."

She didn't run like a little rabbit when I appeared— she seemed to know better than to run from a predator

—but whenever she saw me, her heartbeat began to race, and she'd turn ever so slowly in another direction.

That wouldn't do. I wanted her to run toward me, not from me.

Braxus sent me an image of something in the woods around Ebrus, and I smiled. *Perfect.* It was something I could show her that no one else could. He also suggested a picnic, and I grinned.

"Braxus, you old romantic," I teased the hound, making Alucius chuff and get up to rub her fur along her mate's.

With a plan made, I walked out of my dorm room to see the rest of my Line. It was chaos; animals were lounging in small piles all over the floor and couches, and my kin were doing much the same thing. Some were studying or cleaning their weapons, some were gossiping, others were asleep, spooning their animal companions.

That was the difference between us and the other Lines—the sheer amount of love I felt for these guys. They were my family. I'd lay down my life for any one of them.

Lucio loped over when I appeared, slapping me on the back. Lucio deserved to be my second-in-command. He might be a smiley guy, but inside that impressively hard head was a sharp tactical mind and fighting skills that matched mine.

"Jessia is making that stew with marrow again," he groaned happily, rubbing his stomach. Okay, so maybe Lucio possessed a sharp mind, deadly fighting skills, *and* a bottomless pit for a stomach. "She smacked me with the spoon when I tried to taste it, though. I told her I was just checking it wasn't poisoned. It's my duty to our Line," he whined.

"Suggesting Jessia's food *might* be poisoned is a surefire way to get your ass beat. You're lucky she just whacked you with the spoon for that slight." I sat down heavily, my thoughts still on Avalon. I wanted to know everything there was to know about her, but I wanted her to tell me herself. I wanted her to whisper to me all her hopes and dreams, so I could hold them to my chest, right beside my own.

I shook my head. This feeling was instantaneous, and honestly, kind of intense. I was sure Avalon would feel it too if she just spent a little time with me.

Lucio frowned, sitting beside me. "Brother, what's going on? You've been... off, ever since the conscripts arrived."

I looked around, but everyone else seemed invested in their own shit. Besides, I trusted every single one of these people with my life.

"Lockbox?" I asked softly, and Lucio raised an eyebrow.

Lockbox was the secret word we used when we wanted to discuss things we didn't want our parents to know. We'd used it a few times over the years. Like when Lucio had gotten poison ivy rash all over his dick after rolling around in the woods with Leena Orion, back when we were fourteen. Or when he'd snuck down to the cellar and drank his father's prized whiskey, and we'd had to fill the bottle with tea and hope he never opened it. Or when I'd fought with my brother and knocked him out, and we'd had to convince him that he'd simply tripped and hit his head. Or when I'd asked if he wanted to be my second-in-command and follow me to Boellium, without everyone knowing yet.

Lucio agreed quickly. "Lockbox."

I sighed, leaning forward and lowering my voice even further. "I met my Soul Tie."

"Holy fucking *shit!*" he shouted, and I rolled my eyes. So much for the lockbox. Several people in the dorm turned to stare, and I gritted my teeth back at them.

"We'll discuss it later."

Lucio was on his feet, grabbing me by the arm and dragging me toward my dorm room. Real subtle. "We'll discuss it now. You don't say something like that and expect us not to talk about it *right fucking now.*"

When we were back in my room with the door closed, he stared at me expectantly. He was my opposite in every way, light to my dark. Blond to my brunette. Happy to my brooding. We made a good team.

He shoved me onto the bed. "It's the girl from the Ninth Line, right? The one you've had Braxus tailing for the last week?"

I nodded slowly. "Avalon Halhed. She's…" What was she? I didn't really know her, yet I felt I'd known her all my life. I knew she was brave, and beautiful. I knew she was protective of creatures who needed her, defensive of the new friends she made. That was everything I needed to know. The rest I could learn over our long life together. "She's perfect," I finished.

Lucio groaned. "You look like a lovesick bull in mating season. Does she know?"

I shook my head. "I don't think so. The other Lines don't have Soul Ties. But she's drawn to me. I can feel it."

How could she not feel this pull between us?

Gripping my shoulder, he smiled. "I'm happy for you, Hayle. A Soul Tie is…" He trailed off, because we both knew what it was. It was something special, something gifted to us by the Goddess herself.

I knew Lucio would still look into her, though. He was my second; his job was to protect the interests of our Line if I couldn't.

"So, how are you going to get your mate?"

———

I waited for her at the entrance to the training ring. It felt a little like corralling my prey, but desperate times called for desperate measures. In a rucksack hanging from my shoulder was a blanket, along with enough food to keep the beast inside me happy that we were providing for our mate.

Moving to the side, I waited until Avalon was just past me before I reached out and gently gripped her arm. A pulse of pleasure raced up my own, the connection between us undeniable. She gasped softly, and I assumed she'd draw away. Instead, she moved almost imperceptibly closer, making me want to howl my happiness.

"Avalon," I purred softly. "How are you feeling?" I touched the fading green bruise on her head, the small lump still there underneath her hair.

"I'm fine. Good enough that I don't get excused from sword drills anyway," she grumbled, following me as I led her from the training grounds. She might've been hiding from me, but my Soul Tie clearly trusted me already.

Once we were away from the steady flow of conscripts, I turned to her. "Well enough to come for a short walk into the woods with me? There's something I want to show you."

She narrowed her eyes. "Show me what?"

I grinned. "A surprise."

"I've heard that before. Is the surprise your cock? Because if so, I'm going back to my dorm for a shower instead."

My mouth fell open. I mean, I'd like to show her my cock, but no. I also wanted to rip the cock off any man who wanted to take her into the woods for that reason, and feed it to Alucius.

My hound's agreement was instantaneous. She made some reference to it being chewy, which made me blanch a little. Alucius was terrifying sometimes. People were scared of Braxus because of his size, but Alucius was cunning and brutal. She was definitely the scarier one.

Avalon eyed me. "Is the surprise a shallow grave?"

I blinked slowly. "Uh, no. It's not. It's definitely something you'll enjoy."

She muttered something beneath her breath about cocks again, but finally, she nodded. "Sure. I'll go into the woods with you, even though you're a near-perfect stranger."

Despite the sarcasm, when I tugged her along behind me, she followed. I didn't move my hand away as people watched us walk by. I didn't care if people knew that she was mine; I was glad for it. I wanted everyone to know I'd claimed her.

We walked out through the gates and around the thick fortress walls. Her stolt, Epsy, appeared and climbed her leg, wrapping himself around her neck. He knew where we were going; I'd sent Alucius to find him earlier.

Avalon laughed and scratched the small rodent. "Hey, sweet boy."

I'd gathered all my animal companions to protect us in the woods. Braxus and Alucius were flanking us on either side. My raven, Quarry—who was usually in charge of keeping an eye on the village—had even been called in and was perched in a tree, watching anyone who might venture too close.

Finally, we made it to the clearing. Letting go of Avalon's hand, I unbuckled my rucksack and pulled out the blanket for us to sit on, spreading it out wide. We'd need all the space we could get. I sat and tugged her down onto the blanket beside me.

Sending my consciousness out into the woods, I connected with the creatures I wanted her to meet. Epsy leapt from her shoulder and disappeared into the trees.

"Epsy!" she whisper-shouted, but the little stolt was gone. She looked… heartbroken.

I wrapped an arm around her shoulders and squeezed her tightly. "He'll be back. He's devoted to you—he'll never leave you unless you make him." I could relate to the little rodent.

Letting out a shuddering breath, she leaned into me. The forest around Boellium was beautiful. Not as beautiful as my home, but still, something settled in my chest to be surrounded by animals and wilderness after being cooped inside the walls of the war college.

"It's so peaceful out here," she whispered. She'd be happy in the wilderness around the Third Line Barony. I knew she would.

"It reminds me of home," I said simply. Hearing a rustle in the bushes, I smiled. "Ah, here comes your surprise."

In the blink of an eye, the clearing was consumed by soft purple fur and the sound of Avalon's soft laughter. "Oh my Goddess! Where did they all come from?" There must have been fifty little stolts in the clearing now, from mature adults to the smallest of kits.

"They all come here to den on the island and have their young. No one really knows how they get here, but it's one of the few places in Ebrus where stolts reproduce. They don't live here all year around, though, preferring the mainland forests for food. Your Epsy wanted you to meet his family."

Avalon lay back and allowed the creatures to swirl over her in a soft flurry of fur. Watching the pure joy on her face made happiness bubble in my own chest.

I wanted to make her this happy every day for the rest of my life.

chapter forty-nine

Avalon

HAPPINESS HAD ALWAYS FELT like a fleeting sensation, something so warm and bright that it briefly chased the chill from the cold, dark crevices of my life before disappearing again. I felt like I was forever chasing just a taste of sunshine.

Right now, though, I was basking in that happiness, lying on a blanket in the middle of a forest with a man I barely knew, but who somehow felt like home. In fact, he felt more like home than any other place or person ever had, and I didn't understand why.

At some point, the hounds had joined us in the clearing, and the stolts hadn't been even remotely fazed about the apex predators in their midst. A lack of self-preservation must be a stolt trait, because they played up and over the wiry fur of Braxus's coat, hiding beneath Alucius's legs, and generally playing, like a mass of purple fur.

I laughed as one ran up my torso to curl up on my

"

chest. Within seconds, it was asleep, like someone had flicked an off switch. Hayle stared down at me indulgently, lifting a strawberry to my lips so I could eat without dislodging the stolt. It seemed… intimate. Frighteningly so.

Not because I was scared of Hayle; I was just terrified by the whirl of emotion that had lodged in my chest as I watched him. The joy, the desire… the something else I couldn't name because it would make no sense, but it was *there*, resting deep in my chest.

"Do you believe in soulmates?" The question burst from my lips before I could swallow it back down.

Hayle froze, the berry pausing inches from my lips. He cleared his throat. "Yes. The concept of a soulmate is revered by the Third Line. We call them Soul Ties, though."

I hummed a thoughtful sound, reaching up to take a bite of the strawberry. "What's it like? Being part of the Third Line?"

He chewed his lip, his gaze running all over my face like he was memorizing the lines of it. "It's like the comfort of strong arms. Like having someone you trust at your back, so you can rest."

I closed my eyes against the words, trying to imagine what that felt like, to be able to trust like that. "Sounds nice." I tilted my head toward a small patch of sun, feeling the warmth on my face, the light turning the world pink behind my eyelids. "I don't think I've ever trusted anyone that much."

"Not even your family?" I could hear his frown.

My lips turned down. "Maybe my siblings. Kian especially—he's the Heir. He cared for me the best he could, I guess. He was older when my mother died." I cut off the words. The sun and good vibes were making me a little more free with my past than I should be.

"What about your father? Surely he protected you?" Hayle asked, and I shook my head once. "Anything you tell me stays with me, Avalon Halhed. I swear this on the honor of my Line." His voice was soft, so filled with compassion, that I opened my eyes. He was right there, staring down into my face with an expression that I couldn't understand, but made my heart race.

I believed him. "My father hates me." It was the truth, one that I'd expressed to myself and my siblings many times, the one that was generally accepted by the people of the Ninth Line Barony.

The Baron of the Ninth Line hated his youngest daughter because she'd murdered his wife, the great love of his life, his only guiding light.

Hayle didn't negate my words. Didn't smooth them over with gentle denials that a father could never hate his daughter. "His loss," he said gently. Then he dipped forward and brushed his lips along mine. The kiss was so soft, I wondered if it was just a dream, a desperate hope.

But when he deepened the kiss, something settled in my chest. This was happening, and when I kissed him back, he groaned into my mouth. He leaned over me, pressing his chest to mine, his arms bracketing my shoulders. Pulling back, he stared down at my face as if I wasn't real.

"You feel so fucking perfect. How can you feel this right?" he whispered against my lips, before diving back in and kissing me again. The stolt that had been asleep on my chest wiggled out from between our bodies, then it was just me and Hayle and no space between us. My body curled up toward him, like no space was still too much space.

One of his hands reached down to slide along my side, gripping my hip with firm fingers and dragging me closer, like he too wanted to crawl inside me and be one person. It wasn't my first kiss, but kissing one of the stable boys when I was fifteen had been nothing like this. This was so much more.

Finally, Hayle dragged himself away, moving back a little, his forest-green eyes almost glowing, wild and uncivilized. "I swear this isn't what I brought you out here for."

Embarrassment flooded my cheeks. Was he regretting the kiss? Was I bad? I narrowed my eyes, hiding my self-consciousness behind bravado that felt like a mask. "Why did you bring me out here then, Hayle Taeme?"

His eyes were running across my face again, and he slumped down on the blanket beside me, gathering my stiff body into his side until I was tucked along his own like I belonged there. "You can't tell me you don't feel it too?"

His rock-hard bicep that I was using as a pillow? I

felt that. The way he curled my body over his so my hand was resting on his abs, and my knee was resting on his thigh? Those things I felt down to my core. But I didn't think that was what he meant. I had a feeling I knew, but I didn't want to guess and look like an idiot. Because what if he didn't mean this thrumming energy in my chest? I would be devastated.

"Feel what?" I asked lightly.

Grunting softly, he tugged me until I was blanketed over his body. "This connection between us. This feeling like fate has put us together, that we're meant to be one."

My thighs slid to either side of his waist as I pushed up to look down at him. I did feel those things. Like a golden string was attached from my chest to his.

Vox Vylan's face appeared in my mind. I felt that draw to him too. How did I tell Hayle that I felt that connection too, but not *just* for him?

Maybe we were feeling different things.

Maybe I just had wind?

But when he buried his hands in my hair and pulled me down to kiss me again, I realized that it wasn't gas or any other bodily function causing this. It felt like my soul was reaching for him; there was no denying it.

I just had to work out why it was reaching for Vox Vylan too, and who I was supposed to choose.

And I had to choose, right?

———

We kissed and kissed, as the sun set and the stolts returned to their burrows, and the calls of the day birds gave way to the night creatures. Until I knew the taste of his lips, the feel of his body, the sounds of his pleasure.

He stopped me from taking it further, though. He twined my fingers in his when I tried to unbutton his pants and pulled my hands up until they were caught between our bodies.

Finally, the cold was permeating the air, making me shiver, and Hayle pulled back. He looked… ruffled. His lips were swollen, even as they curled into a satisfied smirk, his eyes hooded and his hair standing up at odd angles.

"I could kiss you forever," he murmured, brushing a hand down my back. "But we should get back."

Nodding, I rolled away from him, curling up on stiff muscles. Hayle glided to his feet like he hadn't spent who even knew how long pressed between my body and the hard ground. Reaching down, he lifted me to my feet with ease. I stood as he gathered up the blanket, along with the remnants of food—which had some suspiciously Epsy-shaped nibbles around the edges— and put it all back in the pack.

Wrapping my hand in his larger one, he walked us slowly back toward the gates of Boellium War College. I ran my hand down my hair, trying to smooth it so I didn't look like I'd spent the better part of the afternoon dry humping in the woods like a horny rabbit.

As we stepped through the gates, I expected Hayle

to drop my hand, but he didn't. He walked beside me, his chin raised and a smirk on his face, no matter how many people turned in our direction to openly stare.

I knew what it was. It was a claiming.

Eyes burned against my skin, and when I looked up at the second floor of the atrium, I could see Vox staring down at me, his expression turned down into a frown. My heart clenched in my chest, but I pushed the feeling down. I meant nothing to Vox Vylan, and he meant nothing to me.

Liar, my brain rebelled. I didn't understand it, but I was drawn to the Heir of the First Line the same way I was drawn to Hayle. No, not the same, but equally as intensely.

As we walked down the stairs toward my dorm room, I pushed thoughts of Vox from my mind. That wasn't fair to Hayle, who'd just given me the happiest afternoon of my life.

Stopping outside my door, Hayle leaned down, kissing me gently once more. I gripped his shirt in my fist and leaned back. "Hayle?"

"Mmm, yes, Avie?"

I smiled at the nickname. I didn't think anyone had ever given me one. Though Father had called me a murderous demon regularly, I doubted that counted.

"I feel it too," I whispered, and he sighed happily against my lips.

"I know."

chapter fifty

Vox

ANGER BUBBLED up inside me as I watched Hayle Taeme hold the hand of the girl from the Ninth. I couldn't explain why it burned the way it did. After all, it was almost inevitable. Taeme ran through the female population of Boellium like a forest fire through a tinderbox. If rumor was to be believed, even some of the male population, though it wasn't a rumor I'd ever chased for confirmation. There were moral boundaries about what could be used as political ammunition, and what Taeme did in his bedroom was one of them.

Though I'm sure my father knew. He had no morals, let alone boundaries.

Something restless in my chest screamed that I needed to make my move, that I needed to secure Avalon Halhed before she was stolen from me.

As I went to sleep that night, I came up with a plan. I wasn't going to just give Taeme what he wanted.

The next morning, I waited in the atrium for the girl

from the Ninth. Avalon. The first step would be remembering to call her by her name. I paced up and down the room, glaring at anyone who stood too long to watch me. Someone was always watching me: other conscripts, my family's spies, my own Line. Back at the Court in Fortaare, it was even worse. I was watched and emulated; every tiny conversation and expression would be dissected by gossips.

At least here in Boellium, I had a little more freedom. I was the king here. These were my subjects, not that a single one of them was loyal.

When she appeared, she was with a group of conscripts from the Twelfth Line. They were easy to spot among the crowds, not just because of their brightly colored clothing, but because some of them still looked half starved. The drought in the West of Ebrus had worsened, and the people were starving.

Helplessness washed over me. There was nothing I could do for the people of the Eleventh and Twelfth Lines. My father would never empty his own coffers to help another Line, despite being the country's de facto leader. I wasn't sure he'd even do it for his own Line.

The only thing the Baron of the First Line cared about was himself and his own power.

"Ninth, could I speak to you?" I called softly, but I may as well have shouted it. All the Twelfth Line conscripts froze like creatures of prey, their faces swivelling in my direction as one.

One of the girls in the middle looked at Avalon. "Is he talking to us?"

Avalon tilted her head. "I think he's just talking to me. Go on ahead. I'll be fine." Despite the wariness I could see etched into the lines of her face, she walked over to me confidently. "You hollered?" Her tone was light, but her eyes were narrowed.

She was pretty in a way that was totally ordinary. Maybe her beauty was in her ordinariness. She wasn't primped and preened until she was walking around in a mask, like the women at court. She wasn't dressed to beguile or fascinate. Her features were soft and classic, unadorned by makeup. Her clothes were stitched together, combined with part of the uniform given to conscripts by the college.

But her eyes sparkled, and her full lips curled at the corners. She was… something. She just stared me down, her tone polite, and that was beguiling in itself.

"I require your assistance, if you'd be willing to give it."

Her expression folded into a mask of confusion. "You need *my* help? With what?"

This was the part where I hoped Shay's informants were as good as they said. "My special interest is astronomy, and it has come to my attention that you are quite a good artist. I would like your help mapping the stars over the coming meteoric period."

She stepped back, like I'd struck her. "How do you know that?"

I shrugged, as if I was some all-seeing demigod, instead of Shay just having a network of kitchen hands who reported to her from across the country. She would make an amazing spymaster, if my father or brother could ever see past her gender.

Stepping closer, I could see the furious flash of something in Avalon's eyes. She didn't like that I'd pried into her life, uncovered her secrets. I didn't give her false platitudes. If I had my way, I'd uncover every single secret she had and use them all to hold her to me, until she wanted to stay by herself.

I froze at my own thoughts, shaking my head imperceptibly as if I could physically dislodge them. There could be nothing between the girl from the Ninth and me; we were incompatible in every way.

Despite the convictions of my head, when I opened my mouth, something entirely different came out. "I know a lot of things, Avalon Halhed, Heir of the Ninth Line." It sounded like a threat, but I didn't pull the words back.

She was silent for a long time, and I worried I'd overplayed my hand. Not that you'd know it from my expression. I worked hard on my uninterested face.

Gritting her teeth at me, she nodded once. "Fine. But I'm not that good. If you want your astrological charts to look like a child's drawing, then so be it."

"Celestial maps," I corrected. "Excellent. We start tonight. I will collect you from your dorms." I forced myself to move away nonchalantly, striding back through the crowds of people with cool confidence, as they parted for me naturally.

This was purely business. I needed to know what she had going on with Taeme, and I really did need someone to draw the celestial maps. This was a neat solution.

So why was my heart beating a million miles a minute?

———

It was ten o'clock that night when I descended below the atrium for the first time… ever. I'd never had a reason to head toward the lower levels of Boellium, but today was a day of firsts.

First time down here.

First time I'd ever had to lie to a girl so I didn't get rejected.

First time I'd wondered if *I* was enough.

Knocking lightly on the door, I was met by one of Taeme's hounds. The mean one. Actually, scratch that, they were both mean. This one was legendary, though. Braxus. He'd once brought down an entire gang of thugs who'd been terrorising the Third Line's outlying villages, and had ripped through their ranks, all by himself.

Even the First Line were impressed by the efficiency of the Third Line's animal companions. It made them fierce warriors, and the whole reason they were such a threat.

I also had my suspicions that they could speak to Taeme somehow. I looked down at the hound. "Tell your master to back the fuck off, or we're going to have a problem," I muttered in a low voice. The giant hound's muzzle came up to my chest, and you'd have to be a fool to look at those flashing teeth and feel nothing. I held my ground, hearing the soft footfalls of Avalon.

"Braxus, it's fine. We've arranged to meet up." She shuffled around the giant beast—who'd taken more lives than most instructors in this college—and stroked behind his ears like he was an overgrown pet. "Stay here. I'll be back." Then she kissed the top of his head.

Kissed it. *Fuck me.*

I gestured toward the stairs. "We are headed to the roof. There's a telescope up there that's one of the most powerful in all of Ebrus."

She followed me without comment, and I was glad that most of the other conscripts had fallen into their beds hours ago. It meant that the atrium was blissfully silent, and as I led her up the stairs to the roof, we didn't run across anyone else.

Not that I thought anyone would say a word, except maybe Taeme. But either his precious hound hadn't been able to get word to him fast enough, or he was biding his time, because no one appeared.

I bypassed the First Line dorms and climbed one extra flight to a door that led to the roof. Technically, this level sat parallel to my room, but the Dome which held my domain sat dark, magic making the glass one way.

The rooftop was pretty; I'd set up a small area with a chair and an easel behind a large brass telescope. I'd also acquired a large amount of artistic supplies and pretty lanterns that set the place in a gentle glow.

I stood to the side as Avalon stepped into the area, her eyes taking in everything in the space. The small burning lights that illuminated her workspace, the pens and inks and brushes and anything else I'd thought she might need. The large telescope.

"It's beautiful up here," she said softly, and I made a hum of agreement.

"It's my favorite place." Not just in Boellium. In all of Ebrus. And sharing it with her felt so right. I waved a hand at the chair. "Your throne, Miss Halhed," I murmured. "Will these tools suffice?"

She snorted rudely. "A box of crayons would suffice, Your Highness," she replied snarkily. "This is more than adequate. I'm not sure what you expect from me, but I think you're going to be disappointed."

I couldn't be disappointed, because I had no expectations, except that she be here. With me, where I could... what? Convince her to go to bed with me? To enter a relationship that was doomed to fail?

Shaking off the thoughts, I gripped her elbow before she even had a chance to sit. "Let me show you the stars first. I think you'll find yourself inspired."

I didn't need all the answers yet. I just needed a chance.

chapter fifty-one

Avalon

VOX VYLAN WAS STANDING REALLY close. The heat from his skin was soaking through my thin, hand-woven shirt as he directed me in the art of using a telescope. When he shifted me into a better position, I went where his hands guided and tried not to think about how big they were, how they spanned my hips easily. How they felt pressing lightly into my flesh.

Fuck me.

"The large glowing discs are stars. There are millions of them across the night sky. So many that we could spend every night for the rest of our lives up here cataloguing and counting them, and we'd die before we were even one percent through." He moved away, giving me a chance to look through the eyepiece. "This telescope is enhanced with magic, and its magnification is second only to the official observatory in Fortaare. They were created by the same engineer, Roulo De

Smaar, and whatever techniques he used were buried with him."

His tone was light, informative, but with a small undercurrent of joy. Like he was excited to share this with me, this little piece of himself, and I found myself relaxing into his tutelage, even if I didn't think I was going to share quite the same passion for astronomy as Vox.

"We'll start at Ebretha, the Goddess of our people. Or at least her celestial constellation. See the star that burns brightly in the center of the view? That's Ebretha's Heart, the brightest star in the sky. Some of the greatest minds in Ebrus think that it is a great sun, similar to our own, and that perhaps there is life out there, flourishing beneath that sun the way we live beneath our own."

When I thought I had a grasp on what I was seeing, I went to the easel and sat down, closing my eyes and drawing the constellation first, then little points. I imagined it like they were freckles on the skin of Ebretha, little marks that enhanced her divine beauty. Then I added further stars, little pieces of stardust around her shoulders and falling down at her feet. While I worked, Vox wrote in a thick journal, and I could see his own scrawled notes from across the table.

We worked in silence, though occasionally I stood and looked back through the telescope, making sure the distances were correct, burning the image behind my eyelids until I was sure it was perfect.

I didn't know how long we were out there, but

eventually, the chill of the sea breeze began to raise goosebumps on my arms. I rubbed them gently, and the movement must have reminded Vox that I was there, because he looked at me and frowned, his metal pen between his teeth.

"You're cold? I thought you were from the mountain tundra of Rewill," he teased.

Scowling, I went back to working on my star grid. "Apparently, these warm southerner temperatures have turned me soft."

Standing, he shrugged off his jacket, coming over to drop it around my shoulders before heading back to his own workspace, diving back into whatever observations he was transcribing. The coat was thick wool and smelled distinctly of Vox. It was hard to explain Vox's scent, which was somehow electric and soothing. Like a sea breeze through a bonfire. Like whiskey on the cliffs of home. It made me snuggle down deeper into the residual heat of his body as I worked.

Finally, when the moon hung high in the sky, Vox snapped his notebook closed. I was basically finished with three sectors, as he called them, and I'd started a small sketch of Ebretha in the corner of the large sheet of parchment. She was naked, her hair spilling down her body, one hand raising a torch to the sky and the other cupped around the glowing heart in her chest.

He stared at it for a long time, and my cheeks began to heat. I shouldn't have been doodling on something he probably wanted to use for official study one day.

"Sorry. I'll erase it," I told him quickly, grabbing the putty from the table beside me.

Quicker than I could fathom, air wrapped around my wrist, stilling my hand before I could reach the page. "Leave it."

I flushed, glad that the darkness hid my flaming cheeks from his view. Still, the air didn't release from my wrists. If anything, it spiraled further up my forearm like caressing tendrils, stroking softly. My eyes flicked to his, trying to read his expression, but his features were shadowed by the moon.

"Vox?" I asked roughly, my breath catching in my lungs. He turned his face from me, and I could finally see his features in the light. His jaw was tense, his full lips turned down. He looked like he was struggling with himself.

Did he want to hurt me? I'd heard all about the cruelty of the Vylans, but as someone who'd had to dodge violence her entire life, I had a pretty good grasp on that tipping point when a person was spiraling into something dangerous. Violence had a flavor I could almost taste, yet I didn't get that feeling from Vox.

His tongue dipped out to wet his lips, and I saw his fist clench and unclench a few times, before a sigh spilled from his lips and the air around my arms dissipated. "Apologies. Thank you for your assistance, Miss Halhed. Same time tomorrow night?"

My mouth fell open. "You want to do this every night?"

Fuck. Me and Vox Vylan, in the darkness together every single night, seemed like a recipe for disaster.

He inclined his head. "Yes."

"And if I say no?" I didn't take orders well—even from the Heir to the entire country, apparently.

His jaw tightened again, but that was the only sign that he was tense. "That is your prerogative, Avalon." The sound of my name on his lips echoed through my soul. He said it softly, without any of the hard edges that normally accompanied his words. "I won't force you to be here if the work doesn't interest you."

I was packing up my tools into a neat little leather rucksack that was laid out on the table. Once everything was stowed away, I looked up into the silent face of Vox and the words came spilling out before I could take them back.

"I'll see you tomorrow, Your Highness." My tone was teasing, hiding the turmoil of my thoughts. The corners of his lips turned up, and he nodded once, turning and leaving the rooftop.

Feeling as if I could finally breathe, I sucked air into my deprived lungs. Leaving the rooftop before someone asked me what the hell I was doing up there, I was two flights below the atrium before I realized I was still wearing Vox's jacket. I turned my nose into the collar of the soft gray fabric like a creep. The smell was so familiar, like the echo of a memory.

When I made it to the Ninth Line dorm, I scratched the disgruntled head of Braxus and headed straight to my room. I laid the jacket along the other side of the bed as I changed into my nightgown, not shifting it to the closet before I climbed beneath the blankets.

When I woke up wrapped in the jacket the following morning, I didn't think about it too hard.

———

Acacia and Viana sat either side of me at breakfast the following morning. They put their trays beside mine, both giving me the kind of look that I figured a mother would give her daughter.

"Uh, morning?"

Viana smiled. "Morning, Avalon."

Acacia drew closer. "Yeah, of course, good morning. What the fuck is going on with you and the Heirs?"

My cheeks flamed, whether I wanted them to or not. "What do you mean?" Playing dumb was my go-to response until I could get a better handle on the situation.

Acacia held up a finger. "One, you're seen walking in the gates of Boellium holding hands with Hayle 'Donkey-Cock' Taeme, after spending the afternoon in the woods. *Alone.*"

Okay, so maybe their expressions weren't exactly maternal.

"I don't think anything happened. Link said he didn't think she was waddling, which would definitely be happening if she'd been dicked down for six hours by Hayle Taeme," Viana pointed out, oh so helpfully.

"Nothing is happening. Well, not really. No one is,

uh, dicking me down, as you say." You could probably see my burning face from one of Vox Vylan's stars at this point. "And I'm just helping Vox map some stars."

"Is that what the First Line are calling it these days?" Viana's laugh tinkled lightly, her eyes sparkling. "If you were just mapping stars, I'd be interested to know why both Taeme and Vylan are switching between eye-fucking you and trying to glare each other into oblivion."

Against my will, I looked between Vox and Hayle, who were indeed glaring like they were trying to kill each other from a distance. Braxus huffed by my feet, and I reached down to scratch him behind the ears reassuringly.

I looked back at my newest friends, already settled deep in the warmth of the Twelfth Line and their sense of community. Apparently, rescuing me from near death had created a bond that they took very seriously. My life was now theirs to hold safe, or something like that. A life debt, though I'd asked why it didn't go the other way, since I'd been the one rescued. Acacia had explained that the Twelfth Line was a follower of the Goddess, and saving one of her children was an honor that the entire Line would uphold.

Honestly, it was unlikely I would have died on the stairs, but it still felt nice to suddenly have this community around me, even if it was under a moral obligation.

Acacia leaned close, bumping my shoulder with hers. "All I'm saying is that if I had the two most powerful men vying for my attention, I'd use it as an opportunity to help the greater good. Most of Ebrus is suffering through drought, and the Eleventh and Twelfth Lines are starving to death in the streets."

Viana slapped her arm. "We aren't pimping out our new friend for social change, Acacia. Let the poor thing get some dick, without the fate of the country resting on her clit."

That sounded painful. "I don't think I hold that kind of sway, but if I do, I'll, uh, drop it into conversation."

Acacia raised a haughty eyebrow at Viana and nodded. "That's all we can ask. Especially if your mouth is full."

"Full of what?"

They both laughed, changing the conversation to one of the Twelfth Line guys trying to take a Tenth Line girl on a date. I ate my breakfast slowly and hoped to the Goddess that neither of the men in question had just heard our conversation.

chapter fifty-two

Hayle

AFTER LISTENING to Avalon's conversation with her friends that morning, I was ready to burst out of my skin and tear out Vylan's throat. It was a delicate balance, though, this ecosystem we'd created inside the walls of Boellium War College. If Vylan died, the power vacuum it'd create would be messy. Plus, his father would probably punish my Line in the most brutal way possible.

No, Vylan and I needed to talk. We tended to avoid it as much as possible, both for optics and because it was hard to be civil with the self-obsessed asshole, without wanting to punch him in the face.

Any issues that needed to be resolved between our Lines were usually discussed between our seconds. They got along far better than we did, but even then, I was pretty sure Shay had to stop herself from tearing out Lucio's tongue at times. I didn't even blame her really; Lucio had that effect on people. Not everyone found him as endearing as I did.

However, this conversation couldn't be done through messengers. I needed to talk to him face to face, preferably somewhere without prying ears. That really narrowed it down, but the roof could be the only place in all of Boellium that the other Lines couldn't access.

I grabbed him as he came out of the Advanced Ethics and Battle Strategies lecture. Looking down at my hand on his arm, he raised a single eyebrow. "Get your hand off me, Taeme, before I remove it permanently."

Fuck, he's a dick. I held my hand there for a beat longer, just so he knew he wasn't my boss, then dropped it to my side. "We need to talk."

He didn't react at all. Not one muscle on his face even twitched. I realized he was waiting for me to continue.

I rolled my eyes. "Obviously, somewhere more private. Preferably with no ears."

We all had our spies. Mine were creatures who'd agreed to share their intel with me, but I had a feeling that the First Line could use their elemental control to pick up sounds far away on the wind. Plus, Shay was resourceful in a way that was terrifying.

No Line fully admitted the extent of their powers, so I was always cautious.

Sighing heavily, Vox turned on his heel, striding down the hall toward the back stairs that would lead directly to the roof. Clearly, he expected me to trot after him like a faithful puppy, and I ground my teeth that I would be forced to do so.

Then I remembered that this was for Avalon, my Soul Tie. I would crawl across broken glass for her.

He was up on the roof by the time I climbed the ladder, and I knew he was flexing his powers. Everything was a show of strength. "Well, Taeme. I'm here, and this is as private as it'll get with all those talismans around your neck."

The *tals* my family had gifted me before I came to Boellium had a range of uses, depending on each charm. The best one, though, was protection against the First Line's magic. It had cost my Line a lot, but had been forged and imbued with some of the strongest magic ever created.

I shrugged at Vylan's annoyed expression. Annoying Vylan was one of the many joys of my life. "This will be fine." Stepping closer, I lowered my voice anyway. We were similar heights, and this close, those ice chips he called eyes were even more cutting. As I watched, his pupils blew wide, and he sucked in a breath.

Interesting.

Keeping my voice low, I tried not to growl as I told him, "Stay away from Avalon Halhed."

His shock was almost comical, but it quickly folded into his normal scowl. "Fuck off, Taeme."

Gritting my teeth, I resisted the urge to headbutt him. "I mean it, Vylan. She's mine, so keep your fucking hands off her."

"No." He raised an eyebrow. "Why should I? She isn't *yours*. She's not of your Line, she's not in a relationship with you, and even if she was, you don't own her. If she decided to stop rolling around with animals and find her way into my bed, you'd have no recourse for it. She's her own person."

I curled my fingers into fists, resisting the urge to throw a punch at his smug face. I couldn't tell him that she was my Soul Tie. The existence of Soul Ties was a Third Line secret. "It's not like that with Avalon."

His snort was dismissive. "Find another new conscript to fuck, Taeme. I happen to like the little Ninth, and she's very... handy." His pause was exaggerated, and the beast inside me rose up, the urge to rip the throat from our rival almost overwhelming.

"You will speak of her with respect," I snarled, making the smug expression on his face falter.

He inclined his head. "I meant no disrespect, Taeme. I find Avalon refreshingly without artifice."

Whirling away, I paced, trying to burn off the rage bubbling in my chest. "She's more than refreshing to me, Vylan. She's more... everything. We have a connection." It was as close to the truth as I'd allow, and even that made me vulnerable.

He paused. "Perhaps I understand the feeling more than you'd think." He sighed. "Stop prowling around. We can have a civilized conversation about these things."

I wasn't convinced we could. Still, I sucked in a deep, calming breath and sat down on one of the long couches that dotted the rooftop. "I'm not sure there's a solution here, unless you agree to release her from whatever arrangement you have going on."

He slumped onto the couch beside me. "Scared she'll like me more?" I snorted, but didn't say anything, and he shook his head. "I understand what you're feeling perhaps *too* well. It's like she's dragging you toward her, even though she hasn't done anything but simply exist?"

He couldn't possibly feel what I did, because the First Line didn't have Soul Ties. The idea of mates was exclusively a Third Line thing. But did the First Line have a similar concept?

I dismissed the idea immediately. They married off their females for political gain, like they were worth the same amount as two mules and a bag of grain. They definitely didn't believe in the idea of divine-ordained soulmates.

Despite that fact, I couldn't discount Vylan's feelings.

Maybe I should just murder him. I could make it look like an accident, right?

"Whatever you might feel for Avalon, nothing can come of it, and we both know it. All you can offer her is heartbreak. Or do you think Daddy Vylan is just going to accept a girl from the Ninth Line as an acceptable wife for you? An Heir she might be, but we both know that your family wouldn't accept her."

It was rhetorical. We both knew they wouldn't. The

way Vylan's jaw audibly cracked from the way he was clenching it told me everything I needed to know.

He crossed his arms over his chest. "Oh, and yours would?"

I gave him a smug-as-fuck expression. "Absolutely."

Vylan was an annoying bastard, but he was smart. He knew there was something I wasn't saying; it was in the calculated way he looked at me. I knew there were things he wasn't saying as well, but I respected the pompous fuck enough not to beat the answers out of him.

"You're right," he said softly, and honestly, I would've been less surprised if he'd taken a swing at me.

"What?"

He huffed something that might have been a laugh. "I said, you're right. Anything I could have with Avalon would have an expiration date. My family wouldn't accept even an Heir from the Ninth." He leaned forward, his hands on his knees. "Even if she'd been from the First Line, she probably *still* wouldn't be acceptable. I won't have a choice in who I marry. I'll be forced to spend my years with some conniving little social climber, or some poor soul who doesn't want to be with me either, and we'll resent each other 'til death do us part. There's no chance of anything as fanciful as love or desire, or even mutual like."

He waved a hand at the rooftop. "These short years are the only freedom I will get, Taeme. This is what has to sustain me for the rest of my long, miserable life. And if that means I have to fight with you to spend time with a woman who makes my blood sing in my veins—for reasons I don't fucking understand—then I will."

His eyes weren't like ice chips anymore. Something was burning inside Vox Vylan, a rage that spoke to the beast inside me. I slumped back against the couch, shaking my head in disbelief. Did I feel pity for him right now?

Unlikely.

Well, maybe. I'd met his family. Met his father, who was a cold, cruel psychopath. Met his mother, who was about as maternal as a dishmop. Met his brother, who made me shudder with revulsion. There was no question in my mind about why Vox had turned out so cold, even though there appeared to be something human left inside him.

However, there was no level of pity I could feel, no amount of empathy in my heart for him, that would make me give up Avalon. I'd rather give him my left hand than step back from my Soul Tie. We only had a year left here at Boellium. Then we would go off to our respective Lines and only ever see each other at Conclaves.

I couldn't step back from Avalon Halhed, but could I share her?

I wet my lower lip, really examining the idea of *sharing* Avalon with Vox. I imagined her hands on him and gritted my teeth. *Maybe not.*

Then I imagined him pleasuring her with his mouth, or holding her legs open with his elemental magic as I fucked her.

My cock twitched. *Well, okay, maybe then.*

I couldn't believe the next words that came out of my mouth. It felt like someone else took possession of my lips and tongue as I said, "Well, I guess we could share her for the next year."

For the first time in my entire life, I saw Vox Vylan truly shocked. His jaw fell open, his eyes went wide, and he puffed out a soft whoosh of air. *"Excuse me?"* His voice must have gone up an entire octave.

I cleared my throat, shaking off my own disbelief. "For the next year—until we graduate and go off to our respective Lines for our familial duties—we share Avalon Halhed. *If* that's what she wants," I added quickly. This might be all extremely redundant, considering pinning down Avalon was like catching a shooting star. She mightn't want either of us, let alone both of us.

Vylan stared at me for so long, I was sure he was going to disagree. In which case, I'd have to sneak into his dorm in the middle of the night, incapacitate him, then take him out to sea and drown him. Consequences be damned.

Finally, as if he was just as shocked, he nodded. "I guess you've got a deal, Taeme."

I smirked, feeling suddenly lighter. This felt right. "If we're going to be co-boyfriends, you should probably call me Hayle."

He groaned, burying his face in his hands. "I take it fucking back already."

Oh, maybe this would be fun.

chapter fifty-three

Avalon

THE MUSCLES of my legs felt like they'd been seared in a firepit as I climbed the stairs to the atrium roof. I'd told Vox that I would meet him there tonight, mainly because I'd wanted to lie in the bathtub and hope that my body magically regenerated. The instructors had drilled us hard to assess our stamina in training today, and now I couldn't feel any of the muscles below my navel.

At least I hadn't vomited over the rail, like half the class. I'd waited until we were dismissed, then puked in a bush just off the path back to our rooms.

Vox's jacket was bundled tightly in my arms, though I'd picked it up and put it down at least three times before leaving my dorm room. I wanted to keep it so bad; something about the scent of Vox that remained in the fibers was soothing. Which was creepy as hell, and borderline stalkerish. It had been that line of thought that had me grabbing it as I walked out the door.

Besides, I wouldn't want to be accused of being a thief, and who would believe that the Heir to the First Line had voluntarily given me his jacket?

No one. Even the concept was ridiculous.

Climbing the stairs to the Upper Line dorms slowly, I kept my head down, but obviously the Goddess wanted to add to my misery today. As I made it to the fifth floor, I had the misfortune of running into Ephily Ingmire and a group of her friends.

Fuck.

Keeping my head down, I tried to scoot around them and up the next set of stairs, but she moved herself into my path. "Um, excuse me, are you lost? What are you doing above ground level? Dirt scrabblers aren't allowed up here. It's the only place the Upper Lines can escape your stink." She curled her lip in disgust as her friends tittered behind her.

Goddess, I hated this entitled little witch.

My brain scrambled for an adequate excuse to be up here. Ephily wouldn't believe that it was at Vox's invitation. Besides, I didn't even want to tell them what he was doing up on the roof. I'd seen how excited he was last night, seen the joy that staring at the stars brought him, and knew that it was something private, something he didn't want to share with anyone else.

So I held up his coat. "I found his jacket and was told that I should bring it up to the First Floor dorms. He insisted on it." My voice sounded higher than normal, but I doubted Ephily would know that.

She reached for the jacket. "I'll take it. I was going to

see Vox anyway," she purred, and I could just imagine her sashaying into the First Floor dorm like she was the savior of outerwear.

I looked at the beautiful woman in front of me, who was definitely the type of person that Vox Vylan would marry. Connected, gorgeous, biddable. I'd never seen her look like anything other than a painting created by a master artist. Her clothes were tailored to fit perfectly, her makeup expertly applied with a practiced hand, making her look naturally flawless.

She'd look so good in those First Line portraits that were distributed to all the Lines, like we were meant to salute their visage every morning. It was how I'd known what Vox Vylan looked like before I even arrived at Boellium. I'd watched him grow through his official family portraits.

However, the Vox of last night, his eyes alight as he described meteor showers and constellations, looked nothing like the boy with the sad eyes in those paintings.

Suddenly, I wanted to deny Ephily any chance of getting her hooks into him. She would smother any joy that was left in Vox Vylan; I knew it in my gut. Shaking my head, I gripped the jacket tighter. "He insisted it should be me. I don't want to be punished."

The lie left my mouth so smoothly, a result of years of practice. Lying to avoid punishments. Lying to avoid my father, or the guards who knew that they could kick me around a little and my father wouldn't care. The ones who hated they weren't in a position of privilege, yet I was, so I was an accessible outlet for that impotent rage.

Ephily glared at me. "I'm sure it will be fine." She tugged at the jacket, and I held it tighter. We weren't outside, so she couldn't use her terraforma powers on me, though someone more powerful from her Line might've been able to bend the stone from the walls. But Ephily wasn't an Heir. She was just like the rest of the conscripts—a sacrifice.

"No." I met her eyes. I would not be moved on this.

She glared back at me, then smirked. "Fine. I'll walk you up. Wouldn't want you getting ideas and stealing from the Upper Lines. I know that's how you dirt scrabblers get by."

I was going to punch Vox in the chest for that stupid name. It was usually used against the Eleventh and Twelfth Lines, because it was very dry out west, where there were vast fields of desert.

However, the Ninth Line Barony was near the mountains. If there was any dirt for us to scrabble in, it was under three feet of snow and frozen solid.

I turned and strode up the stairs, trying to think of what to do next. Maybe I should just hand over the jacket, go back down to my dorm, and apologize to Vox tomorrow. I'd use the downtime to work out a better way to get to the roof, so I didn't have to go up the dorm stairs and be subjected to this fun little interaction again.

We climbed the stairs in silence, with Ephily's little troop of clones behind her. As I reached the door to the

First Line's dorm, I sent out a silent prayer that Vox hadn't left yet and that he'd play along.

Reaching around me, Ephily knocked. She looked smug, which gave me a bad feeling. My stomach sank when it was Shay who answered the door. She looked at me, then at Ephily. "What?"

In the face of Shay's coldness, Ephily seemed to shrink back a little. "Is Vox in?"

Shay sucked on her teeth, continuing to glare at the woman beside me. "No."

Ephily shoved me forward a little. "This girl from the Ninth Line stole Vox's jacket, and I've brought her to you for punishment."

I whipped my head around. "You lying bit—"

"You can't trust those Lower Lines," Ephily continued sweetly, talking over me like I hadn't even spoken.

Shay just gave her a dead-eyed look. Damn, I was glad I wasn't on the other side of that expression. "Indeed. You can go now." She stared down the group until they left. Once they were all down the stairs, she looked back at me. Her eyes were too appraising, as if they'd weighed and measured me, and found me wanting. I resisted the urge to squirm beneath her scrutiny, until finally, she nodded. "You can go now too. Take the jacket with you—it's cold up there tonight."

I blinked at the woman in front of me. She was powerful; I knew that from the rumors that went around Boellium. But the awed whispers were not about her strength, they were about her cunning.

"You're kind of scary, you know?" I told her softly, and she cracked a smile. A genuine smile.

"Thank you. Now go." She waved a hand at me. As I turned, she whispered, "But Avalon? If you betray him, there isn't a corner of Ebrus where I won't find you and make your life a fucking misery."

I nodded, hightailing it out of there before she decided to preemptively cut me down. I didn't exactly know how she thought I could betray him while making maps of the sky, but I'd promise her my left tit to get out from under that all-seeing gaze.

I hurried up the short set of stairs that led to the roof, but stopped dead in my tracks. Vox was at the telescope, which was unsurprising. However, lying on the couch, his feet up on the armrest and a book in his hands, was Hayle.

I blinked and shook my head. This couldn't be right.

They weren't fighting or glaring at each other. Normally, they could hardly be in the same auditorium without sharing barely veiled insults and flexing their powers against one another.

"Did I trip down the stairs and injure my head again?" I asked, and Vox lifted his eye from the telescope.

"You're late."

I shrugged. "Apologies, Your Highness, that I'm late to this unpaid job you demanded of me," I teased, smiling so he knew I didn't mean it. "I had the misfortune of running into Ephily on the stairs."

Hayle grimaced. "Did she try to grope you as you walked past?"

Vox grunted his agreement.

Surely she doesn't actually do that. "Uh, no. She tried to have me punished by Shay for the theft of your jacket. Shay very satisfyingly put her in her place, which was almost worth it." I shuffled over and held out the jacket to Vox. "Here it is, by the way."

Vox looked down at me, his normally piercing eyes dark in the shadowed light. "You still aren't warm enough. You need to bring your own jacket." He held it up for me. "Put it on."

I didn't want to tell him that my father hadn't let me leave for Boellium with my jacket. I'd known I'd have to smuggle out actual clothes, but I thought he'd at least give me the decency of letting me take my coat.

He hadn't.

Luckily, it was spring, so even the mountains were warmish. Except at night. Those first few days, I'd almost frozen to death. But as I moved further south, it had gotten warmer, so I'd forgotten the need for one. Until now.

Not arguing with Vox, I slipped my arms in, and a soft noise behind me had us both looking at Hayle.

"Um, I'm surprised to see you here." *Without bloodshed.* I kept that last bit to myself, not wanting to tempt fate.

Hayle put his book down, standing and stretching lazily like a big cat waking up from a nap. He swaggered over to me, an intimate smile on his face, the one that made my heart pound in my chest. "I enjoy being outside at night, and the rooftop atrium has the best view of the stars. Besides, you're here, which makes it the only place in the world I want to be." He grabbed my hips and brushed his lips across my cheek.

My eyes felt impossibly wide as they bounced between Vox and Hayle, Hayle and Vox. Waiting for something: a fight, an explanation, an exorcism. *Something.*

Vox rolled his eyes and looked back down into the telescope. "Taeme invited himself along to our nightly gatherings."

My brain stuttered. "And you don't mind?"

He looked up again, his gaze drilling into mine with an intensity I didn't understand. "No, Avalon. I don't mind." He dropped his face back down. "As long as he doesn't get in the way of our work."

With a low chuckle, Hayle lifted his hands from my hips and backed away. "You won't even know I'm here."

Vox snorted, then suddenly, he went rigid. "What did you mean you fell down the stairs and hurt your head?"

Damn it.

chapter fifty-four

Avalon

I DID my best to work beneath the collective gaze of Hayle and Vox. Not that they made it difficult on purpose. Vox was making his observations, moving back and forth between the telescope and where he sat across from me, writing in his thick notebook. Hayle just lay on the couch, reading the book in lighting so low that my eyes would have ached in his position.

"Can you even see the words?" I asked softly, and he gave me a crooked grin.

"One of the benefits of being in the Third Line—we have great night vision." He cast a quick look at Vox. I knew the Lines didn't like to discuss their strengths or weaknesses in front of outsiders. Especially if that outsider belonged to a Line that could be considered your rival.

I wasn't an idiot. Something was going on here, and I wanted to know what it was before I got caught up in some political pissing match. That wasn't my thing.

I put down my pen. "All right. What in the Goddess's name is going on?"

Silence echoed around the rooftop as they shared another look. *Nope. Nope, nope, nope.* I wasn't going to be the only person on this rooftop in the dark.

I speared Vox with what I hoped was a withering gaze. He just raised an eyebrow at me, his chin tilted up. Huffing, I looked over at Hayle, who closed his book slowly. Standing with effortless grace, he came and squatted in front of me so we were eye level.

"Avie, as an Heir of the Third Line, I have enhanced senses." That one was general knowledge. They had better hearing, better eyesight, better everything. They were the ultimate warriors. "Which means that I know that when you look at this asshole, your heart beats faster. Your eyes track his movements." He leaned closer to my ear. "And I know that you find him attractive, because I can scent your arousal when you stare at him for too long, like you're imagining how he'd feel sliding inside you."

My eyes felt they were about to pop from my skull, my face flushing red hot. It hadn't even been a week since I'd told Hayle that I felt this thing between us just as strongly as he did. It was one hundred percent the truth; even now, his lips lingering so close to my skin made my heart race. Resisting the urge to tilt my head toward him and steal kisses from those lips was nearly impossible.

Despite all that, I couldn't argue with what Hayle was saying. Vox Vylan did make my stomach bubble with butterflies, my core clench with lust. I wasn't going to insult us both by denying something he could so obviously sense for himself.

Vox looked smug, and I glared at him. "So? There are lots of attractive conscripts in Boellium that make me, uh, moist." I grimaced. "What's your point?"

The smirk fell from Vox's face. "I'm going to need names."

"Names?"

"Of the other conscripts who make you wet."

I frowned at him, because *what?* "Why?"

He went back to looking through his telescope like the conversation was beginning to bore him. At least, until he mumbled, "So I can have them castrated."

Hayle laughed, pulling me to my feet and gripping my chin with gentle fingers. "Let me be clear, Avalon Halhed. You are *mine*. I know right down to the very marrow of my bones that you're the one for me. Nothing will change that. Not even the fact that you so obviously lust after this asshole—even if he does walk around like he's got a silver spoon jammed up his butt." Vox gave him the finger, but there was no anger in it. My lungs had begun to burn from not breathing, but I didn't want to interrupt Hayle. "Because as much as I dislike Vylan, I like you far more. Anything in this world that will make you happy, I'll get it for you."

I just stared at Hayle, the earnest truth written all over his face. How could that be true? How could someone tell me they desired me so badly, and still be willing to share with their archnemesis?

I looked over at Vox. "You agreed to this?" Even more preposterous than the idea of one of the Heirs wanting me, was the idea that Vox would be willing to share *anything*—let alone a lover—with Hayle Taeme. Or anyone else, for that matter.

Instead of answering me, he uncurled from where he was still pretending to look through the telescope and walked over to me. He stood shoulder to shoulder with Hayle, before bending down, gripping my chin, and kissing me.

My eyes fluttered closed as stars burst behind my eyelids. It felt so right. Vox's lips were familiar, like they were made to brush across mine. When he finally pulled away, something had shifted inside my soul.

I didn't understand it. I wasn't sure I even *wanted* to understand it.

Hayle's words about the connection between us resonated with both of them. Like my heart yearned for them both like a greedy bitch, as if one of these beautiful men—who were well out of my league—wasn't enough. She wanted them both.

"You're both crazy," I whispered.

Hayle laughed, leaning down to kiss me as well, his lips overlaying the spot where Vox's had just been, their taste mingling on the tip of my tongue. My brain short-circuited as I stood there, my fingertips gripping the table like I'd float away without it anchoring me.

Trying to shake the lust from my brain and think about this logically was more hard work than I'd like to admit. "What will people say?"

Vox sucked his teeth, his eyes narrowing. "Nothing, if they know what's good for them." He sighed. "Outside of these moments, I wouldn't be able to acknowledge you how I would like. My father..." He trailed off. He didn't need to say more. The last thing I wanted was to be under the all-seeing gaze of the Baron of the First Line. The very idea was terrifying.

"So I'd be your dirty little secret until you move on, go back to Fortaare to marry some Upper Line princess?"

His jaw flexed, and he stared down at me with those mesmerising eyes. "Yes. Trust me, it's for your own safety."

It sounded like a poor excuse, a line you'd spin to some silly little girl to get them into bed, and if I was honest, it hurt a little. But I knew enough about his life that I had no doubt it was the truth.

Looking over at Hayle, I chewed my lip. "And you? Would I be your dirty little secret too?"

He reached out and dragged me into his arms. "Never, Avalon Halhed. You're mine, forever. I don't care who knows it: Boellium, my family—hell, all of damn Ebrus will know you're mine." He buried his face in my neck, giving me ticklish kisses on the sensitive flesh. I honest-to-goddess giggled, but when I looked over at Vox, the longing on his face was truly heartwrenching.

As if he could sense Vox's sadness too, Hayle pulled back and spun me in his arms, burying his nose in my nape. "I could use a hand," he said lightly, but that was unlikely. I knew from experience that Hayle could make me pant with little more than his lips and an index finger.

Vox's eyes caught mine, and I had no doubt he was asking me for permission. I silently granted it with a nod. As he stepped closer, his hands dropping to my hips, I could feel the heat of both their bodies pressing into me from all angles.

He dropped his face to mine, leaning down until his lips were mere inches away. "What magic do you hold, Avalon Halhed, that you have made us yours so completely?"

I just shook my head. I didn't have magic. But what we were creating right now, well, it definitely felt magical.

He dipped down and kissed me again, not as tentatively as the first time. It was full of yearning that singed my skin. His tongue slid into my mouth, chasing mine, owning me as much as he could in a system that was pitted against his happiness. I gripped the front of his shirt in my hands, especially once Hayle's palms began to wander between us.

Hayle stroked and petted, and when his fingertips traced the curves of the underside of my breasts, my breath stuttered in my lungs. I could feel his growing hardness at my back, while Vox's cock nestled against my stomach, making my brain feel like it might explode.

Apparently, they were taking this sharing thing seriously.

Abruptly, in unison, they both pulled away. My skin felt overheated, and I was breathing hard. Vox was staring at me with an intensity that pulsed in my core, his expression so hot, it seared through me.

Hayle nipped my ear, his low, rumbling chuckle like an electric pulse through my veins. "Oh, this is going to be way more fun than I thought."

"But only if it's what she wants." Vox's firm, yet still soft voice held authority that made my body tingle. "Is this something you want, Avalon? I can't promise you anything more than right now."

It sounded like heartbreak, if I was honest. To have Vox and then lose him to the Line system of supremacy. To know how he tasted, the face he made when he came, his laugh, his moans, his whispered words, then to see those stupid portraits one day with his perfect wife at his side? It would be torture.

"Yes. I want this." My stupid heart didn't care. I would have him, even if it was just for now. Even if it was only under the shine of the stars or in the darkness of early morning. Even if it was only with the steady acceptance of Hayle at my back.

I wanted it all.

The smile that pulled at Vox's cheeks was a genuine one. It had been the expression on his face when he'd told me about the stars, when he'd explained his passions. I was now one of those passions, and that was also worth the impending heartache.

Hayle squeezed me in his arms once more, then pulled back, his hands tracing down over the curve of my ass before he turned my face toward him and gave me one soft, final kiss. "Perfect. You're perfect." Then he slapped my ass. "Now, the night is young, and you have stars to draw."

With that, we all resumed our positions, like the world hadn't just erased and redrawn itself into something that was going to change me forever.

chapter fifty-five

Vox

HAYLE'S WORDS and Avalon's taste haunted me all through training and lectures the following day. It did feel like magic, this hold she had over me. Before Avalon, the idea of sharing a table with Taeme would have been abhorrent to me, but now I was okay with sharing a girlfriend? What magic did she hold that she'd taken us under her spell so easily?

My natural scepticism wanted me to suspect that it was all her doing, but the look of dumbfounded surprise on her face when we'd proposed our plan had been too genuine to be faked, unless she was an amazing actor or an even better spy.

No, something wasn't adding up, and I was irritated at myself. Irritated that I couldn't just let myself have this moment, this time, without looking for some kind of subterfuge. I couldn't even go to Shay with this, because she would likely kill Avalon first and ask questions later. She was steadfast in her protection of me, perhaps even a little overzealous. As much as I wanted to trust my gut, I hadn't survived this long without doing my due diligence. Which meant I needed to know more about Avalon Halhed and the Ninth Line.

Actually, I needed to know *everything*.

As always, the best starting point was first-hand knowledge, which was *definitely* the only reason I found myself sneaking down to the lower levels of Boellium in the early hours of the morning. Staying in the shadows, I picked the lock on the dorm door and slid inside.

Only to be met by a giant hound with teeth that glinted in the dim wall sconces.

Lifting my hand, I held him still. "Your master knows about this. No need to take my arm off," I whispered to the mutt.

No, not a mutt. Braxus's breed had been kept by the Third Line for as long as I could remember. They were tall and regal, beautiful and deadly. Even the First Line feared the war creatures of the Third Line.

The hound didn't move for a moment, but eventually, he huffed and stepped away. He trailed me to the bedroom, though, and I doubted that he was about to let me into Avalon's room alone. As if he'd heard my thoughts and agreed, he let out a quick bark, alerting Avalon I was here.

I glared down at him. "Jokes on you, furball, because I was going to wake her anyway."

A sleep-rumpled Avalon emerged from her room, her face screwed up in confusion in the low light of the common room. "Vox? What are you doing here? It's..."

She looked around for some kind of clock, but I realized the dorm didn't have one. How did she make it anywhere on time?

"Four a.m.," I provided. "I wanted to see you." I *needed* to see her. It was a compulsion that resided deep in my chest.

She squinted at me. "At this ungodly hour of the morning?"

I gave her a lopsided smile. "Yes. I want to get to know you, without Taeme being here. This was the only time that was convenient."

"Convenient for whom?" Sighing, she turned back toward the bedroom. "Well, let's do it under the blankets. It's freezing out here."

I hadn't noticed. The First Line prided itself on not feeling anything, let alone mundane things like cold, hot, or love. I didn't tell her that, though, just followed her into her room, hearing the hound huff an aggravated sound as she shut the door. I didn't do anything childish, like poke my tongue out at the beast, but I wanted to.

Avalon stumbled back toward her thin bed, while I looked around the room. It was empty of anything but the bare bones of life. Battered furniture. Scratchy blankets. The difference between our standards of living was stark. Guilt gnawed at my gut, but I pushed it away. I'd fix this, though I couldn't do anything about it right now.

"If you're done staring at my room like it's a filthy

barn, you can either get beneath the blankets or sit in the corner, but talk quick or I'm going back to sleep."

I toed off my shoes and climbed beneath the blankets. I wanted to feel her body pressed to mine. It wasn't polite, or gentlemanly, or appropriate in any way, but I didn't care. I was desperate to feel the curves of her body against mine. I stretched my arm out along the pillow, and she lifted her head to lay it on my bicep. My heart beat a little faster in my chest.

"I'm exhausted," she mumbled. "Why did we have to have back-to-back stamina training?"

I was fairly sure the instructors just liked to torment us. "You can be the best swordsman in the world, but without stamina, you're as good as dead," I told her softly. "Swing while you can, but if you have to retreat, you'll need to be able to run more than a hundred feet without puking."

She grumbled something beneath her breath, but didn't disagree. "What did you want to know, Vox?" My name, murmured in her husky voice that was soft with sleep, made my dick hard. I wanted her to whisper it to the darkness as I pleasured her.

My fingers brushed across the tops of her shoulder almost of their own accord. "Everything." Chuckling, I felt her shoulders lift as she breathed me in.

"You might need to narrow it down a little to start."

"Why'd you come to Boellium?"

She snorted and burrowed closer. "You're so warm."

I could be warmer, cooler, whatever I desired; most

powerful wielders of First Line magic controlled their own body temperature.

"I'm here because of conscription laws. You should know about those," she teased.

"But why you?" I pressed. "Why not your brother, or the stable boy, or some farmer's daughter? Why a female Heir?" I felt the tension stiffen her body, and I wondered if she really was a spy and was about to lie to me.

Instead, she sighed. "It's not a secret—at least, not in the Ninth Line Barony. My father hates me. He blames me for my mother's death."

"She died in childbirth?" It happened all too frequently, especially in the Lower Line Baronies that didn't have access to good physicians. Those wild, barren places where only the desperate people of Ebrus lived had higher mortality rates in general.

The tension in her body increased, like she was bracing herself. "No. It's widely believed that I murdered her."

The fuck?

Using every ounce of training I'd needed to survive my own childhood, I pushed down my reaction, placing it in a tiny box for me to open later, and kept my body language neutral. "Do you believe that? I wouldn't think it was something that could be so ambiguous."

Slipping away from me, she rolled onto her back and stared up at the ceiling. "Sometimes, yes. Sometimes, no. I was three. Logically, I know that there isn't anything a three-year-old can do that could be construed as intent. But sometimes, I have nightmares. Nightmares of me being too close to the edge of those cliffs, of ignoring her words to come back. I was a baby, so there's no way I'm actually remembering the real event. Plus, it changes almost every time.

"Sometimes, if the dreams are good, I come back to her when she calls, but she dies anyway. She trips on a rock and stumbles forward, going over the edge. Sometimes, I ignore her words and start to fall, so she lunges forward and pushes me back, but falls herself. Sometimes, I dream that the maid pushes her instead, but that might just be my mind finding a reason to hate her." As her voice broke, I dragged her a little closer to my body. "It was the maid who informed my father that my mother had fallen. She was entering the clearing with a picnic basket and saw me grab my mother and push her over the edge, like I was possessed by evil spirits."

The scoff that burst from my lips was unbidden. "You were *three*. A baby from the Ninth Line with no magic. Surely your father didn't believe that you'd suddenly gained the strength of a full-grown adult, able to heave your mother over the edge of a cliff?" The very idea was preposterous. You'd have to be deficient in wits to believe that bullshit.

She shrugged. "I don't know if he believed her or not, but he grieved his wife so wholeheartedly that it was whispered around the Barony. He needed a scapegoat, and I was conveniently there, unable to defend myself because my grasp on language was rough."

Because she had been a toddler. Keeping that comment to myself was harder than I imagined. "Surely, after the grief subsided, he could think about it logically?"

Her tiny headshake planted a kernel of something in my chest. Rage? A thirst for revenge?

She let her lips rest against my skin. "I think I became a convenient outlet for his anger. At least until Kian was big enough to stand between us."

Jealousy rose to fill the space of my rage. "Kian?"

"My oldest brother. The Heir."

Feeling like an idiot, I was glad she couldn't see inside my brain. Of course she meant Kian Halhed, Heir to the Ninth Line. I had met him once or twice at events, although he looked nothing like Avalon. He was a quiet, silent man. Serious. So unlike my brother, it was surprising that we even shared a country, let alone ancestors from long ago.

I'd also met the spare Heir of the Ninth Line. Whenever there was a Conclave, we were forced to interact with the other spare Heirs. I'd forgotten the boy's name, but he was much like his older brother, solemn and serious. What had that family seen? Why hadn't they protected Avalon?

"Your father hurt you?" I asked the question, even though I knew the answer. I had to hear her say it.

She shrugged again. "Physically? Yeah, in the early days. After Kian stumbled on my father trying to stab me through the chest in a drunken rage, my brothers worked together to make sure I was never alone with him. I think it shocked even my father, though, whatever Kian said to him that night. After that, he kept his punishments to the verbal variety."

I ground my back teeth so violently, I could hear the scrape in my ears. "I'm going to kill him for you."

She laughed bitterly, like I was kidding. She didn't understand yet the depths of my devotion, but she would. The Baron of the Ninth Line was living on borrowed time.

chapter fifty-six

Avalon

IT WAS odd having Vox Vylan in my bed. If someone had told me a month ago that I'd have the spare Heir to Ebrus beneath the covers of my single bed, that I'd *want* him there, I'd have laughed in their face and taken them to see a healer, because obviously, something would've been severely wrong with them.

Even dredging up all these old hurts was less painful, because his warmth was steady support. His almost dispassionate way of asking questions made me feel validated, and I smiled softly.

"It's ancient history, Vox. If I survive the next two years, I can go home and live up in the mountains by myself. I'll never have to live in the Keep again."

He scoffed, holding me closer to his body. "You're never going home to the Ninth Line, Avalon. Not unless you want to. Hayle won't allow it."

I narrowed my eyes, even though he probably

couldn't see it in the darkness. "Hayle doesn't tell me what to do. Neither do you."

He shook his head, his fingers still brushing gently across the skin of my shoulder. The spot felt like it was electrified. "Of course not. But you have options now, even if you decide you no longer want to pursue this… thing we have. No one in Rewill lifted a finger to help you. If you never want to return home, both Hayle and I will help you settle somewhere else."

Choices. He was giving me choices, something I'd never had before. But at what price? Nothing in Ebrus was ever free.

The thought was like a lead ball in my chest. "What is it you want, Vox? Why are you really here in the middle of the night? Because if it's for sex, I have to warn you, I'm probably not very good." I choked on the words, but he needed to know. This shit was escalating faster than I could have imagined, and while I felt like I was out of control, I liked it. "I've never had sex before." My fingers played across his chest.

His whole body tensed for the first time. I'd told him I murdered my mother—no reaction. Told him my father beat me—total calm as he plotted my father's demise.

Told him I was a virgin, and he got stiffer than a board. *Men.*

"You're a virgin," he said slowly.

"Yes. It's not a fucking big deal. Stop it."

I almost didn't hear his low, drawn-out, "Fuuuck." He slid from the bed, and the rejection stung. At least it did, until he started wrapping me in my blankets, swaddling me tighter than a newborn. Then he lay back down and dragged me on top of his body.

I raised my eyebrows, completely restricted. "Uh, what are you doing?"

He groaned and stared up at the ceiling. "Removing temptation. You're too beautiful. Too fucking tempting. And I owe that fucker Hayle so much for not being a territorial asshole. I'm not going to steal your first time from him."

"Excuse me? It's *my* first time. I can give it to whoever I want." I wanted to poke him in the chest, but my arms were trapped at my sides. "Pompous, bossy asshole."

He kissed me then. Soft, tentative, full of feeling, but way too brief. "Of course you can. And if you choose to let me be your first, I'd be so fucking honored." He sipped at my lips again. "But I can't give you forever, the way Hayle can. He can give you the world and more, but I can only give you this place and tonight. Your first time should be special, with a person who'll love you and take care of you until you're old and gray."

I shook my head. "Hayle doesn't love me."

He laughed. "Maybe not yet, but you've bewitched him completely. The Third Line believe in soulmates, though they think it's some big secret. You better come to terms with the fact that Hayle will follow you around like a faithful hound forever now."

The idea of having someone to rely on seemed like a

pipe dream. I'd had only myself for so long, I didn't know how to be any other way.

I jutted out my chin. "Maybe I want to taste a wide variety of, uh, lovers before I settle down. Maybe I don't just want one special person to love me forever and ever." I didn't even know what I was saying. I was just being combative, because I liked seeing the fire in those normally icy eyes.

He didn't disappoint as he gripped my chin, tilting my face toward his. "No others. Just me and Hayle," he growled, bands of air wrapping around me and lifting me up until we were nose to nose.

"Or what?"

He kissed me again, and being suspended in the air like this was both terrifying and a heady flex of power. "I'll give you so many orgasms, you'll beg me to stop." He lowered me slightly, so his lips brushed mine as he spoke. "And then I'll give you more, until you're a sweaty, incoherent mess. Then it'll be Hayle's turn."

My whole body shuddered, and I was glad I was wrapped in this blanket cocoon, so he couldn't see how his words made my body flush and my skin pebble with goosebumps. His smug grin told me that I wasn't hiding my horniness very well anyway.

He nipped my lower lip, then lowered me back down on the bed beside him with a sigh. "This isn't what I came here for tonight."

Resisting the urge to pout, I looked over at him, trying to shake out my arms. He was definitely holding the blanket closed with bands of air. "What did you come down here for then?" I let out a hiss of indignation. "Free my arms. I feel like I'm suffocating in this thing." He released me immediately, and I reached over and pinched his pec.

He hissed back at me. "Ouch." Now it was his turn to pout.

"You deserved that." I scowled at him. "Now, if you didn't come all the way down here from your golden tower to fuck me, what is it that you want?"

A laugh burst from him like a crack of thunder, making me jump. "You're something, Avalon Halhed. I came down here to see if you were a spy. Or somehow bewitching us with magic."

Now it was my turn to laugh. "A spy for who? The mountain goats of Rewill? Because I promise you, my father doesn't give a fuck about his own Barony, let alone yours. As for magic, no one in my Line has any that I know of. Father can't even predict what time the beer will run out, and it only gets weaker from there. Me included." My bitterness was so strong, I could almost taste it.

Vox pulled me back to his chest, this time entirely unwrapped. His warmth chased away the hurt feelings, the trauma of my past, everything but the feel of him. "I believe you, Avalon, I do. But something is going on. This connection between us is... odd. It feels so right that it makes me suspicious. Nothing's ever given me the same happiness that I feel right now with you in my arms, and I don't trust that emotion. How could I feel like this about a woman I hardly know?"

I nodded, understanding completely. I felt like I was a fish on a hook, being reeled through the waters of fate, unsure where I was going to end up, or on whose rod I'd find myself.

Well, I knew at least two rods I might find myself on, but that was neither here nor there. "You think it's magic?"

"Maybe something residual in your Line? Maybe an outside source who wants to use you to pit me and Taeme against each other, to cause division within the walls of Boellium, perhaps even in Ebrus itself." He huffed a laugh. "I don't think they could have accounted for the fact that Taeme is the sharing-is-caring type, rather than the territorial kind."

A stranger then, because if they thought Hayle was some kind of territorial animal, then they didn't really know him. His empathy and his innate need to care for his people would have prevented him from doing anything as rash as starting a war over me. "So you think we're under some kind of love spell?"

Vox shrugged. "There's no spell I've ever heard of that could do it, and Taeme wears enough *tals* to knock out a horse. But that doesn't mean it can't be done."

My mouth was dry. Was there someone out there messing with our emotions, our lives? "And if there is?"

He dragged me higher. "Then we take them out." He kissed my jaw. "Let me be clear, though, Avalon Halhed. For the next twelve months, you are mine. The yearning might be forced, but the attraction I feel is all me." He pressed his hips against the softness of my stomach, making me suck in a breath at the length of his hardness.

Swallowing hard, I tried not to think about how dauntingly large it was. "How will we find out?" I wiggled against him, feigning the need to get comfortable, but really, I just wanted to watch him squirm. There was something intoxicating about this power I had over him.

He groaned, tilting his head back and closing his eyes. "By going to the place guaranteed to have information. The library."

I knew Boellium had a library, one of the most impressive in all of Ebrus, second only to the one in Fortaare, but I'd never been. I smirked up at Vox. "This hellhole has a library?" I teased, and he nuzzled at my cheek.

"Of course it has a lib—oh my fucking Goddess, what the *fuck* was that?" he screeched, scrambling out of the bed, taking the blankets with him.

There, lying between our bodies, was Epsy. He yawned and stretched, then somehow twisted himself into something resembling knotted bread, and licked his butthole.

"Uh, that's my pet stolt. He doesn't bite." As if to contradict my very words, Epsy bared his teeth at Vox, but when I picked up the temperamental little furball and put him on the other side of me, he curled back up and went to sleep. "Come back to bed, Vox. There's time for a quick nap before the food hall serves breakfast."

Vox grumbled beneath his breath. "One day into an agreement with Hayle, and already I'm in bed with something that's probably covered in fleas." But he still wrapped me in his arms, tucking me beneath his chin.

And when I woke up two hours later, he was still asleep wrapped around me, with Epsy draped across his neck like a fur scarf, snoring gently.

chapter fifty-seven

Hayle

"I THINK we should start our research over in that dark corner between the shelves," I murmured into Avalon's hair. "I'll start by studying the way the current youngest daughter of the Baron of the Ninth Line blushes when I stick my tongue deep inside her p—" She slapped a hand over my mouth, her cheeks flushed, but I could smell her desire. She liked the idea.

"Stop. The Librarian scares the shit out of me, and I don't particularly want to bring her wrath down on our heads." Her eyes flicked around, like the woman in question would just appear. "Besides, we have to wait for Vox." When I frowned, she shrugged. "His rule, not mine."

"What do you mean?"

Someone coughing politely behind me had me looking over my shoulder. The Heir to the First Line moved like a ghost. It was irritating. "She means that she's a virgin, and while ultimately, the choice is hers, *always*"—his tone dared me to argue—"I thought that perhaps it would be best if her first time was with someone who could give her the commitment she deserves."

Avalon crossed her arms over her chest. "And *I* said that if I had to choose, then I would choose both of you."

My brain was emitting a low hum of white noise. The beast inside me rose up to take the reins. I picked her up and set her on my lap, kissing her with more ferocity than I'd intended, but she met my lips with her own desperate need. The primal part of my brain was ecstatic that she would only ever be mine, that I would be the first person to taste her and that one day, long into the future, I would be the last person to taste her too, Goddess willing.

My hands gripped her ass, kneading the firm flesh. If I lifted her a little higher, I could drag her pants down and push my fingers inside—

Vox kicked my knee hard, and I pulled back enough to growl at him. But he wasn't looking at me. He was looking behind me.

A throat clearing had me going still, and Avalon stiffening in my arms. "Mr. Vylan, Mr. Taeme, and Miss Halhed. What a surprise to see you here in my library. Together, at that."

Dragging my face from Avalon's, I set her on the bench seat beside me and turned my most charming smile on the Librarian. She was a no-nonsense woman, but I hoped my charm would get us all out of this predicament. "Librarian, you look lovely tonight."

She rolled her eyes. "Save the charm for someone else, Mr. Taeme. What do three Heirs require inside my library this late at night? I can assure you, there are better places to have an illicit rendezvous."

She was watching us intently, but I had a feeling she was also teasing us. I didn't have a lot of experience with the Librarian, especially not being subject to her hawk-eyed glare.

Luckily, Vox was used to his charm not working, mostly because he had the personality of a wet socks most days. "We are merely here to research, Librarian, of that you have my word. We are researching the historical magics of the genealogical Lines. For a research assignment."

The Librarian didn't blink. She stared at the Heir to the First Line in a way that would have gotten her head removed if she'd been staring at the Baron. Giving her head a small shake, she sucked the back of her teeth. "I see. I've got some texts prepared. Stay here."

She disappeared, and Avalon slapped my arm. "I can't believe you got us caught making out in the library. Fuck, if looks could flay, I'd be fileted on the floor right now."

I nuzzled her neck, unable to get enough of her. I wanted to fight her battles, wage her wars, and fuck her senseless. I wanted to be her everything. "Nah, she totally bought Vylan's pretty lies."

Vox slapped the back of my head. Once upon a time,

that would have ended with my hands around his throat, but it was hard to find anything close to animosity when Avalon was pressed against my side.

Rolling his eyes, Vox sat down too. "They weren't lies. That's what we're here to research." He quietly told me of their suspicions. About magic potentially creating the bond between us, that maybe there was some ulterior motive to the feelings that bubbled between us.

I could see his point of view. It felt too right, too familiar, like life had been lining us up to take the fall and we'd been moved into position like the pawns we were. But I also knew that what I felt for Avalon was greater than magic.

Though maybe this new-found tolerance for Vylan had its roots in magic. That would make sense.

Staring between the two of them, I decided to take a leap of faith. "It's definitely a magical bond between me and Avalon," I said softly, my eyes catching on Avalon's wide pupils and holding there, like I was drowning in their deep blue of her irises. "The Third Line believes we are the favored children of the Goddess, mainly because we have been gifted with soulmates. We call them our Soul Ties, the other half of ourselves. Our one true love. We know them viscerally, deep in our chests."

I gripped her hands as her lips parted. "You're that for me, Avalon Halhed. When I say I'm yours until the day my heart ceases to beat, it's because it belongs to you, and every pump of the muscle is at your whim. There will never, ever be anyone else for me."

The heaviness of the declaration sat between us like

a mantle she didn't know what to do with. She looked like a deer, caught in the sights of a hunter.

I leaned forward, brushing my lips across hers. "I can hear your mind overworking, Avie. There is no pressure for you to love me back like that. Not yet, anyway. I'm also okay that I might never be your all or nothing; I think I've proven I'm very good at sharing."

Her cheeks turned scarlet, and Vox cleared his throat. "The First Line is aware of the Third Line's belief in Soul Ties, Taeme. We're aware of a lot of things. Like not only can you command your beasts, but you can converse with them. It's what makes them amazing spies. You can also see through their eyes."

I froze at that last one—that was another tightly kept secret. What else did the First Line know? Did they know we could shift?

Avalon was tense in my arms. "Soul Tie? Those are the right words?"

I couldn't decipher the expression on her face. Why was she suddenly so pale? "Yes. It's kind of like soul-mates, but more. Our souls are tied together." I squeezed her tighter. "Avie, what's wrong?"

She shook her head. "I've heard that term before. In my dreams."

What the hell did that mean?

Unfortunately, I couldn't ask, because the Librarian reappeared, a stack of books in her arms. Vox raised an eyebrow. "You retrieved all these books this quickly?"

The Librarian sniffed. "It's my job to know what the inhabitants of Boellium might need, before they even know they need it themselves." She laid the books gently on the table between us. "The library in Boellium has been here for a very long time. Long before this was a war college. Long before the Line system. Some say even before Ebrus was named. It has its own magic, older and stronger than many would give it credit for. I belong to the library, not to the college."

With that, she left. That was super fucking weird, but okay. No wonder the Librarian freaked Avalon out.

Vox sat at the table, shifting Avalon until she was pressed beside us both. He ran his fingers down the spines in front of us. There were general titles, like *Genealogical Lines of Ebrus*, *Magic on the Continent*, and even *The Story of the Goddess*, which was a children's book parents read to their kids before bed. But also there were more specific histories of the Ninth Line, even though that wasn't what we'd asked for.

Did the library *know* that's what we wanted? Or did the Librarian know more than she was letting on?

I found my fingers drawn to an older history, the dark-green leather spine cracked, and the embossing worn. It was familiar in a way that I didn't understand. Had I seen it before? I pulled it toward myself and opened it.

An envelope fell out, addressed to the library at the Hall of Ebrus. It was stamped on a date we all knew far too well. The day the First Line had grabbed power, assassinating the entirety of the Second Line in a coup that echoed through the history of Ebrus. We'd all fallen into line after that. None were strong enough to stand against the First Line.

As I opened the envelope, a single sheet of paper fell out. Something about the gently curled script was also familiar, but I couldn't put my finger on where I'd seen it before.

The Ninth. The Ninth. The Ninth.

What did that even mean? The words reverberated through my head, like the knelling of a bell.

Setting it to the side, I looked at the book in my hand. It had a family tree scrawled by hand inside the cover, the different branches spreading across two pages. Someone must have been filling it in, because Avalon's name was there, beside her siblings.

Flicking through the pages, I skimmed the text about her ancestors, their powers, and anecdotes of their deeds, both good and bad. Whoever had written and maintained this book didn't pull their punches either. Stutgord Halhed's gambling addiction and eventual hanging was written about, right below Reginald Halhed's heroics in the Battle of The Coast against the Vylans of Fortaare.

This was before the Baronies had been assigned Line numbers, before we'd become a cohesive, governed country, back when there were borders and squabbles over land. There were accounts on how strong the Halhed family's precognition abilities were, how their foresight had won battles and filled their coffers.

There were pages and pages of much the same thing, following the timeline of the country from when democracy had come to Ebrus, the end of wars between families.

And then something changed. The Ninth Line, known for producing only sons, had a daughter. Ellanora Halhed. The Jewel of Rewill. The First Daughter of the Ninth Line.

She had pages dedicated to her. About her power, which surpassed that of her ancestors. About her suitors and her predictions. Her disappearance. The speculation over her death.

I looked back at the note that had fallen out of the front of the book. The date in the corner was months after her supposed death, no return address, just the name *'Ellanora Halhed'* in cursive.

My brain went round and round in circles, and I didn't realize I'd dragged Avalon back onto my lap and was rubbing my cheek reflexively on her arm until she buried her fingers in my hair, scraping her nails gently against my scalp.

"What did you find?" she asked softly.

I pushed the book in front of her. "Just that your ancestor disappeared, then sent a letter to the one place guaranteed to survive the First Line coup, months after she was gone. My gut says it's important."

The Ninth. The First Daughter of the Ninth Line.

I flicked back to the family tree, following the branches down, finding all the daughters until I got to

Avalon. The Ninth Daughter of the Ninth Line. That had to mean something.

"Maybe it means something. Maybe it doesn't," Vox answered, and I realized I'd been speaking out loud. "I don't think it's any secret that the Ninth Line doesn't have this level of precognition now."

Avalon snorted. "Not even close."

It continued to niggle at the back of my mind, but I finished flicking through the book. When I got to the paragraph on the death of Avalon's mother, she halted my hand. There was a portrait there, and I realized that Malina Halhed had looked almost exactly like Avalon, except where Malina had been blonde, Avalon had the deep brunette tresses of the Halheds.

The scent of her distress burned my nostrils, and I held her closer. Avalon ran her fingers over the image. "I look like her. I've never seen a picture before…"

I hated her father more than ever at that moment. Roman Halhed was living on borrowed oxygen. "She's beautiful," I whispered into her hair, and Vox reached over, gripping her fingers and twining them with his own.

"We'll remember her now. She won't be erased," he told her solemnly, and our gazes clashed over the top of Avalon's head. I knew our thoughts on the Baron of the Ninth Line were in sync. His time as Baron was coming to a very sudden, very bloody end.

Any doubts I had about this little arrangement with Vox were erased. Avalon deserved the whole world and all the love I could give her, even if it was his.

chapter fifty-eight

Avalon

OUR RESEARCH—AS well as, uh, other plans—halted as both Vox and Hayle got called to Fortaare for a Conclave, which was basically a meeting of the Barons and their non-sitting Heirs. Father would be there, as well as my middle brother, Bach. I missed my siblings, more than I'd thought I would. I'd thought that being away from Rewill would feel like such a relief, that I wouldn't miss any part of my life there.

But I missed my brothers, and the hunting dogs, and the cooks. Despite it being filled with bad memories, the Keep had been my home since forever.

"You're fully addicted to Hayle Taeme's cock. You've been useless for the last three days," Acacia told me sternly. "I mean, I don't blame you. I've heard rumors about his magic stick, but girl, snap out of it. No dicking is that good."

Viana bumped my shoulder with hers. "You just

haven't gotten laid in a long time, Cace. Jealousy's turning your hair green," she teased, pointing to Acacia's flaming red hair. "I can say that if I'd been subject to those Third Line *charms* on a regular basis, I might also be looking longingly at the sea, waiting for him to return."

I flushed, realizing I had indeed been looking toward the port. *Awkward.* "Let's go back to training. Besides, I haven't been subject to any Third Line charms or whatever."

"I can remedy that," a voice said, and Lucio appeared beside me.

I'd met him a couple of times now, mostly in passing, and he always watched me with an expression somewhere between awe and suspicion, which led me to believe that Hayle had told him about the Soul Tie thing. If my brother told me he had a magical connection with a random woman from a different Line, I'd probably be suspicious too.

I was trying to think of a polite way to say *no, thank you*, when Shay appeared and slapped the back of Lucio's head. "Not if you want to survive the day, fleabag." She looked at me. "Taeme won't be back for another four days, so I have to agree with the Twelfth—grow some ladyballs and stop pining."

Looking between the four people around me, I frowned. I doubted Boellium had ever seen a more mismatched group of people standing together without bloodshed. "One, I wasn't staring at the ocean," I lied. "Two, what is happening right now?"

Lucio gave me a crooked smile. "As the Third Line's second-in-command, I've been ordered to keep an eye on you. Well, me and Quarry." He nodded toward the raven who sat perched on the gate post, just watching.

Shay didn't say anything, because it was a secret that Vox and I were seeing each other, even from his own Line.

Acacia was watching the woman with suspicion. Her eyes flicked from me to Shay, to Lucio, then back to me. I saw the moment when she added two and two together, and I gave her a tiny shake of my head. I'd explain later, somewhere with no ears or eyes. She stared at me a little longer, before lifting her chin slightly in agreement.

The Twelfth Line might be low in magic, but that didn't make them stupid.

I pasted a smile on my face. "Thank you, but it's really unnecessary. No one cares about me within the walls of Boellium."

Shay snorted. "You aren't that stupid."

I flinched back. Acacia and Viana stepped in front of me—ready to defend my intellect, I guess—but I reached my hands out to stop them. They didn't need to be on the First Line's radar. "What do you mean?" I asked lightly.

Shay raised a taunting eyebrow at my friends, as if challenging them to continue. "You are openly fucking the Third Line Heir. He's committed to you in a way he hasn't ever committed to a person at Boellium, in all the time he's been here. One of his hounds follows you around at all times, and if they aren't here, you have his eyes and ears." She tilted her head at Quarry. "And the somewhat dull wit of his most trusted friend."

She stared at me, her eyes seeing far too much. "You're a target now. Any chance you had at being anonymous is gone, Avalon Halhed, and the more prepared you are for that, the better. If that isn't something you wanted, then I suggest you end your little affair now, because you've been thrust into the world of backstabbing and politics, whether you want to be there or not." She shook her head derisively, something like pity in her expression. "You're a fucking lamb, alone and unprotected, being led to the slaughter."

Blinking dumbly at her, I had no pithy retort as her words rolled over and over in my brain. What she'd said was painfully true.

Acacia stepped forward. "She isn't alone." She stood toe to toe with this woman who was so far above her station; to someone as powerful as Shay, killing Acacia would be little more taxing than swatting an annoying gnat. "She has the Twelfth Line. We don't forsake our friends." There was an underlying taunt in there, and I reached out, gripping her elbow before she got herself frozen into an ice statue on my behalf.

Shay continued to stare Acacia down, until to my surprise, she smiled. Shay Vylan *smiled*. It was a disconcerting expression. "Loyalty is something she'll need," Vox's cousin—and the second most powerful person at Boellium—said softly.

They held each other's eyes for a moment longer,

until the stubborn standoff turned from angry to something more charged. I definitely got the impression there was more subtext going on here than I could understand. You didn't have to be an emotional empath to feel the sexual tension so thick, you could cut it with a knife.

Just then, the instructor blew the whistle that released us from training, but no one moved. Shay straightened her face into the same imperious mask that Vox used as she flicked her gaze back to me. "Be careful." Her eyes slid back to Acacia. "Twelfth."

"My name is Acacia," she purred, but there was a little bite to it too.

Shay nodded once and turned on her heel, striding out of the ring. I blinked, my eyes flicking between her and Acacia.

Lucio whistled low. "That was so fucking hot."

Acacia raised a bright red eyebrow at him. "Be a good boy and run along."

He groaned beneath his breath, looking over at me. "I'll leave Leviat with you." He pointed to his war cat, who was licking her paw with an expression that might have been disdain for us all. Lucio looked back at my friend with heart eyes. "Nice to meet you, Acacia."

She gazed at him haughtily. "You can call me Twelfth."

With a lopsided smirk, he clutched his chest. "Yes, ma'am. I'll be seeing you, Twelfth." He strode off in the same direction Shay had gone.

Viana was fanning her face. "I'm not sure what just happened, but I'm going to need a cold shower."

Acacia's face finally flushed pink, clashing with the red of her hair. "Hush. Let's go. Our little Ninth Line adoptee has been keeping secrets." She dragged me back toward the atrium, dodging the people heading to the food hall.

"What about lunch?"

"Clancy made meal cakes. You won't want to miss them. Now, stop stalling," Acacia ordered.

I looked back at Viana. "Has she always been this bossy?"

Viana snorted a laugh and nodded. "The First Line is lucky she can't back it up with magic. Otherwise, we'd all be bending the knee before her throne."

The girl in question rolled her eyes. We descended the stairs in silence, and it wasn't until we made it to the bowels, striding through the common area and into Acacia's room, that I was content that there were no listening ears. No one would waste spies down here, because they believed that the Twelfth Line conscripts were little better than rabbits, prone to breeding and not worth much.

They were so wrong. I'd found more warmth, acceptance, and beauty down here than I'd ever seen in the Upper Lines. From the wall mural of the rolling sand dunes of Western Ebrus, to Clancy's culinary masterpieces that made my eyes roll back in my head, to the clothes and jewellery that were basically pieces of art—every single thing they did was with intention to create a community of appreciation, joy, and togetherness.

In my opinion, it was worth more than magic.

As Viana shut the door, Acacia put her hands on her hips. "You're fucking them both? Do you know what a dangerous game you're playing? If they find out, they'll tear each other apart, and then you. They're *powerful*, Avalon. The Third Line is territorial, and if Hayle Taeme finds out you're fucking his archnemesis..." She swallowed hard. "You're just a Ninth Line conscript, not a powerful Heir. You'll bear the brunt of their rage."

Her words were stern, but I saw real fear on her face. Fear for me. It warmed something deep inside my chest.

I shook my head. "I'm not having sex with either of them, but what we have is... something else." Something more than meaningless sex, anyway. "And I'm not doing it behind anyone's back, especially not Hayle's. It was his idea."

That dumbfounded them both. "Hayle Taeme had the idea to share you with Vox Vylan?" Viana reached out and grabbed my fingers tightly. "Are you on drugs? Some of the shit peddled by those Upper Lines can cause serious brain damage. We can help you get clean—"

Raising my other hand to stop her, I shook my head. "I'm not on drugs, V. I was just as surprised as you, I promise." I squeezed her hand in mine. "This can never leave this room, okay? Swear it?"

Viana swore immediately, but Acacia hesitated. "I

swear, unless I feel like your life is in imminent danger."

Was that good enough? I needed friends, and a friendship couldn't survive if it was based on half-truths and lies of omission. I'd have to take a leap of faith.

"Hayle says I'm his soulmate. He said he just wants me to be as happy as possible."

Viana let out a little whoosh of breath. "Well, getting double-teamed by two hot, powerful guys would defi-nitely make one part of you happy."

"And Vox?" Acacia prompted.

"Vox believes that there's some kind of magic at work, but we can't figure out who or what would benefit from us being... together. We've decided to roll with it, because one day he'll leave and have to enter into a political marriage with someone from the Upper Lines, and he'll live in miserably married convenience forevermore. I think he just wants to have this moment of happiness, without political maneuvering and social climbing. To be desired as Vox Vylan the man, not the Heir."

They both stared at me silently for a long time. Finally, Acacia spoke. "And Shay knows?" I nodded. "And Lucio?"

"I think the whole Third Line knows that Hayle is my boyfriend, but only Lucio knows that I'm their version of, like, a soulmate. Neither of them know that we suspect some kind of magic is at play. They wouldn't take that well."

Viana let out a long whistle. "Adopting you is the most interesting thing the Twelfth Line's ever done." She wrapped me in a hug. "Just know that whatever happens, we've got your back."

Acacia hugged me from the other side. "Even if we do think you're fucking insane."

chapter fifty-nine

Vox

I HATED that I was expected to attend the Conclaves. I had no input into the outcomes; I was just a ceremonial weapon my father trotted out to all the other Barons. *Look at my son. Even he is more powerful than you can ever imagine.*

It was true. I was probably stronger than all the other people in this room, and though I wouldn't admit it—even under punishment of death—that included my father. I was probably stronger than even my brother, though I'd never attempted to go head to head with him, mostly because I didn't want his First Heir mantle any more than I'd like my cock chopped off with a rusty spoon. So I showed my magic at seventy percent of my full capabilities and never fought back when my father exercised his own against me.

Irrespective of all my family baggage, today's Conclave was worse than most. The Eleventh and

Twelfth Lines had called it concurrently, and the topic was the effect of the extended drought in the Western Baronies. As usual, my father was being a condescending prick about it, even though he considered himself the ruler of all of Ebrus. He only ever wanted to rule the people he deemed worthy, and no one after the Sixth Line made the cut in his eyes.

Maybe once upon a time, I'd been the same. Apparently, Avalon's little friends had softened me to their plight.

No, possibly even before Avalon. It was hard to sit in the food hall every Conscription Day and not be affected by their sunken cheeks, or the way they fell on their food like they might never see it again. You'd have to be a monster not to have pity, at least.

Unfortunately for the Eleventh and Twelfth Lines, my father was indeed a monster.

"The management of the Baronies are the purview of each Line, Baroness Ulsen. We don't want to start a precedent of interference," he said with faux sympathy.

Ingrid Ulsen might have been the only female Baron on the Conclave, but it didn't make her soft. She was a ballbuster who would happily go into battle for her people, and wasn't cowed by the fact she was the only person around the table who had no magic. Although most of the Lower Lines had barely discernible magic, the Twelfth Line had none.

My father hated Ingrid Ulsen. Partly because he didn't think the Twelfth Line should even have a place at the Conclave, partly because she was a woman, but mostly because she didn't cower in his presence. I respected her all the more for it. If only I could exhibit that much spine.

Baron Jacob Abaster, of the Eleventh Line, glared with barely concealed venom at my father and his closest cronies. "Devastating weather conditions can hardly be considered a management issue, Baron Vylan. This is a once-in-a-hundred-year drought that affects us mainly in the Western edges of Ebrus. If you could send us even a moderate amount of aid, we could survive until the drought breaks. People are dying—the elderly, the sick, and the young. Our livestock are starving." He looked stricken. "Our people are *starving*. We need help."

Baron Ingmire of the Fifth Line was tapping his glass impatiently. "And what kind of aid is it you require?" His tone was bored, like he was trying to hurry this all along. A sentiment I might have agreed with, once upon a time.

Jacob Abaster looked between all. "Food would be ideal, especially things like grain, dried legumes, anything that can last for a long time in dry storage. Dried meat. Powdered milk for the young. Money, if that is simpler." He looked at Baron Rovan from the Fourth Line. "Barring that, we'd like to borrow some strong magic users from the Fourth Line to break the drought over the western peninsula."

Roderick Rovan was a weasel of a man. Powerful

enough to have ideas of grandeur, he was of the same ilk as my father. He curled his lip at the Barons of the Eleventh and Twelfth Lines. "Once-in-a-hundred-year drought, you say? What did you do last time this happened?"

Baroness Ulsen speared him with a glare so hot, it was a wonder he didn't incinerate on the spot. "We died, Baron Rovan. Both Lines dwindled to barely a hundred people from each Line."

Someone muttered about them not taking long to replenish their population, and I did my best not to frown. It was a bias long held by the Upper Lines—that the Eleventh and Twelfth Lines had no talents, except lying on their backs and procreating.

Baron Rovan gave her a smarmy expression. "Perhaps that's the Goddess's will. My Line is loath to interfere in the plans of a higher power."

He was taunting them. The Upper Lines didn't really care about the will of anyone except themselves, but the Lower Lines—especially the Twelfth Line—rooted much of their society in their honoring of the Goddess Ebretha.

My eyes slid to Hayle and his father, Viktor. Hayle's jaw was clenched, but he was doing a good job of burying his real thoughts deep down. It was only because I'd spent so much time with him recently that I knew he was imagining flaying Rovan alive, or perhaps letting his hounds feast on the man's entrails.

He looked at his father, and once again, jealousy

pierced me in the chest. A person would have to be blind to miss the way Baron Taeme adored his sons. He was proud of them, not just as extensions of himself, but of the men they were.

Hayle and his father had a silent conversation, their eyes meeting, but I was paying close enough attention that I saw Baron Taeme give a nearly imperceptible nod. Maybe they could speak to each other mentally? Maybe they just knew each other well enough to convey their thoughts with an expression alone?

"I find it hard to believe that the Goddess would wish her progeny dead, Rovan. And if she did, I find it hard to believe that it would be her most devout followers. Others, perhaps, would be more understandable." Well, you didn't have to be a genius to hear that jab at the Fourth Line by Baron Taeme. "The Third Line will send aid to the West. If the Baron of the Seventh Line is amiable, we could send food directly across the ocean from our stores in Hamor and save weeks of transportation."

Everyone turned to look at Baron Lunderov. The Seventh Line lived on the island of Bine, in the middle of the Alutian Sea, right between the Eastern and Western portions of Ebrus, yet somehow, not a part of either. They were enigmatic people, prone to staying in their own world and leaving politics to the rest of us. They were mostly fishermen, who caught the vast majority of Ebrus's seafood. With their ocean-reading abilities, even their small amount of magic kept their Line prosperous.

Lunderov narrowed his eyes on Baron Taeme. Clearly, he didn't like being put on the spot. But I could see his eyes soften as he looked over at the Barons of the Eleventh and Twelfth Lines. "Of course. The Seventh will also provide aid and transportation."

After that, more and more of the Lines offered aid, and I watched my father's face get stormier and stormier. In the end, almost everyone from the Fifth Line onwards offered aid, with the notable exception of the Ninth Line.

Avalon's father was a large man with a sickly pallor, probably from years of heavy drinking. I couldn't see any resemblance to Avalon at all. She was beautiful and light, yet this man looked like he sucked the goodness —and the ale—from every room he entered.

Beside him, looking angrily at the table beneath his hands, must have been one of Avalon's older brothers. I'd never paid much attention to him before, but now, I appraised him critically. Though there was nothing of Avalon in her father, there was definitely a small familial resemblance with the brother. I'd forgotten his name, and it was irritating me. Bart? Brett?

No, Bach. As if he could feel my eyes on him, he looked up, his irises the same dark blue as Avalon's. His lips thinned, and he gave me a cool expression. I gave him my own haughty one in return. I couldn't let on that I knew his sister. If my father got even a whiff of an idea that anyone mattered to me, he'd make their life hell.

Finally, the Conclave concluded. We all stood

quickly—the urge to be away from this place and the other Barons was almost universal. I watched the Ninth Line as they left, and it looked like the younger Halhed was trying to convince his father to offer aid, but I knew from my spies there was no aid to offer. They had no discernable crops, and Baron Halhed had drunk most of his Barony's coffers dry.

At least Bach Halhed was trying to do the right thing. It took everything inside me not to steal the air from Roman Halhed's lungs and let him suffocate to death, but now wasn't the time. Not in front of the rest of the Conclave. Not with a power that was so easily traced back to my Line.

But he was living on borrowed time.

My eyes slid to Hayle again, and I saw he was also glaring at the Halheds, his eyes flashing with a rage I knew viscerally.

Following my father down the hall, I could tell from the posture of his spine that he was angry. Livid, even. He didn't like it when the Conclave moved against him, even if it was to save the lives of other citizens of Ebrus. In his mind, he'd made a declaration, and what Viktor Taeme had done was tantamount to treason.

Our palace was connected to the Hall of Ebrus by a long marble walkway. In between the two buildings was a courtyard, complete with large fountains and topiaries so high, it felt like they spiraled into the sky. Manicured gardens perched in neat square beds and were maintained almost to death. Not even a stray leaf dared to grow out of place.

As soon as we were through the doors of the palace, my father swiped a hand and launched a vase across the room. Selling that vase would have fed a village in the West for a month. My father really was a psychopath.

"Those fucking *leeches*," he seethed. "Always wanting more. They shouldn't even have their own Baronies. If I wanted some fucking wasteland in the middle of nowhere, I'd take it from them and burn it to the ground."

I pushed down the disgust I felt about sharing DNA with this man. "At least the Conclave ended in a win-win. They get their aid from someone else's pocket, and we don't have to lift a single finger."

My father whirled on me, and immediately, I knew I'd said the wrong thing. I felt his air snake around my throat, lifting me high, until only the tips of my toes touched the ground. Enough to strangle me, but not kill me. It was his favorite position to punish me in.

"Win-win?" he growled. "What part of that fucking fiasco felt like winning to you?"

I was prepared for the airlash—one of hundreds I'd received in my life—but still, I flinched. I hated that I flinched.

"They went against *me*, their ruler. Their First Line. They forget their place, but I can bide my time. A couple of misplaced ships full of food going down will end this dissension once and for all." His air power gripped my throat tighter, and my vision started to go splotchy around the edges. "You forget your place too.

But reminding you will be much easier and far more enjoyable."

The lashes began in earnest, one after another with no reprieve in between, and I screwed my eyes shut. I couldn't be sure when they ended, because consciousness escaped me first.

chapter sixty

Hayle

I CHEWED the inside of my cheek raw while standing in the corner of the banquet room, watching the Barons drink and eat, like we hadn't just had an entire meeting about people starving. I could see the guilt on the faces of the Barons of the Eleventh and Twelfth Lines, like they wanted to box it all up and take it back to their people.

I'd overheard the Baron of the Eighth Line, Zier Tarrin, telling them to eat. That their Lines needed them to be strong, and denying themselves out of guilt wouldn't help their people.

Zier Tarrin was the youngest Baron at the table, and his Barony was both the most magical and the most wealthy in West Ebrus. He'd been quick to pledge aid at the Conclave, but I had a feeling he'd been doing it long before the Eleventh and Twelfth Lines had come here to beg.

Avalon's father was drunk, spilling ale down his

chest and eating food messily. He was talking too loudly to some of the guards, most of whom were humoring him as they did their job. I wanted to punch that fucker until he threw up all the ale he'd imbibed. I wanted to beat him for every moment of sadness that he'd given Avalon.

Her brother was nowhere to be seen, and I was glad for that too. Seeing one of her brothers made me feel conflicted, because while Avalon seemed to love them and didn't blame them for what had happened to her, none of them had stood between her and their father.

If my father was treating one of my siblings the way Roman Halhed had treated his youngest daughter, he would either be exiled or six feet in the fucking ground. As far as I was concerned, the Halhed brothers were spineless, and I had no time for people who wouldn't stand up for their family.

Growling low, I left the banquet room. Maybe I'd try looking in the library here at the Hall of Ebrus for answers to Vox's hypothesis. They'd have better records of whether or not someone had the power to influence behavior. No one since the more powerful members of the Second Line had been able to do that, and they were long gone.

The First Line had been nothing if not thorough in their eradication. They'd used the Lines of heraldry like hit lists. They'd murdered every man, woman, and child with even a hint of Second Line blood running through their veins in the space of forty-eight hours.

I met my father's eyes as I left, and he lifted his chin,

recognizing that I was skipping out on the niceties of the banquet. It wasn't like I was the only one. Along with Bach Halhed, Vox wasn't here either. Maybe they were having a party somewhere and hadn't invited me. Or maybe Vox was torturing him for being a spineless fuck for so long. Either way, I might have been a little jealous.

My footsteps echoed on the marble floors as I moved from one area of the Hall of Ebrus to another. It was the grandest building in the country, but I hated it. It was cold and loud, and filled with assholes. How did the First Line live, surrounded by all this white stone? It was like somewhere a person would go to die.

I was nearly at the large doors to the library when my nose twitched. There was a scent in the air that shouldn't be there.

Blood.

Blood and Vox.

Following my nose, I found him in one of the darkened alcoves that had once been used as a place to light candles and ask favors of the Goddess. I doubted they got much use anymore—at least, not here in Fortaare.

As soon as I saw Vox, I knew something was wrong. He looked pale and sweaty, his face screwed up like he was in pain as he twisted to one side.

"Vox? What the fuck?" I hissed, hurrying deeper into the shadows. As I got closer, I knew the blood I could smell was his.

His eyes rolled up to meet mine, and he grimaced. "I'm fine, Taeme."

"Like fuck you are. You're bleeding." I stepped even closer, but he put up a hand to stop me.

"Go. We shouldn't be seen together."

I snarled at him. "I don't give a fuck. You're injured."

He just shook his head weakly. "I'll be fine. I've healed from much worse. I just needed to be somewhere quiet."

Fuck me. "Get up. I'm taking you to my room."

He shook his head again. "Can't. Probably bugged."

This was bullshit. "I don't care." I reached out and grabbed him under his arms, pulling him to his feet. "Is there anywhere in this Goddess-forsaken city that's private?" He hissed in pain, and I felt bad. I needed to see his injuries.

"Probably the library. Father tried to install spies in there, but they always disappear within hours," he said weakly. I'd never heard Vox sound weak a day in his life. It was making me feel anxious.

I gripped his chin. We were similar heights, but he always seemed so much bigger, with that giant stick up his ass. When he was this vulnerable, he seemed smaller, and I hated it.

"I'm going to walk out of here, and in exactly two minutes, you're going to walk out after me. You're going to meet me in the library in one of the private meeting areas. If you take more than two minutes, I'm going to come back and find you, and when I do, I won't give a fuck who sees. Understand?"

Seeing his glare actually made me feel better. "Even injured, I could kick your ass, Taeme."

Grinning, I just pointed my finger in his face. "Two minutes. I'm counting. One... Two... Three..." Hurrying down the hall, I didn't have time to appreciate the intricately carved doorways, similar to the ones back at Boellium. I didn't stop to look for the Librarian, just moved off to the side to one of the many soundproof rooms.

And then I waited.

Thirty seconds.

Sixty seconds.

Ninety seconds.

He still hadn't appeared.

I was getting ready to stand and go back into the hall to fetch that stubborn fucker when the door opened and he slid inside. He looked even worse; his skin had turned gray, his lips now thin and tight with pain.

"Show me where you're injured." It wasn't a question. I wasn't sure why I needed to see, but I knew Avalon would be upset if anything happened to this asshole. That's why I cared. The only reason.

Vox rolled his eyes. "No. I'm okay, and its none of your fucking business."

Stepping closer to him, I grabbed his cheeks, squeezing his face between my palms. "Despite how I feel about you personally, we're all in this together. Avalon is my Soul Tie, and I'll protect her at any cost. And for some unfathomable reason, she really likes you, which means you're mine to protect and care for too—at least until whatever you guys have runs its course. Now show me, or I swear I'll strip your clothes off and find it myself."

There was a flash of something in Vox's eyes, but it was quickly chased away by pain. He unbuttoned his shirt agonizingly slowly, then allowed the silky fabric to fall from his shoulders. He held my gaze defiantly, but I walked around him, checking for the wounds I could smell so easily.

I didn't have to look hard. There had to be fifty raised welts on his back. Some were so vicious, they'd split the skin and were still gently oozing blood.

It was a punishment the Third Line would give to its worst betrayer, not to its most prized Heir.

"Who the fuck *did* this?" Even as I said it, I knew. There were only two people in all of Ebrus who could do this to Vox Vylan. His father and his brother.

Vox's expression was his usual shuttered mask. "Doesn't matter who. You can't do anything about it."

I hated that he was right. "Why?" There was no good reason to brutalize anyone like this, let alone someone who was your flesh and blood. The why didn't matter, but I had to know.

"I had the audacity to agree that everyone got the outcome they desired from today's Conclave."

My teeth ached with how hard I was grinding them. His father. I hated that fucker. "We'll go back to Boellium tonight. I don't care if I have to manufacture drama to make it happen. Fuck it, I'll manufacture a whole damn Line war, if it means you don't have to come back here." I gripped his face again. "Never again, Vox."

He shook his head slowly, defeat curling him in on himself. "And when our time at Boellium is up? You can't keep that promise, Hayle, but I appreciate the thought."

There was a knock on the door, and we both froze. I moved between Vox and the doorway, my eyes narrowed like I had X-ray vision. In my head, I called for my hounds, who were close by. They'd tell me who was out there and if they were a threat.

They sent me back an image of the Librarian.

I walked slowly up to the door, opening it just a crack. I didn't trust anyone in this place, except my father. "Can I help you?" My voice was haughty. Obviously, I was channeling Vox's normally cool demeanour.

The Librarian was of indeterminate age. I suspected mid-thirties, but she had fine lines around her eyes that could've been from the passage of time or from squinting while reading tiny texts. "Such a loaded question, Heir Taeme. But in this instance, I believe I can help Heir Vylan." She lifted a jar of healing balm. "From the supply of traditional healing medicine that I regularly order from the Twelfth Line. It will stop the bleeding and aid in reducing the swelling and pain."

How could she possibly know about that? Did she have this room under surveillance? "I'm sure I don't know what you're talking about."

She shook her head at me, like I was an errant child.

"Undoubtedly. However, it is my job to know all things. It was my Goddess-gifted purpose in life." She stared at me, until I felt about three inches tall. "I promise you that my intentions are honorable."

I narrowed my eyes, trying to look for the deceit. In my experience, nothing came for nothing, especially not here in Fortaare. "In exchange?"

She shook her head again. "No strings. But if you'd like to exchange favors, I have a parcel of books that need to go to the library in Boellium. If you could take them with you on your return travels, I would consider it a fair trade. I believe Librarian Enora might be in need of them soon."

I hadn't realized the Librarians had names. I mean, obviously they did, but we never called them by anything other than their honorific.

I could take some books back with me. In fact, it might give us an excuse to leave. Everyone was wary of the Librarians. There was power in knowledge.

"Sure, we can do that, in return for your discretion."

The Librarian gave me a determined, if somewhat sympathetic, expression. "The library is a place that prides itself on the gathering and safekeeping of knowledge, Heir Taeme. But we also value privacy and the right for people to research topics without political backlash." She gave me a look that saw far too much. "Your secrets, and that of those you hold dear, are safe in the library."

To the wrong ears, her words would be considered

treasonous. That was enough of a reassurance to me. "Thank you, Librarian."

She gave me a soft look, not quite a smile but something warm, before folding her face back into severe neutrality. "The answer is always in the library, Heir Taeme. It's a valuable lesson that I believe that Ebrus has forgotten." She turned and walked back toward one of the many darkened corners of the library. "Collect the parcel of books from the front desk on your way out," she said over her shoulder, not waiting for my response. She disappeared into the rows of shadows and began shelving before I could reply.

Clutching the balm in my hand, I turned back to Vox. The Librarians really freaked me out.

chapter sixty-one

Avalon

MASTER PROXIUS WAS PERSONALLY TEACHING our History of the Line System lecture, which was new. One of the instructors had been called home for a family emergency, and apparently, Master Proxius had volunteered.

"As you can see from the maps, not all of Ebrus was populated until after the Line system was introduced by the Vylan family six hundred years ago, when Hopus Vylan was at the family's helm. The most powerful family of elemental wielders, they held a great amount of control over the running of Ebrus, even prior to the Line system. In fact, they could have set themselves up as a monarchy, rulers of the country, yet they didn't. Does anyone know why?"

The silence around the room was deafening, and Master Proxius looked vaguely disappointed. I'd read about this somewhere, but I didn't want to answer and be wrong. I already had too many eyes on me.

Still, no one else answered.

Finally, I raised my hand. "Because he wanted the country to be united, and believed in every person having a say in a democratically run system."

Master Proxius gave me a proud smile. "Excellent, Miss Halhed. Yes, Hopus Vylan believed that we were stronger together, and that no one person should exercise absolute power over the lives of others. Does anyone know why this was?"

This time, I had no idea.

"No, I guess this one might have been struck from your school's teaching materials. It was because Hopus Vylan was in love with—and would later marry—Aurelia Hanovan. The Vylan and Hanovan families had feuded for generations, but the marriage between Hopus and Aurelia heralded a century of peace. The Line system was set up, giving all the major families a place at the table when it came to issues governing the country. Trade routes were opened, with Lines moving freely across the country for the first time in memory. It was an age of prosperity, and many of the great cities were built in this time. Fortaare, Hamor, and of course, the war college, although the Dome and atrium were already here."

His face grew serious. "However, as with any age of both economic and societal growth, there is always eventual unrest. It's a slow, insidious thing. The idea that someone else has more than you, even though you deserve it. The idea that more power, more magic, should come with more boons. As if by not subjugating those around you entitles you to some kind of reward for your restraint. These ill feelings festered between the Lines, until one event changed the shape of Ebrus again forever. Does anyone know what it was?"

Eugene raised his hand. I fucking hated Eugene on sight, though I didn't know why. We'd barely exchanged a single word, but there was something about his slimy, reptilian eyes that put me on edge.

"The First Line uprising."

Master Proxius nodded. I wonder if he'd chosen to have this lesson today because Vox wasn't here. Shay was sitting in her section, surrounded by the other First Line conscripts, looking bored.

"Indeed. The First Line uprising. It was two nights of carnage, but eventually, the First Line emerged victorious, and they have led this country since. But an uprising of this brutality doesn't just come from nowhere. Much like the love between Hopus and Aurelia created an era of peace, it was love—or perhaps obsession—that brought low what they'd created, hundreds of years later. Does anyone know what I'm speaking of?"

Shay raised her hand. "I assume you're speaking of Ivan Vylan and Oris Hanovan. They both wanted the same woman as a wife."

Master Proxius nodded his head. "Correct, Miss Vylan. They had both requested the hand of Ellanora Halhed, of the Ninth Line. Despite being rebuffed by the lady herself, they both believed that it was due to the other man, and not that they personally lacked the charms to woo her. She was quite the beauty, though," Master Proxius said softly, his eyes on me. "Unfortunately, her life was cut short, and she disappeared, believed to have been murdered quite soon after their rejection. Both men believed the other had stolen Ellanora, or had her killed so no one could have her. They blamed each other. Tensions festered, first between the men and then between the Lines, until a few months after Ellanora's death, it bubbled over into violence. The First Line uprising happened."

Ephily snickered quietly. "Poor Ninth. You missed out on the magic *and* the looks from your ancestors, apparently. Ugly, talentless bitch." Fortunately, no one else could hear her words as everyone was engrossed in the lecture.

Silence fell, and Master Proxius spent a moment looking at all the faces in the room. "At the end of the uprising, every last person from the Second Line was eradicated. Whole villages were burned to the ground. Mass graves were dug all through the Second Line Barony. When it came time for the Conclave to come together, the Barony borders were redrawn and whole Lines found themselves uprooted and moved to somewhere else, especially those who were seen to be aligned with the Second Line or deemed not strong enough to protest."

So the Eleventh and Twelfth Lines, then.

Master Proxius moved on, and I sat back in my

chair, turning over his words. I was glad Ellanora hadn't lived to see the fact that her rejection had caused the death of so many. I couldn't even imagine the guilt that would've come from that.

I thought about the note that Hayle had found, addressed to the library at the Hall of Ebrus. Had she seen what would happen and killed herself in an attempt to stop the bloodshed?

There were so many answers lost to history. There was nothing any of us could do about it now; we were stuck in a reality that two men who couldn't take no for an answer had created.

The class was eventually dismissed, and Quarry hopped from my desk to my shoulder. I scratched his head, and he made a soft cooing sound by my ear. Hayle's animal companions had accepted me whole-heartedly, which made me feel, well, special.

I missed Hayle, though. And Vox.

Stepping out of the classroom, I smiled. It was a beautiful day, clear with only light winds. If I were a raven, it would be the perfect day for flying. "Go and stretch your wings. Leviat will be here soon to walk me to dinner."

Cawing, Quarry launched himself into the sky, but I saw him circling around. He wouldn't go far.

The Twelfth Line had some kind of religious festival today, so they'd been excused from all their classes, and I missed them. In such a short amount of time, I'd become accustomed to not being alone anymore.

Someone grabbed me from behind, and clearly, I'd

also become complacent because I smiled as I turned, thinking it was Viana or Acacia. But when I spun, it was Eugene Rovan.

His grip on my arm was almost painful. "Can I help you?" I hissed, and he swung me against the wall, pressing his forearm to my throat.

"No. You can't help me, or anyone." He was looking down at me with such barely contained venom, I wondered if I'd accidentally pissed in his eggs this morning. "I just wanted to see what had turned Hayle Taeme into a pussy, but quite frankly, I don't understand it." He leaned closer, his hand going from where it was clenched around my bicep to being wrapped painfully in my hair. "You're ugly, fat, and magicless. You must have a fucking amazing vagina to make him go all starry-eyed. Master Proxius was eye-fucking you too. Are you spreading those legs for the Headmaster, Ninth?"

His face was briefly overlaid by my father's, and my knees turned to water. Old fear made my body numb, paralysed by wounds that were deeply entrenched in my soul.

"Weak and useless. It makes no sense," the person above me said, not with my father's deep baritone, but with a nasal whine.

This man wasn't my father. He was *nothing*. It was enough to shake me from the fear that had a hold on me.

"Get the fuck off me," I hissed, pushing at his chest. Quarry was suddenly there, his huge claws aiming right at the side of Eugene's face, scoring deep cuts as if he was trying to fly off with the flesh of Eugene's cheek.

The man in question screamed, not just at Quarry slicing open skin, but the fact that Leviat had arrived and was tearing flesh from his ass muscle. The giant war cat snarled as she swung her head, ripping him away from me and onto the ground.

Clouds quickly formed over the school. *Fuck.* He was going to use his weather abilities. No one knew the perils of bad weather like someone raised in the North, and I didn't want to see what Eugene would conjure if he feared for his life.

Leaping toward Leviat, I trusted that she wouldn't take my arm off as I grabbed her by the scruff of her neck. "Leviat, stop! He isn't worth eating. Goddess knows where he's been," I said cajolingly. "Come on, drop him now. I don't want you to get into trouble."

To my surprise, Leviat dropped him. *Huh.* I'd thought it would be harder to get her to give up her prey. Maybe he tasted as vile physically as he was mentally.

A low growl behind me made my heart pound in my chest. "Oh, the trouble has already arrived," a familiar voice purred, and I spun to launch myself straight into Hayle's arms. He'd returned.

Braxus and Alucius stepped between us and Eugene, and Braxus took Eugene's throat between his jaws. Hayle held me gently as he glared down at Eugene.

"One wrong move, and Braxus is going to rip your

throat out. I'll call it an accident. It happens." He set me down, and Leviat immediately curled around my thighs. We watched as Hayle prowled closer, squatting down in front of the bleeding man. "Your time is done, Eugene. You can live, and swear on your own pathetic life that you won't so much as look in Avalon's direction again, or you can be the brainless fucker I know you are and mouth off at me so I can end you now. Your choice."

There was hatred in Eugene's eyes when he looked at me, but eventually, he showed what a coward he was, turning his face away.

Hayle gripped his chin. "You're going to swear it on your life, Eugene."

"I swear it," he spat out, ripping his face from Hayle's grasp.

Standing, Hayle kicked him in the ribs. "I almost hope you're lying, so I can put you down like the rabid animal you are." Then, like someone had flicked a switch, he gave Eugene his normal charming, cocky grin. "You might want to get that bite checked out. War cat bites can cause some seriously nasty infections."

With that, he picked me up in his arms and carried me away. He didn't stop until we were through the atrium, down the stairs to the lower levels and in my dorm room. I didn't argue. Being pressed into his chest eased an ache that I hadn't even known was there, like an injury that just festered before it was cut out.

What *was* surprising was that Vox was sitting on my

couch in the middle of the day, looking disheveled. Something about his demeanour seemed… off.

Hayle walked to the couch and dropped me down beside Vox. I looked between them. "Is everything okay?"

Vox dragged me into his lap, burying his face in my hair. "It is now."

chapter sixty-two

Avalon

I PULLED Vox closer to my body, wrapping him tightly against me. There was a desperate feeling in the air; something had happened. It was in the tense way that Hayle was holding himself, and in the air of desolation sitting on Vox's shoulders like an ugly cloak.

Reaching over, I gripped Hayle's fingers, but my attention was still on Vox. "What happened?"

Vox shook his head, tilting his face so his lips were close to mine. "Nothing unusual. I'm just happy to be back. Even happier to have you in my lap." He closed the gap between our lips and kissed me softly, but it was infused with so much feeling, it almost tasted like a goodbye.

Clutching him closer, I deepened the kiss. He groaned into my mouth and buried his fingers in my hair, holding me so close, I wasn't sure I could come up for air unless he allowed it. I didn't care.

Hayle's hand started to roam my body, up the curve

of my hip until his thumb brushed the underside of my breast. I ripped my mouth away from Vox's and looked between them. Two sets of eyes looked at me filled with desire; one forest green and one ice blue. "Is it time?"

Tilting his head back and staring at the ceiling, Hayle inhaled several deep breaths before he looked back at me. "It's time, Avie. Let us show you how good it can be."

Vox's hand trailed up my thigh, squeezing the flesh gently. "We can give you a first time that none of us will ever forget."

Nerves buzzed along my veins, but were quickly quietened by anticipation. I knew in my gut this was perfect. The perfect moment, the perfect people—even if there was one more person than I'd traditionally expected.

"Yes please," I breathed, and it was like I'd released the beasts from their cages. Vox lifted me easily in ribbons of air, floating me between them as he kissed me fervently.

Hayle pressed against my back, his hands every-where. "Bedroom. I need a large, soft surface to do my best work," he rumbled, his voice rough with lust.

Vox snorted. "Not me. I could just…" I squealed as he shifted me with his air, until I was lying horizontal, my legs spread wide, with Vox positioned between them. My body was completely cushioned, and if I didn't know better, I'd think I was lying on a bed.

Whistling between his teeth, Hayle moved so he was standing by my head, leaning over to kiss me. "Well, this could be even more fun than I thought. I'm not second-guessing my decision to allow you to horn your way into my relationship now, Vylan."

Rolling his eyes, Vox flipped me back upright and set me on my feet. "Come on, Ninth. I want to be nose-deep in your cunt within the next five minutes, or I might actually go insane."

My core clenched at his words, and I almost sprinted to my dorm bed. With the two of them in my room, it seemed tiny, little bigger than a closet.

Laughing as he pulled off his shirt, Hayle nudged Vox with his elbow. "Fuck, I forgot how small the lower level dorm rooms are. Hope you don't mind if our junk touches, Vylan, because there isn't enough room to swing a cat in here, let alone my massive cock."

"You know what they say about people who boast about their dick size, Taeme. They're usually full of shi —" Vox trailed off as Hayle dropped his pants, and his long, naked length was right there, on display.

My jaw dropped. There was no way that fucking thing would fit inside me.

Vox raised a brow. "I stand corrected."

I was still staring at Hayle's dick. Mesmerized and terrified. Like I was going to watch a steam train try and go through a storm drain.

Hayle groaned. "Baby, if you don't stop looking at it like that, I'm only going to last half as long as I want." He stepped toward me and lifted me into his arms, pressing me right along his naked body. His shoulders were broad and his torso was solid, and I wrapped my legs tightly around his waist. The feel of his muscles flexing beneath my fingers made me lose all higher reasoning beyond holding on tight as he captured my lips, fucking my mouth with his tongue. As he walked me back to the bed, I could feel his fingers fumbling with my buttons, though he didn't lift his head.

I felt the air on my overheated skin cooling me down, and I didn't know if it was just because I was running so hot, or if it was Vox's breeze giving me what I needed. It didn't matter; it had the same effect. My nipples pebbled behind my bra, my skin breaking out in goosebumps, and I groaned as everything became a hundred times more sensitive.

Gripping my bra in his fists, Hayle snapped it in half. I slapped his shoulder, but he grinned at me unapologetically. "I'll get you a new one. Maybe I'll get you ten, because I fucking love these glorious tits." As if to prove his own point, he buried his face between them with a happy sigh, but he didn't stay still for long. His mouth moved up the curve of my breast, sucking and nibbling at the soft flesh until he reached my nipple. He sucked it between his lips, and I felt my soul leave my body.

It felt so fucking *good*.

"Oh baby, I've only just started," Hayle murmured, pausing to look over his shoulder. "I mean, we've only just started."

I lifted my eyes from his mesmerizing green ones to see that Vox had used my distraction to get naked. Fuck, he was beautiful. Like white marble, he was all hard lines and edges. A weapon honed, until it was both alluring and dangerous. He was also packing a giant cock, and I started to wonder if maybe I'd just misjudged the size of men's penises in my mind. Like when you see a picture of a sea otter and imagine they're cute and small, but in reality, they're huge.

"He's kind of pretty, isn't he?" Hayle murmured into my ear. "Not as beautiful as you, but I can't wait to watch him fuck you. The Ice Prince and my fiery mate —mmmph." He was roaming again then, his hands and mouth mapping my skin.

Vox knelt at the foot of the bed, wrapping air around my ankles. He ran his fingers up the insides of my legs, tracing them like he was committing the lines of them to memory, then hooked his fingers in my pants. Lifting me lightly, he dragged them down my thighs and over my knees, until he could slide them off my feet and toss them to the side.

The whole time, his eyes flicked from my face to my core and back again. "I'm going to taste you now, Ninth. I've wanted to know if you taste as sweet as you look since the first moment I saw you in the courtyard."

We all collectively held our breath as he leaned forward, biting me gently on the fleshy part of my thigh before running his tongue up my center like I was ice cream. He hummed a happy sound, and I realized that Hayle was watching him with as much intensity as I was.

I gasped as Vox stopped at my clit and swirled his tongue around it, making my body strain and jolt like

I'd been struck by lightning. I hadn't thought anything could feel as good as Hayle's mouth on my nipples, but apparently, I was wrong.

I buried my fingers in Vox's inky hair, holding it tightly in case he decided to get up and run away or something. Maybe I was just holding on for dear life.

He continued to suck me gently. On and on and on, until I felt like my whole body was tingling, on the precipice of something… life-altering.

Just when I thought I was walking on the ledge, teetering toward the edge of an abyss, Hayle put his mouth back over my nipple and sucked hard. "FUCK!" I screamed, my leg shooting out and slamming into Vox's gut.

His, "*Oof,*" vibrated against my clit, which in turn made my thighs clench around his head. I felt like a contortionist as wave after wave of soul-rending plea-sure rolled through me, bending me in odd ways. Should my toes curl like that?

Vox looked up at me smugly. "Quite the kick you have there," he groaned, but I could see the humor mixing with the straight lust in his eyes. "We aren't done yet, Ninth. I'm going to slide my fingers inside this tight little channel and make you ready for us. No way you could take either of us yet, Avie." His fingers gripped my thighs, and he stared at the most intimate part of me, like I was a painting by a master artist. "Fucking beautiful. What I'd give to climb between these thighs every day and feast." He slid one finger inside me, and I gasped at the intrusion. "Hot and snug. Got to stretch you out for us."

Hayle was groaning, and I noticed he had one hand wrapped around his cock. He looked like sex personified. "Who knew our little prince had such a dirty mouth? I like it." There was desire in his eyes, and I wasn't sure it was only for me anymore.

I didn't have the brainpower to follow that train of thought, because Vox was stealing all my attention, sliding in another finger and then another in quick succession. His fingers felt cool and soothing, and I realized he'd lowered his body temperature.

He was so unbelievably powerful, and he was *mine*.

I was climbing higher and higher, pleasure making me squirm, so close to the edge, and then Vox stopped. "She's ready for you," he murmured to Hayle, and I whined. The whine turned into a whimper as he withdrew his fingers from me. "Don't worry, Avie. You won't be empty for long."

Hayle climbed onto the bed beside me, lifting me up until I was sprawled across his body. As I straddled his hips with my knees, my wet core ran up and down his wildly hard dick.

"Are you sure that will fit?" I asked, because I couldn't imagine what I'd tell the healers if it got stuck in there, or he split me in half.

"We're gonna go so slow," Hayle told me softly. His eyes were filled with something that I was scared to acknowledge. A feeling so all-encompassing that one wrong step might leave me broken and bleeding. "This is the first in a lifetime of moments that'll be just like this. You're mine, Avalon Halhed, and I promise that I will love you and keep you safe from anything that might hurt you—even my giant dick." Vox snorted a laugh, and I couldn't help but roll my eyes.

Kneeling behind me, in between Hayle's thighs, Vox pressed close to my back. "Let me help you," he whispered. He slid a hand between us, sliding those cool fingers through my wet folds. When his fingers were dripping, he reached down and gripped Hayle's cock, making the man in question jerk in his hand. "Gotta get you both nice and wet. Smooth the way," Vox murmured in my ear, still stroking Hayle. My eyes were so wide, they felt like they'd pop out of my head. "There we go." Then a tight band of air wrapped around my ribs, lifting me slowly until I was poised over Hayle's cock. The blunt head notched tightly against me. "Slowly now."

My chest was heaving in air, my nails pressing savagely into Hayle's chest, but the comfort of Vox at my back, holding me steady, soothed the nervous energy. As I pressed lower and lower, the pinch of Hayle filling me, spreading me, made me hiss. I could feel him *everywhere*.

"I can't take any more," I lamented softly, feeling like a failure, but Vox kissed my nape, his hands coming back around between us.

"Oh, you can, baby. You can take so much more. You're doing so fucking good right now. Look at your mate. You've melted his brain. The only person who'll ever put that look on his face again is you. My sweet, powerful, little dirt scrabbler," he teased. "Until you're ready, though, I'm here to help." Once again, he reached around me and wrapped his hand around Hayle's dick, right at the base this time. He must have squeezed, because Hayle groaned, his eyes rolling back in his head.

"Fuck, Vox, I won't last. Fucking asshole," he muttered, but he didn't tell him to stop. Didn't tell him to move his hand. I could feel the muscled circle of Vox's fist brushing my pussy.

Vox was chuckling low, like a master puppeteer who had us both where he wanted us. "Slide up, Avie, then move back down. Take as much of him as you can, and I'll take care of the rest."

At his words, I did as I was told, the perfect little marionette. Up and back down, until I reached the flesh of his fist, and up again.

The sensation. The pleasure. It was mind-wiping. I could think of nothing but the pleasure that was making my skin prickle, making electricity race through my veins. I chased that feeling like I was chasing down my prey.

More, more, more…

Sweat was trickling down my body, until the sensation changed from the hard fist of Vox's hand to the wiry curls of Hayle's groin. I was seated all the way, with Hayle buried so deep, I'd swear he was in my womb.

He was sweating, like he'd run ten miles under the

blinding heat. "Fuck, Avie, *fuck*. I love you so much," he groaned, his hands on my hips, lifting me up and down the long length of his cock. "Look how good you take me."

It was too much. I came on a wave of pleasure that made lights dance behind my eyelids. I screamed my release, as my orgasm pulsed through me. Vox came all over my back, and I felt the warm slide of it over my ass cheeks. Hayle jerked inside me as he came, his hands clenching my hips tight enough that I'd probably have finger-shaped bruises tomorrow.

Finally, I collapsed against his chest, suddenly noticing the gouges in his pecs. I kissed the one closest to my face. "Sorry."

He shook his head. "There isn't a single thing you should be sorry for right now. That was fucking perfect." He looked over my shoulder, then shifted more to the right so we were closer to the wall. I felt Vox collapse onto the bed beside us. He ran his shirt over my back, cleaning up his mess.

"Hottest thing I've ever seen," Vox murmured, kissing my shoulder, seemingly uncaring that he was pressed shoulder to hip, naked, with someone who'd once been his enemy.

Smirking, Hayle lifted his chin. "Thanks for the assist. I'll be sure to return the favor."

My eyes were sliding closed when I heard Vox's chuckle, his fingers ghosting over my spine. "I'm counting on it."

chapter sixty-three

Hayle

IT HAD BEEN three days before we'd emerged from Avalon's dorm rooms. Three days of sweat-soaked skin, of sharing, of pleasure and release. It had been the best three days of my life, and judging by the gooey smile on Vox Vylan's face, the best three days of his life too.

We'd done our best to ensure that Avalon was boneless with pleasure, or asleep because we'd wrung orgasm after orgasm from her body. But even now, weeks later, she was still smiling like she'd discovered the secret to life.

Fuck, I love her. It had slipped out the first time we'd had sex, but I'd told her over and over again since then. I never wanted her to doubt my feelings, not even for a moment. I knew it would be hard for her to say it back, but I could wait. She had trauma that she needed to work through, and I'd be here for her every step of the way.

The other great thing about our self-inflicted banishment into Avalon's dorm of ill repute was that no one had seen Vox arrive; most had thought him still in Fortaare. It had been a blissful escape from duty for the both of us, and by the end of the third day, Vox had seemed so much lighter that he was almost hard to recognize.

Shay had known he was down there, of course—as had Lucio—but she'd kept the news to herself. No one wanted Vox's happiness more than Shay. Well, except for Avalon and me now.

Which made the fact that this three-way relationship we had was on a countdown clock, endlessly ticking toward its expiration. I fucking hated it.

I didn't want Vox to return to Fortaare, to that fucking psychopath who'd brutalized him for his own weaknesses. To live a miserable life. There had to be a way to extract him from that life, I knew, but two weeks later, I was no closer to a solution.

Whenever I thought of the Baron of the First Line, I felt a rage so incandescent, it threatened to set me on fire. Not only had he fucked up his own son so casually, but a shipment of food, sailing from the stores of my home in Hamor to the capital of the Eleventh Barony, Tenby, had sunk in the middle of the Alutian sea last week. Tons of grain and dried fruit and meat were now at the bottom of the sea, due to "unseasonable" gale-force winds.

Vox had warned me that his father would try and sabotage the boats. I'd tried to warn my father too, in a way that didn't incriminate Vox as the source of information, and while my father had taken it seriously, there wasn't much any of us could have done in the face of that power.

Hell, we couldn't even pin it on the First Line. It could have been storm magic from the Fourth Line. The ambiguity meant no one could point fingers, so the Baron of the First Line got away with it, again.

We could send more grain, the other half of the shipment. But it wouldn't be enough to last the Eleventh and Twelfth Lines through the rest of the drought season. It was half of what they'd need, and it might keep them from dying, but it wouldn't keep them from starving.

I attacked a little harder, and the instructor in front of me grunted. "Easy there, Taeme. I like my head attached to my body," the older man muttered. He was another former soldier from the Dawn Army. A lot of the former soldiers would train with the First and Third Line conscripts. It kept their own training up, and they could call it "teaching."

I'd learned the arts of war at the feet of my father and his most trusted seconds; there wasn't much about fighting that this place could teach me.

"Sorry, Beury. Got caught up in the movements." I gave the man an affable grin. "Good to keep you on your toes anyway. Don't want you getting slow in your old age."

"Old?" Beury rumbled indignantly at my teasing. Honestly, he was probably no more than forty-five, but an assignment at Boellium had probably made him a little more fat and happy than his former comrades still in the Dawn Army. "I'll show you old, kid." He raised his sword and shifted his stance.

"If I could have a moment with Heir Taeme before you attack, Instructor Beury?" a soft, yet firm voice asked.

We both dropped our swords as we watched Librarian Enora pick her way across the sand of the training ring. It was weird to see the Librarian out of the library, let alone outside in the training ring.

Beury nodded quickly. "Of course, Librarian." He moved away, and I stepped hesitantly toward her.

"Can I help you, ma'am?"

She scoffed. "You can start by not calling me 'ma'am.' Do I look like I'm a hundred years old?"

Out in the light, away from the shadows of the library, she did look a lot younger than my original estimation, though I still wouldn't put a number on it out loud. I liked my balls attached.

"I need to see you, Miss Halhed, and Mr. Vylan as soon as possible in the library. It would be... beneficial if you came post-haste."

She didn't want to be called old, but she still used terms like post-haste. "Of course, ma—Librarian. I'll find them and bring them to you as soon as I can."

Librarian Enora looked worried, gnawing at her lower lip, but she nodded firmly. "I will see you as soon as possible, Heir Taeme."

With that, she turned on soft silk slippers that were not made for the training ring and hurried back inside the heavy stone buildings of Boellium. Her midnight-blue skirts flared behind her, barely touching the sand.

I wondered what Line the Librarian was from; much like the instructors here at Boellium, Librarians gave up their allegiance to their Line, to devote themselves to the libraries and knowledge. But they maintained their powers, and given the way the bottoms of her skirt seemed to stay a mere breath above the sand, my money was that Librarian Enora was from the First Line.

Interesting.

I looked over at Beury. "Raincheck? I have to run an errand for the Librarian."

He nodded and bowed lightly. I bowed back. It was a gesture of respect at the end of any battle.

"Of course. Between two soldiers, that woman scares the shit out of me."

Laughing, I slapped him on the back and went in search of Avalon. Then I'd have to find Lucio, who'd have to find Shay, who'd need to get a message to Vox. I hated the need for subterfuge.

I kind of missed the surly fucker, now we couldn't be seen together. But every night, we still climbed onto the roof of the atrium so Vox and Avalon could do their star charts and I could nap. Well, napped until we snuck inside the Dome, then fucked under a cone of silence until the sun lit the horizon.

I was sleep deprived, but I wouldn't change a single moment.

Avalon was training with her friends from the

Twelfth Line, and it was cute. She sucked. She was never going to be a swordsman, but she had pretty good aim, so I thought I might buy her a crossbow. Long-range weapons might be a better fit.

I didn't interrupt as they worked through the remainder of the battle, Avalon eventually yielding. Viana was a good swordsman, but even better with daggers. She'd nearly taken out Ephily's eye when she was badmouthing one of her friends a few weeks ago, and I doubted that Viana had missed accidentally. It had been a warning, and Ephily had kept her mouth shut since.

Viana said something to my girl, and Avalon looked over at me, her face lighting up. My heart squeezed in my chest at the joy in her expression. I wouldn't ever get tired of her looking at me like that. Like I was the best thing she'd seen all day.

She bounded over to me, and I wrapped her up in my arms. I didn't care who saw; the more people who knew she was mine, the better.

"Well, well. If it isn't Avalon Halhed, the one and only love of my life." I kissed her loudly as I spun her around. "Your sword skills are getting so much better," I said into the curve between her shoulder and neck.

"Liar," she admonished, but her tone was light and happy.

If I did nothing else but make her this level of happy for the rest of my life, then I'd go into the Great Beyond satisfied. I pressed closer, and she tapped my shoulder.

"Careful, I'm still holding my sword. Though I have

to admit, it's a novelty that I'm poking *you* with something long and hard for once."

My laughter echoed around the training ring, though no one really even looked anymore. Sure, there were still some expressions of disbelief, some of outright disgust, and more than a little jealousy, but it was becoming the norm now.

"The Librarian wants to see us. She says it's of extreme importance. I have to go find Lucio to tell Shay that the other one has been requested also," I whispered in her ear.

"I think I saw Lucio flirting wi—" She was cut off by Quarry cawing loudly overhead, sending me notes of alarm. I tensed, my mind connecting instantly with my raven.

Boats.

Guns.

Soldiers.

Surrounding Boellium?

That made no sense. *Who?* I asked, and he sent me images of an army I didn't recognize. Dark uniforms shot through with amber, an insignia I didn't know. How could a foreign invading army get so close without anyone sighting them?

"We're under attack," I told Avalon quietly. I had to tell the instructors. I had to tell Master Proxius.

Sirens sounded around the training ring, coming from speakers I couldn't even see. *"Boellium is under attack. Please return inside the walls."* More loud whooping.

What the fuck was happening? Gripping Avalon's hand, I called all my animal companions to me as I pulled her back toward the atrium. Braxus and Alucius came immediately. I looked down at Braxus. "Until we know what's happening, you stay with her *at all times.* You understand? She is your priority."

They both acknowledged my request. Braxus moved to Avalon's side, and she buried her fingers in his fur.

Fear like I'd never felt gripped me. Not fear for myself, but fear for her. Because if anything happened to Avalon, I knew I wouldn't be able to live without her.

chapter sixty-four

Vox

WHILE EVERYONE WAS OUT TRAINING, I was sitting in Svenna's gloomy office. The woman in question looked pissed as she paced back and forth. "What exactly did you want me to do about this, Vylan?"

I raised an eyebrow. Very few people would have the balls to speak to me that way. I could count them on one hand, really. "I didn't want *you* to do anything. If you cast your mind back to fifteen minutes ago, you'll remember that I asked to speak to Master Proxius."

She huffed. "Wouldn't we fucking all like that. Unfortunately, he had urgent business that took him away yesterday. Otherwise, he could deal with your… claims."

I'd wanted to warn Master Proxius about my father sabotaging the drought relief. I couldn't in good conscience let him kill hundreds of people over his pride. Hayle had said he'd told Baron Taeme, but that hadn't gone so well. I needed to warn someone who could speak openly, without it sounding like a political maneuver.

"I can't let them starve for ego, Svenna. I thought you, of all people, would understand that."

Defiance flashed in her eyes. "Don't patronise me, Vylan. I do understand. And just like you, my hands are tied. I can speak to my contacts in the Dawn Army, but what good would that do? Do you know who the army answers to, for all its perceived neutrality?"

The question was rhetorical. We both knew they answered to the Baron of the First Line. The shadow king of this Goddess-forsaken rock we called home.

Appraising her, I watched for tells, for even the hint she'd run and tell my father about this. Because despite the fact that he was the one killing the citizens of Ebrus, I was the one committing treason. "Surely there's an underground network we can utilize? I'm not an id—"

A siren sounded, making my heart leap into my throat. *Fuck.* Had this conversation made it back to my father already?

A soldier ran into the room, his eyes wild. "Where is Master Proxius?" he demanded, and Svenna held back a snarl. Barely.

"Not here. What is it?"

"We're under attack. There's an army off the shores of Boemouthe."

We both stared at him like he'd lost his mind. "The Dawn Army?"

The soldier was whipping his head back and forth so furiously, I was worried it would snap right off. "No.

I don't know the colors or banners. They just appeared out of nowhere."

How could an invading army just appear from thin air?

Svenna cast me a quick glance, and then I was forgotten. "Use the announcement system to get all the conscripts back inside the walls. *Now*, Redford!" she snapped.

She rushed to one of the ledgers, hauling it down and opening up a small compartment behind it, pulling out maps. She unfurled one on her desk, and I looked down at an image I'd never seen before. A map in which Ebrus was tiny, surrounded by the ocean to the east, west and south, but with what looked like a giant sheet of permafrost to the north.

That wasn't the surprising part, though. At the bottom of the map were other land masses, names printed neatly across them which were entirely foreign to me.

Bellineaux.

Ryland.

Ajix.

Veria.

None of those places meant anything to me. "What in the Goddess's name is this?" I breathed, and Svenna looked at me with disappointment.

"I thought you were a stargazer, Vylan. Surely, with all your study of celestial space, you didn't think we were the only people on this rock?" She pointed to a country whose shape I knew well. "Ebrus. History goes that during a catastrophic weather event, the ocean rose exponentially, wiping out half the landforms and life on the planet. Only the very top and very bottom of the globe survived. The ocean in between became uncrossable. No landmass survived in the space between. No islands. No atolls. Nothing but ocean. No boat could carry enough stores to make the distance, and why would they? There was basically nothing left up here but us, and we're hardly worth the effort needed to cross. We have no great resources. No gems or jewels."

"We have magic."

She shrugged. "According to historical records, so did they. So they forgot us, and by extension, we forgot them. Only the maps and histories in the libraries, and here in Boellium, speak of the times before the great flood." She ran her finger over the landmasses at the bottom. "It could be one of these countries, but why?"

I shook my head; I definitely didn't know.

Someone banged on Svenna's door, and she straightened. Gone was the surly administrator and in her place was the warrior who'd once been the pride of the Dawn Army for decades. "Enter."

There were several members of faculty here now, and not one of them seemed perturbed that I, a conscript, was there too. "Svenna, they've alighted on the beach. What do we do?"

There was a fire burning in her eyes now. "Call for aid from Ovl and Eaglehoth. Get word to the Third Line, if possible. They might be our only form of communication. We'll go down to the shore and see who the *fuck* dares to invade our island. Someone better prepare the conscripts for the possibility of a fight."

They rushed off to do her bidding, following her orders. Clearly, no one else wanted the mantle of responsibility.

I needed to find Avalon and Hayle. I needed to warn Shay and the rest of my Line. But Svenna was strapping on armor like she was going to go out there alone, and that wasn't going to happen.

I stared at the woman in front of me, one of the few people in this institution I respected. "I'm not letting you head out there alone."

Svenna had the audacity to roll her eyes at me. "You don't *let* me do anything." She strode out of the office and down through the atrium. Hundreds of students were there, looking freaked out, their whispers like a consistent hum through the room. Svenna paused. "We're under siege. Listen to the instructors and stay within the walls." Then she moved quickly toward the exit.

Shay appeared at my side. "What's going on?"

"Invading army, I think."

She looked at me like I'd lost my mind. "Invading from where? How'd they get all the way to Boemouthe without anyone being any the wiser?"

I leaned in close. "In Svenna's office is a map. Go there now and copy it down. We'll need it for later. Then get together with the First Line and inform them of what's happening. I want them to be prepared, in case we have to fight. Talk to Hayle or Lucio; tell them everything you know. Now isn't the time for Line squabbles." I hesitated, lowering my voice. "Make sure Avalon is safe."

Shay set her jaw as we made it to the doors of the atrium. "I'm going out there with you."

Shaking my head, I tilted my chin back toward the office. "Do as I ask. We aren't going out there to swing dicks. It's just fact finding, and I promise to let Svenna speak. Proxius is gone. She's the best we have for a commander right now, until the Dawn Army mobilizes." I nudged her with my air. "Go, Shay."

Glaring at me, she huffed. "If you die, I'm going to fucking piss on your corpse, Vox Vylan."

I smiled reassuringly at her. "I'll be safe, I promise." I hurried to catch up with Svenna, who reached out her one arm as we made it to the gates.

"Stay here, Vylan. If anything happens to me, Boellium will need your strength." I started to protest, and she quelled it with a look. "You can see me well enough through the gates, and we both know you have enough magic to put them down from here. So just fucking *stay*."

Clenching my jaw, I nodded and watched as she walked down the path toward the shore. She stayed in sight, like she'd said, but I was surprised when a young guy in a black-and-amber uniform climbed up the path from the beach, a smile on his face.

He spoke to her softly, but even stroking the wind toward me, I couldn't hear what they were saying. I frowned when Svenna turned, though, leading them up toward the college.

What the fuck?

Svenna was smiling as they got to the gates, ushering them through. What the hell was she doing?

"Svenna?" I called, and she looked at me softly.

That wasn't Svenna. She didn't have a soft bone in her body.

I pulled my gun and pointed it at the intruder. Up close, he was beautiful, which was an odd thing to recognize about an enemy. He had hair that looked like spun gold, burnished skin, and eyes that were almost black.

"Stop," I ordered, aiming the gun at his head. "I can kill you in the time it takes for you to blink. Who the fuck are you?"

The guy smiled, and it made me break out in a sweat that I hoped to the Goddess I kept hidden. "You first."

"Vox Vylan, Heir to the First Line," I replied haughtily.

The handsome guy laughed, like that was the greatest thing he'd ever heard. He turned to the man following him, who shared his coloring but looked more like he'd been through a meat grinder. "Did you hear that, Iker? First day here, and we already found the Heir to the throne." The guy turned back to me. "I wouldn't want to be rude to the progeny of a man who would murder babies in their cribs. Let me introduce myself. My name is Lierick Hanovan, Heir to the

Second Line, and I think you should turn that gun toward yourself and shoot yourself in the heart."

As if he'd taken control of my hands, the gun began to turn.

Hanovan. The Second Line. It was impossible. They were all dead.

Lierick just smirked. "Not dead, my blood-soaked Prince. Just waiting. Welcome to the first day of the revolution. Unfortunately, it'll also be your last."

The gun was facing me now, and with my power hijacked by the person in front of me, I stood no chance at resisting as I pulled the trigger, propelling the bullet right into my own chest.

The last thing I saw as I fell to the ground was Avalon running toward me, her screams echoing around the courtyard like the wail of the spirit of death.

chapter sixty-five

Avalon

thirty minutes earlier

"I HAVE to go and find Lucio or Vox. I need to know what's going on." Hayle was still clutching my hand tightly.

"Heir Taeme!" The Librarian appeared, and Hayle shook his head at her.

"I'm sorry, Librarian, but we're under siege. We won't have time—"

The Librarian's jaw tightened. "You will make time. Come."

Hayle looked between the crowd and the Librarian. I pushed at his chest. "Go. Find Vox and Lucio, and figure out what's going on. I'll go with the Librarian to see what's so important."

He hesitated. "You won't leave the library without me or Vox?"

I shook my head. "Braxus will be by my side the whole time too. Go, your Line needs you."

He kissed me hard, then dipped his head respectfully at the Librarian before rushing off, Quarry on his shoulder and Alucius at his heels.

The Librarian watched him go and nodded approvingly. "You've chosen consorts well. Come, time is of the essence." She hurried through the crowds of conscripts, while I followed along behind her. It helped that people moved out of her way, though I doubted even a tenth of the conscripts had even met the Librarian. She just had that kind of presence.

The crowds grew more and more sparse, until the corridor to the library was basically empty. She pushed through the doors into the tranquility of the large shelves, filled with knowledge. In a crisis, the library was the perfect place to be, but apparently, I was the only one in Boellium who felt that way.

"Mr. Vylan and Mr. Taeme brought me a package of books back from the library in the Hall of Ebrus. I've only just gotten around to reading them, which I regret." She muttered that last part more to herself than to me. "I wish we'd had more time."

She stopped and pulled a few things off a shelf. The first book was a weathered tome, with gold embossing reading *A Future History of Ebrus*. I raised an eyebrow. I wasn't sure that was even grammatically correct.

The second tome was titled *Reconstructionists and the Hands of the Goddess*.

The last thing was a letter with my name on it. It

was weathered, the edges of the folded paper yellowing. It looked old.

"This is for you. I haven't read it, but I believe I might have an inkling about its author, and I knew it would be important." The Librarian pushed it into my hands. It felt heavy, and not just physically.

I recognised the handwriting, though that was impossible. Opening the back flap, I carefully removed the letter from the envelope. Several thick sheets of paper were folded neatly within, and I gently opened them.

Dear Avalon,

If you're reading this, your stars are beginning to align and your future is being set into motion. It annoys me that it took so many resets for me to be able to send this, but that is the will of the Goddess and her greater plan.

Our family was once incredibly powerful, Avalon, and you, the Ninth Daughter of the Ninth Line, will be the most powerful of all, if not the one steeped in the most pain. Because the universe is about balance, and the Goddess gifts with both hands.

What I'm about to tell you is of the utmost importance, Avalon. You control the fate of Ebrus. The lives of hundreds of thousands of people rests on your shoulders and will be decided by your decisions.

You are a Recreationist. Long before the Line system, before even the Halhed name, our ancestors were the hands of Fate, directed by the Goddess herself. She used us to shape her favored children into something that could be great. Something she was proud of.

But as with every child, they eventually grow and change, no longer yours to control. Some flourish and some fail. That's the nature of life.

However, for thousands of years, we failed more than we flourished, until even our family's powers dwindled far from what we once were. The last women in our Line gave themselves to the Goddess's temples to keep Her knowledge, cursing our Line to bear only sons.

For centuries, it remained the same. Enough power to influence pivotal points, shifting small fates, but not restoring what we once were. Until Hopus Vylan gave us hope, and I was born, a herald of a new age. But love, like hope, is fickle. Ivan Vylan ripped it away once more, and I fled. The vision of the future where I stayed was too bleak to contemplate.

Then I saw you. The Ninth Daughter of the Ninth Line, so full of promise and power. A life filled with tragedy, but a soul that remained so pure and ready to love. You were the next turning point, and so much hung on your shoulders.

Although I can't be there for you—I am probably just dust on the Veria ice plains by now—I can give you the knowledge gifted to me by our Goddess, through the magic of our Line.

I can't tell you what will happen. I can only tell you what has happened before, so you aren't doomed to repeat the same mistakes over and over.

Read the books. Learn from our mistakes.

Eternally yours,

Ellanora Halhed.

I stared at the paper, letting the sheets slip through my fingers. What did that all even mean?

I reached for the books, but the doors to the library banged open. Instructor Perot appeared, his expression harried. "Librarian, we have a problem. You have to get to safety."

She shook her head. "There is nowhere safer than the library." She said it with such conviction, I couldn't help but be in complete agreement.

"Enora, please," he whispered, and I realized that he wasn't just asking as another staff member. The Librarian and Instructor Perot were a thing. Lovers?

I screwed up my nose. I didn't want to think about that too hard.

"It's fine. I promise," she murmured to him softly.

He gripped her shoulders. "It isn't. Svenna and the Vylan Heir are out on the beach, trying to work out who—"

I didn't hear the rest. I was already running, Braxus at my side. I should've known Vox would put himself in danger. I should've known he wouldn't be like the rest of us, following orders and staying inside the atrium.

Where was Master Proxius? Why was it Vox, and not one of the instructors out there with Svenna?

Pushing my way through the crowd, I couldn't see

through the windows, though I could hear the confused murmuring.

"What's she doing?"

"Who is that?"

"Is Svenna a traitor?"

I didn't pause to see what they were talking about. Something inside me was pushing me to get out of the atrium. I needed to have Vox's back.

I slammed through the doors that led to the courtyard too late. My eyes had to be lying to me, as Vox turned the gun in his hand and pointed it at his chest.

Why was he *doing* that?

I was running across the cobblestones before I even heard the gunshot. I screamed, the sound ricocheting around the thick stone walls, and the man in front of Vox whipped his head toward me. I didn't even pay attention to him, my eyes focused solely on the crumbling body of Vox.

"No!" I sobbed, skidding to a stop beside him. Braxus growled, leaping between the man and me, snarling and snapping, his bark drowning out my pleas to the Goddess. "No, Vox. Please, please, please, stay with me." I pressed my hand to his chest, blood and shredded flesh oozing through the gaps in my fingers. I almost knew the pain he was feeling, an echo of it in my own chest. "Goddess, *please.*"

People were yelling, and there were soldiers coming up the path behind the man who'd killed Vox. I didn't know how, but I knew it was his fault.

Standing, I spun to face the threat. He was beautiful,

and I fucking *hated* it. He'd killed someone I loved, and I'd make him so ugly, he'd regret the day he was born.

"No!" I screamed at him. Wind started to swirl around him, around us both, and he stood there, eyes wide and full lips parted. The word *Recreationist* spun in my brain, over and over and over again.

This wasn't right. This couldn't have been the plan. I refused to accept it.

Light began to seep from the pores of my skin, burning through the space around us in the courtyard. "*NO!*" I screamed again, but the guy just stood there, awe on his face.

"You're real," he breathed. "It's really you."

I didn't know what that meant. I didn't care. Because there wouldn't—couldn't—be a world without Vox. The streaks of light, the burning wind, they all pressed close to me.

The guy in front of me grinned. "I'll see you in the next life, Ninth Daughter of the Ninth Line."

The burning fires that surrounded me exploded outwards, demolishing everything in its path, until there was nothing.

No lifeless body of the man I loved.

No beautiful killer.

No Avalon Halhed, Recreationist.

chapter sixty-six

Avalon

the first day of the revolution

"WELL, well. If it isn't Avalon Halhed, the one and only love of my life." Hayle kissed me as he picked me up and spun me around. "Your sword skills are getting so much better," he murmured as he buried his face in my neck.

I snorted, because there was no way. "Liar." I hugged him back. "Careful, I'm still holding my sword. Though I have to admit, it's a novelty that I'm poking *you* with something long and hard for once."

He chuckled. I loved his laugh. "The Librarian wants to see us. Says it's of extreme importance. I have to go find Lucio to tell Shay that the other one has been requested also."

I looked over to the corner of the training ring. I'd seen Lucio flirting with Acacia earlier, so maybe he knew where Shay was. Having to go around in a circle to speak to Vox hurt my heart. "I think I saw Lucio flirting wi—"

Quarry cawed loudly, coming down to land on Hayle's shoulder, and I could tell from the rigid line of Hayle's shoulder that whatever news he carried was bad. Hayle was silent as he and his raven companion conversed, before he turned a pale face toward me.

"We're under attack," he said quietly, but almost as soon as he finished the words, a siren wailed.

"Boellium is under attack. Please return inside the walls."

Who the hell would be attacking Boellium?

Braxus appeared at my side, and I buried my fingers in his comforting fur. People were yelling and rushing toward the atrium, and we got swept up in the crowd. Somehow, the Third Line conscripts who'd been in the training ring formed a circle around us, moving as one cohesive unit of animals and humans.

We'd barely stepped through the doors when we were swamped by people. It was madness inside the atrium, of a sort that I hadn't seen since the day I'd arrived. People were panicking, while instructors were trying—and failing—to restore order.

I needed to find Vox. "Come on, we'll see if we can spot Lucio or Shay," Hayle yelled over the sound of people's panic.

We hadn't made it three steps when we were approached by the Librarian. "Heir Taeme!" she shouted, making her way toward us from ten feet away. Hayle huffed, his anxiety to find and care for his people making him short on patience. When she finally made it to the space in front of us, her cheeks were pink, and she too looked annoyed. "Heir Taeme, I need you to come with me. It's a matter of urgency."

"I'm sorry, Librarian, but we're under siege. I haven't had time to find Vox—"

"Don't worry about that." She hustled us back toward the door. "Quick, we must hurry, or this will end badly. At least, that's what the book says."

What book?

I must have asked the question out loud, because the Librarian gripped my arm and was now tugging me to the atrium door. Braxus stepped between us and gave a warning growl.

The Librarian looked down at the hound and raised a brow. "Deep down, you know what I'm saying is true. Follow those instincts," she said to the hound, which was super freaking weird.

But Braxus, for a reason I couldn't comprehend— and one that left Hayle completely dumbfounded— stepped aside to let the Librarian drag me toward the door.

"I'll explain about the book later. I'll explain every- thing later. But we must hurry, or the Heir to the First Line dies."

As we stepped out of the atrium, Vox was standing by the gates, face to face with a beautiful blond man dressed in black and amer.

Vox held a gun—I hadn't even realized he owned one—on the man in front of him, though it kept pointing to the ground and lifting again. The Librarian hurried me over to the stranger, but not before I noticed Svenna standing off to the side, looking dazed.

Something wasn't right.

The stranger stared at the Librarian with a blindingly white smile. His eyes were an abyss so dark, it was nearly impossible to see his pupils. He was young enough he probably could have been a conscript at Boellium War College.

"Don't fear, Librarian. We too have a copy of *A Future History of Ebrus*. We learn from our mistakes." His eyes shifted from Librarian Enora to me. "Avalon Halhed, Ninth Daughter of the Ninth Line, it's so good to finally meet you."

Vox stepped between us, blocking me from the view of the man in front of us. Hayle also tugged me behind him.

"Don't look at her," Hayle growled, and the guy laughed.

"And who are you?" he asked.

"Hayle Taeme, Heir to the Third Line."

The guy leaned around him so he could meet my eyes again. "Really? A matching set? Interesting." He raised both hands in the air. "Where are my manners? My name is Lierick Hanovan, and I'm here to surrender."

afterword

This novella is Part Three of a title I am writing chapter by chapter over on Patreon. It is the final part in **Daughter of the Ninth Line**, and now I'll move on to the second book in the *Lines of Ebrus* duet, **Heir to the Second Line**.

If you are desperate to know what happens next, to talk about dreams and theories with others who are reading along too, think about checking it out.

Grace McGinty Writes - Patreon

Thank you for reading.

- Grace x

about the author

Grace McGinty is eclectic. She has worked as a chocolatier, a librarian, a forensic accountant, and finally, a writer. Like her professional career, the genres she writes are chaotic and out of control. From contemporary new adult to smutty reverse harem novels of every sub-genre, if you like it, she's probably written it.

Except dark romance. She's a marshmallow, and somehow the mean guys always end up cinnamon rolls.

Grace lives in rural Australia with her crazy family, an entire menagerie of pets, and will one day be crushed by the giant piles of books that litter every room.

Head over to www.gracemcginty.com and join the mailing list for sneak previews into what she is working on and to stay up-to-date with new releases and giveaways!

www.ingramcontent.com/pod-product-compliance
Lightning Source LLC
Chambersburg PA
CBHW031729180726
48283CB00005B/1434